THE JUBILEE ACCOUNT

A WILLIAM BARNWELL NOVEL

A Monje Press Book

 MP

Published by Monje Press, an imprint of Le Monocle Publishing Group, LLC Boston. Library of Congress Cataloging-in-Publication Data Barnwell, William. The Jubilee Account:/ William Barnwell ISBN 9798649708807.

Vesel, Neap; Joliard, Jessie; Patrimos, Henry; (fictitious characters— fiction) Printed in the United States of America 987654321

p. cm

First E-book Edition October 2019

Book Design by Tanja Prokop

Distribution by Amazon.

ACKNOWLEDGMENTS

For Jo Ann, and for all who have ever supported me, called me, written me, or emailed me as a fan. Thanks to those in my gym world who have over the years said good and bad things about everything, the world, and all expressions of it, like earlier versions of this book. From the tireless soldier Leon Frishman to the inimitable Phillip Johnson; and for Bob Keivit, who read an early plot summary and helped get the wheels going. They were all an education.

This is also for Marshall Fallwell and Walter Brown, old friends, both now ghosts.

For Al and Nancy Johnston, together again, who helped start this journey years ago.

And thanks, as always, to Monje Press for advice in this new medium.

By WILLIAM BARNWELL

The Blessing Papers

Imram

The Sigma Curve

Book of the Romes

The Scheme-of-the-Month Club

Death of the Camel's Child

The Dungeon Below Bling-Bling High

I, Lord Several

The Jubilee Account

See williambarnwell.net

PROLOGUE:

THE EMPIRE STATE BUILDING

MAY 1, 1931

Before his death in 1913, America's most successful Robber Baron John Pierpont Morgan said that he was the only man who knew how to run this country, and he may have been right. But after that, and after the Great War, the nineteen twenties seemed a gifted time that ran easily like sand through the fingers of many of those who believed in it. And yet its consequences were worse than all the foreign wars through which they would eventually have to suffer; it brought stark reality to America's front door and gave witness to a financial beast that waged a predatory war from door to door, alley to alley, city to city, state to state and country to country for decades, and it remained a continual threat.

So on the cold and rainy evening of May 1, 1931, when a fake button pushed by President Herbert Clark Hoover in Washington, D.C., officially opened the one hundred and two story Empire State Building in New York City, raw gusts of wind whipped violently around the structure from the northeast as if to test its strength. Inside, electricians engaged real switches and full lights began to illuminate the interior. Walter Leeds Patrimos on the Observation Deck was watching, and he took it as the sign to jump.

He knew of no way to go back in time and undo what he had done. It was what it was. Hurt was built in. That was it. That was the secret. He had seen the future and could do absolutely nothing about it. Except the one thing.

An influential editor of *Essays on Commerce in the Midwest*, Patrimos had deposited a dry bundle wrapped in oilskin next to the inner wall of the Observation Room. He was now at the southern edge of the eighty sixth floor and looked down carefully over its parapet. His nostrils flared, and his eyes squinted because of the chill wind at his back; his skull was matted with balding red hair, and his bone-white face had tiny brown freckles over its nose and under its eyes. His glasses had long since been abandoned.

He thought he heard a door open behind him, drew a lung full of air and scrambled up and over the enclosure built to prevent anyone from falling by accident. Since he had read that he would probably be dead from shock halfway down, he believed the jump would not be a fall to mere brick or asphalt, rather it would be a dive into the River Styx, the river of forgetfulness, for which he yearned.

Leaping from the building like an Olympic swimmer, his legs bunching then thrusting forward, his hands grasping at air, his body rolling on its back, and his four limbs blowing upward as if held by wire. The rear winds curving around the sides lofted him away from the building's lower facings and buffeted and numbed him as he glimpsed out of the corners of his blunt eyes full lights clicking on floor by floor inside the behemoth from which he was falling.

The nine-second dive ended with brief thunder when at near ground level he smashed through the top of a 1930 Packard sedan parked at 11 West 33rd Street and lay sprawled forward in the front seat wreckage. His face was the only part of him left intact and it seemed to be smiling. Some few bystanders, hands to their mouths, began to gather and look at Patrimos and up at the top of the Empire State Building, which they could not see.

A strolling reporter with a Speed Graphic took the shot, angling the camera on the face to advantage, and the flash-lit picture later appeared in Life magazine as the *Smiling Jumper*.

After the red tape ran its course, a bureaucrat from the New York City Chief Medical Examiner's Office sent an overcoat, a wallet, a tweed jacket, and a proof copy of his *Essays*, Patrimos's last, unpublished journal issue, already with foxed edges, to his family in Palatine, Illinois. There was also a plugged brass urn containing Patrimos's ashes.

In the spirit of the times, the city sent the package COD.

1

A DARK ALLEY

Sammy Beguiles felt the moment was either heaven or hell: The *heaven* was that he was by himself and out on one of the Friday night adventures he liked best, when he would sneak out of his house to find things on his moped; *hell* came as he watched with horror when, in the hot delivery alley of the Murphy Mall, night lights from a closed 7/11 across the Atlantic Highway unexpectedly flickered on and off, exposing near him a large figure carrying what seemed to be a stiff mannikin, or a dead body.

It was 9:30 p.m., June 6, 2007, and the New Moon gave no light. Sammy thought then that the darkness was a good thing. He was frightened by the person he saw with the body, a muscular person, or maybe a hunchback, but he could not see its face. He was scared, but he squeezed his mouth shut and hid like a stone in the darkest shadows he could find and still be able to see what was happening.

The Murphy Mall was a standard strip mall. Its ends faced east and west, and the front faced north. The back-delivery alley was close and humid. That, along with the unusually hot June temperature, made the night seem as liquid as steam cleaning. Sammy's cheeks were as red as apples and his black T-shirt was soaked with sweat. His haircut was fashionable for male freshmen at Fleckner High School: A one-inch tall Mohawk in a three-inch wide band, which for him was the color of a broom, running from front to back of his otherwise mostly shaved scalp. Wearing it made him feel good, like a savage. But that night he thought that he might have to *be* one to escape what he saw. The bulky figure in the dim light was sinister. Standing by the unmoving body, it touched the white face it carried almost tenderly and suddenly glanced in Sammy's direction. But the figure must have been satisfied and left, putting down the body and walking out of the west end of the mall with an odd but steady stride.

Sammy waited and then moved slowly toward the body, pausing, breathing quietly, looking around, advancing. Up closer, he could tell that the dead man was sitting against the back wall of the Red Serpent Hibachi Grill as if he were enjoying the evening after buying everybody inside a drink, as his father had once told him occasionally he did.

Between the index and middle finger of his right hand the body held a cigarette. Closer yet, Sammy could tell that the man wore a white shirt, a blue-and-white seersucker sportscoat, and a shiny gold watch on his left wrist. He also noted that the dead man had dark spots on his white face.

Sammy's eyes widened when he saw that the man had no body below the waist. Was he cut in two? The young teenager had seen movies and TV programs that suggested they revealed real blood, but he did not believe them. His father did not let him see slasher movies, so naturally he wanted to know what a *real* cut person looked like. He thought it would surely be revealing, yet the man seemed to have left no blood at all behind, real or fake. He also wondered why the hunchback that had brought it left no tracks he could see.

His usual curiosity growing hot again, Sammy went farther down the alley and looked around the corner at the extreme west end of the mall where the murderer went, and where the big HVAC fans were humming steadily together like two different but unchanging pitches of minimalist music.

A derelict looking like a load of Goodwill clothing donations lay catercorner to the alley where a chain-link fence picked up the mall perimeter, and tall sulfur lamps from the parking lot in front of the mall lay a tangerine blanket over the homeless person. Sammy quickly thought that it must be the killer, and maybe it was just bulky clothes he had seen, not muscle. But was there a gun? Did the man still have it on him? Maybe he could find it if he approached....

The mass of clothes stood and headed for him.

"Who the hell do you think you are?" it shouted.

Sammy could not take any chances here. He turned and sprinted past the half-man. He thought that what he needed right then was what he had wished for on his next birthday, the last day in July, when he would be fifteen.

He did not need a newer moped, as his father had suggested. Sammy wanted a black semiautomatic with a rough plastic handle. His dream was to have such a gun and pull it in front of his friends who would surround him like curious dogs, sniff at him with approval, and keep a respectful distance. After seeing what he had seen, Sammy believed he would do everything he could to get such a gun.

Slowing, still running behind the mall, he wondered what he would tell his parents about the dead man. Probably nothing. His father may have once been an LA cop, but the half-body was, after all, his discovery. It might be there the next day, and he might go back to see it. *Sweet,* he thought.

Still half-running, glancing behind himself every now and then until he came out the east end of the alley, where he had left his red moped chained to one of the few parking meters left in town. Unlocking and cranking the bike, he headed home. He felt better and swore he would later tell himself the truth about what he had done out of curiosity in the dark alley, and what he had not done because of cowardice.

2

A large sign in front of the sheriff's office was illuminated at night by floodlights:

FLECKNER COUNTY

SHERIFF'S DEPARTMENT

SHERIFF BLUTHER WALSH

CHIEF DEPUTY NEOPOLITAN VESEL

The departmental building was two-stories of white-washed concrete block with an arched green vinyl roof, gray double front steel doors, and a reception room and visitor counter just inside to the left. There was a third steel door to the rear of the building, and a slow elevator near the front entrance to the right. Offices were on the bottom floor; the cells and interrogation rooms were on the top floor. Lately people in Fleckner were using the otherwise empty cells to sleep off drunken nights of depression, and before leaving the next morning they would eat breakfast made with real sausage and eggs.

Currently, only one person was in any of the cells: Marvin Allan Macy, who was an alcoholic insurance agent with floppy gray hair and a slight hunchback. Sheriff Walsh had picked him up earlier that evening from his parked car and put him safely in a cell before going to the 10:00 p.m. weekly assignments review with Chief Deputy Neap Vesel. Macy would be released as usual when he was sober the next morning.

Sheriff Bluther Walsh, whose nickname was Blue, and his Chief Deputy Neapolitan Vesel, Neap, were in his office late to discuss the incident reports for the week's assignments, which were increasingly involved in holding back the growth of activities that had only recently arrived in the town: theft, rape, material destruction, random violence, and drug runners with sophisticated computer setups.

To counter this growth in crime, Blue Walsh wanted the Fleckner Sheriff's Department to be as high-tech as it could get. There was an Apple computer on every desk. There had been classes in the use of digital phones, software, and internet communications; enough money was squirreled away in the budget to keep up with the newest equipment.

Before 2007, no one in Fleckner thought that all the shocking news they heard or saw on national TV would come to their town. They were wrong. Fleckner was no longer a lazy place situated beside a slow winding river that led west to a small dam and picturesque lake, and then east on out to the sandy Atlantic Ocean beaches fifty miles away.

The Sheriff sat in a black leather chair behind his desk, which was stacked with paperwork next to his monitor and printer, and on the wall behind him was a Norman Rockwell print with a June calendar showing a barber in red slippers, a young boy sitting in the barber's chair happily having his abundant hair shaved for summer freedom, and a patient dog waiting in a chair beside them with its ears puckered, watching for the boy to join him for a season of wild fun.

Chief Blue Walsh had silver whiskers on his cheeks and chin and short, balding gray hair, a dusky skin, and a crooked nose gotten when he was younger and had been a bouncer somewhere in Hawaii, where he was born. It made him look like a real fighter, a pug; since then, he had put on a lot of weight and lost the hand-eye coordination for good fighting, although he had in fact willingly given it up and never fought again after leaving the islands.

Neap Vesel, 29, had his back to the office door and projected the taut confidence of a highly trained soldier with a big frame, full of rounded muscle, and, although he still ran long distances in the mountains like he once did, his strength had grown less during the last few years on his new job as a Chief Deputy. This was alright with him, since, like the sheriff, Vesel was trying to avoid using the raw violence he possessed.

That might be a contrarian's view of law enforcement, he thought, but it was the similarity between the two men that had attracted Neap to the job. They were alike, although the Sheriff was at the end of his career and Vesel was at the beginning.

People liked the chief deputy without knowing why. He seemed dangerous and big, but his face seemed to suggest that you could get his help if you asked him carefully enough, and then he might do what he had always done as a football player for girls at Fleckner High School. And he would mean it. His tight routes would merge and he would burst free into the open, streaking toward the far goal posts, and after the school annuals came out, he would sign his name at pictures of him slanting across the goal line and add in a scribble that, *This one's for you!"*

The two officers were discussing the department's late answering service for 911 calls. Because of the bad situation rising in town, on-call hours for the departmental force had moved further and further into the night and, unless they had time off, they had to keep their cell phones on, and their hours free. The department paid them overtime for this service.

"No calls tonight, though," the Sheriff said.

"That may be a good thing."

"Well, Jacoby will take over for you tonight, Neap. You are off tonight and tomorrow, so enjoy."

"Already doing that, Blue."

Blue tried to envision Vesel having fun but usually saw him attacking a giant pinata, going at a huge stuffed donkey with a massive ax.

"Let's at least finish up this week's reports," he said, trying not to laugh.

He had grown to like Vesel very much, and he would do nothing to make him think that he did not.

3

Val Coombs thought going to school and working for a living was basically a waste of time. After all, it cost money to go to school, and making filthy money just to make more filthy money was not one of her goals. That was for her mother and father to do. She meant this sincerely.

And yet Val had learned that the next meal was always going to be a balancing act in finding the delicacies thrown out at night, maybe pieces of some Mediterranean dish on Main, or some Chinese raw fish with pieces of little green and orange vegetables sprinkled on top at the mall, or some woman's small T-bone, only partially eaten, smeared with an orange-brown sauce.

She recalled that she broke her left arm one night several years before while clamoring over the top of an empty dumpster by herself and falling inside, hitting hard at the bottom. She screamed as loud as she could, but nobody heard her until the next morning when the astonished owner of one of the few shops left at the mall called 911. They got her out, delirious, and took her to the free Fleckner Clinic. A young emergency-room doctor gave her pain medication and put a cast on her arm, but after that the arm was not as good and before they left, her friends ribbed her by calling her *ole one-arm.* After that, she knew that death for her was going to be at the bottom of a Dempsey dumpster.

But that night she had expectations of a feast. The garbage truck had come twice that night, and that meant something big was up. She had to check the two dumpsters at the mall again for remains that were usually left behind. Chinese restaurants supposedly threw nothing away, but still, they did. Oh, she had a nose for that, knew what was coming most of the time, and from where. The Hibachi Grill was just around the corner.

She sat with her back to a chain link fence as she waited, and her memory wandered. She remembered a class in high school before she left for good at sixteen. Her science teacher told them about the geographical line that ran north and south right through Fleckner. On the west side of the line a cliff of granite ran for nine-hundred miles from Maine through Georgia; on the east side was nothing but soft dirt, sand, and the ocean. It was distinctive.

Val looked at her feet. She might be straddling the line right there, and it made her dizzy. She thought she might fall into it, right through into the time when there was no town, no trees, no animals, nothing but torn rock at the sheered border of broken continents, a part of which floated away to be New England, and the other part floated away to become northwest Africa, Morocco, Western Sahara, Mauritania. She looked up across the imaginary border of time and saw some kid looking back at her. In the half-light she could see only a round face, but she remembered that was the alley where she was going to resume looking twice for food, her food. Growing angry, she rolled over, got to her feet, and started for the alley.

"Who the hell do you think you are?" She yelled at the kid.

The kid ran. Val was the second innocent person to find the dead body in Fleckner that night, and she knew right then, after looking closely at the half-man in the alley, she would be unable, or unwilling to catch the boy.

4

After the late meeting, and before Vesel left for his date with Grace Sallice, the Sheriff observed there had to be something new going on in the mountains, but he had no idea what it was. Vesel was not yet sure either, although he felt a military sense about a coming battle of some sort.

The Sheriff stretched his arms. "Well, go on, Neap. I'll stay. There is only one person upstairs anyway."

Vesel smiled and this was unusual for him. "If there is any trouble, Blue, don't call. I do have plans," he said.

Blue smiled, which was not unusual for him.

At 9:50 p.m., Vesel left the office building. He was thinking of the evening ahead with the beautiful Grace, who made him feel light-hearted and safe, and therefore, as he was driving home, he also thought about the tough Tajiks who inhabited the northeastern mountains of Afghanistan, and who had ended there his final tour of duty. His fire team had been ambushed in such a way that he had been neatly cut off from the others, and the Tajiks hustled him to their temporary camp over a rocky trail that would be difficult to track. Vesel did not try to leave clues because he knew what the deal was. It had been set up by the CIA section chief to mollify the Pakistanis ISI, who wanted Vesel out of their way for his refusals to deal with the Taliban as ISI friends in their battle for control in Afghanistan. Since he wanted to go home and break any connections with the CIA anyway, Vesel agreed to the idea.

The deal was simple. He would be captured by the Taliban with close ties to the ISI, then rescued and discharged on some field medical charge and sent home immediately. It was to be called the Wizard of Oz Op.

Vesel's Afghanistan duties had included liaising with not only the Taliban agents representing groups that wanted struggle on the battlefield, but also with those who wanted peace. The shifty third rail was the Pakistani Intelligence agency, the ISI, that was called *a state within a state*. His job with them had been to appear to be nothing more than SO muscle they could trust and control, but now they wanted him gone.

They then set up what was to become a major event in his life. The Wizard Oz Op would let him out, but at a high and unexpected price because of the wrath of a fellow soldier.

After the operation started, and Vesel was captured, the Army determined that a counter-terror Delta Force soldier, who lisped slightly and had been assigned to the SF fire team for a top-secret task, had lied about where Vesel had been taken. Jordan Manse Fellestre admitted to having told the attacking Tajik group how best to capture Vesel, because he believed that Vesel had caused the death of his Afghanistan woman with one of his fireteam's explosives.

Fellestre had compromised the operation and almost cost Vesel his life. He had lied about where the capturing party would take him, and his capture had already overlapped the operation's timeframe of safety. His fireteam was notified of the different site at the last minute, and they left for it immediately.

* * *

Stretched on a slanted stone table with grooves carved out for blood to run down and away from him, Vesel's forearms were bound by ropes over the top of the table behind him, and his ankles were held by cords from each side of the lower part of the table. He had already been through an hour or more of very delicate flaying under his right armpit, where, for some reason, the Taliban flaying master wanted to begin.

The only words Vesel had spoken were as a question at the beginning.

"Are you the Wizard of Oz?"

The old man had stared at Vesel for a minute. The man's black eyes had a mineral quality to them that glinted fanatically in the firelight as if nothing could change his mind.

After that, except for heavy breathing, Vesel did not utter a sound.

The old man, with the help of a special razor-sharp Afghani knife shaped like a cheese cutter, peeled off small horizontal pieces of Vesel's skin. The top strip was level with his sternum and a vertical strip moved down his side to a point level with his navel, a total of about twelve square inches so far. It represented the first letter of the old man's name, he said, and it looked like a capital *T.*

The old man, evidently a master in his craft, spoke the Taliban language, Pashto, one of the two national languages of Afghanistan. As an SF soldier, Vesel had to learn a basic form of both Pashto and Dari. But Vesel did not care enough to respond to the man's questions. The old man said to Vesel that he admired his silence. He stared at Vesel, considered something, and went to his hut nearby.

When he returned and reached for Vesel's bound hands. Vesel instinctively tried to grab him, but the man popped Vesel's hands with his fingertips and placed something that seemed small in Vesel's huge left hand. It was a ball of some kind and Vesel closed his fingers gratefully around it.

"*Hun Gabon,*" the old man said.

If the words were either Pashto or Dari, Vesel was unfamiliar with them. He did not know if *Hun Gabon* was a noun or a verb, or both, but it sounded good, and he felt good holding something warm, round, and solid, as a respite from the pain which he yet would not acknowledge. He almost believed it was a gift, as his agony seemed to bleed into the ball. But the official flayer resumed his task like a hair stylist whose job was cutting and shaping hair, slowly unrolling and rewinding it into shape, working with thin layers of skin that could be cut and peeled away only so deeply without ruining the overall effect.

Flaying was not new to Afghanistan. Vesel knew it had come from East Asia and been brought back to Europe by Crusaders in the Fourteenth Century. It was used when necessary by Christian Heresy Courts conducted in open-air markets for anyone to see how important it was to stick to the right faith. Vesel later learned that such torturers usually peeled off facial skin first and slowly worked their way down to the feet, but most victims died of shock before the flayer or flayers reached the waist.

Before moving on to the next section to be flayed, the old man took a short break to eat something light and drink some dark wine to refresh himself, as the Prophet Muhammad had done on occasion. He contemplated the pattern of the initial letter and stopped to tell Vesel about its origin, while three of the Taliban who had come to watch tried to hurry the flayer along, so the big American would do what others did, scream and beg. The only thing Vesel did, however, was to sweat while his chest heaved in the cool air. The three Taliban were each wearing parts of his uniform. One of them wore his pants up to his armpits; the Tajik's head with the helmet looked tiny; another one was dwarfed by the bulky field jacket.

As the flaying master achieved the big capital letter on Vesel's right side, he apologized to Vesel but explained that he was then ready to branch out and go for much bigger blocks of his skin. He would begin by making the 'T' a solid vertical bar like a thick 'I,' and roll it on across his chest. Neap's body would, he said, truly feel what was happening to it and shock would come.

The old man said he needed different tools from his hut. He bowed to Vesel and left. He did not return. Vesel's fire team arrived and started killing everybody in the camp.

When his team cut him loose, Vesel sought and killed the three Tajiks who had mocked him. He recovered his entire uniform. Some of the other soldiers paused to watch Neap's naked body like a Greek god's, tear the three Tajiks apart while holding a ball of some kind in one hand, hitting them with it, using as he did so every scream he had held back during the flaying.

After that Vesel was different, and the other men in his fireteam did not goad him about what had happened. The action triggered a Court Martial that decided on a Dishonorable Discharge, stripping the man, Fellestre, of his rank and privileges in the U.S. Army and sending him home.

Vesel dealt with himself as he healed. He kept the Hun Gabon with his most personal possessions. He still did not know what type of wood it consisted of, just that it had been carved into a perfect sphere by hand. He wanted to ask the old man how that was done and about its uses, so that he could replace it if necessary.

But he never saw the flayer again. As a reminder of his past agony, he felt a constant fire under his armpit like a tattoo, a T, made of gun powder. It became a constant reminder of his new promise to himself: *After the killing of the three observers in the Tajik camp, he would not knowingly kill again.*

His subsequent feelings about violence dated to that night after the flaying, and at the time it sounded like a promise he could keep.

5

DISCOVERY

At 10:00 p.m. a homeless person flagged down a patrol car in the parking lot at the Murphy Mall and led a new deputy, LeMace Jacoby, to a body placed up against the back wall of the Red Serpent Hibachi Grill. According to the deputy, there was some gibberish from the homeless person about a kid doing it. When he arrived behind the Murphy Mall, Sheriff Blue Walsh played a flashlight over the body, or what was left of it, the head, arms, and torso.

"Why the hell did somebody cut the damn body in half, Jacoby?"

"I don't know," Deputy Jacoby said. He was still in training with Neap Vesel, who was not there, and he felt uneasy being alone with the Sheriff.

"And why was it left right here?"

"I don't know that either, Sheriff."

"There are no footsteps around the body," the Sheriff observed.

Jacoby remained silent for that one.

"But these footprints going around farther out here, and then slipping in here next to the body, they look like a girl's, don't they, or a kid's?"

The deputy had an answer for that one.

"That's what the homeless girl was saying, Sheriff. The kid also says she knows who the victim is: David Knight Joliard."

The Sheriff glanced at the deputy. "Damn. Get Neap down here to spearhead this."

"I tried to get him already. He doesn't answer his phone."

"Well, goddamn it," Sheriff Walsh said, scratching his head. "I let him take tonight off. He is probably right now at his house with his new girlfriend. But this is big. Go get him."

"He is not going to like this," Jacoby said with a bit of fear in his voice. He knew how Vesel could radiate intimidation with his body tensed in a fight- or- flight pattern, but ready to go only to fight. No flight.

When irritated, Chief Deputy Vesel showed that side of himself too, and Jacoby had learned not to irritate him. Nevertheless, he knew that his partner had a sense of duty that would override any bad move before it acted out fully.

The Sheriff looked at Jacoby and shook his head. He knew how it could be, and he hoped the young man could stay in the ring until he completed his training. Given what they faced in the county now, the department needed all the good men it could find.

"He's not going to eat you, LeMace. Go get him. Tell him I said we got a Joliard murder down here at the mall and we need him, bad."

"Yes, sir."

After Jacoby left, the Sheriff waited for the part-time crime-scene technician and coroner, Frost Nellums, who was retired from Minnesota. Being a part-time coroner in a county with a lake, and only an hour or so from the ocean, seemed an easy bet for the coroner to take. He said he had moved to Fleckner for the best fishing anywhere in the USA, right on Lake Joliard, where he owned a big cabin. He had bought two lots and built on them as if they were one lot.

The man must have retired with money in his back pocket, the Sheriff thought at the time. Lucky bastard. He also wondered where he found that best fishing in the USA business. He would have to check on that, maybe to use for more PR for Fleckner. He knew that helped the economy.

Still reluctant to admit that his zero-murder rate was now over, he repeated an old motto in his head: *A place without murder is a place to stay.* Half serious, but with some chagrin, the Sheriff realized things had surely changed. He could no longer use that motto. Not anymore.

But maybe he could invent a new motto. Maybe this one, *Fleckner: Where retirees come to fish, play, and stay.* Yes. That would help. He wondered why the Joliards had not thought of it, and he would suggest it to Nellums when he arrived.

Frost Nellums was sleepy and sullen and did not respond well to the new motto. He was carrying his examination kit, a big black bag, and a camping lamp.

"I'll study the upper half of the body and let you know what I find in a day or two, Blue," he said. That was the usual routine.

But the Sheriff felt edgy and told Nellums to drop the *two* part of that statement and see him in his office the next morning.

"Well, okay then," Nellums said.

The Sheriff gestured at the body.

"As a matter of fact, start now," he said. "What do you see?"

"Well, there are a few obvious things," Nellums said. Shrugging his shoulders, he pointed to the base where the top of the body sat.

"First, the bag he is mounted on here is made of burlap."

"Burlap?"

"Well...."

Nellums pulled two blue cotton shoe covers and two white kneepads from his bag, put them on and knelt in front of the half-body.

The Sheriff knew that Nellums was a lot brighter than he looked. He had come with excellent recommendations. He was short and bald, with a bulging stomach, huge love handles, and cheeks as baggy as pouches.

"Second, the jute in it is absorbent and that's probably why it's there," Nellums pointed out. "To contain any leakage. The murderer evidently did not want to spoil the effect with stains.

"And third, that's probably how the top half was brought in here, in the burlap bag, then it was taken out and the bag was folded neatly and put here. Then somebody set the top of the body upright on it right like that, arranging it, putting a Pall Mall long in one hand there, and making the head look satisfied. The rest will have to wait until I finish the lab work, Blue."

"I will see you tomorrow morning," the Sheriff said. "Something will turn up by then, I'm sure."

"Well, the only thing most people can be sure about turning up," Nellums said, "is that if they are going to blow their noses, they better take their glasses off."

Silence.

"Hey, that's a good one, Frost," the Sheriff said, pointing his right index finger at him, chuckling despite himself.

Nellums smiled. Setting up his standing exam lamp, he began the preliminary examination. He pulled on latex gloves stretched out thin as onion skin and started work on the body while kneeling in front of it on his kneepads, one hand braced on the left shoulder of the half-body and the other palpating something on the right neckline. He seemed to be comforting a fallen, grief-stricken friend, or maybe congratulating him on a job well done.

When one eye of the head snapped open and stared at him, Walsh dropped his flashlight.

"What the hell!" he said.

"Just a postmortem reaction, Blue. The lids haven't been stitched together yet. Don't let it bother you."

"It's not still alive?"

"Of course not," Nellums said. "With no murders ever here, you are not used to seeing bodies like this. But the eyes may have been rigged to do that, Blue. If there are more murders, you'll get used to it."

"Jesus! See you in the morning, Frost," the Sheriff said, as he realized that he was like many who could not fully agree to death unless it was displayed with firmly closed eyes, primly folded arms, or exposed in a full skeletal mode.

"Bye, Sheriff," Nellums said, already preoccupied, just as the other eye popped open.

When Chief Deputy Vesel arrived at the first scene, Nellums was still there. The two talked. Nellums shut the eyes of the dead man and put him back into the burlap sack. He left with the half-body in his white Crime Scene van, which was also his fishing van. Inside, it always smelled of fish.

Vesel stayed for a while looking at things and then followed Nellums, shaking his head. He reflected that he better be more careful. Something new was happening, and it did not seem right in Fleckner.

He was uncertain about this. But he had after all agreed to keep an ear to the ground about three things in his home town that might affect terrorist operations: *Jessie Joliard*, whose fiancé was a US Senator who was pushing for new war funding that might trigger more terrorist activities in the states; *James Parsons*, his old quarterback, the banker in town who might be laundering money, with large amounts turning over in the bank without clear knowledge of where the money came from or was going; and the drug operations of *the Joliard brothers*, who evidently had money problems since the dot.com crash.

Vesel agreed to do this because they were Joliards, but it was for another reason altogether, an even more urgent one for him. The thing was, deep down, he loved *Jessie Joliard*, whom he had not seen for fifteen years. He cared nothing about the other matters, so he paid little attention to them until it was almost too late.

6

PATRIMOS

Private Investigator Henry Patrimos's closely cropped hair had a rusty color. He seemed as hard as iron, with a sharply narrow face like a hatchet with freckles, his eyes close set, wary, as if they were considering the best angle to hit something, or somebody. He normally wore a daytime uniform of pullover golf shirts, khaki pants, maroon sweaters in season, and Bass Weejun loafers with no socks. Just like at Yale. But when investigating in deep cover, he always wore black.

He had good management skills when they involved suspects in a case. He identified a certain type of person and could probe until the facts came out, although he was not always proud of hiding from Mitch Stein the kind of Black Ops intimidation he sometimes used to get at those facts.

But then, for some reason, Stein never pressed him hard on the subject; Patrimos thought that perhaps it was beyond the attorney's imagination to consider doing things like that. After all, Stein felt that the ends did not justify the means, while Patrimos did in fact believe the opposite, that the ends did indeed justify the means.

And yet Stein was his legal partner and between the two of them they had won every case they had accepted over the years. They were famous working together, *cool* even. People Magazine had published several articles on them, how they worked with movie stars. Within certain circles they seemed hand in glove, step by step, like Astaire & Rogers, Holmes & Watson, Woodward and Bernstein, or–and this is the simile Patrimos told friends he liked best–like Steve McQueen & a '68 Ford Mustang, with him being the Mustang.

But beneath everything else, Patrimos sought the truth surrounding his paternal grandfather's jump from the Empire State Building on its opening night of May 1, 1931. Walter Patrimos went off the southern side of the Observation Deck and landed by chance face forward in the driver's seat of a brand-new maroon Packard. His face was still in enough shape to look like it was smiling. A picture was taken at the right angle, and Life magazine published it in the summer of 1931 as *The Smiling Jumper*.

But did he jump, or was he pushed?

After serving in the marines in Vietnam, where he met Stein, Henry Patrimos discovered his ability to find meaningful facts hidden in great troves of data, and he was soon accepted by Stein as probably one of the best hackers in the country, a hacker who specialized in catching hacker criminals by counter-hacking them, which he had demonstrated in many of their early cases. The PI had his own tool sets and his own algorithms.

This later led Patrimos to become a recognized Internet Investigator, which allowed him access to government and private systems he normally could not get into, being hard-nosed in searching for other facts he might need once inside. Early on, it was slogging through a haystack of coded lines. Since then, computer hacking was easier. It was like a private sport for him. He would give appropriate data to Mitch Stein, who would then use it to win cases. He and Henry would bat the facts back and forth until the defense jelled and a trial was over and won. It was his genius to find something, and Mitch Stein's to use it.

But for many years, little of that data had helped Patrimos in his main mission. So far, he had file cabinets and disc space full of facts but with fewer and fewer connections to the Smiling Jumper. The road toward an answer would bounce off rock walls and flop on the floor.

Yet when he felt the stirrings of grief about this, he would get back up like an old dog and sniff the wind. This had occurred in his recent retirement traveling the globe, during which nothing was interesting to him except the Ville Borghese in Rome, the statue of Apollo and Daphne in particular, lust-chasing and chastity-stonewalling, which seemed to him to be a symbol of everything in life, the appealing to and denying of very strong forces. He noted Daphne's top turning into limbs and leaves, and yet the long graceful toes of her right foot, were still human in form. How could Bernini, or anybody, form images of such forces out of slick marble?

Now he believed that sculpting seemed harder to do than hacking a computer system and presented much more of an appeal. Maybe he would take it up. But then, by chance, he heard a news story about a small town in America called Fleckner.

7

At 9:30 a.m., Sunday, 8 June 2008, in Oslo, Norway, Patrimos phoned Defense Attorney Mitchell Stein in Boston. Stein's phone rang at 3:30 a.m.

"Yes?" Stein whispered into the speaker.

"Mitch, this is Henry."

"Henry...I thought you were in Oslo."

"I'll be on a jet back to Boston this afternoon."

"So why did you call?" Stein said, rubbing his eyes.

"Did you listen to the morning news?" Patrimos asked.

"Henry, we are not all retired like you, nor are we always in a different time zone."

"It was a story in a small town somewhere on the East Coast Fall Line. It was about a bizarre murder, Mitch."

Stein was silent for a moment.

"Mitch...?"

"Why does that interest you, Henry?"

"The dead man was, and I quote, *one of the two remaining grandsons of Calvin Murphy Joliard.* It was on BBC World News."

"Well, I did expect to hear from you, Henry, one way or the other."

"Oh, so you did hear about it."

"Maybe I'm just thinking about it now, Henry."

"Hey, you're growing old with me Mitch, but I want you to exit with glory. I want you to defend the man who killed David Joliard, just to get us there and working together again. This may be our last case."

"I don't like the sound of *exiting with glory,*" Stein said.

"Mitch, you know that all we have is two choices in life. One is to deny death, and the other is to get out on the street and say let's do this. Am I right?"

"I thought you had made peace with your work, Henry. You are younger than me, and you're already retired."

"Well, it's a Joliard, Mitch, and I think this time it is the right Joliard. Old man Calvin changed his name and then buried himself, but I am going to dig him back up. And if we are on Joliard's trail again, I am out of retirement, and this time I am going to find the financial conspiracy behind the Great Depression in 1929 and its connection to the death of my grandfather in 1931. When this search is finished, then I can retire for real, Mitch."

"Alright, Henry, but listen to me. Real conspiracies are based on facts underwritten by evidence, otherwise it is all craziness, and we've got to call it that or why should I be a lawyer, charged to find the truth; or you, to find it so I can use it? I've told you this before."

"Still a good point. And I am going to find that evidence before I am through, Mitch."

"Well, since you know about it already, I must confess something. You are not the only one wanting me to defend the killer, Henry."

"Good. Who is it?"

"An old friend of mine who lives in that same town, Fleckner, called me last night," Stein said. "She also wants me to defend the suspect who is supposed to have killed David Joliard, one of her brothers."

Patrimos made a guess.

"*She?* Is that person, by any chance, the same one you met in England in '96?"

"It is."

"Well, that explains that. So, you are not just thinking about doing it, Mitch, you are actually going to do it, and I also assume that you are going to defend the man charged with the murders *pro bono.*"

"Yes, for her, Henry. If you are coming, you are *pro bono* too. I am already packed and intend to be in Fleckner tomorrow. For several reasons, the District Attorney's office has decided that discovery is going to be short, only two weeks, so we have to start running hard right now."

"*Two* weeks?"

"The murder is the first one in Fleckner in thirty years. It looks like they want to get it over with quickly. It may be cut-and-dried, or maybe not, but the Joliard angle makes the case unique, as you just pointed out."

"I'll stop by my office to gather some things I may need. I'll see you in a few days, Mitch. I'll need some insider tips. Yahoo me a list of people to see and things to do while I'm in Fleckner, because I may be in and out of town as usual."

"If we make it through, Henry, win or lose, it could be interesting again."

"It's about time," Patrimos said.

Stein agreed and hung up to finish what he could of his night's sleep. Ten minutes later he got up and went to his kitchen to brew some Peets coffee. It was 3:45 am.

8

Neap Vesel was having breakfast after a few hours of studying the half-body, when he got a call from Sheriff Walsh.

"Get on back in here, Neap," the Sheriff said with excitement in his voice.

"We've got a suspect!"

"A what?"

"A *suspect.*"

"Be there in ten minutes," Vesel said. He had had little sleep, but he was used to that. On the way to the department, Vesel noticed clouds already darkening the sun. Shadows gave relief from the heat, and he welcomed them. When he got there, he saw the Sheriff waiting for him outside.

Blue walked to the truck and as Vesel got out, the Sheriff banged his right index finger up and down on his other palm in cadence with the syllables of his words.

"Neap, we... have... a... suspect... right... here... in... this... god...damn... jail... right... now!"

He stopped jabbing his palm with the finger and motioned toward the building.

"It's Marvin Macy," the Sheriff said.

"Who?" Vesel asked.

"Marvin Macy! The guy that looks like a skinny hunchback with a mass of gray-white hair on top. Last night I brought him in on a courtesy DUI right before our meeting and gave him the breathalyzer test. He was sleeping off a big one in his car parked at the side of the road near Fleckner High School."

"I know him. Where is he now?"

"Up in Cell 3."

"What evidence do you have?"

"He had two watches on him, a Walmart something or other and a gold Rolex. Ebba thought it was funny that he had two watches on his wrist at the same time, and she looked at the gold Rolex getting ready to give it back to him in a personal possession bag. But she spotted the initials D.K.J. engraved on the back cover of the watch and alerted me. I figured that it's got to be the initials for *David Knight Joliard.*

"He also had a dried bloody rag in his pocket, and I'll bet the blood matches Joliard's."

"Macy had that too?"

"Yes, and the Rolex he had was a real one, and it is expensive. It has a little crown sitting on top of an R. Ebba says it's worth $26,000. It is real gold, so it's maybe worth even more. Gerald Medford downtown used to sell them, and he just authenticated it a while ago. He even recalls engraving it for Joliard when he bought it from him in 1998 right before the dot.com bubble burst.

"Macy must have taken it off Joliard after killing him, wiped his hands clean with his own handkerchief, and then started drinking. We have him clean. As usual, even guests like Macy must take a breathalyzer test when incoming. He did not pass the test, of course, so he's here to stay legally until arraignment, which will be very soon."

Vesel thought about that for a minute. "Macy would have to think straight for some length of time to work out all the angles of something like this, Blue. Can he really be guilty of any of that? And did he have any other of David Joliard's possessions on him?"

"No other Joliard stuff that we could find. You and Jacoby go to David Joliard's place and see if anything else is missing. We'll talk to Marvin when he's over his hangover."

"Okay."

"And listen to this, Neap. The assistant district attorney was over here just now after I called them, and he said the grand jury was going to bring a bill of indictment against Macy *this afternoon.* He would not say why it was so important to do it this quickly, but that's his job. Marvin Macy is going to stand trial for the murder, and soon."

"Really?"

"It's not for us to question why, Neap, but my understanding is that the push comes all the way from the State Attorney General's office. Somebody must know something we don't. But it is the jury here that will decide his guilt or innocence. That is what I am after, and by God, it will be done."

"Blue, we're going to have to investigate Macy's story too."

"Of course, Neap. We do need the facts for both sides. Get on this big time and let's find out for sure what's going on. You are now the official investigator for this office. I already told you that discovery is going to start quickly, and we need to be ready. Tell me what you need. We will have some money left in this fiscal year's budget to pay for more overtime. That's the least I can do."

"I'll call LeMace," Vesel said.

Vesel felt sorry for Macy. As he returned to his office in the south wing of the building and sat down, he thought about the situation. Several odd events: an alcoholic hunchback caught with an expensive watch he could not possibly have bought on his own; handkerchiefs with blood from somebody; and a quicker than normal indictment with a rapid conviction probable. There must be a good reason for all that.

But Vesel knew TV Vans would soon be pulling up outside in the parking lot, and the people inside the vans would be asking lots of questions and Vesel knew correct answers would not be easy to find.

That morning, he had noted thick layers of bruised clouds gathering over the mountains to the west and moving slowly overhead. They were good for cloud shade in June, sucking up water and dark color as they came, destined to be darker and heavier than a blast furnace before they reached the long flat farms on the other side of U.S. 1 to the east, beyond Fleckner, heading toward the huge Atlantic Ocean that did not need water.

9

THE MURDERER

Monday morning, driving her rusty, red-paint-curling car south down US 1, enjoying the sun, the woman could see Murphy Mall coming up on the right. A strip mall facing north, it was the first and only mall in Fleckner and it was named after *Calvin Jay Murphy*, or as she knew even before the town did, *Calvin Murphy Joliard Senior*, and that it was the first thing in Fleckner he had built. That was in 1950, just before the dam was started by the US Army Corps of Engineers.

However, in 2007, after another economic collapse had blasted the town, things were slow in the mall. She thought Fleckner was rapidly becoming a charnel house filled with the dead and those wishing to be dead, and sympathy rose in her heart, but not much.

Now she was hungry. There were several small restaurants and fast food eateries near the mall, but the better Tea Shoppe was downtown. There was only one good Oriental food restaurant left in Fleckner, and it was at the mall. The Red Serpent Hibachi Grill, behind which she had placed David Joliard.

However, the murderer, as she thought of herself, because of the nature of her deeds, a fact being a fact, pulled into the drive-through of a Cap'n Mariners in the parking lot at the mall, and looked over the menu board. She chose a cod sandwich combo and pushed the speaker button.

"Yes, sir... ma'am, what can I get for you?" said a high school student on vacation duty, wearing a seaman's cap and a little white apron with a blue and white Cap'n Mariner logo stamped on it. His name tag read *Harmon*.

"What's your best deal here, Harmon?" she asked.

"Well damn, the one you just punched up, I think. Excuse my English. All that happened yesterday, you know. Bad stuff."

"The dead man?"

"Yes, ma'am."

"Does that worry you?" she said.

"Well, sure it does. I don't want to be cut in two."

"It's just somebody out to make a buck. The publicity you know, Harmon."

"*Make a buck.* You really think that? Where did you hear that? Hey, Marshall," Harmon said to the store manager who was standing right behind him. Marshall's father owned the Cap'n Mariners franchise in Fleckner, and Marshall was listening to music on his brand-new Apple iPhone.

Harmon shook the manager's sleeve to get his attention.

"What?" the manager said, annoyed.

"She said that the killer is just out there to make a buck, and that's it, maybe put it all on cassette and sell it."

Harmon had added that last part on his own, and he was not far wrong.

"Really?" Marshall said.

The iPhone had been introduced January the year before, and it was still selling hot despite things growing tighter and tougher in the economic downturn. Marshall's dad had gotten two in New York, and Marshall did not really care about the customer. He was listening to the Rolling Stones.

"Can I have some lettuce with it?" the murderer asked, as the attendant handed her a medium-size coke.

"What? Oh, sure. Any relish or mayo?"

"Why not. And listen, that murderer? I hear it's a woman."

"What? Marshall, hey Marshall, it's a woman doing that," Harmon said, turning back to Marshall and pulling at the sleeve of his store uniform again.

"A woman?" Marshall said, lifting off his earphones. "Are you kidding me? No woman could cut up a man like that. He would take her down first. Easy."

"Did you hear that, lady?" the attendant said. "It's definitely not a woman."

"Do I get fries with the sandwich too?" she asked.

"Yes," he said, handing her a brown bag with a sandwich, fries, and napkins. There were some hard-to-open packets of ketchup, mayo, and Tartar Sauce inside too.

"Thank you," she said.

"Hey," he said, noticing her large biceps. He thought to himself, *wow she's ripped! Is it a she?*

"Yes?" she said.

"Uh, how can you eat at a time like this?"

Smiling, the murderer pulled out and kept driving down U. S. Highway 1, called the Atlantic Road, watching, biting off a mouthful of sandwich, chewing.

She liked the way the car moved. The exterior was sloppy, but the inside was something else. The entire drive chain was less than a year old. Under the hood was a clean Coyote Mustang Engine that could deliver 435 HP on premium fuel. It was good enough to beat a new Crown Victoria sedan. So were the tires.

After finishing a step on her activity sheet, she liked prowling suburbs and mobile home parks along the Atlantic Road and racing the car on small mountain roads, gaining ever more experience coming out of fast curves. The car was a wordless world and she was a rolling eyeball. It encouraged her to feel that her car and her eyes served her as means to help satisfy her goals. And if any law people wanted to pull her over to ask about it, well, good luck to them.

The Sheriff's Department would by then have the news about David Joliard. She had missed getting him a few years earlier when she shot Calvin II in his hunting fields. One Joliard was enough then, but David's number had come up this time. So that was two down, one to go. Damn, she was almost there, she thought, chuckling. A few more visits out to one of the main microlabs should do it. Whatever sexual pyrotechnics those little immigrants wanted her to do, she did it. What did she care, if she got what she wanted: To kill another Joliard. She even gave them the right gun to use.

The murderer dabbed her thin lips with a napkin, rolled the papers into a ball, and put it back inside the white Cap'n Mariners bag. She balled that up too and tossed it in the floor of the passenger side of the car. She did not want to litter US 1 by throwing it out the window; the Atlantic Road was an historic highway connecting Maine to Miami. She would throw the bag in the garbage when she got home; littering probably added to climate change. Some things were more important than others.

Reflecting on the situation, she thought that it was easy to know where you were going when the end was a certainty, and there was nothing more certain than death, which was a big black piano no one ever played, sitting in a quiet, dusty room with light seeping in through thin window shades.

The rolling eyeball left the neighborhood and sped up the western hills toward Lake Murphy, which had grown richer and more intriguing as the years went by. People and their living spaces had grown first around the eastern tip where the dam was located, and the southern curve and southeastern edges of the lake, but not so much so in the dense northeast, or many sites in the thick woods of the western or northwestern sections yet, either.

But closure for her was even more urgent now. Neap Vesel would be looking for her soon.

10

WASHINGTON DC

Jessie Joliard heard from the mayor in Fleckner, Jimmy Givens, about David, her younger brother, and she tried to remember whether he wanted to be embalmed or cremated. That was immediate. Right, embalmed. She would bury David in Joliard ground at the Maynooth Presbyterian Church. At first she was not certain about the dates, but she learned that the trial for the murder would come very quickly afterwards.

She would be back for that, too, after hashing out her money problems with her potential husband, Senator Jackson Miles. She had also just learned from Parsons at the Fleckner First Bank that a mortgage payment of two hundred and fifty thousand dollars on the family mansion was due. This was a surprise to her.

Jessie had gone from a college graduate to a writer of high-level corporate grants to a top position in the Smithsonian before she was thirty-five. She was now an advisor for a major Midwestern senator, to whom she had been engaged for over a year.

When she called him to pass along the news about David, she asked Senator Miles to meet her before leaving. He suggested they meet at his place in Penn North for supper that night. He would have Harriman, his personal Chef, get fresh Dungeness Crabs at a seafood market on the bay in Baltimore to the east.

Miles looked like a rich merchant with graying hair always combed and brushed, but with one ear bent outward on the left side. Sometimes Miles would point to that and say that was a bond they had together, meaning the similarity between his ear's odd bent appearance and her singular face. She was not amused when he did that. Overall, she was a 9.5, as Miles would say when introducing her to supporters or colleagues, to throw off the obvious, that her facial variations kept her from being a full 10.

After lovemaking, they lay on a huge bed with Venus and Mars carved on the headboard and Jessie thinking how best to bring up the subject of the money.

It was more complicated than that. In fact, each of them had a secret that neither wanted to talk about. It was like a Mexican standoff of secrets. Each had something the other wanted, but neither wanted to tell what his or her secret was first. For her, it was the secret of the Joliard treasure and where it was. For him, it was the secret of where he got all his political Pac money; it seemed inexhaustible, and he kept being re—elected with it.

Jessie knew that night better be the night for her to find out his secret and then leverage her request with it. If that did not work, she might just stay in Fleckner and go down with the ship.

"Jackson, we have to do something," she said. "I'm losing out at home. As I told you, David is dead, but he just followed what Kurt was doing, and Kurt is, I'm sure, still doing it. My share of what is left of the Joliard estate may be losing more air than the Hindenburg."

"Damn, Jessie," Miles laughed. "I have a large personal loan repayment due next month, and you still have at least one old Fed Note. You're ahead of me."

Jessie thought to herself, probably not, but her grandfather's *Chicago Diary* was something about which she had not told the Senator, and she had not mentioned that she had *nine* Federal Reserve Notes left, not one, and each one was valued by collectors at close to half a million, or higher. She had always been good at arithmetic in her head and she rapidly ran nine times half a million. Four and a half million. But she also knew how the high-end collectibles market worked. If too many of a valuable item came up for bid at the same time, collectors would quickly grow skeptical. So, she could not move on her bills immediately, and they were therefore of no real help to her at that time. She needed another way to solve that problem.

If Jackson did not loan her the money she needed—something she had never asked of him before, she would turn to solving her own problem without him, and even beyond the matter of the printed Federal Reserve Notes that might be hidden somewhere on the estate somewhere. She also had a clue about something else in Fleckner she believed was worth even more than the hidden bills.

"I know what you're saying, Jessie. If you have at least one Note, then it's clear that your grandfather did print at least some of them, right? And so, one assumes there are more. But one hundred thousand of them? Where would he put them? They would weigh about two-hundred pounds, right?" he said.

The Senator seemed relaxed and pensive, as he usually did after intercourse, but Jessie wanted to boil the pot some more. Since Neap Vesel had once explained to her that an active offense was the best defense, she attacked Jackson. It was time for the big surprise.

"In the early years, Jackson, we all knew there were rumors about what had happened in Chicago with my grandfather during the Great Depression. Chicago was really where the depression got its start, in the futures market, with pork, and I believe I am the only one to whom Pawpaw told anything true about it."

"Pawpaw?" Miles said, with a grin on his face.

Jessie was nonplussed. "That is what I called my grandfather when I was little, and he liked it. He was a very tenderhearted man, at least to me, not a hardnosed capitalist as you hear about people around Washington now. So, if you really love me, you can help me act in my family's best interests here, Jackson. I want to pay off the last loan my brothers put on the place and keep Kurt from doing anything worse to the family name."

Miles nodded his head but said nothing.

"I need your help, Jackson," she said. "I need to cover the loan on the house and grounds. I need one hundred and fifty thousand dollars to take back to Fleckner with me this week."

"Woo, Jessie, that's more than I have liquid. I can't do anything like that for maybe two months."

"Oh?" Jessie said, taken aback by his cavalier reply to her request. "I suppose, although..."

"Wait," he said, turning on her. "You *suppose*? I have gone well out of my way to help you against Kurt on the hill here, Jessie, even carrying around a micro-lab bill by hand to combat drugs on your estate grounds. You wanted that to stop Kurt from making drugs on your property with a chance of the government confiscating it. Right? That has raised some eyebrows, I can tell you, but I want you to be able to help me in return. Christ! Can I count on that?"

"Of course, Jackson," Jessie said, consciously trying to relax, feeling better. When Miles got agitated about something, he could be led to a conclusion. It looked like she was going to be able to lead him up to the clincher and the money after all.

"Now if you tell me what it is you are working on that requires my help so badly in return, Jackson, I can tell you if I can really help you in the long run or not," she said.

"Are you talking about all that lost money your family is supposed to have hidden somewhere but nobody can find?"

"More than that," she said.

"Mine's Top Secret," he said.

"Well," Jessie said, still leading him. "So is mine, and if you give me some more incentive here, maybe I can help you in a bigger way than you might guess."

"Ah, how's that?" Miles said, intrigued.

"Maybe we can find the Notes' original printing plates."

Senator Miles was immediately on his feet and at Jessie's throat. This was the first time he had heard about a *real* treasure. He clapped a hand over her mouth.

"*Plates?* There are printing plates for the Notes?" he whispered, as if someone were listening. "Why didn't you tell me about them before? Jesus Christ, Jessie, with plates we do not need your goddamn Note at all. We can print as many as we want!"

"Well, I think I know where the plates might be, Jackson," she said, peeling his hand from her mouth.

He put his fingers to his lips and indicated to her that she should also whisper.

"I have a good clue, but I can't get to the plates by myself. I would have to have help that I know can keep quiet. Now that is *my* secret. But before I give you my clues, I need you to answer my question. What is your secret, and can you help me here?"

Miles stood and looked around. He started walking in a tight circle. "Now, listen, Jessie. This is only between you and me. Years ago, when I was first a representative for a house seat in Kansas, I used my own money to get elected. I was effective and worked my way up the ladder with some help from a mentor I was lucky to have.

"But when I decided to run for the Senate, I had talks with lots of donors, you know, to weed out the crazies. I settled on several deep pocket groups, but one was a very deep pocket group. I chose that one for the long haul. It was called the *Jubilee Trust* and, as I have learned, it is backed by a determined group.

"I asked for ten million to fund my first Senate race and they did not even blink. All they asked in return was for me to introduce legislation on a variety of unconnected regulations, and to help kill certain bills. That seemed straightforward enough to me. Hell, none of the regulations or bills they were after seemed anything I would not naturally oppose anyway. It seemed a good arrangement."

"That's it?"

"Not quite. Years came and went. I received whatever I needed to keep being re-elected, including grants, scholarships, underwriting for new schools, that sort of bread-and-butter stuff I had to keep up with for my state. The reason was to sway anybody and everybody to keep voting for *Military Miles.*"

"*Military Miles?*"

"That's what I was called early on when we were beefing up the military for all those sandy wars in the Middle East in the nineties. I did not let up. I was out front parading all the time for the military. It was always more, more, more for the military. I even talked several times with President H.W. Bush about it.

"Oh?"

"Things were moving well for me."

"A lot of politicians did that, Jackson. Hell, I bet when that war started, they fell into line like flies after a gob of chicken fat."

"Funny, Jessie, funny, but true. However, after that I was asked by this group to push legislation that would d undermine the military in one way or another. I said hell, no, I am not going to do that. I love my country."

"So?"

"This was before you and I met, Jessie, so you probably won't remember the time when I went skiing in Crystal Valley, a very swank place in Utah. I broke my leg and gave up skiing."

"That's true, Jackson," she whispered, and nodded her head. "That was before we met, but I do remember you talking about your broken leg once."

"But what you weren't told, Jessie, is that I did not break it while skiing," Miles whispered.

"You mean..."

"Yes, I do mean. The JT finally made it known what would happen if I crossed the queen. They not only did to a US Senator, they did it to the consitution. "

"My, God, Jackson. You mean..."

"They did that to a man in a *goddamn blood oath.*"

The next day Jessie headed home to Fleckner with a cashier check for two-hundred and fifty thousand dollars.

11

At age fourteen, Neapolitan Vesel was looking at the tips of his scuffed Reeboks, kicking at small brown and white sandstone and quartz rocks. The weather was hot, and he was breathing hard. He had on gray gym shorts and a white T-shirt cut short across his large dimpled navel. He had just run up and down a rocky slope as if it was the Greek amphitheater at Delphi and he was an actor playing some tragic part requiring him for all eternity to run up and down the semi-circular rows of stone seats carved out of the mountain.

Indeed, running was all young Vesel thought about. He loved running in the foothills, absorbing the world of his father who had taught him about challenge, bounding from rock to rock, guessing what the rocks a few feet ahead were going to be like, adapting on the run, pushing his leg muscles hard, honing his eye-foot coordination. He was already playing ball in Junior Varsity and excelling. People in town heard rumors about him and for the first time ever, non-parents went to see Junior Varsity games. He was good at it; in fact, sensational, and it was his as well as his father's great achievement.

Vesel had no brothers or sisters, and he was growing rapidly. His mother Margo Ricci accused him of eating enough for three brothers. He loved his mother as one loved the moon: she was always there, never leaving, although changing from time to time to remain interesting and fun.

Feeling drained as he cooled down, the young Neap was ready to drift back homeward when he heard what he thought was a muffled shout. He looked up, glanced around, and heard it again from the next rise over, near a grove of Loblolly pines of which he could just see the tops.

Vesel knew that he was on Murphy land and he hesitated to do anything, but when he reached the ridge, he saw someone he thought he knew lying about fifty yards away: It was Jessie Murphy. He thought he remembered her for some reason. The Murphy's at the time lived up on top of the tallest of the foothills surrounding Fleckner, along with a few other wealthy families not far from where he was crouching.

He did not know closely any of the Murphy brothers, one of whom, the oldest, had gone missing years before and become a legend by which to warn children to stay close to home: *The mountain hag will get you like Calvin 3, if you don't watch out and if you don't really see.*

It seemed uncertain if anybody was really lost that way, other than Calvin III.

But now Vesel saw the Murphy girl pinned to the ground by a man lying on his left side with his back to Vesel. His balding head exposed frayed hairs; he wore old hiking boots, a picture of a gray airship in flames was on the back of his faded T-shirt, and the back of his blue jeans exposed white briefs and the obscene V of his fat buttocks. Vesel could not see the man's face. A lavender panty was hanging on one of Jessie's slender ankles; the man had bunched up around her neck her grey Bryn Mawr T-shirt and white bra.

The man had braced himself against Jessie's right arm, shoulder, and leg to hold her flat on her back, and his left arm was under her neck and a large dirty hand looped up and over her mouth, forcing her to squeal, their cheeks almost touching. He was using his free right hand to reach between her thighs, although Jessie fought with her legs and free hand as best she could, flailing at the man's face awkwardly.

Despite the shock of what he was seeing, Vesel noted that Jessie's hair with red highlights seemed to have a life of its own, like a basket of snakes whipping and curling as she struggled. He thought that if the hair got within striking range of the attacker's neck, as they were then, they would go for his jugular vein.

The girl was tough, Vesel could see that, but not enough to force the attacker to retreat. The man had large upper body mass, and young Vesel, as big as he was, was unsure if he could successfully chase him away. But he saw the man was opening his pants and giving full attention to what he was doing.

Vesel seized a large piece of quartz rock covered with tan dust. Clutching the jagged rock in both hands like a large brown, uncut diamond, Vesel crept up behind the rapist. He caught Jessie's eyes as she turned to him and they bulged as she increased her muted cries.

Alerted, the man glanced over his shoulder and saw Vesel just raising the rock above his head. Quicker than it looked possible to do, he pulled a switchblade from one blue jean pocket and made a threatening motion with it first toward him and then toward Jessie's throat.

But there was nothing to haggle about and Vesel moved faster. His choice was made in a fraction of a second as he brought the rock down hard and true on the top right side of the attacker's skull. The man's eyes bulged for a second like Jessie's, right before there was the sound of a ripened watermelon hitting concrete. The blow forced the man to slump across Jessie as his legs shot out straight, shook for a few seconds, and then went limp across her.

"Neap, Neap!" Jessie screamed with her mouth free now.

Vesel tossed the rock to one side, gripped the man's feet, and twisted him away from her.

Before she dressed, she stood and cried, splattered with gore on her face and neck and clothes. She had a half smile through her tears that seemed to beg Vesel for forgiveness, as if all this were her fault. He stared at her snow-white nakedness, and she allowed it. He would remember that moment as if it were a grace glimpse of life; she was beautiful and he felt a stirring in his loins, which for him was not unfamiliar.

At almost the same moment, when he looked at the dead man covered with blood, his head in crooked white and grey pieces, Vesel faced the ground, his hands on his knees, feeling nauseous. He would remember that too.

My God! What have I done?

For some reason, it was as if the two acts were the same: One was a vision of beauty; but the other was an ugly penance for having witnessed beauty's desecration, which had required vengeance.

Vesel wiped Jessie's face and neck with his T-shirt as best as he could. When Jessie was dressed, he was curious.

"How did you know my name?"

"Your father would come up here to work for my daddy and sometimes he would bring you. Don't you remember? We played under the cedar tree in front of the house. My daddy told me to take care of you since I was bigger."

"Yes," Vesel said, his eyes brightening. He did remember her.

Jessie gestured for Vesel to follow her to her house, but Vesel told her he would have to do something with the body first. TV shows and movies showed him that. The body had to be hidden. There was a gully about five feet deep nearby and Vesel took the knife, pulled the body toward the gully, and rolled it in. He wiped the knife clean on his shirt, gathered the skull and brain fragments together and threw them into the gully with the body.

Collecting large rocks of numerous sizes, Vesel covered up the gully and the man in it. He made it look as normal as possible. There was little chance that the rocky terrain would leave any foot- or fingerprints, especially after the next rain, which was probably the next day, he thought, looking up at the skies. He collected handfuls of rock dust to toss across spilled blood on the ground. The next hard rain would take care of that too. It would wear out.

When he finished with the makeshift cairn, Vesel walked silently with Jessie to her big house. Coming in from behind it, she showed Vesel where a green hose lay coiled behind the garage. He could wash the blood off his clothes and himself, and she would bring out towels with which to dry.

As he sprayed himself, he thought he saw a black face standing at a big window to the rear of the house upstairs, watching.

When she came back out, Jessie had showered and put on a new shirt and jeans. Even though he was now as exposed as she had been, with a straight face she handed him a big red towel with a gold

J on it. She admired his muscular shoulders and upper legs, and had a strange feeling of involvement, a future goal.

He asked if she was all right now.

"Better. Thank-you, Neap. I won't tell anybody if you don't," she said.

"I understand."

"Can you keep a secret?"

"Yes."

"Even a bad secret like this?"

"Sure," he said, envisioning the event, the man and the knife and what he might have done to Jessie with it.

He dressed in his still wet shorts and tennis shoes, and the T-shirt which was almost dry again. He felt Jessie's eyes upon him. When he was finished, he smiled and handed her back the towel, wondering what the letter J stood for.

"It's another secret, Neap, okay?"

"Okay," Neap said, hoping he could remember all the promises he had just made.

"My family's last name is really Joliard, not Murphy. It was paw-paw's decision to change it. He told us it could be bad for us if the word got out. So, we became Murphy's. Do you swear to keep this secret too, Neap?"

"Yes," he said.

"Thank-you," Jessie said, handing him a big green bill. "I want you to have this."

Vesel took it and almost dropped it. It was bigger than a dollar bill in size and very much bigger in value. It was a $10,000 bill.

"Did you make this?" he asked.

"No," Jessie said. She looked back at the house. "It's real. Keep it."

The thought of attaching money as a reward for or against violence was for Vesel a new thought. There was a better way he could think about it. It was tit for tat. He was too young to figure the moral weakness of the thought, but much later he did, from Machiavelli, who noted that revenge was the prince's choice, not that of someone lesser.

"I just couldn't let that man do that to you," Vesel said truthfully.

Jessie shrugged. "Okay, Neap."

"I'm glad you're better," Vesel said, looking again at the big green bill that had a man's picture and a blue certificate on the front and what looked like kneeling Thanksgiving pilgrims on the back. He noticed that she had not crumbled the bill; she had treated it like real money, folding it carefully. Vesel was skeptical, but he folded it the same way she did and put it carefully into the driest pocket in his running shorts.

As he did so, Jessie leaned forward and kissed Vesel on the cheek. He smiled and was glad he had been able to clean his face.

"Remember, just you and I know about this," Jessie said.

"Okay."

She turned and ran back to her house.

As he watched her go, her elbows flapping like a bird's wings, Neap guessed that to do something like that to a girl in the right way, you had to earn it, not take it without purchase the way the homeless man had tried to do. *That was bad. Earning it was the best way.* In a moment of insight, Vesel knew deep down that running in the mountains had just taken second place in his life to Jessie Joliard.

Yet, he could not think of himself doing that with Jessie. No, she was above that, and he wanted it to be that way. For all his animal nature, he believed she had descended into flesh, which he could only admire and even worship through his memories of seeing her in a moment in which she had been almost desecrated but was saved.

There would be many other women for Vesel, but he would feel that each carried a small piece of Jessie with her, and he would receive it from all of them each time in a sacramental mystery.

* * *

Jessie made a scrapbook of Vesel's high school football career and kept it with her wherever she went, yelling for him loudly at games in town if she were there, or was able to hear one on an AM radio station in Pennsylvania near Philadelphia where she was in college. His success was becoming famous on the east coast. People would bring binoculars to watch him run. At times he looked as if he were running *from* something, instead of *toward* the other goalpost, and that seemed to make him run faster.

Jessie Joliard's own memories about Vesel were riddled by an interaction of thoughts good and bad. A boy of good intent defeated a man of evil intent, and if she were writing a story, and telling it to her grandchildren, she would assert that the villain was the homeless man who wanted to take her youth by force, and the hero was the young boy who denied the other man his wish by beating him to death with a rock. In reflecting on that act many times, she asked herself how the story could be any different than it was, when the struggle that gave it birth was of a short duration in both their lives.

She felt, rather than thought, that something truly unspeakable had happened, and that it was a complex mixture of moral and personal conflicts that had, out of all other places in the world, found Fleckner in which to blossom.

12

Marvin Macy put his face into his soft hands and moaned. All he did was buy a watch from a homeless nit downtown. The homeless nit was the one who ought to be in the cell there, not him. It was almost a week since then, and he was still there, in jail!

Macy wondered why Melody Turner had recommended this Mitch Stein to defend him. His one call had been to her, and he wound up with a famous lawyer who told him he could get him off and that he would not require legal fees. Being desperate, Macy had agreed. Why not? It sounded simple enough, especially the part about no legal fees. He just hoped Mr. Stein knew what he was doing, because sitting in a cell for some homeless bum was not good.

He felt like a bug in a corner, waiting for some very disturbed homemaker to smash him with a stiff broom. In addition, his ex-wife was on him again about money. He recalled something he read once and with which he now gleefully agreed: *his wife would have been a good wife, if there had been someone there to shoot her every day of her life.*

And what was her harangue about this opportunity to get some big money to serve time for a noble cause? The noble cause was for her, it seemed to him. She would know what the money would be in a few days, she said, and for Macy to say nothing about it. Later she said the money might be a lot more, maybe one hundred thousand bucks. This, of course, got his attention.

On her last visit, she told him to shut up and they would get him off with a half-million if he ate his sentence and said absolutely nothing about it while in prison.

In fact, the Head of the program–probably, he thought, some liberal philanthropist–told her directly that if he told no one anything, ever, the amount rose to one million dollars, and protection while in prison too. Christ! Who was he going to tell? The cockroaches in his cell, who were like cryptic little messengers, leery of being caught and tortured, signatories from the pope perhaps, with wings like dried and bloodstained papal robes, and the pusillanimous ability to weasel away from anything, just under and through the thinnest of cracks?

He tried to believe his wife, of course. Even though he wanted out, it was a big temptation. If offered, he guessed he would take the money faster than a thirsty dog at a water bucket.

The next day he learned from her that there had to be a decision made no later than the first day of the trial when they would give him an action plan and part of the money, with the rest coming after serving at least three years. Well, no problem, he thought, and he passed that along to his ex-wife, who took charge of the operation *in toto*. She told a friend that the two might be making up and might re-marry.

13

Angry and anxious for his country and its people, especially his Ricci Italian relatives in New York City who had been in the wrong place at the wrong time and fell with the two towers, Neap Vesel joined the army two years later and left on a bus for basic training in Fort Jackson, South Carolina; and then SO training at Fort Bragg, North Carolina, and later counterterrorist training at Ft Benning, Georgia.

He finished two tours of duty in Afghanistan during which he went to Italy, land of his ancestors, only once, and toured the ancient Ricci places of interest along narrow pearl and bruise-colored cobblestone streets in Naples where his ancestors had walked.

For the obvious reason, he also went to the Flecknerspitze, a peak of the Alps mountain range near South Tyrol, where he found a high-altitude symbol, a large wooden cross, which suggested to him a great if barren suffering, with nothing else but snow and ice nearby.

Vesel tried for connections with his ancestors, but he felt instead only a desire to be back at the home his ancestors had left Italy for two centuries before: America, where he had been told repeatedly that he was a hero for being in a war.

When he came home, the reasons for doing so were not at first made clear to others in town. He seemed to owe fealty to something in the woods and hills there, either their innocent motions or stillnesses. Up in the hills he met people who had forgotten where they came from and did not know their names. They were like wild game that, when they saw a human being, vanished to avoid being shot for food. Vesel wondered if the bare economics unveiled by the war, and the Great Recession, had forced most of them back in time to the state of the early settlers, chronically hungry, sick, and quick to run from danger.

Vesel cleaned up and joined the Sheriff's Department in Fleckner. He believed the Sheriff was willing to take a chance on an ex-high school football star who had never lost a game, and a Special-Ops soldier who had a high kill-rate in SF operations.

Many believed that Vesel was just the type of man they needed to fight common crime such as there was in Fleckner. With his experience, they believed he was a hard man to be feared by others. If there was any brawling at the local bar on Saturday nights, Vesel could clean out the place in a matter of minutes, tossing rough men outside with impunity. With domestic violence calls, the perps would raise their hands to the ceiling when Vesel walked in the front door.

Over time, the people of the town had accepted that he was in fact a good man who did a good job, until the dead half-man turned up. Thirty years without a murder, and then BLAM. At that point people began to wonder again. Was this man, this deputy, good or bad?

14

Blue was angry and frustrated. "I just heard that the Feds are coming in soon about problems with drugs here in Fleckner County," he said. "And they are serious about all this, Neap. They will get in the way of the murder investigation, and there will be lots more work to do. I'm getting too old for this. You can have it all now if you want it."

"No, sir," Vesel said, still standing at the door. He leaned forward and tossed his empty cola cup perfectly into the wastebasket beside Walsh's desk.

"For what, me not being too old, or you don't want it?"

"You still have what it takes to do the job, sir," Vesel replied, sitting down in the folding chair.

The Sheriff stared at Vesel for another second then grunted.

"Huh, well maybe I have it, or maybe I don't. But you know I am going to retire soon, and the closer I get to it, the less I want to have anything new or unusual like this going on here."

"No, sir."

"As Sheriff, I'm going to start depending on you more and more, Neap. You know that, right? I believe you are next in this barrel, and I want you to be ready."

"Yes, sir, I do too."

"Now, you want to hear what Nellums told me?"

Vesel nodded his head. "I do."

"Okay. According to Nellums, he wasn't killed where he was found. The bumps on top of the head were made by a hammer of some kind. Bruises on the face probably occurred when he fell from the blows, which came from behind. The body was cut evenly across the middle, at the spine just above the hips, and right below the kidneys here," he said, pointing to his side.

"Good sew-up at the bottom. Very neat. A professional job. No blood remained. We don't know where the other half is."

"And the Band-Aid on the back of the hand?" Vesel asked.

"An injection of some kind had been made not long before they died. Nellums has no idea why a Band-Aid for sanitation purposes was added. The man was going to be dead soon anyway."

Vesel frowned but grew animated. This was the sort of logic he had gotten used to in battle.

"Anesthetized maybe?" he asked. "After the hammer blow, a portable IV to make him easier to handle? Done by a doctor, or a nurse? The man did not live in such a way that allowed anybody to believe he was missing, even after a week. But cutting up a body might take at least two or three days. I wonder if he made a video of it."

"A video?" the Sheriff responded.

"A video for the record," Neap said. "Bleed him out and then cut him in half and dress the top of the body the way it was? Edit himself out. Make a TV special, or a video how-to manual. Dodge the issue of murder, make himself look good. Los Zetas would like that for instructional purposes, or maybe to intimidate buyers and sellers alike. The Taliban would do that too, if they could."

"I don't know, Neap, that's creepy. Anyway, the murderer was certainly concerned about hygiene and that would account for a lack of fingerprints with blood on them. The killer must have used plastic gloves the whole time.

He was careful."

"I suppose so," Vesel said.

"But how did the body get there without anybody noticing? And why does something so unnatural happen here in Fleckner in the first place?"

Vesel shrugged. "There were no satanic symbols on them anywhere, no harsh secret messages hidden in the fabric of their coats? In Afghanistan, we would find threaded codes in the perahan tunban shirts, the long ones that fall below the knees? There were lots of places to carry colored threads of code in thick fabric like that."

"No, they were clean. No tattoos that said Mama either," said the sheriff, chuckling.

"Nothing out of the ordinary is what Frost told me at the crime scene last night," Vesel replied. "It was nothing out of the ordinary, except for David Joliard's top half sitting right there staring at me while I was listening to Frost."

"I saw it."

"So, do you think there is druggie stuff involved here like the Feds do?" Vesel asked.

"I don't know. But it was bizarre that a perp just walked in there with the top of David Joliard and set it down without leaving footprints," the Sheriff noted.

"Maybe the perp wore socks over his shoes," Vesel said. "Frost guessed that the small shoe prints just out of range near the half-body at the mall were made by a   woman or a kid who may have seen the whole thing."

"An eyewitness, Neap? A kid in town? That could be a big problem if the murderer hears about it."

"It could be, but that's way down on my list at the moment, Blue."

"I hear you."

Vesel rubbed one palm over the thick pectorals of his chest. "I see Mason Corson first, and then check on the footprints again, sir, but it's possible something more is going on here."

Mason Corson was the Fleckner County Waste Control Officer.

"You think Mason knows something?" the Sheriff asked.

Vesel nodded. "His garbage truck comes to the rear alley of the mall on the east and west sides three nights a week to pick up garbage. Has for years. I remember the truck from when I was here in high school. Nobody pays it any mind. It's a fixture."

Vesel wondered how that could happen without him knowing about it. He knew Mason kept a close eye on his truck; he washed it and petted it. But when Neap looked at the Sheriff, he saw in his face a hesitancy about this crime.

"I'm sure going to ask him about it though," Vesel said.

15

CHICAGO

Henry Patrimos had two important things on his mind. One was his grandfather's strange death, and the other was the trial that would be coming up soon. As to what had happened to his grandfather, Patrimos almost knew the answer. Bending the photos with his fingers, he surmised that two things had become one. His grandfather's fate met with the movement of large money in the country. He did not mean hundred-dollar bills either. Something big had to be behind it, and he knew this was his last chance to prove it. He looked up at the crown-molded ceiling in his office and shook his head. He thought:

This case needs to start exposing the answers I am after, and soon, or I am a dead man who never fulfilled his promise to his family.

The promise was for revenge.

He put the photos back in the file and put the file back in a drawer in his desk. He locked the drawer with a key he carried around with other keys to his house, his office, his car, his gun cabinet.

He kept out the last photo in the pile. It was of a slim woman with blond hair down to her shoulders. She was smiling at whomever took the picture. On the back of the photo were two names: Millie Masters and Byron Crumb. He did not know when it was taken, but when he first saw the photo in 1982, he knew Millie Masters was the woman in the picture.

The picture had been taken in front of the house next to 221 Parlor Street: 223 Parlor Street. Millie was a friend of his Grandmother Gertrude who lived next door, and who had grieved a long time for her husband Walter, and in fact endured the rest of her time in the one house until she died and the house was sold.

Patrimos remembered that the much younger Millie Masters would take things to his grandmother and they would sit and talk for hours about everything, and even after they had long since exhausted the subject of her dead husband. Patrimos thought it was therapy for his grandmother, and he remembered that he was grateful to Millie for doing it. Over the years, he guessed his Grandmother had spent more time with Millie than with him.

Byron Crumb was a close friend of the widow Patrimos in the furtive way men are who are not a widow's husband. At that time Patrimos had not cared about Byron, nor where he worked, nor how inextricably he was caught up in the same web as his grandfather, when he had first known Millie; but at the time, Vesel did not have the right question.

He tucked the picture of Millie in his briefcase with his Ruger .38 snub nosed revolver, the one he had used for years. He was a licensed PI, and he would declare it at the airport and get it back, no problem. He called the airport and booked a flight to his old neighborhood in Palatine, Illinois, leaving late that afternoon.

As he flew and watched the lights from the earth far below, Patrimos recalled that there was only one thing he ever wanted from a woman, but he had never shared it, nor asked for it, because of his obsession with finding out who had been behind the death of his grandfather Walter. His job had made him rough over the years, and he could not let that edge go. His driving need was still to find the people who were responsible, and that need always got in the way of his relationships with women. He could not sit content, and the inability to do that broke down any bond he could have had. It was an obsession and he knew it, but it would not be over until he found the facts, any way he could get them.

For him, two things stood in stark contrast—the need to share a life, and to be alone to pursue truth—and that basic division motivated his daily actions. The struggle made him conflicted, but good at what he did. Who better to search and ask questions about normal things and seek hidden answers than someone who, because he was never a part of them, knew about such things intimately?

16

THE JUBILEE ACCOUNT

Ebba rang Vesel's office. He had come in that morning and made the comment that he had spent a night in the mountains to refresh himself, and it had not worked. Ebba usually did not ask the obvious question: Why not? She was good that way. But she usually called early when only a bad act had occurred. When she rang him, Vesel instantly thought: *My God, don't tell me somebody else has been shot in Fleckner!*

"Hey, Ebba," he said.

"Neap, there's someone up here who says she needs to talk to you. It seems very important in the sense that it may very well be important, if you know what I mean."

Vesel was not in the mood to talk with anybody.

"Who is it?" he asked.

"Melody Turner."

"Bartram Turner's daughter?"

"She's retired now," Ebba whispered.

"She taught most everybody here at the station except you, the Sheriff, and me, I think, since we never talk about her, and the others never quit talking about her."

"Send her back."

He at least owed Ms. Turner the department's regrets for her father's death, which may or may not have had anything to do with the half-body. It was probably an unintended meeting of landowner and drug manufacturer, and the landowner had lost.

He did stand at the door to meet her.

"Come in, please," Vesel said, motioning her to a chair in front of his desk.

"Have a seat."

"Merci beaucoup," she said in a clear voice with a lilting cadence.

It was not a boring voice, like those of many teachers he knew; hers had suggestion in it, a bit of mischief even. He had never been in one of her classes, nor had he officially met her when he played football there. He did recognize her now, however. She was still beautiful in a burnished, old museum type way. Brass and polished mahogany kept clean every day.

She in turn immediately noticed his hands. "Neap! Did you injure your hands?"

Neap? He guessed that the only person who could always call you by your first name, even if you were the pope, was a high school English teacher.

She put out one of her hands over the desk towards him, and Vesel let her take one of his to look at.

"It's nothing," he said. "We have been dealing with the homicides in town. My mind is on about six different things right now. This is a time when I went too far. I took out my frustration on the top of my desk."

"I can see that. Well, then, Neap, we will get to the point immediately. I bet your mind is preoccupied," she said in a way that told Vesel that she knew what else he had been thinking about: Her.

She released his hand.

"I'm sorry about your father," Vesel said. "We believe we know how he died, but not yet why."

"Daddy always was stubborn. He loved it out there in the woods and the lake. It was his retirement place. I offered to move him in with me when mother died, but he did not want any of that, or to go to an assisted-living place. It just was not in him to do that. It may be questionable how he died, but he was at least older than the elder Calvin when he went."

"He knew Calvin Joliard?"

"He was younger than Calvin Senior, but they talked a lot, and they played poker together, him and several other men who are all gone now, I think. He knew early that Murphy was Calvin's real middle name and Joliard was his real last name. So, did I. But no one else in town did, I don't think. That grand old man just wanted it that way."

"That must have been interesting."

"Oh, it was. Poppa had many stories about Calvin. But, listen. This is why I came, Neap. Do you have a good suspect for the killing in town?"

"Yes. Marvin Macy. He's in custody."

"Ah, no," Melody said. "I said a *good* suspect; somebody who might really have done it."

"You know who the killer is?" he asked.

Ms. Turner laughed a soft sound in her throat like a lower register b flat. It was appealing and dismissive at the same time.

"You know the sexes are still not really allowed to be equal today, Neap, although I do what I can. I cannot easily snoop around without giving it all away. I have no idea who the real murderer is, I just know it isn't Marvin, and I'll testify to that in court and tell why. But I'm not here about that, either."

"You would do that in court?" Vesel said. "Then why are you here...."

"I also saw LeMace the night he was killed," she said.

Vesel jumped forward in his chair. "Where?"

"At my house. Many of my old students, and part-students like Marvin, often drop by just to chat when they have something important about which to talk. I welcome them all. He stopped by and told me about some of what you and he had been doing about the case. He said he thought he knew who the killer in town was, and he was going to confirm that suspicion that night. He was confident."

"Who was it?"

"He wouldn't tell me, of course. He said he had found some evidence, and he was on his way there after leaving my house."

"He came by to see you before confronting a serial killer?"

Vesel was leaning forward aggressively toward Ms. Turner. She did not move and seemed unflustered.

"I couldn't restrain him, Neap. That's what he did and what he said. I thought you would want to know the facts, given what we know about his fate."

"Ah, Ms. Turner, I'm sorry, you're right," he said, sitting back. "That's all he said that he knew who it was—he was sure about that--and he was going there then?"

"As they say, Neap, it is what it is. I hope it helps in some way. His death, and other recent ones, has us all looking for comfort of some kind, I will bet, even the teens at my school."

Vesel looked up. He had suddenly recalled where Jacoby might very well have been going that night:

The Beguiles' house, about Sammy.

"It has helped, Ms. Turner. I...thank you so much for coming by," he said eagerly.

"Let me know when you catch the real person who did this, Neap. Okay?"

"The world will know, Ms. Turner, but you will know first, because I think you have just helped me greatly."

"And one last point," she laughed. "Teachers always have one last point, and sometimes it's the best one."

"Yes?"

"You know James Parsons over at the Fleckner First Bank on the corner of South and Main? He was a good student, in business classes at least. You played ball with him. As a school sponsor, I went to most of the games, but not all. You were tremendous at the time, of course."

Vesel nodded his head. "We called him the General. He was the quarterback my freshman and sophomore years. Why?"

"Before the trial is over, I would suggest that you talk with him about the *Jubilee Account.*

"What?"

"It's still called the *Jubilee Account,* I believe. I think you may learn something new about the Joliards and the larger world old Calvin played in if you approach James with the right attitude. It has something to do with how we live here in Fleckner."

"How do you know about that?"

"Did I mention that my father used to play poker with Calvin Joliard the first?"

"I believe you did," Vesel said.

"Well, good day to you, Neap."

The gracefully aging schoolteacher rose, bowed slightly, and left. Vesel stepped out of his office and watched her move regally up the hall, past Ebba's desk, and out the double front doors of the Sheriff's Department. There seemed nothing false about her, and, because of her, Vesel now believed he had the piece of information he needed to complete the puzzle about his deputy trainee, Jacoby, and what he had tried to do.

Before he came home, he had been tasked to check into possible money laundering at Parson's bank, but his heart was not in it. He believed that the General would not have been involved in anything illegal at his family bank. He guessed he would see Parsons about the Jubilee Account business soon enough, but he would have to put it on a back burner for now to follow up on the Jacoby shooting, and Larry Beguiles' possible role in it.

17

In Chicago O'Hare International Airport it was supper time and people were lined up at various national brand outlets, eating, talking on their phones, laughing, looking around, gesturing with their hands.

Henry Patrimos stood in the atrium beyond the limit of ropes that said:

NO SMOKING. THANK-YOU.

He was smoking. He would eat later. Staying there long enough to finish three Natural Spirits cigarettes, walking to and fro as if waiting for someone, his left hand perched up on his left hip, he noticed a man in a navy-blue serge suit who was there as he left the plane and gone down the steps into the causeway. It was plain enough. The man was big and probably armed. He was just the type. He would find out soon enough if the man followed him into the nearest rest room.

When he finished the third cigarette, he went to the Men's room he had already checked into. It was clean and polished, pale green walls, five stalls, filtered fans overhead. He went in and waited near the door. When the man tried to push his way in, Patrimos shoved the door back into him, apologized, then yanked him quickly into the room by his lapels, whirled him around into a stall, the man's right hand captured in one of the big pockets of his own coat.

That's when the man started to react.

"What the hell... uh...you do..."

Patrimos was sitting on the man's lap with his left elbow stuck up under the man's chin so he could barely talk, and the man's right hand could not easily get to him because it was jammed in his right pocket.

"Who sent you?" Patrimos asked.

"Fug you."

"Wrong answer," Patrimos said and with his right hand hit the man in his left ear, three, four times, rapidly.

The man was stunned.

"Who sent you?" Patrimos repeated.

"Goddamn..."

"Wrong answer again," Patrimos said. With his right hand, he popped the man in his Adam's apple.

The man choked and tried to breathe.

"Who sent you?"

This time the man believed Patrimos just might leave him dead in the stall. He blinked his eyes rapidly and said JT.

"What?"

"JT."

"The TV?"

"TJT!"

Patrimos released his left arm from the man's chin and with a solid right left the man lying beside the commode. He looked through his pockets and found nothing except the nine mm semiautomatic pistol about which he had guessed. He left the pistol, locked the bathroom door, and stayed inside for a minute brushing his hair in the opposite direction, and bathing his knuckles. He took his jacket off and put it into the trash barrel along with his tie.

He rolled up his sleeves and looked in the closet, which had been locked until he popped it open. He found some brown shoe polish and a white apron, smoothed the polish over his hair and poured some water and cleaner into a bucket on wheels with a mop. He prepared himself with the proper hangdog attitude and left. At least they knew he was coming, he thought, pushing the bucket through the rest room door.

He did not look exactly like a hard-bitten worker of the world, but close enough. With his face down, and his new and slick brown hair showing, he walked slowly to the other end of the terminal and saw two men who looked like the man on the toilet, but they were not looking at him. Entering another rest room, he ditched the apron and bucket of water. He went out front to take a taxi downtown, the polish on his hair annoying him.

In the taxi, Patrimos thought over the fact that he was an agnostic in morals. He believed the bar of justice had been moved to the rear, and he felt freer to move onto the edges of justice as he had done in the airport restroom. He always felt ready for the next step, and so there he was. Such action seemed to prove to him that he was right to use that tactic in his PI activity. For him, the ends justified the means. Back at his hotel room, he showered the brown shoe polish out of his hair.

The next morning, he dressed and in a rental car drove through the old neighborhood of Parlor Street where his grandparents had lived, and he reflected on the series of neighborhood types that had developed there over the years. The first was 1921 when it was brand new; then in 1931 came a long downturn into a slum with union members and Afro-Americans from the South after work in the North; then there was a time in the seventies and eighties when gentrification was a fad that slowly decayed into a place where seniors on Medicare and Social Security lived for the end in a quiet fashion.

He wondered what type of group would move in next after they all died. He then drove his car slowly past his grandfather's family home. There were large poplar trees, maples and oaks looking as if they still believed they lived where it mattered. There were older car models in similar types of driveways. He could see no pets.

He stopped at Millie's mailbox, which was still a vintage early box the color and material of a tin gutter. He walked slowly up the stained concrete slabs of the walkway to the front door giving anybody in the house fair warning that somebody was coming. He rang several times. Inside, he heard a TV program channeling an auction.

The door opened and through the years Patrimos saw Millie Masters, maybe forty, her blonde hair playing down over her shoulders, her chest full, her back unbent. She was still beautiful.

"Millie?" Patrimos said, astounded. He was certain she should be closer to one hundred.

"She's not alive anymore, sir. I am her daughter Ginger. What can I do for you?"

"Ginger? Ah, Ginger. I'm Henry Patrimos. You were barely a teenager when I was here last. You have grown up."

"With that and two divorces," she said, smiling now. "I remember you Mr. Patrimos. Same haircut and color, and it still looks good on you. You were an investigator of some kind. Is that right?"

"Something like that. Call me Henry. May I come in?"

"Sure."

Patrimos went in and knew right away that the house had not changed since 1921, or at least its skeletal structure had not. He knew it was almost an exact replica of the house next door, his grandparent's, with arched doorways inside, dark wood floors with colorful rugs from Mexico, and a big square coffee table covered with magazines, loitering between a sofa and two chairs.

"You all right, Ginger?"

"Well, I inherited mother's house with no mortgage, and I was lucky enough to have no kids."

Since she did not seem serious about it, Patrimos laughed. Strangely, he felt the same way.

"I have a job at Walmart out on the interstate. A manager. I am good at it, and I am happy. This is an off-day for me."

"When did Millie die?"

"In 1992. She was lucky, with a pension and government money coming in regular for medical care. God bless the US Government."

"The pension was from that company she and her husband worked with?"

This was a guess.

"Crown Imports/Exports?" Ginger asked.

"Yes, that's the name. It was their pension?"

"She did not work there long enough to get a pension, I don't think. When daddy died in 1943 in the war, she started seeing a worker from out there, Byron Crumb, who knew daddy. Crumb set up an investment-savings account for her years before he died. He evidently put a lot of money into the account. She had no idea he had done that, but she was delighted when he told her about it. He also saw that she got part of her husband's social security income too, so she was able to pay off the mortgage and live well later into the nineties using that money."

"Where is Byron today?"

"Byron's dead too, Henry, maybe ten years after Mom. I think he and my mother loved one another. He would come by every now and then and stay for supper and for a while afterwards. I thought of him as an uncle. In high school I called him *Lord Byron*. I can guess what the deal really was, but that was fine with me.

"After mother died, he had a stroke and lived for maybe another year like that, and then had another stroke that took him off. He was an attorney for that company, Crown Imports/Exports, and there were many people at his funeral, which I went to. I had a feeling that it was mainly the people he worked with. But Byron and Millie had some good times together. Trips to the Great Lakes, the Grand Canyon, British Columbia."

"Sounds like it," Patrimos said.

"What did you want to know beyond what mother already told you about your grandfather? I recall both of you back at the kitchen table talking and talking. Did you ever find what you were looking for?"

"Not yet, Ginger. I'm still looking."

"Really?"

"Your mother told me about Byron spending a lot of time with people he worked with, and I need to know about one of them now. A man named Gaylon Starks."

"Gaylon Starks? Hmmm...maybe...it was after his funeral, Byron's. Somebody came by and gave me some papers to sign. I believe it had to do with closing his pension business, part of which had been going to mother. I said something like: *Thanks, Mr. Snarks*, or something like that. He smiled at me when he left. I never saw him again."

"And they worked together at Crown Imports/Exports?"

"That's right. So, you knew Byron, but now you want to know about Gaylon Starks too?"

"Yes. When I was here the last time, you were not here. But now I also need to know more about that company Byron was with. Aren't they down on Henshall Street?"

"They moved into Chicago, Henry, near the docks, I think they said. The name may have changed too. I really don't know anything about them now."

Patrimos looked at his watch. "Well, I...."

"But wait a minute, Henry," Ginger said. "Mother left something for you. I had to hide it to be sure I never threw it away. Give me a few minutes." Ginger jumped up and went upstairs where things were stored in the dormer room.

Patrimos looked around the house remembering when he was young, and he would come with his father to see his grandmother. It always felt like a church service as they tiptoed around the subject of the Empire State Building. His father stayed to talk, but as a kid he would go next door to see Ginger's mother Millie. He told his father she was funny; and when he was with her, he felt relieved of a heavy burden, whatever that was, although he guessed it was the Empire State Building business.

Ginger returned ten minutes later with a smile on her face. She was carrying a green shoebox.

"Here, it must have meant something to her for you to have it. I have no idea what is in it, although I was tempted a few times after mother died to look, you know. But you had come by every now and then and so I kept it for when you came next. And here you are.

"But there is another reason I hid your stuff. There have been at least two break-ins here in the last year. I checked. Nothing was taken, but the place was searched. They were looking for something. I had the feeling that the box you are holding is what they might have been after."

After she called a taxi for him, Patrimos thanked Ginger and wished her the best of luck. He said he might come back sometime. He enjoyed talking with her. She looked a lot like her mother, Millie.

"I know you'll be back, Henry. It seems you're on a wheel."

Patrimos nodded his head. When the taxi arrived, they shook hands and Patrimos went back to his hotel room, thinking about what she had said. The box was wrapped tightly with clear but yellowing scotch tape and he could see his name written on an address label under the tape.

The box was heavier than Patrimos thought it should be, and he put it on his bed carefully and went to the bathroom to splash cold water on his face. He investigated his face in the mirror for a time and then wiped it dry.

He slipped off his shoes, picked up the box, and took it to a small desk in the room. He sat down and used the knife on his keychain to cut through the scotch tape and release the top. He opened it and put the top aside. Under some personal items of his father that he had left there at her place, was a letter to him from Millie.

After reading the letter, Patrimos knew he would have a long day the next day. He stripped and took a hot shower. He ordered a 5:00 a.m. wakeup call and crawled gratefully into bed. In the letter, Millie had just answered his prayers about a friend of the man who was her secret lover for many years, and what he did in the company, and why.

At 5:10 a.m. Patrimos put on black pants and gym shoes, a black V-neck shirt, and a black leather coat. He put the letter from Millie in his briefcase along with the .38 and took a cab to the Chicago Import/Export Bank near the Chicago River.

To the rear of the Chicago Bank there were three warehouses jutting out on the waterfront parallel with each other. The one in the middle had an unobtrusive sign: Crown Imports. Close enough. He took his briefcase and told the driver to wait thirty minutes. The driver nodded his head and asked Patrimos if he really wanted to go into the warehouse section, especially that early in the morning.

"Bad guys in there, pal. I'd hate to wait for nothing."

Patrimos gave him a hundred-dollar bill. "I'll be back in a half hour. Wait for me, and I'll double that."

Once out of the cab, Patrimos vanished into the darkness. The .38 was stuck in his belt in the back, and his briefcase had several special tools in it. He wanted information from the Crown Imports personnel files on their hard drive, which meant he had to hack it, and that would then give him wider latitude in tracking down Gaylon Starks.

There was a light on in the top floor of the warehouse. Patrimos moved from black point to black point, watching for floodlights. He reached the narrow door at the top of three flights of stairs in ten minutes. He bent and worked the door with a picklock. No alarm.

Inside, the light was bright in one corner of a large room near the windows but dim in the rest of the area. An old man sat in the light over a desk and seemed to be slowly checking off numbers.

The old man had more fight in him than Patrimos thought, but he soon had him in a neck and forearm lock and was slowly cutting off blood to the man's brain. Before he let him black out, he whispered to him, close, at the ear.

"I need something here. No trouble. No robbery. Just some copied information."

"Is that...uh...so?"

Patrimos pushed down with his forearm.

"I can do it quick and be out with no man the wiser; or I can put you out and search for a while, find nothing, get mad, and shoot you in both knee caps before I leave, which will wake you up and hurt a lot. So, which will it be?"

"Mister, I've got liver cancer, prostatic and lymphatic cancer. You think I care...what you do?"

"You would if it looked like you weren't doing your job. I think what you are doing here is charity work by the company that allows you to sink into the ground as pleasantly as possible. I think you want to keep this job, which might not happen if the place is a mess in the morning, and it's clear you'd been sleeping in one corner while all that was happening. What do you say?"

The old man stopped struggling. "Talk to me," he said in an old, tired voice.

"First, tell me where the company's servers are located. Then you're going to get me there, and then show me out the nearest door when I'm through; and then you will go back to whatever you were doing day in and day out without saying a word."

"We have to go downstairs, and there are alarms that can go off if you're not careful," the old man said. "So, watch how I move. The main servers are there, but otherwise it's an empty room."

"I thought so. Lay on, Macduff," Patrimos said.

The old man had obviously bought into Patrimos's narrative. He wanted to die easy with easy work and a regular check, which was the only way to pay for the expensive pills he had to have to die painlessly.

Exactly twenty-nine minutes after he left, Patrimos opened the door of the taxi and got in. He reminded the surprised Taxi Driver of the name of his motel. He was there by 7:00 a.m. and made a series of quick out-of-state phone calls. He knew the trial in Fleckner was growing closer and closer, but he almost had what he was after.

* * *

Gaylon Starks had retired to Fairfax, Ohio, near the small Clover River. He was still receiving a check from Crown Exports, and it was not a bad check. He lived on a curve in Nightly Boulevard across from a small city park that drew drug pushers who came there on Sundays to sell to Senior Citizens wanting to escape their golden years for one reason or another and found that hallucinogens from their college days in the sixties and seventies would do it. No opioids, no heroin, no speed. It was the mellow mushroom alone they were after. The police did not bother them.

Starks was in his late eighties and already in a transcendent state sitting on a blue park bench when Patrimos found him. The PI pointed out to Starks that an old friend had persuaded him to find Starks and thank him for years of friendship. Starks thought he remembered the old friend and so agreed to take Patrimos back to his room so they could share what Patrimos had brought with him, which was supposed to be the derivative of a rare mushroom, Lily Pons, and then they would talk.

"About what?" Starks asked.

"About the mellow fucking Submarine of course," Patrimos said.

Starks fell off his park bench chair laughing. "That's a good one," he said. "*Mellow fucking submarine!*"

"You like it, huh?" Patrimos said. "I got more. I am a goddamn reservoir of sixties jokes. Okay?"

Patrimos helped Starks up.

"Okay, but follow me," Starks said. "It may take a while until I remember where my room is exactly."

The two laughed and sang as best they could, *We are Sailing* by Crosby, Stills and Nash, until they reached Starks's low-rent apartment. He opened the door and Patrimos kicked him from the rear and sent him sprawling on the floor inside. Patrimos closed and locked the door and turned to Starks.

"Hey, that was fun," Starks said.

"Sure, sure. You're going to like the next thing even better."

"Okay, what is it?"

"Where I tie you to your bed and singe every hair off your body as a starter, although that sounds like more fun for you than for me."

Starks seemed to sober up a bit and asked Patrimos who he was.

"I'm from Crown Export."

"From what?"

"You remember, Starks, you worked for us, and so did your father until 1998 and you retired and are still receiving our money. But you forgot something."

"What? What did I forget?"

"We need to ask you about an event almost seventy years ago now. We, the Crown Export, put out a hit contract in early 1931 for one Walter Patrimos. Your father took it and later told you about it. About how much fun it was driving some poor fool over the edge of a tall building. Remember? Do you remember that?"

"Ah...of course. That was good money for him. It was the guy who went off the Empire State Building, right?"

"Right. Why did you do that, and who signed for it?"

"You're not with Crown Export."

"You're right. I'm worse."

It took a while, but eventually Starks was sitting naked in the cold bathtub, his wrists taped to his ankles. Patrimos turned on the hot water and sat down on the narrow side of the old tub that had old claw feet at each corner. Starks moved to get himself as far away from the water as possible. His mellow mood had passed, and he was not happy, but neither was Patrimos, who had learned from the Army how to interrogate.

"I'm not married, Starks, never wanted to be. It's a duty I owe my offspring, for I cannot guarantee them anything in this life. Do you understand that?"

"O, yes, sir, I do, I do, although I have five kids with twenty grandchildren."

"Do they all live well, Starks, with good educations and income and no debilitating diseases?"

"I can't say that's quite true, sir. You know how things happen."

"Exactly what I'm talking about, Starks. Exactly. So, let's have that name. Okay? The water will soon be maybe up to your balls, and it will be very hot. We can sit and wait for it to rise on up to your chest and then over your face, when I push you down in it, or we can discuss the name I need right now."

"I don't know shit, really, sir, I don't. I really don't. It's been so long ago now. I was so young and all."

"I understand that, Gaylon. Can you excuse me a minute?"

Patrimos walked out of the bathroom and sat on the bed. He placed several green mints in his mouth and listened to the water rising. He started to hear Starks yelling.

Oops, he forgot something. He took some duct tape into the bathroom and taped Stark's mouth shut. He left again.

"Mmmmmmmm. Mmmmmmmmmmmm! Mmmmm huh huh huh."

Patrimos looked at his nails. He would have to have a manicure first chance he got.

A few minutes later, Starks was banging around in the tub trying uselessly to get out.

"MMMMMMMMMMMKKKKKKKKKKKKKKKKKKKKKKK KKK."

Patrimos smiled and stood up, taking his time to reach the bathroom.

"What did you say, Starks? Did I hear something?"

"MMMMKKKK.MMMMKKKKK."

Starks was almost blood red from the waist down. Boils were appearing here and there, especially around the fat navel.

Patrimos stopped the water. He sat down on the narrow edge of the old white tub again. He could feel the heat rising from the water as he pulled the tape from Starks' mouth.

"*Ah, Jesus, man! Christ! Let me out. Let me out.*"

"Mr. Starks, I am a demon looking for one good man, or woman, I forget which. Are you that person?"

"What? Ah, no...yes...*I mean it hurts, it hurts!*"

"Well, that's the idea, Gaylon, and if I have to put this tape back on your mouth because of the lack of anything worth hearing, I will turn the water back on, leave the room, and go home. You are wasting my time."

"I'm burnt. You have to get me to the hospital, please... please, it hurts!"

"Listen, Mr. Starks," Patrimos said, grabbing him by the cheeks and twisting them. "He was killed because you wanted him dead. He was getting in your way. I'm sure it hurt like hell when my grandfather hit the ground. Now give me names!"

Starks' eyes widened. "That was your grandfather?"

"I'm waiting, Mr. Starks."

"So you really don't know?"

"Know what?"

"Your grandfather was the one who pushed hardest for the *Jubilee Trust* to succeed. It had something to do with the need to show the limits of reason in financial affairs. The force of nature was not reason, he believed, and it would always win. He wanted it to balance off things which I could not understand. That was beyond my scope. But he wanted the Jubilee Trust to do well to make that point. I don't know why he jumped. I really don't.

"Look Starks, I have something I have to do right now. So, give me this quick. When the hit request was sent around to the supervisors, the document was signed by one person. That would have told you who initiated the contract. If you don't recall the name, then you are in very deep shit, my friend."

"OK. OK. That man is dead, the one you are talking about. Fifteen years ago, at least. His son took over. He's still around as one of the top people at Crown Exports in charge of cons...."

"His name?"

"Hector Rulotto, Jr."

Patrimos was now almost certain of the next answer.

"What does Crown Export do?"

"Cons and extortion."

"Small?"

"Very big Cons."

Patrimos dropped Starks off wrapped in a wet towel near the Emergency Room of the Fairfax Community Hospital and promised him they would give him some good morphine for his red legs, arms, buttocks, and waist. However, if Starks said anything other than it was an accident, it would happen to him all over again. Did he understand?

"Yes. Oh, yes, sir," said Starks as he sat shivering in the car looking longingly at the Emergency sign. He was almost in shock.

Patrimos watched him in the rearview mirror dodder across the new pavement toward the hospital.

All the way back to the motel, he wondered what Starks had meant about his father wanting the Jubilee Trust to win. Was it true, and what the hell did it mean to Walter Patrimos in 1931?

18

The spiral staircase in the Joliard mansion in Fleckner rose gracefully to the second floor like a conductor about to direct a large orchestra. The air of the first floor was thick and dark with several aromas working their way around and through it, apples, floor wax, tobacco, medicinal products.

The large living room to the right had a very tall ceiling. Jessie Joliard stood in front of a fireplace that was used in winter, and sometimes on cool nights, like that one. A Lifesize oil painting from the knees up of her grandfather Calvin Murphy Joliard hung over the mantelpiece behind her. The Joliard patriarch was standing and looking straight out from the painting with rumpled white hair; he was leaning forward with one hand resting on the back of a big red leather chair. There was about him an air of concern, and the suggestion that he wanted to guard his granddaughter from that concern.

Jessie was expecting them. She was wearing a light green sweater, beige pants, and cordovan Weejuns.

"Neap!" she cried.

She walked to him with her arms open, hugged him, and stepped back.

"Are you in Fleckner for good?" he asked.

"Because of David, for a while at least. It is good to see you, Neap. And you have added even more muscle too. Wow. The army made a man out of you, huh?"

Vesel smiled and saw Jacoby staring at Jessie. He knew that for many who met her for the first time, she could be odd looking. With rich, thick auburn hair, her face was strangely appealing despite some differences in balance and structure of the eyes and skin. The eyebrows were plucked and shaped to balance the differences, but hers was a face out of kilter. On the left side of her face, the skin sagged a bit, almost as if she had had a stroke, while the right was tight and clean as marble.

It was not yet determined that this division was a correct diagnosis of Bell's palsy that would eventually go away. The diagnosis had been made by a New York doctor when she was thirteen years old. But later in life Jessie had accepted the bifurcation in her face, and even liked it for its slight shock effect. This made for a delicate screening process about the sincerity of emotions toward her and, with years of experience, she was certain that it worked.

For men, her body was cause enough for them to catch their breaths, then step back and mull things over. Where was her true appeal, where not?

"Jacoby, this is Jessie Joliard. I've known her from when I was a kid here in Fleckner," Vesel said.

"Miss Joliard?" Jacoby said, nodding his head.

"Yes, Deputy. It is still Miss. How are you?"

Jacoby was flustered. "Good, thank you," he said.

"You are here about David, right?" she said to both men.

"Yes," Vesel said. "His room is still upstairs?"

"It is. Deputy Jacoby, why don't you go on up and start doing what you do. David won't mind now. Neap let's go out back and talk just a minute first. Okay?"

"Sure," Vesel said and pointed out of the living room. "LeMace, go up the stairs to the next floor. Turn to the right. David's room is the first room on the right. Look for anything not in place where it should be, showing empty spots maybe. I'll be up directly."

* * *

Outside, Vesel and Joliard walked for a minute in silence. Wind moved slowly through the limbs and needles of the pines and there was the suggestion of pine resin in the summer heat.

"I hear you were kept busy overseas, Neap," Jessie said at last.

"You mean in the Second Afghanistan War," Vesel said.

"I heard you did as good over there as you did at football here," she said, smiling warmly. "More commendations than anybody else."

"The body count was higher; but yes, I was good at what I did. The thing is, I won't do it anymore."

"Is there a reason?"

Vesel started to tell her about the *Hun Gabon*, but he believed he could do that later, at a better time.

"I wanted to stop killing," he said.

They were now strolling slowly into the English garden behind the mansion. Vesel could see the hothouse on one edge of the backyard and the big double compost bin covered with black tarps beside it.

"You know, I really, really owe you a lot, Neap," Jessie said.

"No, you don't owe me a thing."

"You never told anyone?" she asked.

"Never. You?"

"Nobody real, Neap. I talked with a psychiatrist once at school about an anxiety issue I had, and she asked about any big secrets I was hiding. I finally told her about it, but I said I didn't know you or your name. We had a confidentiality firewall and I was a victim in the crime anyway, according to the psychiatrist."

"I see."

"I quit with the psychiatrist shortly after that, but it was all obscured by 9/11 and never came up again."

"Speaking of that, have you seen what's happened to Fleckner since we left?" Vesel asked.

"I have. I drove around and saw things that made me very sad. I wish I could do something about it. I do contribute to the Red Cross for overseas, but the Joliard fortune seems to be evaporating, Neap. I do not look forward to going to the bank and seeing what a mess Kurt and David have made of it. It worries me a lot about what would happen if it was gone and this house had to be sold by the bank. I have no idea what I would do."

"That's a possibility?" Vesel asked.

"Yes, it is. I think you know I am engaged to Senator Jackson Miles of Kansas. He is sweet to me and shows a lot of affection. I hate to say it, but I think I'm going to marry him for security, even though he's a bit weaselly sometimes."

"I've heard of him," Vesel said. "He is supposed to be to the right of Genghis Kahn. Military Miles."

"Neap," she said, laughing and slapping him on his sleeve. "That's not true. Well, maybe some."

"He's the one making a lot of noise about beefing up the army again rather than keeping the boots off the ground in that part of the world," Vesel said. "If he wants to fight overseas in the Middle East, I can help him get a job on the front lines."

"I heard you had a tough time at the end over there. If I could have come out of nowhere and helped you, like you did me, you know I would have."

"That's all over now," he lied. "I do want you to call me quick if you think anything suspicious is going on up here, though. I can't help but be worried about your connection to the murders by way of your brothers."

"Thanks for your concern, Neap. I will take care, even though the dogs give us good warning about anybody coming anywhere near the house. Abejundio is a good marksman, and he can give us time to at least call 911," she said. "He and his boys who stayed with us are all now a part of the Joliard family. He knows how to do many things well, although I am not sure where he learned how to do them all. Kurt told me that he had once been a part of a cartel in Mexico."

"That would explain it," Vesel said, who already knew that.

"I want to thank you for something else, Neap. I have wanted to do it for a long time."

"Okay," he said. "What?"

"At no time whenever we met and talked together back then, and even now, have I ever felt you thinking the same thing about me almost every man I meet does, and half the women. You know, my face and the rest of me."

"I don't know what to say, Jessie. I never felt the need."

Jessie leaned toward Vesel to kiss him on the cheek as she had once before after he had saved her life in the mountains. Then, whether by chance or design, Vesel made a shift so that their lips met. They were lost for a moment in time.

Their eyes met as they pulled apart.

"We can't do this, Neap," Jessie said. "I...."

But Vesel had felt the full attraction of love's powerful sweetness, and now he was awake to it. He kissed her again on the neck.

"Ah, Neap," she said. "You are already much more than a friend, you know that."

"Will this be like before? Keeping a secret?" he asked.

"This is a bad time to think about this," she said.

"I know."

When they got back to the house, both walking slowly as if discussing the weightiest of issues, and thinking only the deepest of thoughts, Jacoby told them he had found in David Joliard's room a few old unpaid checks for gambling debts at Simmo's Poker Bar. He found expensive Italian suits and shoes, but there seemed to be nothing otherwise that could help in the investigation.

They would go through David's First Fleckner bank records later. They had found nothing on his computer, no recent ledgers, balance sheets, or tax returns. The computer hard drive was blank, with evidence that someone might have wiped it clean. The two deputies took the computer and hard drive with them and they would let Ebba, who was also a computer whiz, analyze it, and maybe make something of it.

Vesel would work on that problem with Patrimos who was also supposed to be a computer whiz. He said a reluctant goodbye to Jessie, and he and Jacoby left.

Pauley was outside, down the road, waiting for them. She was leaning on a mahogany walking stick by the side of the road. It was unusual for the house manager to be outside like that, and Vesel raised his eyebrows.

"Neap, Mr. Deputy," she said, when Vesel stopped and powered down his window.

"I need to tell you something."

"What is it, Pauley?"

She looked at Jacoby who looked away. "I'm old and can't talk as good anymore, but my folks been here a long, long time at this place. They worked building this house. They are ghosts with good memories. Myself, I'm stuck here like a tick on a dog's belly. I won't let go."

Vesel stared at her. "What are you saying, Pauley?"

"She tell you she going to lose this place?"

"She said it might come to that, but it did not sound urgent."

"Well, that damn urgency already come."

"What do you mean?"

"An appraiser come out, and the bank, it's called several times. No, don't you look back at the house now," Pauley said. "It may be too late already, Deputy, and I think you might think on that. When people get desperate, they do desperate things. They marry wrong for one thing. Do something for her, Mr. Neap Deputy. I seen you when you was young. She loves you, not that damn senator, and you love her."

"Whoa, wait a minute, Pauley, I..."

"I got to get back now, Mr. Neap. Ponder on that."

Vesel watched Pauley walk back to the house with a rolling gait using the stick as if she was at sea, with her elbows and shoulders serving as part of a balancing act, the walking stick like another limb awkwardly serving its purpose.

He knew there was truth in what Pauley had said about his connection to Jessie, although he had never thought of it in quite that way, of hooks sunk, hearts torn, droplets of blood witnessed. But the power he had just felt with her in the yard was manifest.

Now that he thought about it, however, maybe he did understand something like that, and as he thought of it, heated feelings emerged like subtle lava. Each time he thought of her, he saw her as a nineteen-year-old girl in trouble. That had been then. But sometimes his nighttime dreams of her were far more disturbing: She would be drowning, and he could not reach her in time, and he knew it. But he believed, when he let the thought happen, that through the agency of sleep's magic he could one day reach out and save her from the water and they would come together, saved.

Recalling these matters later, however, he opined how absurd they were. With all he had experienced, and the goals he sought, he could not have her. And he did not know what he could do for her house. He could not ask Blue not to deliver an eviction notice when it was worked up.

Perhaps she might after all find the treasure that her grandfather had supposedly hidden in the hills. That would certainly help, if it were true, but he believed that it was not.

But for all that, and despite his desire to do the right thing, he also wanted to draw closer to the consuming labor of love with her, even if for only a short time. He could see their bodies writhing together like sinners in hell, and he wanted it. He knew if Jessie called, he would be back up faster than a startled whip snake, and that would be it.

Yet he knew as he nodded his head that he had Grace waiting for him at home, and that thought yanked another string, and he winced as if he had felt the fierce burning of a broken intestinal wound.

19

Working the case, Vesel and Jacoby were skeptical about Marvin Macy being the killer, and they were aware of the growing gossip about the Sheriff's inability to investigate the murder. The evidence was not complex. There was the Rolex, a cloth with blood on it found in Macy's pocket at the time, and old stories of how David Joliard had repeatedly screwed Macy financially back in the eighties. There were sharp tools found in, and collected from, Macy's garage. It was unclear if any blood had been found on the tools, and if so, whether there were matches with Joliard.

But the Rolex seemed to make the case solid for the Gazettes' readers: It was robbery and murder, pure and simple, and could Blue Walsh handle it.

"Neap, did you see this morning's Gazette story?" LeMace asked.

"That Blue's good record on murders for thirty years makes him unable to investigate a murder because of his lack of experience?"

"That's the one."

"Odd attitude, but I did see it, LeMace. Did you see the story on WNBA-TV last night?"

"Same thing. They were thinking that somebody else ought to take over the investigation. The state's people might want to do that, Neap, and they will be hard to ignore."

"Yes, well, this is clearly in Fleckner's jurisdiction," Vesel said. "So, this is where it will stay, and I am the chief Investigator."

"Good, but something else does bother me though, Neap."

"What part of it?"

"What could be the outcome of a capital case with only circumstantial evidence?"

"We'll find out, LeMace. Somebody wants this case to go to the mat, and I do not think that decision was made on the local level. We will find out why that is somewhere down the road. But until then, we are the ones handling the case on the ground, and that's what we are going to do."

20

After the first killings in town, rumors ran through Fleckner like Cheetahs in South Africa, and Jason Deeds III, the editor of the Fleckner Gazette, was frustrated and wanted to track down all the Cheetahs.

"This will be a very big story, Puck," Deeds said. "The trial is about to begin, and I have got everybody here working on it, but that's not nearly enough. You have got to help us here. You know him. I have seen you and Vesel together at your office. We need some insider information."

"Why can't the Sheriff catch the killer?" Puck asked.

A young woman just out of college, Puck Magran was both stocky and slim. She had played women's soccer at VPI as a Central Midfielder, and she taught geography at the local high school. She was in the best shape of her life, she thought, and she liked her summer job at the Fall Line Park in the middle of town.

She often came early in the morning to study quietly at the park, and then she would go over for lunch with Jason Deeds. If tourists showed up during park hours after lunch, she took them for tours of the park, explaining the geographical nature of the Atlantic Coastal Fall Line that was 900 miles of solid elevated granite running north and south right through Fleckner.

"Can the Sheriff catch him? Probably not, but Neap Vesel might be able to," Deeds said. "Hell, he was in every Special Forces training program there was. Before he was a prisoner for a brief time overseas, he had an all-time high body count, and then he just quit. He does not talk about it, I have tried, but as far as I can tell, he is the Audie Murphy of the Afghan war. If true, we need to get the story out there. People always like heroes who live in their own town."

"*Audie Murphy?*"

"In World War II, a GI by name of Audie Leon Murphy had the all-time decoration rate in that war with every medal the US Army had to give, and he came to represent rampant heroism for readers of American newspapers. He said he was killing all those Germans because they were killing his friends. War murder in the movies was a big thing then. They wanted to glorify Murphy and his righteous deeds. Now, not so much, but Neap was on the same path."

"So, you think Neap can catch this local murderer?" she asked.

"If he does not, the Department of Homeland Security is going to be really mad and get all over this like rice on chocolet. I am surprised they aren't here already. Maybe they are. Who would know? To catch a thief, you need a thief. To catch a murdering terrorist, I guess you need a murdering terrorist."

"What?"

"Homeland Security has been looking for terrorists in the states ever since 2001, Puck, and they are disappointed they can't find all that many. I think they are picking up overseas terrorists and turning them loose here, and then hunting them down for PR on TV news."

"You think one of those terrorists is doing this in Fleckner?"

"Well," Deeds said, shaking his head. "You've got to back up that kind of story with evidence, of course. But how hard is that? The murder was bizarre, like all wars.

Editor Deeds's face was filling out. His big sideburns had a few gray hairs turning up, and his square, rimless glasses had the tendency to glide halfway down his long nose while he talked with both hands in motion.

He liked Puck, who liked him. Puck thought Deeds might go on to do bigger things one day, if newspapers were still around.

She looked at her watch, stood up and stretched her arms.

"Okay, it's time to pick up my tourists, if there are any," she said.

"Talk to Vesel if you can?"

"Sure, I'll try."

"See you for lunch tomorrow?"

"Okay," she said.

After talking about the crime story with the Gazette's editor, Puck left the Gazette building on the west corner of Main and started across the street toward the Fall Line Park, which was behind the Bibliotheca Restaurant whose brick walls inside were covered with worthless old books bought by the pound, yet people asked the waiters to pick one out for them so they could read it before the food came. It was almost a literary event at lunch time.

Puck was at the South end of Main Street, and the Sheriff's Department was to the direct north at the other end, three miles away. Both streets stopped right in place like ends of a ruler, and at the crossways of Main and Algonquin Street stood the Courthouse. West was where the Joliards lived with other wealthy inhabitants, and Lake Murphy was behind them, now slowly being called Lake Joliard. To the East fifty miles away was the Atlantic Ocean.

The median of Main Street had walking paths and black lamplighter poles, which the town had built using terrorism grants in 2004. Maybe she would ask Neap about the editor's concerns when she saw him the next time to talk philosophy, which he liked to do, although so much was going on in town, the halfway murder to start it, she was sure it was hard for him to find the time to do that anymore. During murder investigations, she guessed there was little time for philosophy.

Neap seemed a serious man behind the gorilla body, she thought, and while his remarks about various things were thought-provoking, he was now so deeply involved in finding the murderer, or murderers, he could give no attention to the little things that occurred in Fleckner.

But she knew they were important. Even tourism had fallen off since the murder; people out of fear did not want to be anywhere near where they might be murdered. She guessed the mind scattered at the thought of such a thing, since the senses would be lost all at once, where otherwise a normal death dragged things out and took the senses only one or two at a time. She shrugged and, without looking in either direction, headed across South Main for her small Fall Line Office.

She was thinking of Neap Vesel's favorite question: *Was the consciousness of the One conscious?*

When she was halfway across the street, the brakes of a cherry red car squealed and stopped the car right before it might have hit Puck. She jumped away as adrenalin came fast. She was pissed. She wanted to fight.

"What the hell!" she screamed.

A tall man who looked lean and heavy at the same time got out of the car and nodded to Puck.

"A close call, young lady," he said. "You should look before you leap."

"What?"

"How do I get to Algonquin Street?" he said.

She was cooling down now, but Puck still wanted to hit the man, even though he seemed to have a handicap, a lisp, and was much bigger than she was.

"Who are you looking for?" she asked.

"The Joliards."

"Okay, turn left down there the way you came in on Algonquin and go up four or five miles. Turn off right on a gravel switchback and zigzag up to the end. That will be the Joliard place. But David Joliard was just murdered. I don't think they are open to strangers. Are you a stranger?"

"I'm sorry to hear that," the man said, although Puck could see no sympathetic response from him. He seemed to ignore her questions.

"Is there anything else I can help you with?" she asked.

"Where can I buy some jelly donuts?"

"*Jelly Donuts?*"

"Yes."

"Well, you may have passed the Dunkin' Donut place out on US 1. I think they have them."

"Thanks," Jordan Manse Fellestre said. "You have been very helpful."

Puck watched as the man stepped back into his cherry-red car and drove off, turned at the end of South Main and headed back toward Algonquin Street. But at Algonquin, he turned in the opposite direction Puck had given him. She guessed that the man must have wanted jelly donuts more than the Joliard's.

Puck forgot the cherry-red car and her close call with death. She hoped she would have at least a few interesting visitors to the Fall Line Park that day, and maybe a new Audie Leon Murphy would be amongst them.

21

When she first arrived home after the halfway murder occurred, Jessie Joliard noted that everything in her bedroom was still tasteful and in place, like House and Garden pictures with fashionable colors and the latest fabrics and designs. Pauley saw to that, just as she oversaw the routines of the house like a forest ranger at a national park, keeping bad bears where they were supposed to be. Pauley knew a classy house to work in when she saw one, and it was going to stay that way.

After Calvin Joliard bought the house and moved there in the summer of 1929, a separate three-car garage using masonry as close to the original as could be found was added at an angle to the rear of the house. A covered walkway connected the garage to the main house. All minor tools were stored in the garage with plenty of space left for her car, and David and Kurt's Mercedes Benz sports cars.

There was a separate place on the grounds for the larger landscaping tools Abejundio used.

Pauley was preparing for the burial of David Joliard. The first of the week after the murder, the remaining Joliard family, Kurt and Jessie, held funeral services in the Maynooth Presbyterian Church and buried what they had left of David in the sloping churchyard full of old cedars, where all the Joliards had plots. The only other church in town was the Catholic Blood of Christ Mount Church just outside the town limits.

Jessie was in a hurry to finish all that business and go back to Washington, so she got with James Parsons at the bank. She gave him the check from Jackson Miles for covering the short-term needs for the house, but when he showed her the Joliard financial paperwork she was flabbergasted. Even with the recent money, the house might still be lost through financial mismanagement. When the brothers last refinanced the family mansion, which she did not know about, they had made her tax-free utility bonds part of the collateral, although they had agreed at their father's death that she would receive the bonds that should last her, they said, forever.

She understood that it was an allowance, and agreed reluctantly, because she had to. In a patriarchy the males came first. They killed opponents, preserved bloodlines, and gathered necessities like food as hunting forays into deep forests. While it was the first-born son who inherited everything, the eldest Joliard son had vanished when he was twenty-one and about to come into the estate. No one ever learned why, nor ever saw him again.

When the youngest, David, was killed, there was still one male Joliard left in the family, Kurt, and Jessie was in line behind him.

Nevertheless, Jessie was mad about the state of the big house, and she confronted Kurt as soon as she found him.

"Kurt, what is going on? You and David mortgaged the house with my tax-free bonds?"

"We had to, Jessie. David started up a string of antique stores, which he did not know anything about, and notes came due and he did not have it. So, we had to put up the bonds to satisfy the bank. David thought it was all supposed to be run like a Cracker Barrel franchise, with antique rip-offs and sentimental duplicates readily available from a cheap antiques factory somewhere. He filled all his stores with the same stuff. After a time, nobody bought anything, even from a Joliard. Daddy usually bailed him out, but this time Daddy wasn't there, was he?"

"How could he borrow that money all by himself?" she asked, furious. Her cheeks felt like a red beard.

"Just because he was a Joliard, he could borrow just about anything," Kurt said. "The bank probably assumed that big gold did lurk somewhere. You know about that, Jessie."

"What happens when the note on this house comes due again soon?"

"You mean, what happens when the house note comes due *again*? Not a problem, Jessie," Kurt said. "We have a deal papa set up with a South American drug cartel before he died. Abejundio has been helpful in that regard. I mean, money has already started pouring in. I am picking up more next week. That should carry the house for another six months or so."

"Money from a *drug cartel?* Jesus, Kurt, no damn wonder," Jessie said, startled. Finances had never really been a concern of Jessie, not since her grandfather, Calvin Senior, had given her ten old Federal Reserve Notes and assured her that things would be fine for her if she kept them secret and sold them out, if necessary, only one at a time. But her father, Calvin II, was a different and careless man, and she was thankful that she had kept knowledge of those Notes from him.

She did wonder if Abejundio had helped her brother set up any drug deals, though. That did not sound like the Abejundio she knew. She would have to ask him, although her plate was already full of things to do, like returning to Washington soon to finish giving her fiancé the clue to the golden eggs so she could maybe save her possible marriage and the estate if her brother could not.

She drifted down the old winding stairs of her home, her hand gliding on the cherry banister that was as polished as a sea creature, to the original wide-plank hardwood floors of the house. She could see her split face in the shine of the bannister, if she wanted to, and she was happy.

But later that night, a man named Fellestre called Jessie and told her to do nothing about the notes or plates until he had a chance to see them. Angry and confused, she hung up on him.

22

Vesel and Jacoby were on their way a mile north of town to the county landfill to check on the garbage truck that may have played a role in the Joliard murder. They had put it off for obvious reasons—there were other leads, and it was bound to be a smelly recon, but that day was the day to do it.

Vesel drove the Sheriff Department's bronze Crown Vic with a star on the front door and parked it next to a one-story white building with a flat black roof. He could see Mason Corson inside on the phone.

Corson was the Fleckner Garbage Control Engineer and the only employee. A short bald man with a chubby chin and suspenders, usually green, that hugged his round shoulders and belly, Corson saw the Sheriff's car, hung up the phone and stood, hitched up his pants, and walked out to meet the two deputies standing beside their car.

"What can I do for you, Neap?" Corson said.

"Mason, I have to ask you a few questions," Vesel responded.

"Anything, Neap."

"You ever lose your truck?"

The dump manager turned toward the machine that looked like an alien with a huge green head resting just behind the cabin, its huge mouth open to the rear, ready to eat anything. There were places on it where garbage seemed permanently smeared, and places of impact that showed scraped-off paint and dents; but it was holding up, load after load.

"Aw, that the one?" Mason said.

"How many you got, Mason?" Vesel said.

"Just the one."

"So, who has the keys to it?"

"I do, Neap, you know that. The only other one is the key down at City Hall. What is the problem? Has one of the drunks downtown seen it in their dreams, or what?"

"Does it ever go out after dark?" Jacoby asked.

Corson turned his attention to Jacoby.

"Sometimes after dark in winter maybe, but hell, you know that Neap," Corson said, turning his attention back to Vesel. "But at night it stays locked up here in the compound, and I go home with the key."

"Why did you mention the drunks downtown?" Vesel asked.

"Huh?" Corson said.

"The drunks downtown, you just mentioned them," Vesel said to Corson.

"Well, just because it is stupid to think the truck would be downtown at night unless the drunks saw it as an illusion maybe," Corson said, looking nervous. "You would have to be drunk to think that."

"When do you add the load from the day's haul to the landfill?"

"Right when I come back in. It is better that way. Does not offer a smell as much later it does. Different aromas of course."

"Can I look at the truck? Is the key in it?" Jacoby asked.

"Aw, no," Corson said. "I have it."

He reached into one of his pants' pockets.

"Here it is. Go ahead, I guess," Corson said, keeping his eye on Vesel. "But be careful. It could flatten my office if it got away from you."

"Let me just ask you a few more questions until he's through with it, Mason, okay?"

"Neap, what is this all about?" Corson whispered, glancing back over his shoulder where Jacoby was nearing the truck.

"Where did you dump the garbage from Friday, the sixth of June, Mason?"

"Let me think. It is just garbage, Neap. Oh, right over there by those five pines. You see them?"

Vesel knew that Corson considered the landfill his place, and he kept it like a favored landscape, or even a museum. He pointed to the opposite side of the dump toward a mound of garbage where sure enough there stood five sorry looking pines as if very unhappy with what they had settled for in life.

Vesel nodded. "Mind if we look around out there for a minute?"

"Aw, it has already been compacted, Neap. That is the ordinance. I can break it up a little for you if you like. But help yourself."

Jacoby had fired up the big truck and was clumsily maneuvering it into the landfill. When he turned around, Vesel motioned to him.

Vesel walked out toward the dump truck in the landfill with Corson, who was fearless with rotting stuff all around him since he was used to it. Corson scrambled up into the truck which Jacoby happily abandoned. He manipulated the controls, turned and drove the big truck toward the five pines on the outer rim of the landfill, growling and swaying here and there like a ship in a gale, his green suspenders clearly visible, wobbling in the front seat.

Corson knew where everything was up to ten years down, or more, and could go right to it, Vesel thought, like him and the truck were a goddam garbage time machine, wherein waste of the past could be measured precisely.

Vesel shook his head and followed the machine through the stinking piles as he recalled ancient villages he had seen in the Hindu Kush Mountains, all clean as whistles.

23

The day was still and hot with a greasy white sky. It was the worst kind of day there was, she thought in irritation, looking high overhead. It seemed cool with the sun smudged, but it still burned you, still made you sweat more than most. It confused the senses, like hot ice or cold fire. It was confused and confusing, although the murderer had come to accept it as being a part of everything else.

She was about a half-mile away from the Fleckner landfill, lying on top of an old Indian mound with binoculars. The mound was supposed to contain all kinds of Indian things, pottery, bones, arrowheads, tattered leather bits. The mound was on an historical listing of some kind and there were laws against any digging in or developing of it. That was where she kept stuff buried that she just did not want to keep lying around elsewhere, like the results of her early practice of sawing through flesh and bone.

In the distance, she saw Jacoby and Vesel stop and point at something. The two men looked like clay figures in some impressionistic landscape. They were old men in a new wasteland, or maybe future men in an old wasteland. It did not matter to her. She had no future. But it was like a graveyard out there, and they were digging up the dead, raising them to the smells surrounding them. She thought you could quickly see if Lazarus was going to be grateful for resurrection in a place of such stench. But why should the dead be let off the hook? Everybody should share the same patch of manure, she thought.

She saw some movement and guessed Vesel and Jacoby had found something interesting in the dump right where she had put it, a leg maybe, one of her old ones. She stored her binoculars and went back to her car. She leaned against it for a while and smoked a small cigar, a Macanudo Whiff, thinking about an odd feeling she had just had.

For a while there it felt like she was being watched, and not by Vesel or the other deputy.

She glanced around in a wide arc that side of the Indian Mound and could see nothing out of the ordinary. She knew by experience that to observe without being seen, one had to know the psychology of whomever was being watched; one had to be invisible, yet somehow tied to the observed, so that the observed felt some small piece of the connection.

She felt that now. This person knew her. Could it be that detective Patrimos, or that new guy with a ponytail, the Delta soldier? So, she was watching Vesel, and somebody else was watching her, and so on in a circle that was almost metaphysical.

However, she had business to attend to in town, and other chores to perform. She thought things just withered on the vine if you did not pay attention to them. She would deal with the metaphysical problem later. As for the Fleckner Garbage Control Engineer, Corson, she shook her head in amazement. Was there anything she would not do to reach her goal? Her legs had held him hard, and he had grunted happy as a pig and had seemed infinitely grateful for her presence. He rode her hard and fainted when he was through. Afterward, he taught her how to drive his beloved truck.

Starting her car, she drove slowly through the mud back to the paved road a half-mile to the west and stopped at the Hyper-Spray just outside town to wash the mud off the car.

24

It was clear to Jessie Joliard that while she knew what her own needs were, she was still unsure about the needs of her fiancé Senator Jackson Miles. She was about to find out. She had decided to be back in Fleckner for the trial in two weeks and be available in Fleckner if anyone there should need her before then. However, she had to be back in Washington right then to sink the hook.

Miles had always been interested in what he called her *golden eggs* letter, but while the plates had really ignited his interest, that interest also seemed to arouse shadows for him. She wanted to be sure he did not scare off.

It was also clear to Jessie that the bargain could go either way now, and the more she thought about it, the more she was in favor of what might happen: Marriage. That might be good, even with Jackson. After all, being a senator's wife had its perquisites, even if she could not get all she wanted from him right then. She believed by doing so she could at least solve the problem of the upcoming payment for the mortgage. Maybe Jim Parsons at the Fleckner First Bank could help her keep the house in limbo for a while longer.

But pending that, as far as repayment deadlines go, soon meant soon, and she was feeling an acid stomach about it. She knew if they found the plates and handled them correctly, both she and Jackson would never want for anything ever again. They could safely marry, and she could live forever in a secluded English garden, like the backyard of her house in Fleckner, and that softened all the geo-political-carnival thoughts for her. She would not have to do anything out of necessity ever again, although she knew she might grow bored like that. Still, it was her heritage and garden they were talking about, not the senator's.

But maybe she would not need Miles. There was little else she could do in that world, which she had always considered a man's world; but she figured that with the clue about the printing plates, she probably had the upper hand in the situation, and it felt good.

With this renewed effort, she believed at least the plates could be found soon. Pawpaw would not have lied to her about the money involved. She knew he would have disabused her of the lie if nothing real were there to be found. Pawpaw would not be that cruel to her. The clue had come down through him and it had stopped with her. She had memorized it and then burned the piece of paper it was written on.

For her own reasons, she decided she would tell Miles most, but not all the clue. She wanted to spook things out into the open. She would give him four lines out of five and see what happened, see if that alone would work. If not, she would add the last line. Miles was ready to leap for the bait, and her golden eggs were the lure. All she had to do was reel him in and hope she was doing the right thing for herself.

The full clue went like this:

In the house of three pines it is best

To be cautious of the box below.

Rise up to secure the chest

With plates which you should know

Are for my family, the Joliard nest.

Pawpaw liked what he called doggerel, and he would write some down and sometimes laugh and sometimes cry. She repeated for Miles all the lines except the second one. He wrote them down. She did not know what the second line might mean, but she would hold it back for later, just in case.

The site of the house in the doggerel was doubly important. *Our house*, for example, referred to a photograph that her grandfather showed her when he gave her the poem. She could still point out the important three pine stubs from the dirt road that ran around the lake.

It was a house as big as hers but with a different look, more relaxed maybe. The plates were in the house, Calvin had said, and he pointed out in the picture the three huge pine trees standing right in front of the house. He told her whose house it was, and where it was now because of her father, Calvin II. She remembered this vividly, because that was a year after her older brother–Calvin III–had left town for good after a big fight with her father. She thought it had been about the way the lake planning was being handled, but it was still a mystery.

* * *

Senator Miles was not ignorant, and he knew the set of clues as he heard it had a standard *abab* rhyme scheme. He was unaware of the *ababa* the full poem had. He was elated about it, as he dreamed of a good and long war to come in North Africa that could well be started by the old Federal Reserve plate financing he had just discovered.

He was divided of course between a true love of country and the need to make a good living out of it, but every other senator he knew was a multimillionaire except him, only a millionaire, and that had to change. The old plates would certainly ensure a victory for him in that respect, one collectible Note at a time. He knew the difference between face values and collector values. He wondered if Jessie did, but he would not bring it up.

He would have to find the right man for the job, too, maybe use somebody already on the ground there. Probably that man Fellestre, who still did good work even if he had been put on a blacklist by the Army. As a sitting senator, Miles could not be implicated at all. Although he did not want to give up Jessie, the muted uneven shifts in her appearance, and now her awareness of what he was involved in, begged the question as to whether he would ever really marry her at all.

Nevertheless, he believed the Easter egg hunt was on for real now, and he would do nothing about her until the hunt was over and he had all the eggs.

25

THE FIRST DESCENT

When the unfortunate man, Norris Everson, who looked like a pencil but was supposed to be a first-rate underwater explorer, said he wanted to be paid before going down, Fellestre told him he wasn't going down by himself anyway, and Everson said to him, *I'm gone.*

"Are you sure?"

"This is not what I thought it would be. I don't know what you are after but screw it."

Fellestre nodded and told him to follow him to the operation treasury box to be paid a percentage of the amount. The two went up past vision of the water's edge and near a small creek near the big trucks.

Fellestre drew his knife and slit Everson's throat. He let the body go and it fell halfway into the creek, releasing into the water blood that looked like red worms.

"Nobody beats me in a debate," Fellestre said.

The man with the ponytail turned and headed back to the rest of his men. Ordinarily he would have used the man as an example to the others, but time was running out. He could not kill any more of his men. The optics could be bad.

Later, two of his men went down in SCUBA gear and only one came back up, carrying a small safe that had two plates in it. The other man had been impaled by a two-by-four when he had tried to pull out the safe from one of the walls in the basement. Fellestre shook off his fatigue.

He had the old plates, but now where were the old Notes, already printed? They were next.

He selected two men and they stole away to the Joliard Mansion.

* * *

At the Beguiles house, the garden gate was unlocked. No guard dog was visible. LeMace Jacoby opened the gate, bypassed the little garden plot, and walked through the lawn to the workshop door, stepping carefully. There were no windows in the workshop, but a single air-conditioning unit was sticking out on the top side facing him. It was on.

He walked around to the side and the back of the workshop, which he could not get to. No windows. He could not see what was inside if anything. Lawn equipment? Storage boxes? Several half-bodies? He might have to get a search warrant for the workshop too if it was in fact a workshop.

Again, it was a strong gut feeling he had about Larry Beguiles, and Neap Vesel seemed to agree. Eager, he checked the front door of the workshop, but it was locked. Jacoby wanted to pick the lock. Why not? Then he could get a warrant. He would worry later about that poison fruit business, about evidence thrown out of court because of the unlawful way by which it was obtained. He did not think Vesel would do that sort of thing, so there was no hope for calling in support from him. He was alone, but he could not let this opportunity to solve a case himself pass. It would take at least one problem off Vesel's back, big as it was.

As he bent forward working with his tools, his own scratching seemed to be louder in the warm night silence, and an unseen light inside the small workshop suddenly went out.

Later, the footsteps on the lawn behind him were very quiet.

* * *

When early evening had come to the Joliard Mansion, Abejundio knew he was not the only person there. The dogs were barking. Abejundio saw the first man looking in the gardening shed, and he thought the terrible past he had left in Mexico had found him at last. He knew the time might come.

He loved the Joliard family for what old man Calvin Murphy Joliard had done for him. During the Ronald Reagan administration, which Joliard had supported, he had taken Abejundio from the Sinaloa cartel, protected him and his family, brought them to America, and finally made them citizens. In his will, old Calvin had given them title to their compound to the north of the estate to stay in or sell. He did the same for the cook and the housekeeper, Jimmie and Pauley, and all remained at the place they knew and had come to love, and even though some of their sons had wandered elsewhere, they returned.

Abejundio had never given up the fighting skills he had gained in the cartel world. He had stayed in shape over the years by landscaping, and he knew he could kill as well as ever. Now he must protect the Joliard family, or what remained of it. Miss Jessie had just left for Washington, but she said she would be back soon.

However, there was Kurt. Abejundio sadly regretted his efforts to help Kurt, the only Joliard male left in the family. He should not have told him how to set up a drug network, or who to call to get started, but Kurt had seemed so desperate. Abejundio knew what would result. Thinking of this, in the present, Abejundio picked out a triangular spade. He walked slowly to the potting shed where the first man had gone inside and was looking around. He saw a second man slip toward the house from behind the garage.

One at a time, Abejundio thought.

The one man in the shed was easy to take because he had unwisely dismissed the gardener as what he appeared to be, a mere worker of the grounds, a shy and useless Latino. He brushed by him on the way out without a word, the letters DEA on the back of his jacket.

Abejundio buried his gardening tool in the base of the man's skull. Hiding him for when the others would surely come, Abejundio placed the man on top of a compost bin beside the hothouse and covered him with several black leafing bags. A bag covered the top of Abejundio's body as well. There would be blood, and he knew he had to be ready for it.

The other man was already inside the house. Abejundio heard him upstairs pulling out drawers, ripping things apart, and going through Miss Jessie's closet. He did not know what the man was looking for, but he was doing it with an obvious violence as if it were all very personal.

Knowing he might need other tools, Abejundio brought with him to the house a Dutch hoe with a very sharp flat blade at one end. He crept up the stairs, stopping every few steps to listen. Abejundio made it to the entrance of Miss Jessie's room. He strained to determine if there was only one man inside, but it did not matter. He took up a position against the wall next to the door and waited. Soon the noise stopped and Abejundio could hear hard breathing inside the room. He prepared the hoe at half-mast.

When the man came out of the room, Abejundio almost severed his head with the hard thrust of the Dutch hoe against the front of his neck. Blood sprayed the walls as the man fell back. There was no one else in Miss Jessie's room. Walking quietly back down the stairs, Abejundio entered old man Calvin's den carefully and saw that it, too, had been wrecked, but not as badly. He was sorry, and he went to the windows in the den open to the rear of the house.

To his dismay, he saw a tall man with long hair running into the woods behind the house. On the back of his jacket were the same letters as the others: DEA. It was, he knew, America's drug army made to confront Mexico's drug army; one to give, and the other to refuse, in one long battle. They were the same.

Abejundio thought the longhaired man must have come in while he was killing the man upstairs. There was nothing in his hands and he was carrying no bags. Maybe he had seen Abejundio at work in the killing mode and was a coward and was running away.

Soon the two men he had killed were sleeping in a deep pit of manure and mulch at the bottom of the compost bin that he would not open until the next spring. The smells during the summer, fall and winter to come would not matter.

Satisfied, Abejundio went to his cottage at the other end of the large front yard and prepared himself a light lunch. He would have to be ready and strong if more men came. Then he would clean up Miss Jessie's room.

He sensed an end coming. How could he not? The world of money was tiny and mean, but men were still rushing to engorge it. Deputy Vesel, whom he liked greatly ever since he had given signed footballs to his grandsons, and who could handle these matters, seemed however to be going mad with his own affairs, as if forces of darkness were invading Fleckner to get at the last Joliard through him. He knew more might come. He did not believe that he could defeat all of the evil. What else could happen?

26

Sammy Beguiles finished the video game that had stumped millions. He did not know what deconstruction was, but he thought it was going on in the game he was playing; there was not a human being in sight, and Sammy was pleased that he was on this side of the screen. Thing was, he was deep-down glad it was only a game. Tanks were obliterating whatever got in their way.

After the game was over, Sammy went outside. With his mother increasingly busy again, he had to do something. Grabbing his father's Israeli Army Combat knife David, and a fishing pole, he took off past the next-door neighbor's house where his mother was visiting. She had taught him to be self-reliant while she was gone. She made him learn and memorize stuff like, *elevating his life by a conscious endeavor.* He was not sure what that meant, but he had it memorized in case anybody asked what he wanted to do with himself: *Elevate my life by a conscious endeavor, by Henry Thoreau,* he would say.

The field behind his neighborhood arched upward through black, brown, and gray boulders that soon became as big as cars until it reached old groves of pine with a litter of broken limbs and black bark all over the ground from the last hurricane to come through. From there, Sammy knew the mountains stretched upward toward another hill even taller yet; they then merged with the largest of them all. He had never been up that far.

On his side of the hill was a small valley with a stream of water flowing through it. That is where he headed. Sammy had no clear idea what flora and fauna were, but he was aware of most of it. Something had put it there for him, and he was grateful. He whacked at limbs with his pole and chased squirrels with his knife like he was a kid again. He had never caught a squirrel. They were too fast. And, after looking at the harsh gripping claws of an already dead squirrel, rotting, he figured he did not really need to catch one after all. He trudged on upward, slanting toward the ground.

When he got there, what he found at the stream gave him chills. It was something black lying half in the water of the stream. Sammy slowed and looked around.

What is this, he thought. I am finding bodies right and left! First at the back of the mall, and now one right here. That is what it was. Another body!

The body looked like a cop in riot gear, Sammy thought, or maybe a SWAT team member like the ones he saw on TV. There were yellow letters on his back that said DEA. The man—he assumed it was a man—looked asleep in the water, his head under it. He could see no bubbles. At the man's waist was a holstered black gun—the kind he wanted!

He put down his fishing gear and leaned over to look at the whole man, but all he could see was that he had a stiff mustache, puffy lips, and wireless equipment stuck all over him. Sammy knew about wireless things. He had moved past the wonder of wired stuff. There had been few wires in his world, although he wondered what he hell that had to do with this situation.

He poked the man with his knife. He poked the gun. No response there either, except some mild motion in the water. Sammy carefully positioned himself so he could pull the gun out of the holster without touching the dead man's skin or falling into the creek.

He was soon holding the sweetest gun he could imagine, the symbol stamped right there on the barrel: Glock. The man's trousers were not wet. There were two clips of bullets in a pouch on the left leg. Sammy smiled as he found them. There was one clip already in the gun, with one round chambered, and then the two more clips of seventeen rounds each. He did not know what exact version of Glock the gun was, but he could sure find out on Google. He would study the Glock until he knew everything about it. He was amazed. *This is way better than my birthday is going to be!* he thought. *And now I have some bullets too!*

27

The man forced the lock and moved silently into the interior of the small house. Dressed in black, he heard the woman in the next room singing along with a pharmaceutical TV commercial about brown spots on white skin. He moved toward her room and listened as she sang.

Grace Sallice looked in the mirror and still saw a lot she liked. Her lips were naturally puffy, and her straight black hair seemed Egyptian. Her breasts were a handful, the nipples like ripe olives. She was happy that her stomach and upper legs were still firm.

She could tell when men liked her, downtown where she shopped at the grocery store, or had her nails done at the Vietnamese salon on Main Street. They would look at her, not at her face so much as at the rest of her. She knew they were lying if they looked only in her eyes. She could tell. She knew Neap Vesel felt about her the same way. Feeling happy, she stepped from the bathroom to the big bed where her night robe was lying.

The intruder was staring at her buttocks as she slipped the robe over her head and let it fall around her. He could wait no longer. Three long strides and his big left hand covered her mouth, as the other arm tightened around her arms and shoulders.

"Don't scream," he whispered. "Or I'll hurt you bad."

"MMMMMMM," she said and shook her head.

Fellestre threw Sallice on the bed. "That's good," he said.

Afterwards, Grace Sallice was lying in bed with Fellestre. She had been with him since college, and she thought she had been happy to leave West Virginia after they almost married. They still might. She had not wanted to stop over too long in Fleckner, either, although his plans claimed an awful lot of money had been stashed there somewhere, and she was willing to stay on a while just for that.

However, there were now several problems.

Fellestre had tasked her to learn what Vesel was going to do about the ICE people in town, and she knew little or nothing about that except that one time she saw Vesel downtown talking quietly with Agent Phillip Rainwater of ICE.

When she told him, he had seemed quite interested in that. And she was to pass on to him whatever her ex-classmate, Jessie, told her about her grandfather's activities before 1929, and she was to keep sleeping with Vesel to learn what he was going to do next. What happened next was not surprising. She fell in love with Vesel. Love, she knew, was a more than complicated thing, and she now wanted nothing to happen to him.

But the violence in the town disturbed her. Both men were involved in it, Fellestre as a perpetrator no doubt, and Vesel as someone who could put a lid on it. Grace felt uncertain about things she had taken for granted, like where to park, what to avoid doing out in the open if it was not necessary, that sort of thing. All this was brand- new business for her, she thought. Jordan had not told her about what happens to a person after the trained violence of an SO soldier occurs, except in the abstract.

Another problem was how she felt after her rough treatment by Fellestre. That rape business was a good example. It was not a new thing for him. He seemed to like it, and he always laughed about it later. But she had felt truly afraid from the first, and she knew she would be sore later. She thought that recently his games had been going a bit too far. Being a highly trained soldier, he knew where all the bad nerves were and how to affect them without showing any outward harm, but she would be in pain for several days. Sometimes she had to lie to Vesel about it.

On the other hand, Neap Vesel had been open to her about everything; he believed that SO people lived to serve all Americans, even though he said that was all over for him now.

Grace sat up. She saw how Fellestre's long cigar-yellow hair splayed out over his pillow. It seemed grotesque. She pushed him away and pulled the sheets around herself.

"Hey! Jordan! Don't sleep. Neap sometimes calls during his work hours or comes around to surprise me. If he does and you are here, he will turn on you and me both, and I'm not so sure you're a match for him."

"Bullshit, Babe," Fellestre said, yawning. "I have had the same training and more experience in the dark arts, if you know what I mean."

"*Harry Potter*? You've seen the movie more times than him?"

"Are you kidding me? Christ, Grace, sometimes I don't know where your head is."

"What?"

"But good news! You and me, we are going to very soon be richer than ole King Cole," Fellestre said.

"You, what—? You found the money?"

"The senator got a good clue about where the printing plates were, and I've *got* them. I have a question about them, but they look good. We will be long gone before Neap Vesel, or Phillip Rainwater know which way their piss is blowing. We may be off to Bermuda, or maybe the Seychelles."

"Oh?"

Fellestre smiled but at the same time gripped Grace's face with one tough hand.

"I love you, Babe," he said.

"I love you, too, Jordan," she said, her lips pooched out by his fingers.

His smile faded as he stared at her. "You damn well better. I did not bring you here with me just to work over Neap Vesel all day."

"It's not like that."

"If I catch any vibes about that being any more than a job, especially with that cocksucker, Vesel, I will decorate your face with one of my tattoos, which you will not like, and it will be permanent. Do you understand?"

Grace shook her head up and down. There was real fear in her eyes. She knew what Fellestre could do. She had seen it.

"All right, then," he said.

Without a word, Fellestre dressed in his SO camos, left by the back entrance to Grace's rented house, and disappeared into the woods.

After being reminded of Fellestre's tattoo work, Grace was alarmed that she suddenly realized who might have killed David Joliard. It was not Fellestre; she knew his work. It was someone she had thought of, based on some things she had heard, and some things said amongst new friends.

Damn, she thought.

She had all kinds of things to do, but this was important because it might help Vesel capture the Fleckner murderer, and maybe then she and Neap Vesel could be together.

A confession would help. She promptly left that person a phone invitation to meet at the Fall Line Park that morning.

28

The old courthouse was cater-corner to the Fleckner First Bank in the center of town. The gray and pink marble floors inside the courthouse were well polished; thick white columns held up the second floor, and a wide and circling staircase in the middle of the first floor wound up to offices on the next floor. Benches in the hallways were of mahogany, and old but clean brass spittoons filled with sand were scattered around the wide marble corridors like brass balloons.

Beautiful as it was, the entire courthouse always needed maintenance. There was dusting, the securing of replacements for old items that were hard to find, keeping up the original marble floor polishing machine, and the frosty, opaque glass in the doors of each office that displayed on it the function of the office in black archaic printing.

Patrimos found the Records office and went inside. The wooden counter was chest high; old pens lay at intervals along the counter anchored by proud, sturdy chains that may never have needed to be replaced, he reasoned, since the place was built. A woman with a good face, no make-up, gray hair carefully framed and curled up in the rear perhaps to resemble the way it looked when she was a teenager, came to the counter. A tag on her shirt read, *Ms. Haggar.*

"May I help you?"

"Yes, Ms. Haggar. I'm Henry Patrimos, an investigator with the defense in the State v. Marvin Lee Macy case."

"Ah, yes."

"I cannot find records about Calvin Murphy Joliard Sr. on your computer files here. I need court records that go back to the twenties and come up through the fifties."

"He would be listed under *Murphy*, you know, on every book in here about him. But now he appears here as *CM Joliard*. Which name do you want me to look under for your book."

"CM Joliard. The twenties through the fifties."

"Okay. Do you keep records that far back?"

Ms. Haggar smiled, and a mischievous glint grew in her eyes. She put her index finger to her lips. "I'm sure we do. However, it has been a while since anyone has asked. And there have been floods. Write down what you need and let me go check."

"Thank-you," Patrimos said. He passed her a note of what he thought he might need.

He watched her wend her way through a path of desks, standing files and rotating fans, and an old water cooler with maybe a quarter of a bottle of clear water left. She opened a door with its opaque glass showing behind it a cold white glow.

Patrimos stood patiently and tapped his fingertips on the counter. He turned and saw the corkboard on the wall and the signs about government programs and dire warnings about discrimination of any kind in government jobs. The office was warm, and he rubbed his eyes. The air itself seemed permeated with age. He could imagine the same office in intervening years, yellowed dust motes falling slowly through lazy air and him standing there in laced-up muddy boots and a vest with the chain of a gold pocket watch strung across his flat belly.

Fifteen minutes later, Ms. Haggar returned. She carried a thick ledger with a forest-green binder and gray-cloth cover. The ledger was maybe a half-foot thick. The weight of it did not seem to bother her.

"I could not find exactly what you asked for," she said. "But look at this. I think you ought to know something about this particular file."

"Okay. What?"

Patrimos was growing impatient. He was ready to go. A good scotch would help, and then he could work up his report for Stein and take off for Chicago again.

"Well, look at the name on the spine," Ms. Haggar said.

Patrimos did. He blinked. "Wasn't this supposed to be catalogued in 1929 as Murphy?" he said.

"And the name as you gave it to me?" Ms. Haggar asked

"Calvin Murphy Joliard."

"I think you know that Joliard changed his name in 1929 when he moved here," Ms. Haggar said. "He assumed the last name Murphy, which was his middle name, and all subsequent material was tagged as Murphy. But this one book was clearly filed under that old name, Joliard. I don't know why."

"This ledger has been back there for more than, what, eighty or so years under the name of Joliard instead of Murphy? Has nobody seen it for that long?" Patrimos asked.

"Apparently not."

"How did that happen?"

"Someone early must have put that name Joliard on the label. You see that the name is handwritten. That was done before even typewriters were widely available. I would say that the Great Depression caused that problem. The workers in these offices must have been poorly educated to begin with, half the lawyers too. But look at the reader label on the back of the front cover."

Patrimos did. "It was used one time, in 1985," he said. "By a *V. M. Harris and Samuel Harris.*"

"They were the plaintiffs in the second case we were just talking about," Ms. Haggar said.

"Oh?"

"Yes. As I recall, at the second trial there was a young girl who sat with an older man on the plaintiff side. But other than those two, and you today, nobody has ever asked for, nor read from this file as C. M. Joliard. No one could have found it in the card catalogue. I noticed it quite by accident while I was looking under the name, Murphy."

"May I check this out?"

"Ah, no. Not books like this. These are research books."

"Ms. Haggard. This may be urgent."

"You can't take it out, but let's go to that desk over there near the window. You can read it there and take notes and then I can Xerox about twenty pages you can keep for personal use. Library policy."

"Thanks."

At the desk, Patrimos carefully arranged a pile of green mints in front of him like a stack of poker chips and studied the ledger for most of three hours, taking notes.

When he finished, Patrimos believed he knew what had happened in Fleckner County. Being cast out of paradise was grim, he thought. He hoped that it would not be repeated. But who knew? The right economic conditions could prove to be as vicious as an expulsion from Eden. A general chaos in the making and selling of things in the marketplace could again quickly separate the haves from the have-nots, making a bad situation worse.

He believed he knew, along with the murderer, what the problem was, and he was certain now about who the murderer was. He had only one more thing to nail down. The MO. This would be more interesting than he had thought. It would be a labyrinthine case, but he and Stein could work through it, giving him even more time to consider his own pursuits, the affairs of Walter Leeds Patrimos, his grandfather.

29

To be certain about his new thoughts concerning the Joliard case, Patrimos would have to eliminate other thoughts. After doing the initial local research in Fleckner, Henry Patrimos called Elias Ford, an old friend he had worked with in the murder/homicide division at the LAPD in the eighties, before he went to law school. It was now Monday night, the 16th of June. Time was growing short.

"Elias?"

"Yeah. Who is this?"

"Henry Patrimos."

"Henry? Henry 'the Brain' Patrimos?"

"Yes, goddamn it."

"Well, it has been a while. You in the city?"

"Going to be tomorrow. I need to search some LAPD files."

"This is not about old times?"

"I am working a case on the East coast with Mitch Stein."

"Really? You are, what, still working with him? Aren't you getting a bit old for that? You could set up a Corporate Security company any day. Terrorism is big business now."

"I am restricting my activity, Elias, but I find working with Mitch lubricating."

"Lubricating? You still drinking?"

"Not as much. I mean the work keeps me moving, keeps the arthritic knees from rusting out."

"Ah, good, good."

"But there is something you can do for me, Elias. I need to know about a LAPD cop who said he was once assigned to a unit out there."

"You're investigating an LAPD Officer?"

"Black-and-white. He was there in '85 or '86. Turned up on the east coast in 2003. I need to know a few things about his work in LA. For example, he said he worked on what turned out to be the Grim Sleeper murder case."

"What's his name?"

"Larry Raymond Beguiles."

"Ramon? Beguiles? Is that a Latino name?"

"I don't know. Flat vowels. Raymond. First name. Beguiles is the last name. I've heard two-syllables for both names. He said he grew up out here on the east coast, not exactly a Latino stronghold."

"When will you be in?"

"Tomorrow afternoon."

"Can you find the PAB?"

"I haven't exiled myself totally from that coast, Elias."

"Okay, well ask for me up front. I'll be doing paperwork all morning, but I'll see if I can get to his records by then. 1985. That goes way back. I may have to step on some toes, but who cares, I'm already one-year past retirement."

"Thanks, Elias."

"No problem. I'll take you to the *Angelini Osteria* in West Hollywood when we're through, if we can get in. It's tough to get a table even two months ahead. But I will try. I recall you liked the place. Didn't you do a big favor for the owner one time?"

"I've called Gino. We're already in," Patrimos said. "Tomorrow night. 8:00 p.m."

"Hey! I'll see you tomorrow," Elias said.

Elias later told him that not only was there no pension being paid to a Raymond Beguiles, there was nobody by that name that had ever been shot or disabled either. The same was true for the

Grim Sleeper case. No connection. A Raymond Beguiles was there in 1985, but only for a year and he was careless with the rules.

However, Elias gave him a big clue: Beguiles was gay, which it said in his file was the reason he left. Patrimos called Stein and gave him the information. He asked him to pass it along to Neap Vesel. They now had a major local suspect in Fleckner: Larry Beguiles. They would, however, continue their search for outside suspects. That would be the idea behind the defense: There were several possible murderers involved in the halfway killing, not just Marvin Macy. He was after reasonable doubt.

That night he and Elias went to the restaurant Angelini Osteria and had white wine with the Linguine and Sea Urchins, Garlic and Chives. After supper, the two men shared old stories about their first years in law enforcement until late in the night. Before bedtime at his motel, Patrimos Googled for all articles about Calvin Joliard. The next day, the 12th, he was on his way back to Chicago.

* * *

Henry Patrimos was looking for Harris Hall in the Weinberg College of Arts & Sciences on Sheridan Road, Northwestern University, forty-five minutes northwest of Chicago. The campus was bright green with late spring growth; after the rain, it seemed as hot and moist as a sauna, even with winds off Lake Michigan.

At the office of the History Department, the secretary at the front desk told Patrimos that Dr. Oates had not come in yet, and for him to have a seat and wait. It should not be long. The secretary looked very efficient, and he believed she had a great smile. He spent the time reading a paperback he had bought at the airport. He read for an hour. When he looked up and checked the time, he reflected that the only reason he had called Oates in the first place was about an article by him the detective had found on his laptop the night before in which the name Calvin Murphy Joliard had appeared. He had called Oates and set up a meeting that morning.

The PI stood and walked to the secretary's desk.

"We had a definite meeting this morning, Dr. Oates and I," he said, looking at his watch as if it had an answer. "I'm going to have to leave soon."

"I'm sorry sir, if you would leave your name, I'll let him know you were here."

"Henry Patrimos," he said.

"Henry...Patrimos?" She asked, pulling open a drawer in her polished desk.

"Yes," Patrimos said.

"I'm sorry, sir, I guess I was not listening clearly when you came in. He said yesterday that if he was late, to give you this."

"Ah, thank you," Patrimos said, smiling broadly as he accepted a sealed letter with his name on it. He sat back down and opened it. He waited for another hour and left. Back in his car, Patrimos re-read the letter.

Dear Mr. Patrimos:

I am sorry I may be late. I have a very tight schedule between classes, committees, dissertation directing, and my own research.

However, you asked me a good question. You wanted to know if there was anybody named Calvin Murphy Joliard connected with the Chicago Federal Reserve Bank during the late twenties.

Yes, there was, but I am unsure of his job description beyond being a board member. He would have had to work in some fashion with the Region 7 Chicago Fed Governor James B. McDougal, known admiringly then as the Quiet Man of LaSalle Street. While completing my book, I heard the name Joliard used several times as a young genius of finance, but I had no real reason to pursue it; however, if what you say has merit, it should be investigated. It would add to our knowledge of what exactly was going on in the Federal Reserve System right before the GD, the Great Depression, or the Goddamn Depression, as we call it here.

You might also try a colleague of mine, Dr. Loretta Long in the Graduate Program in History at NYU. She is working in that period too and may be able to help you better than I can.

Looking forward to meeting you,

Dr. Stickler Oates

Department of History

Northwestern University

Eager and now pressed for time, Patrimos canceled his flight to Fleckner, called Stein, left a message on his phone, and was soon on his way to New York to see Dr. Maria Long at NYU, who said she would be happy to tell him what she knew, and that there were some people she knew in Philadelphia who had had old family contacts with Calvin Joliard, and Patrimos probably needed to meet them too.

Patrimos was pleased. He thought this came at a crucial time for the defense. It seemed clear that much of it would be financial in nature and they needed all the help they could find in that field. He believed Mitch would be pleased too, and he hoped there would be something worthwhile to be had in New York. He had recently found a lot of meat for his own search, but, other than knowing who the murderer was, he had only bones with scraps for the trial of Marvin Macy. But now he could throw a few things from his search onto Henry's plate. Maybe for now he could use the financial business and the business about Larry Beguiles being gay. That should do it, although he had appointments in Fleckner he still had to follow through on.

30

The day was dead still, its heat quivering the air with what seemed like a new dimension as hazy waves rose from the paved streets. It was 8:30 a.m. Driving into the departmental office, Vesel was lost in thought when his phone rang.

"Hello," he said,

It was Ebba at the office.

"Come on in now to see the Sheriff, please, Neap." Her voice sounded muffled and, for her, strange.

"I'm already on my way, Ebba. What's happened?"

"Just come on in, Neap," she said.

Normally quick in taking in what was going on around him, Vesel was emotionally flat that morning. When he came in, Ebba was blowing her nose in her handkerchief. On the C-board there were no daily pictures of bad felons she normally liked to put up. There were no cute quotes for the day, either.

She pointed Vesel down towards the Sheriff's office but said nothing.

Vesel went to the Sheriff's office to find out what was up.

The Sheriff had his regulation hat on, and a tan tie was in a perfect Windsor knot in the center of his thick neck. He was sitting in his chair upright and pensive. His working glasses lay on a white blotter on his desk. The phone was off the hook, and it seemed gloomy where he sat.

"Sheriff?" Vesel asked. He figured some member of the Sheriff's family must have died. The Sheriff was at retirement age and Vesel understood that his parents were still alive in their late nineties somewhere. Maybe the problem was with one of them.

"Sheriff?" he repeated. "You asked to see me?"

Sheriff Walsh looked up. "What? Ah, yes, Neap. Have a seat." He pointed in front of him, but there was no chair there.

Vesel pulled over the old folding chair from next to the wall, opened it and sat down.

"Neap?"

"Yes, sir."

"I've been here most of my life it seems sometimes," said the Sheriff. "Almost thirty years now. No unusual crimes, really, only cyclic events, the coming and going of personnel. These are my things, Neap. This town has been my small Garden of Eden, you know that? There have been many sweet moments here."

"Yes, sir."

"And then there are the times of wanting to give it all up as vanity, Neap."

"Sir?"

"It seems this town has blundered its way into some other landscape I do not recognize, and I must take some responsibility for it. I...."

"I'm sorry, Sheriff, but I don't believe I am following you on this."

"Ah, sorry, Neap, just trying to put off the moment."

"Sir?"

"Himons found Jacoby early this morning propped up in the west wing of the same alley where we found David Joliard. His cruiser was blocking the alley. At least he had not been cleaved. The only thing missing was his reporting folder."

Vesel sat speechless, his mouth open, as he stared at the Sheriff whose face seemed to be flushing into the pale red color of a young radish.

As he left for his office on the other wing of the building, he was still speechless. Once there, he rolled up the sleeves of his tan shirt and began beating in the top of his metal desk. Soon Vesel's large knuckles were almost raw; he was pounding them hard on the gray metal desk, creating potholes until the knuckles bled.

No one came down to find out what the problem was. They already knew. He sat down at last. He believed the death of LeMace Jacoby was a fatal inattention on his part. Obviously, someone had caught Jacoby getting too close to an answer. But to which question? In which case? Was Jacoby dead because he knew who committed the killing in town?

But the thing was, did it matter now? People were dying in Fleckner despite anything he could do.

31

THE TRIAL BEGINS

It was Monday morning, the 23rd of June 2008, at 9:00 a.m. in Fleckner County Sixth Circuit Court, Circuit Judge Bob Hayes Warren presiding, and the capital trial of Marvin Lee Macy for the murder of David Knight Joliard began. Some thought it would last one day; others said maybe a week and a half at most.

The town was ready.

High overhead, large fans with dark walnut blades moved air slowly though the courtroom and people sat in the public gallery and used wooden hand fans that looked like Ping-Pong paddles. The people of the town were not backward, but they had long before voted against putting central air in the courthouse. As in their churches, if their grandparents had used only hand fans in court, then by God, they would too; there was a strong connection in Fleckner with the past, and it was enhanced by being observed in their churches and courthouses at least. Everywhere else, in summer, air conditioners served up strong, cold air.

The two sides picked jurors quickly as neither Gregor nor Stein had seen a lot of difference in the ravaged jury pool, and Stein had made only one challenge; Alex Gregor made two. Since this was the first capital case scheduled in Fleckner since Richard Nixon, and with a limited jury pool, the county used a six-member jury that consisted of one white male, one black male, one black female, and three white women. A Latino and one white male served as reserves. Stein felt they were appropriately representative of Fleckner and would give few surprises.

The Bailiff started things moving: "All rise for the Honorable Judge Robert Hayes Warren!"

Everyone in the courtroom stood. The judge entered and sat. He was slim and his hair was slicked back. He had a light high-yellow color and wore black frame glasses with circular lenses. Stein knew that Warren was a lawyer who was good enough at the old-boy system to be elected a judge, and he had already been elected for three terms. But it was known in the county that the judge had an attitude of curiosity that opened the doors to many side alleys in his trials, and he had never had a case overturned on appeal.

Stein guessed that when he reached middle age, the judge must have decided that one had to look at things a tad beyond the evidence and think about them in terms of large patterns recognized or read about. If there were curious back alleys in evidence, they needed to be explored, and Mitch Stein was counting on this judge to allow such lines of attack.

Judge Warren banged his Gavel. "The courtroom will now come to order. You may be seated. This court is now in session. This is an action brought by the people of the state against the defendant, Marvin Macy, for the crime of First-Degree Murder. Is the prosecution ready?"

"Ready for the people, Your Honor," Gregor said, standing.

"Is the defense ready?"

Stein and the rest of the defense team stood. "Ready for the defendant, Your Honor," Stein said.

The bailiff then swore in the jury and the trial was underway.

As Gregor made his opening statement, the jury cast several angry looks at the defense table. Gregor spoke of an underhanded, despicable, opportunistic murderer, and like a carnival barker, he pointed right at Macy and shook his finger.

"Marvin Macy grew up in this community," Gregor said in a booming voice that suggested he was correct in his opinions. "I suspect he loved it as most of you do. He was happy in the schools and became a normal young man. We have spoken to Fleckner inhabitants who will swear to this. One of his teachers is in this courtroom today to tell us about him, if we ask," he said, pointing back toward where Melody Turner sat in an outfit that looked made for the courts of the world, not a courtroom in Fleckner. She smiled demurely and nodded her head slightly.

When Stein looked at Melody, what he saw was the ambiguous Mona Lisa smile he was familiar with; yet he knew which side of the case she favored. He also knew she was on both lists of witnesses; prosecution and defense, and he noticed that Macy slouched a bit as the prosecutor talked about her. Stein wondered: What did he not know about what she might witness to? Certain off-campus activities? Melody had hinted to him of her philosophy of life, but without confessing anything. To him, it had made her even more mysterious and attractive. They had met on a tour of the English Lake Country at the William Wordsworth cottage in Grasmere. Strangely enough, readings of the great English poet of nature had brought an attorney and an English schoolteacher together in spirit and kept them connected over the years.

When he thought of her, it was the singular lines of Wordsworth he remembered most:

She was a phantom of delight,

When first she gleam'd upon my sight.

And there they were again, in Fleckner, and she still gleamed upon his sight. For this reason, they had agreed not to speak to, nor see one another until the trial was over.

Looking at the existing evidence of the case, however, Stein agreed with Gregor who thought it seemed a slam-dunk for the defense. The District Attorney had built the case on nothing but circumstantial evidence. Who would convict on just a Rolex watch or a bloody piece of cloth--even if the blood was from one of the victims? Stein would challenge both of those things. Patrimos had already discovered that the bloody rag was from Macy's garage workshop and the blood on it was his, not the victim's.

There were, however, many unknowns. Stein did not want to overestimate the intelligence of the jurors, nor underestimate the role of unknowns in the case, any of which might explode in his face. However, Stein had the best man in the field looking for just such explosive evidence for the defense. Henry Patrimos knew what they needed, and he was getting it.

Meanwhile, Alex Gregor was continuing his opening remarks.

"And yet at some point something happened to Marvin Macy that turned him into a man riddled with hate. We will prove beyond any reasonable doubt that Marvin Macy with malice aforethought decided to kill the youngest son of Calvin Murphy Joliard Jr., David Knight Joliard, in a bizarre manner and leave his upper body behind the Murphy Mall as a statement to Fleckner. In addition, a once successful businessman, Marvin Macy is an alcoholic who has been financially ruined in schemes that..."

"Your Honor," Stein said, sliding his chair back and coming to his feet. "Name-calling is neither a policy nor evidence."

Opening statements were usually allowed to go uncontested, but Stein wanted to cut off quickly the line of reasoning that Macy was a failure who automatically killed for that reason.

"Make your points clearer, Mr. Gregor. This is not a movie set."

"Yes, Your Honor," Gregor said. "We know from county records that David Knight Joliard and the defendant engaged in financial schemes before the death of Calvin Joliard II in 2003. Marvin Macy had hoped to make a lot of money on these schemes, but instead, through bankruptcy, he lost everything. His money, his house, and later, his wife.

"This man was determined to leave a message: *That he could seek revenge and take it when and where he wanted.* He decided it was time on the sixth of June of this year, and he acted in cold blood."

Stein was fine with the jury knowing about the money side of the matter. During the defense argument, he would point out that Macy had worked through his bad times and was now a producing member of Tradd Insurance, the firm of a commercial insurance broker. Why did he need to kill David Joliard long after the negative events of the nineties had passed?

However, Gregor lengthened his statement to include the alleged threats Macy had made against David Joliard in the nineties, all of which would come out during the trial, and he stressed that only the death penalty would do in such a heinous crime.

The death penalty was a divisive political issue in the community, and the jury looked a bit queasy when Gregor raised the subject. He must have known that would happen, since that was the usual reaction to the announcement of the death penalty, execution by lethal injection, if the state could find the right drugs. But Gregor believed that most of the people in the jury pool would vote for that penalty once he detailed the horrendous details of the crime.

"Marvin Lee Macy is guilty of a major crime and we will seek the death penalty for it," Gregor concluded.

Stein knew that Gregor was prepared to detail the grisly and deliberate work that must have gone into the physical division of David Joliard. The coroner had been working on that for him, and Stein was sure Gregor planned to spread out his case in that fashion. He suspected that the more horrendous the visual aspect of the crime, the better for the prosecution's case.

However, after a long morning of seeing a corpse cut in two, illustrated by slides taken at the autopsy, the jury had had enough. The judge noted that, and at 11:39 a.m. instructed the prosecutor that he might want to move on, and a recess for lunch was called, although no one was certain that they were very hungry.

* * *

After lunch, Alex Gregor called Valerie Coombs to the stand. A cleaned- up version of Val rose in the public gallery. She shuffled to the witness stand, put her hand on the bible and took the oath. She smiled shyly at the jurors, one of whom turned away and seemed to be looking out a window. However, they were all surprised at how symmetrical a face Val had; it was almost beautiful, with very thin lips. It was a fresh, naïve face with freckles, best for a TV soap commercial perhaps, and not a homeless girl.

Val scratched the top of her head. Yellow strands of hair ran across her forehead. The Maynooth Presbyterian Church had clothed her in some nicer things they kept on hand for the homeless and had given her a haircut. Although she still had some of the characteristic raw look of the homeless, she seemed acceptable on the witness stand. It was obvious, however, that something was wrong with her left arm, as she carried it awkwardly. She sat down and rubbed her hands together as best she could.

"Ms. Coombs, how are you today?" Gregor asked.

"Okay, I guess."

"Ms. Coombs, did you know the deceased David Joliard?"

"I did."

"Did you know him well?"

"I know everybody."

"But how well did you know him?" Gregor repeated.

"Sometimes we would talk. He would give me lunch money for doing things for him."

At his desk, Stein scribbled a note.

"Okay. Now tell us what you saw the night of June 6, of this year," Gregor continued.

"I was at the mall. Lots of people were there, eating, waiting. Before I left, I read in school about solitary warriors standing guard against the fall of their castle. I do that. I stand guard. I do."

"Against what, Ms. Coombs?"

"Whoever tries to get my food."

"Your food?"

"Yes. You know, restaurants throw cooked food out back when they close at night. They have to do that, you know."

"The previously served food, you mean?"

"That too," she said.

"So, you have a pretty good knowledge of what goes on in the back of the mall, is that right?"

"Oh, yes. Usually."

"Let's return to the night of Friday, the 6th of June, as far as the back of the mall goes."

"What day?"

"It was a Friday night."

"Okay. Let's see. You and me have gone over this a number of times, so I hope I get it...?"

Stein was up. "Your Honor, has the district attorney been coaching a witness?"

"Mr. Gregor?"

"Your Honor, only in terms of the straight narrative of her remembrances. She tends to wander, as you can tell."

"Then let's get it laid out, Mr. Gregor. Overruled for now, Mr. Stein. You'll have your turn."

"Yes, Your Honor."

Gregor smiled benignly at the jury, without blinking. It was like a zombie at a garden party.

"Now, Ms. Coombs, we were talking about that night, a very hot night, as I was told."

"Yes."

"Okay. So, did you see anything unusual that night, Ms. Coombs?"

Val hesitated. She was thinking of an answer to the Prosecutor's question.

"I sure did."

She looked shyly at the jury just for a moment, but Stein saw it. Did she know one of the jurors? How did that get through? He made a note and kept a sharp watch for where Val was looking. She glanced at one person on the jury several times. It was a man who was used to hard work outdoors. A farmer?

There was also a woman in the public gallery who was watching Val closely and put a handkerchief to her eyes every now and then. Val looked at her too. Friends on the jury and in the gallery? Stein could almost hear the word *mistrial* echo in the courtroom. He thought the prosecutor's case was never good, but with jury tampering, this trial could be over the next day.

Stein made more notes to himself.

"Now, in the mall delivery alley, what was it you saw the night of June 6th?" Gregor asked.

"The garbage truck came twice that night."

"Twice?"

"It never does that. I remember it like it was yesterday. It came twice, but the food wasn't twice as much to get in the first place, so he needn't have come at all."

"Okay. What else happened with the garbage truck?"

"Ah, I don't know. I left for another spot until he was gone."

"Who was gone?"

"The garbage man."

"Okay."

"The boy was there. But he ran away when I saw him. I thought he was after my food too."

"A boy? You mean a small man?"

"No, a boy, it was a boy, I don't know who he was, but he was there."

"And what else?"

"When I went to ask the boy if he was taking my food, I found a man propped against the wall back there."

"At the west end of the mall?"

"Wherever it was."

"Your Honor, the state stipulates that a part of the body of David Joliard was found at the west end of the mall."

"So noted," Judge Rawlins said.

"What did you do when you found the body, Ms. Coombs?"

"Well, I knew the man," Val said. "He was always out at the mall doing something, making deals, meeting people. It was Mr. David Joliard."

"What was different about Mr. David Joliard that night?"

"There was only half of him there."

Thinking of the coroner slides they had just seen, some jurors winced. One chuckled. Gregor looked at them and nodded his head.

"It wasn't pretty, was it, Ms. Coombs?"

"What? Ah, no, it wasn't."

"What did you do then, Ms. Coombs?"

"I went back around to the front of the mall and waited until I saw a deputy's car about to drive through out there in the big lot. I ran and waved and told him about it and he came over and stopped with his lights on. Blue and red and all. Pretty. I took him to see the half-man."

"The dead man."

"Yes."

"Did you take anything from the dead man?"

"I didn't touch him."

More notes by Stein.

"Okay. Now, think carefully, Ms. Coombs. Did you kill Mr. Joliard?"

Val's eyes shifted from side to side. She knew what the question meant. But they told her she was not a suspect. What should she do?

"Ms. Coombs?"

"No!"

"So, you didn't cut him in half, sew him up, and leave him sitting there?"

"No!" Val said, arching up straight, and then suddenly banging on the armrest of the witness chair. "I told you no, I don't do that kind of thing! I don't. I don't! I told you that!"

Stein knew Gregor was trying to eliminate others who were in town that night who might have killed David Joliard other than Macy. Val may have just put herself right in the suspect box. The sudden anger raised red flags, and Val's face lost its naïve and sympathetic look and became something else, something almost predatory.

"Okay," Gregor said, trying to lower the decibel level. "So, the deputy– LeMace Jacoby–called the Fleckner coroner?"

Val calmed and drew her neck in, growing shy again.

"Yes, sir, I guess."

"That's all for now, Your Honor," Gregor said, stopping on a high note.

"Mr. Stein?"

Stein was thinking that he hoped Patrimos was finding more evidence in their favor to use in the case. Although the prosecution's case was only circumstantial, it was stacked against his client, even though a real problem for the prosecutor had just opened with an agitated witness and a possible mistrial involving jury tampering.

He would ask the Sheriff's Department to investigate that last part immediately, and he reached for another yellow note pad to write down the request. He realized he had not slept well the night before. He remembered when his maternal grandmother turned ninety and was sick. She advised any who would listen to her to, *Abandon ship!* Now he thought he understood why she had said that.

Nevertheless, he had responsibilities and he would force his way through any barrier to do the best job for his client, Marvin Macy, and right then it meant for him to secure the correct evidence for the record.

He was a nationally known criminal attorney, and he needed to continue the persona of a strong man who was also the smartest man in the room, not a man who was falling apart.

"Yes, Your Honor," he said. "May I approach the witness?"

"Your purpose, Mr. Stein?"

"I have a question to ask, and given her wandering statements, as the prosecutor said, I want to be sure she understands it."

"Granted."

Stein wanted a few points solidly noted on record, so he could impeach her testimony later if it came to that. And there was that other angle the witness had raised about what David Joliard did for her.

He walked to Valerie Coombs and looked her in the eye.

"You said you did not touch Mr. Macy. Is that correct?"

"Yes, sir," Val said, nodding her head calmly.

"So, you took nothing from Mr. Macy? You did not take a gold Rolex watch from his left wrist?"

"That's right, sir, yes, I took nothing. And I didn't kill him, or anything nasty like that. He never touched my food."

"Thank you, Ms. Coombs, now let's return to a comment you just made about Mr. David Joliard. You said he would give you money for doing things for him. Would you tell us what some of those things were?"

"Get a newspaper, look for something he had lost, have me stay with one of his clients, watch out for people."

"*Stay with one of his clients?* What did that mean for you?"

Gregor rose: "Your Honor, is the Defense Attorney trying to have the witness testify against herself?"

"Mr. Stein?"

"No, Your Honor, but I do want to know what David Joliard was paying her for."

"Answer, Ms. Coombs."

"It wasn't like that," Val said. "He didn't like women. He liked men. I could hear them back in the alley sometimes while I was watching out for him, you know, scuffling, grunting, so nobody would find them by surprise."

"Did you recognize at any time any of the men with Mr. David Joliard?"

"They were out of town people mostly. Just pick-ups. Like that."

"Thank you, Miss Coombs. Your Honor, I reserve the right to cross later if necessary," Stein said.

"So, noted. Miss Coombs, you can step down now. "Thank-you for your testimony. You're dismissed for today."

Coombs stepped down and shuffled slowly back to the exit in the public gallery. The woman Coombs had been looking at in the gallery was crying softly and he noticed that after a time she rose and followed Val outside.

* * *

Stein had a specific point about Val Coombs to clear up, but he did not need her for that.

"Your Honor, the defense calls the Chief Deputy Sheriff of Fleckner, Neapolitan Vesel for cross concerning Valerie Coombs's testimony."

Vesel came to the stand and the bailiff swore him in. Stein immediately worked toward the point he needed.

"Chief Deputy Vesel, how much experience have you had working with Valerie Coombs, who just testified about her lifestyle in garbage cans?"

"Ever since I've been a deputy here," he said.

"About two, three years?"

"Yes, sir."

"All right. In your experience, is Valerie capable of murder?"

"No, sir. Not at all."

"How about stealing?"

"Small things. Nothing big. She calls it *finding* things, not stealing."

There were a few titters in the gallery.

"Is Val capable of taking a watch off the deceased Mr. David Joliard and keeping or selling it?"

"I believe so," Vesel replied.

"You believe so, sir, or do you know so?"

"I would have to say I know she is capable of that, Mr. Stein. Yes, sir."

Gregor rose.

"Your Honor, Mr. Stein is leading the witness, and mind-reading is not admissible."

"Thank you, Deputy. That will be all," Stein said.

Vesel stood up and moved through the courtroom. The people there marveled at Vesel's sun-darkened scars. But remembering stories they had heard, some of the people still wondered deep down which in fact he was, a good man, or a bad man? Maybe he was a bad, good man, or maybe even a good, bad one? As he left the courtroom, no one wanted to stop him to ask those questions.

Stein turned toward his defense desk and felt a sharp pain in his left hamstring; it wanted to spasm. It was the rain maybe, he knew that, but it was also an old and nagging nervous pain in his spine that was getting worse. Henry had warned him about this. Old age. Old man. A shriveled neck in a loose collar.

He really did not think this applied to him yet, if it ever would, but his MD in Maryland had wanted to send him for more tests before this trial. He had refused until the trial was over.

Pain hit him again quickly while sitting down in his counsel chair and leaning forward to say something to his legal secretary. He grimaced and knew he could not for the moment easily stand in the courtroom even if he had to. He would look weak and would make his case look that way too.

For a moment he felt uncharacteristically like an injured bird, its wings drooping on the ground, hopping to safety, or at least a safe place from which to launch back into the air. He was uncertain what to do and tried massaging his leg under the defense table without seeming lewd. He knew he could not pause, call 911, or ask the judge for a continuance on the first day of trial defense.

He shook off the hamstring problem and put his attention back on court proceedings. At least current events in the courtroom—paperwork– were boring people enough that they would not necessarily look to him for excitement or able to notice anything odd going on at the defense table.

To change his thoughts, he glanced down at the list of witnesses that the prosecution may or may not call for the remainder of testimony. He knew both sides often put more than enough witnesses on the list as distractions for the other side to make wrong guesses as to priorities, which made him wonder if he was guessing wrong about the prosecutor's priorities, but he did not think so. Gregor wanted to whittle down any pool of suspects to isolate Marvin Macy. Period.

There were a few names he did not know on the prosecutor's list. Others had already played parts in the trial, some were involved with small issues, or asserted a minor fact or two about events that might be of some use later. He had passed the list onto Henry and had received a paragraph and a big picture shot for each one. He was amazed that his PI could do that so easily and lace them as they were with his out-of-town trips. He only hoped that this effort remained at the front of his mind instead of with that financial conspiracy surrounding the death of his grandfather, which Stein had never really understood, although he recognized the often-hidden rage that drove Patrimos about it.

The pain in his leg was fading. Making a note to Patrimos, Stein stressed with exclamation marks that Michael Houston had to be ready to testify for the Defense by Thursday morning. There were other questions he had. For example, was there ever a drug connection with the Joliard's? Certainly not in strict old Calvin

Senior's time maybe, but did his sons ever deal in drugs? Was there ever a connection with major drug cartels out of South America that would provoke murders like the ones the court was considering? Lord, he thought. There was still a lot to be done, and he was already tired.

He indicated to the judge that he did not need Deputy Vesel anymore that day, and Judge Rawlins hit the pad with his gavel and announced an end to the first day of the trial.

32

Mitch Stein had sent Henry Patrimos a folder of pertinent information including newspaper stories in Fleckner, a local Rotary Club's Bio work-up of its members' families and civic activities. Patrimos scanned the information, and then set up interviews. He thought he would start from the top, as far up as the locals thought the top to be.

Jessie Joliard, whose brother David was the man killed, was the first. He knew that she had just returned from Washington where she lived. When he visited her, he could tell from the large front porch of the Joliard mansion with its white rockers and huge bronze pots of topiary designed by the Latino lawn manager, there was a breath-taking view of Fleckner to be had.

He could tell that the sun rising from the Atlantic Ocean about sixty miles away would come up facing the front door of the mansion. US 1 ran north and south, left to right in the distance, from Maine to Florida. He knew that the mansion was in the hills directly to the west of the highway, and that Lake Murphy was beyond that to the west in a straight line behind the mansion. The house seemed to sit right in the middle of a huge well-run compass, and Patrimos mulled that over as he waited for coffee to be brought out.

Jessie and Patrimos finished their cups of coffee and were still sitting on the front porch talking about the murders in town.

"I'm glad you're here, Mr. Patrimos," Jessie said. Vesel had given her a brief bio of Patrimos. "I'm scared."

She told Patrimos about the man who called her and had a voice that sounded like a baritone snake, and it suggested that he could do what he said he would do, which was to get his hands on some valuable objects of hers. But while Fellestre had warned her to stay away from Fleckner and the Notes while he was looking for them, that was exactly what she was not going to do.

"Anyone would be frightened, Ms. Joliard," Patrimos said. "But as I hear, you have a very good Chief Deputy here in Fleckner."

Jessie smiled. "Neap Vesel and I have known each other all our lives, although not together. He'll help me if I need him here, but he has the rest of the town to care for too."

"So, I hear," he said. "But let's get started on events here at your home, and the theft of what you called some familial and legal documents. Is that right?"

"Yes. Some documents that mean a lot to me and might in some way be connected to the murders in town, my younger brother David in particular."

"All right, but I am going to have to ask you about the nature of the documents, and in what way they might be connected, as you say, to the murders."

"Must I?"

"Well, no, unless you want to get them back."

Jessie told him, and the PI seemed unsurprised. Had he already heard the rumors about gold being stored there somewhere? Did he already know that it was not gold, that it was one hundred thousand old Federal Reserve Notes with a face value of $10,000 each?

"All right," Patrimos said. "I want to get a taste of what was happening here in the house and then build on that."

"Of course."

"You told me earlier about the cook, Tommie, and the housekeeper, Pauley," Patrimos said. "Let me take them to the study where you say your Grandfather used to rail on about not being able to get good help before Abejundio Gutierrez arrived, right? That was Ronald Reagan's time, and he gave citizenship to Gutiérrez's family at your grandfather's request?"

"That's right."

"Speaking of Abejundio, I will need to speak with him too. Wasn't he in the Sinaloa Cartel?"

"Yes, in the eighties before Grandfather saw the good in him and brought him up here. Grandfather was glad to have him around a couple of times I can remember when we had rowdy people show up here for outdoor parties. Abejundio took them away and afterwards, if they came back at all, they came as very polite guests. He is at the gardening supply outlet down the road, right now, but he'll be here soon if you want to wait afterwards."

"Good."

The two went inside where Pauley and Tommie were waiting.

"Follow Mr. Patrimos, please," she said to them. She smiled and opened her palm in Patrimos's direction. She followed to listen at the door.

In the study, Patrimos took a spot beside the tall bookcases full of good hardback books directly behind the large cherry desk of the Joliard patriarch. He turned to the housekeeper who had on a clean gray-and-white striped pinafore. She loved the pinafore and kept it clean and pressed neatly, even though her old hips and style of forced walking like a sailor caused her to make any clothing to look awkward on her.

"Thank you for coming," Patrimos said.

"Of course," the housemaid said in a high, scratchy voice.

"Do you know why I asked for you two to be here?" Patrimos asked.

"No," Tommie said.

"No," Pauley said.

"Has anybody strange been here or up in Miss Joliard's rooms in the last few weeks, before the death of David?"

The cook and the housemaid looked at one another again.

"Strange?" they asked.

"Somebody you have never seen before up here, who visited here for the first time."

Tommie the cook put his eyebrows up high over his eyes. He was tall and thin, wearing a long white apron over jeans and a T-shirt. His head was orange and wavy with tight hair twists, covered by gauze netting. He wore white socks in well-worn open-toed slippers.

"You talking about us going up there?" he asked, pointing with one bent finger straight up in the air.

"Have you been up there?"

"I don't go up there," Tommie said, shaking his jaw from side to side. The short remains of a cigarette lay rigid on his lower lip as if stitched on.

"No need to. No. I stay in the kitchen. I cook gumbo and etouffee like I was taught. Now, she go up all the time, to clean. That's all she do, for sixty, seventy years, gone up there and clean. But the family about all gone now."

"That's right," Pauley said. "I dusts, change sheets, keep it up under duvets, ready for them when they come home. I must. My great-great grandpa built those stairs, you know. That's why I must walk on 'em a lot, going up and down."

"He did?" Patrimos said. He looked at Jessie who nodded her head.

"He probably did," she said. "The house dates back to 1849."

"Who is this *them* you are talking about?" Patrimos asked the two.

"Just Kurt and Jessie, now," the housemaid said, rolling on her hips to keep her balance.

"From four to two," Patrimos said.

"What are you saying?" Jessie asked him.

"A surmise," Patrimos answered, his brows knitted into thought. "It may be that...."

"Wait!" Pauley shouted.

Jessie and both men looked at her, startled.

"Was Mr. David before Miss Jessie come home axe me to look for a book of his in Mr. Joliard's study right in here, at that desk you standing by right now. I come in and look around and look around and could not find a thing with his name on it, and when I come out to tell him, he gone, like a ghost, like he never been here, but he was. That's right. I remember that now. Uhhuh. That's who it was. Mr. David."

"David Joliard?"

"The poor child sliced in half," she said.

"That's right," Tommie agreed. "Mr. David. She tell me. I forgot."

"And he had a strong woman with him," Pauley added. "Blond, tough, deceitful, like white girls on Fox News."

"She didn't tell me that," the cook said.

"How tall was she, and why did you say strong?" Patrimos asked Pauley.

"Because she was, you could see the arms bulging, like some women in one of them workout videos Tommie like to watch. She about Miss Jessie's height."

"Strong like a bodybuilder?" Patrimos asked.

"No, like a woman with muscle, you know, working in a big gym with weights and bags?"

"I don't watch no videos," Tommie said.

"They can change things on those videos," Pauley said.

"But she was big."

"That's it!" Patrimos said.

The others now turned to him.

"What?" they said together.

"Changing things on videos."

"What does that mean?"

"An MO," Patrimos said.

"A what?" Jessie said.

"The key to the jeweled chest of mystery."

"Mr. Neap said you be strange," Pauley said.

But Patrimos only nodded thoughtfully and told the small staff of two they could leave. He had to discuss with Ms. Joliard the need to hire some private security for her and her house, although he had been told that Jessie Joliard could be stubborn.

She was, but he stayed and discussed the matter with Abejundio, whom Patrimos believed could protect the grounds well by himself, with his boys there and the dogs and his collection of sawed-off shotguns from his old days in the cartel.

Stein and the legal defense of Macy was important now. Patrimos believed he knew the rough details of the Fleckner murders, and only a small part of it had anything to do with Fleckner.

But it was that small part he had to uncover for Mitch Stein, and he knew where to look and that included his business in Chicago.

33

Starks had given Patrimos the address and telephone number of Hector Rulotto, Jr.'s divorced wife. Her Condo was on the Chicago North Side in the Parlor Plaza. The place sounded familiar to Patrimos, and he got through the front gate by showing his PI badge to the door attendant whom, as it happened, he knew.

"Jimmy! You still here?" Patrimos said.

"Where else would I be, dude?"

"Of course, Jimmy, and I have in my pocket a fold of $100 bills that will change hands with the right moves."

"That ought to be something to watch," he said.

"But if you don't see that happening, I'll have to show you the Old Ball game trick."

"Jesus, Henry. I got a real job here. I want to keep it. Man, I've had five jobs in the last two years, and this is the best one."

"Ah, gee, and what I'm asking is not allowed here?"

"Yeah, yeah, that's right."

"Oh, I'm genuinely sorry bothering you like this, Jimmy. I think I'll turn around and find someone else called Jimmy Madera to go to the North Side police with me, and then the truth will out, and they can put that person in jail."

"Please, Henry."

"I don't give a damn if your mother's life depended on it, Jimmy. I need to get into an apartment and get out again. That's where you come in."

"Who is it?"

"Dolores Rulotto."

"Oh, no, not him, man, not Rulotto's wife. I...."

"And if I am interrupted while doing so by several shady men who want to ask me some questions about my being there, I will shoot them all and leave enough of your blood scattered around that it will look like triple homicide by you. And there you are in a Federal prison. Wow. What fun."

"Ah, man," Jimmy Medera said.

* * *

Dolores Rulotto was a blonde-haired woman with enough chemicals in her hair that Patrimos thought she could have gotten into the export business all by herself. She still had some of the looks that had kept her married to Hector Rulotto for thirty-five years, but she showed her age now. Hector was a man who had to give parties for his backers, good parties, and he needed a young, good-looking hostess for the parties. Patrimos could understand that. A young person who gave good parties. That was her.

But when her good looks went away, so did Hector. To keep her in line, he paid alimony that kept her in the style for which she craved: Aesthetic views of Lake Michigan, trips to Niagara Falls on the Grand Sturmer, dinner out every night. All for which she would keep her mouth shut and certain things hidden.

Patrimos bet that she was afraid her husband would lose patience one day and kill her. For that night at least, Patrimos was going to make her dreams come true, or almost true.

He called her on the house phone. "Hey, Dolores, he told me to call you, get with you, talk things over with you awhile."

"Who did you say asked you to call me?" the ex-Mrs. Rulotto said.

"See if you can guess. His first name rhymes with *jerked her.*"

"Hector sent you."

"That's right," Patrimos said.

"I'll call management," she said.

"I already have. I told them the real ex-Mrs. Rulotto forgot to tell them about the bad checks she wrote in the eighties as a teenager and that the State of California was still after her for about $35,000."

"How did you...you told them about that?"

"Well, not yet. Let's talk about it first."

"Tell them to let you up," she said.

"Oh, I'm already up. Just open your front door."

When he walked in, Patrimos looked around as if he were getting ready to auction at a clearance sale. Looking under things; looking down inside lamps, checking for dust balls in the corners of the crown molding, exhibiting an air of distaste.

"Why didn't he come?" Delores asked, trailing Patrimos around the room.

"Why should he? He's having fun in British Columbia with two of the better-looking bump girls in the casino."

"I thought he went out east somewhere on a fall line job or something," Mrs. Rulotto said.

Patrimos stopped and thought about that for a minute. He was *out east on a fall line job?*

"Why would he do that?" he said.

"I don't know. He got a call maybe. Somebody else to fleece? What they do, somebody sets up the deal and then calls in Hector. Ask him. What do you want from me, money or jelly roll?"

Patrimos laughed. "Jelly roll? Where did you pick that up?"

"When I worked in New Orleans."

"Why should I want some? You're still all right, but you are not that super teenager you once were when the boss met you."

"Thanks."

"You are welcome."

"You're going to kill me, aren't you?"

"Maybe."

"That son of a bitch," she said. "He was always like that. I always put on the best luncheons most of them were ever at. And for that, I get this."

My, Patrimos thought: You can take the girl out of the Holiday Inn, but you can't take the Holiday Inn out of the girl. *Luncheons?*

"All right let's get down to business, Dolores. He needs his accounting sheets for the last thirty years."

"His what?"

"You know: his work agendas, his girls, the gambling books."

Mrs. Rulotto grew suspicious. "He should have those," she said.

"Not his old ones. They are somewhere in this apartment, and unless you want me to take it apart bad paint job by bad paint job, you'd better get them now. The Boss gave me until tomorrow afternoon to get them back to him. I can call some local friends if necessary. But they are very big and very clumsy and likely to mess up a nice place like this. You know?"

"Jesus.... Okay. Do you mean those old boxes with dates written all over them?"

"That's them," Patrimos said, smiling. "Where are they?"

"They're up in the attic."

"Let's go get them."

"Us?"

"You didn't think I expected you to make tea for us while I was getting sweaty up there, did you?"

"Me? No," she said.

Dolores Rulotto's Condo had a ladder pull-down in the long hallway to the bedrooms. The halls were painted purple and the crown molding painted a deep yellow to suggest gold. A goddamn faux palace, Patrimos thought. The attic was not an attic but a minimum crawlspace between stories to allow for extra space for client storage.

Down the hallway, Dolores walked in front. She showed some good curves, but Patrimos acted uninterested.

"Here, I'll get that," he said and reached up to grab the pulley. As he did so, Dolores jumped at him and rammed her hand down into his coat where the .38 was. She almost got it, but Patrimos was faster.

"Jeez," he said, releasing the pulley and striking Dolores across the face. She fell and tried to get away by crawling on her hands and knees.

Patrimos grabbed her by the cuff of her robe. It ripped away, and she rolled over onto her back holding the front of the pajama top to her chest. Patrimos was pissed and he grabbed that and tore that away from her too. She lay naked on the hall carpet and looked up at Patrimos.

"Look. Okay. Please," she said.

"Why not," he said.

Later the boxes were in Patrimos's van, and he was ready to go. He and Dolores had come to an understanding. He would not kill her, and she would not tell the Boss that he had been there. She also invited him back for a visit anytime he was in Chicago. He thought he might take her up on that sometime. He gave her a fictitious home address and phone number.

After going through the boxes in his motel room, Patrimos was ready to head back to Fleckner. Rulotto was in fact going to be in Fleckner too, and now he knew why. All this had to do with making money, but he had to be sure where Neap Vesel and Hector Rulotto would be at any one time, because he was going to kill Hector for the honor of his family, and he would rather Vesel not be there.

That is what it has come down to for me? he thought. Me, shooting some guy in some small town somewhere in the east of America. Would his Grandfather, Walter Patrimos, think that suitable enough for revenge?

34

Another surprise for Fleckner came on the 23rd of June. Father Tim had been at the Murphy Clinic all day and most of the night. He was tired. Three of his parishioners were inpatients, and he had to write down things to get for them as well as other things to do. That was especially bad since he was not right-handed enough to compensate for the loss of his left thumb, which was still hurting from an accident putting up a poster in the Parish office the week before, when a hammer missed the mark and flattened his thumb nail.

He supposed this brought up a point about the group good versus the individual good: One person must lose the utility of a thumb so that the large group could gain larger information on a poster. Funny but interesting. Perhaps he could elaborate on the implications of that in a discussion of the current events group he had recently set up for interested adults in the church. His old Jesuit teachers, wherever they were now, would like that one. He believed people needed to know the significance of such events in their everyday lives, and how to connect themselves meaningfully to an encompassing event.

But his stomach was empty and growling. Maybe he could stop by the all-night waffle house out on the highway. As he was about to leave, however, Father Tim heard the paging announcer call his name.

"Father Tim, Father Tim," said the disembodied voice of a female announcer. "Father Tim, report to the Emergency Room, please. Father Tim."

Father Tim sighed. He was in front of the reception desk in the lobby, and he could hardly walk on out the front door as if he had not heard the announcement. They would see him leave and word would spread, rapidly, and for the wrong reason, he thought.

He wondered if his failure was not due to walking out on duties, but perhaps being too alert to his parishioners' needs.

He sighed and headed to the rear of the hospital, following the red markers on the floor. When he arrived at the ER, there were two state highway patrol officers standing at the entrance. The officers saw the priest's white clerical collar and they waved him inside through the automated doors.

He entered the inner sanctum of the emergency room where the staff did its helpful, bloody work. He saw the Sheriff talking with several nurses gathered in a hive beside a half-open curtain and even the Sheriff seemed shaken. He could hear Doc Bevel inside ordering procedures. All of them had a look of concern on their faces.

Sheriff Walsh saw the priest and nodded at him. "You had to see this, father. I thought some prayers might be good for him, and I knew you were in the hospital already. Glad you could come."

"Who is it?" the priest asked.

"Larry Beguiles."

"Ah," Father Tim said. "Yes. He is of my church. Is he alive?"

"Yes, but barely."

"What happened?" Father Tim asked.

"Hard to say," Walsh answered.

Father Tim looked for Neap Vesel but could not see him. He was probably back in the hills again. Father Tim thought him to be a big, rough man who was quite interesting when he talked about his experiences in Afghanistan with the Taliban. He especially recalled the deputy explaining the word *Taliban* for him, that it was a Pashto word meaning *students* trained in madrasahs, religious schools that had been established in northern Pakistan for Afghan refugees in the 1980s, during the Russian invasion of Afghanistan. America backed them to fight the Russians, and therefore helped create the hardened Taliban who later waged war against the American invasion after 9/11.

"Is Neap Vessel here?" he asked the Sheriff. "And what exactly happened?"

The Sheriff shook his head at Father Tim's two questions. "First, no. And two, Beguiles's thumbs were tied behind his back with wire. It looks like somebody then used him for archery practice. There were four arrows shot in odd positions. Then there were small gashes made on his skin just about everywhere you could think of. I cannot imagine anything like that.

"But whatever is happening, I don't have a lot of help left to investigate it. That's why Neap is not here. This is the sixth murder we know of in just over two weeks, and that is not counting the Latinos shot by the DEA in recent drug busts. Vesel is investigating all of them. Prayer may help."

Doc Bevel heard them talking outside the ICU and he came out to join them.

"I don't understand why Beguiles can be anything but dead," he said, loosening his white smock. "They found him out on I-95. He was evidently dumped out of a car and left there. We have no idea how long he had been there. That's why the troopers are here, they found him on their Interstate. The man was unconscious, barely alive. For some reason, his wallet was lying right there beside him, so the First Responders knew where to bring him. He had no money, but he did have a Joliard Clinic card. At first we thought it was robbery."

"Okay, good," Father Tim said, although his thoughts were rattled.

"We were trying to do something with him," Doc Bevel said, nodding with his chin to the curtain. "See what you can do Father."

"Yes, of course," said Father Tim, and started for the white drapes.

He moved aside the curtain and stepped in, followed by Doc Bevel. The staff had spread Beguiles out on the arms of the gurney like a sacrifice: a victim with a calm, resigned face. Father Tim stepped to one side and tried not to retch. He breathed in as little as he could the familiar smells of a hospital at work: sweat, urine, alcohol, fecal matter, the iron smell of blood.

"My God," he whispered.

Doc Bevel overheard him. "We'd rather hoped that you would bring Him here with you, Father."

Father Tim did not react to that. He was noticing that they did not have Beguiles receiving blood.

"Can you not do anything further for him?"

Doc Bevel pointed toward the arrow wounds on Beguiles. "He had four arrows in him, Father, not quite deadly in themselves. One in the chest, one through the neck, and two there in the left shoulder. We removed those already, and the Sheriff and the coroner has them as evidence."

"What did you make of the arrows, Doc?"

"At first I thought they were random shots."

"But...?"

"A nurse who was a Renaissance Art major before she saw the light, said the array of the four arrows made him look like a copy of the portrait of Saint Sebastian by Peter Paul Rubens. We took that for what it was worth, but she had a new iPhone and she showed us the picture online. She was right.

"But what is not a part of that picture are those small gashes in the armpits and groin and over his chest and stomach and up and down his thighs there. They seem to be the work of one of those old beer can openers, with a nasty tip on it. Why that too?"

"I'm not sure...," mumbled Father Tim.

Doc Bevel nodded his head. "Neither am I. Except for the neck wounds the arrows did not do severe damage. There does seem to be some internal bleeding. The smaller gashes were made for much slower bleeding, not too much, not too little, maybe just enough for a Goldilocks murder, almost as if whoever did this wanted him to be found alive, but not stay that way for long. Odd thing was, he was sedated before this happened to him. Still is."

"Drugged?"

"Yes, Father. Heavily. Probably with Fentanyl. We could bring him out of it, but it would kill him. Severe shock would set in immediately and...poof."

Father Tim cleared his throat. He did not know about drugs. He was more aware of renaissance pictures of martyred saints, and he knew that the medieval world believed Saint Sebastian to be a protector against such plagues. He wondered if the small marks were an allusion to the ruptured buboes of the Bubonic Plague, from which Saint Sebastian was supposed to protect them.

"The Black Death of the lymphatic kind made you look a bit like that," Father Tim said at last. "After the boils spread and ruptured and bled open."

"You say the Black Death?" Doc Bevel said. "I'll admit it is suggestive, but I don't know. The autopsy will tell us about that. But I do suggest if you are going to give him the last rites, now is the time."

Father Tim nodded. "Yes, of course. I'll have to go to my car to get some things, however."

For his part, the Sheriff was curious not only by the way Beguiles died, but also why. He seemed puzzled about why Beguiles was killed at all. If Beguiles was considered the lead suspect for the murderer by his deputies, who had murdered Beguiles, and why?

But he had no answer he could use in the stark face of what had happened.

* * *

The burial for Larry Beguiles was the same as for LeMace Jacoby. Both were Catholic. The ceremony was at the Blood of Jesus Mount Chapel too. Father Tim presided over both, and Deputy Vesel attended them.

When he went to the funeral across town, Chief Deputy Vesel noted that Sammy's semi-Mohawk haircut stood out. He was trying to stray from his mother's side, but she sternly held to him. He noted that Mrs. Beguiles was wearing a large black dress, hat, veil, and open-toed shoes. He could not help but notice that she had red toenails.

As if hearing his thoughts, Mrs. Beguiles turned her face and looked in his direction. Vesel nodded at her. Coming to the morgue earlier while he was there, she had identified the torn corpse of her husband, and she had almost fainted. She had slumped on the steel gurney he was on and grasped one of his hands. *Good-bye*, she had said.

She was tough, and she had not cried. Vesel had been impressed.

After the ceremony, Vesel sat in his car and used his cell phone for about an hour before it ran out of juice. He had work to do. He had looked at everything the department had on the murdered men to see if there were any further connections between them. There seemed to be connections, but none to the actual half-body cases.

There was a cold case about the death of a member of a prominent family in Fleckner County who had accidentally shot himself trying to step over a barbed wire fence. Then during the investigation of what they called the Half-Body Case, they found an old man, Abe Turner, the interesting teacher, Melody Turner's father, dead in a cabin near a meth lab.

And then of course there was the unfortunate case of LeMace Jacoby, his partner, and now Larry Beguiles. They all seemed connected by the geographical circumstances of the fall line, but that was it.

***

For Henry Patrimos, if the output from his research did not directly key on the murder trial, the facts and data merged in his head and often presented some interesting answers. Standard tactics of following a suspect helped. In the first Arab war, the Army had given him the equivalent of the Q course the Special Forces used for training. Oddly, he knew that made at least three other people in town who had probably gone through the course: Neap Vesel, the Murderer, Fellestre, the man with a ponytail who was working with the DEA, and himself. Four in all.

But facts were not exactly what he was searching for. He was looking for reasons why things were done, in hopes of finding information about who killed his grandfather. There was a bigger picture emerging, and the murderer was only one piece of it. He knew the DEA and ICE teams were not there just to investigate meth labs, either. Something else was going on, and he wondered if there was some crossover from the Joliard case.

Patrimos knew that Phillip Rainwater and Neap Vesel had been talking. That was fine if it did not interfere with his business. However, if there were a conflict between ICE and DEA concerning these cases, he and Stein did not want to be caught in the middle. The feds could be like bulls at a cow-milking contest.

35

THE TRIAL, TUESDAY MORNING

The old Fleckner courthouse stood in profound self-possession at the crossing of the two axes of N/S and E/W. Almost in deference to such a spirit, the prosecution started strong Tuesday.

"I would like to call Vicky Beguiles, Your Honor," Gregor said in the same loud and prophetic voice he had used the first day.

The courtroom rustled as the new widow rose from her chair in the public gallery and, wearing flats, walked clumsily to the witness stand. With little makeup, she looked full of bald grief and her fluffy sleeves and full dress without a belt revealed nothing about her figure, if she had one, the men thought. Was she pregnant? That would be a hell of a thing.

She took the witness seat and swore on the Bible to tell the truth, the whole truth, and nothing but the truth. Some card-playing friends were sitting in the public gallery, puzzled at why the court had called her about the halfway murders with her own husband just freshly dead.

"Mrs. Beguiles," said Gregor, walking toward her, a look of sympathy on his face. He was going to quickly eliminate some other possible killers from the list so that Macy stood out even more to the jury as the murderer.

He knew that Val's statements could be overlooked as mere gibberish. He hoped Mrs. Beguiles would be an easier witness to question. Her story seemed straightforward enough yet touched with enough tragedy to give her an edge with the jury.

"The court wishes to sympathize with you about your recent loss," Gregor said.

"Thank you," Mrs. Beguiles said, her eyes wet.

"Now, Mrs. Beguiles, I want to ask just a few questions to see if there may have been any connection between your husband and David Joliard. Do you know of any?"

"No," replied Mrs. Beguiles.

"Okay. You were aware of Mr. Beguiles' background, were you not?"

"You mean as a police officer?"

"In LA, yes."

"Of course, I was," she said. "But he had given all that up, so he could have a family...."

Vicky Beguiles broke down for a few minutes and Gregor waited patiently, as did the jury.

"I'm sorry," she said at last. Tears streaked her face.

"Did he ever put money into any of Mr. Joliard's investment opportunities?"

"We really didn't have any extra money for that, Mr. Gregor. He had his income from his accounting practice and a small retirement pension from the LA Police Department, because, you know, he had been shot in action."

"We are sorry to hear that, Mrs. Beguiles," Gregor said in sympathy, although this was news to him. He wondered if Stein knew. He looked over at him and noticed the stupid stare people have when caught by surprise. Such news did not help Gregor any, though. It meant more places and more people that might have something to do with the murders, which he was trying to avoid.

"Shot in the line of duty. Did he ever have any reason to worry about threats from LA since then?"

"No, sir."

"Thank you, Ms. Beguiles. That's all, Your Honor."

"Cross, Mr. Stein?"

Mitch Stein stood and moved slowly toward the Witness Box, thinking aloud.

"So, you had no money worries, Mrs. Beguiles?" he asked.

"As I said, what we had left over from expenses was being saved so that Sammy would be able to go to college."

"Quite right, Mrs. Beguiles," Stein said.

"But did Larry, your husband, take any particular precautions about anything from his past because of what had happened during early June of this year in Fleckner?"

"Since the two men were killed, he kept a gun next to our bed. He's licensed to carry. A *Clock*, I think."

"A *Glock*. So, he did feel a threat from somebody or something outside his family. Had he ever before kept a weapon of any kind in your bedroom?"

"Not near the bed, no, never."

"Had you seen it before?"

"It was left over from his police days in LA, or he may have bought one like it to keep. He had it packed away up in the attic to that point. He didn't want our son Sammy to find it and maybe hurt himself."

"I see. But did he ever tell you about worries other than an unknown murderer?"

"He tried to protect me and Sammy, Mr. Stein. He never spoke of things that worried him."

"You can think of no one who might have wanted to kill him in the way that happened?"

Mrs. Beguiles paused and seemed about to sob again but held it in.

"No," she said.

"Now Mrs. Beguiles," Stein said. "Tell us again about how your husband was shot in action on the west coast."

"He worked on a serial killer case in LA. He was shot when he went undercover. It was before I met him. He did not talk about it much."

"I see," Stein said.

Stein was thinking why that business about being shot on duty with a small pension had not come up when Henry was investigating in LA. This was the first time he was aware of that Patrimos had seemed to overlook something important, and that disturbed Stein. As a defense attorney, he needed to check on things outside the courtroom, and he needed reliable legs, eyes, and ears to do that.

Patrimos was out of town, but Neap Vesel was in court. Spotting him, Stein made a sign that meant stay close. Vesel's testimony about Beguiles might help him here, and so he asked the judge for a lunch recess to prepare for it.

"So ordered," the judge said and hammered the gavel.

36

TUESDAY AFTERNOON

Back in session after lunch, Mitch Stein seemed back to his old self, like a curious bird pecking in a yard, seeing everything, pulling at just the right spot for a meal, a worm, or a few delicious bugs. He continued with his questioning of Vicky beguiles. He had learned more during lunch about the Beguiles situation and felt much better about it.

"The Glock your husband owned. Do you know where it is now?" Stein asked.

Vicky Beguiles stared at Stein for a moment. "I gave it to the Sheriff back when he asked for it. To check it, you know, to see if it was safe. I don't know anything about guns."

"Okay. One last question you might be able to help us with, Mrs. Beguiles."

"Yes?"

"My Investigator Henry Patrimos—have you met him before?"

"No, I haven't," she said, shaking her head.

"Well, as I said, he has talked with people he knows out in LA about possible connections to what may have happened there concerning this trial, and he uncovered some facts about your husband. I would like you to clarify them for us. We would call your husband now, of course, if he weren't already..."

Mrs. Beguiles frowned. "What kind of facts?"

"My investigator was unsure about some of the things you mentioned this morning. The LAPD pension for being wounded out there, for example. They didn't know anything about that at the LA Police Department. I'm sure you have receipts for it, or tax records, to clear the matter up, but he also said that your husband had displayed a certain lifestyle choice that seemed to make Henry wonder why he would choose to...later...marry...and...have children."

The jurors were looking at each other. *Lifestyle choice?*

"I don't know what you're talking about, Mr. Stein."

"Henry was told that your husband was in a situation that would make an ordinary marriage with you almost impossible, the birth of Sammy especially."

"Your Honor, what is this?" Gregor bellowed "What does a situation the dead man was in have anything to do with Fleckner, or his marriage to Ms. Beguiles?"

The judge motioned to them both.

"Mr. Stein, Mr. Gregor, sidebar, please."

The two attorneys went to the bench and leaned in toward the judge, who put his hand over the microphone.

"What exactly are you doing, Mr. Stein?" he whispered, glancing at Mrs. Beguiles in the witness chair.

"Your Honor, we have been trying all along to establish that there were others who may have been involved in the death of the deceased man, which is the reason for this court case. Ms. Beguiles is on the witness list. Mr. Gregor knows that."

"You are suggesting that the widow here was involved in this?"

"No, Your Honor, but there has been testimony from Val Coombs, a recent prosecution witness, that connects David Joliard to the same lifestyle choice as Larry Beguiles'. He and Beguiles may have both been gay and had a relationship with each other, or even with others in town, and if any of that went sour for some reason, that was a conflict that might have ended in the murder of Joliard right there.

"We did not think this was important until we connected those two similar remarks, the first time when my PI discovered it in LA, that Mr. Beguiles might likely be gay; the other time when Ms. Coombs made the same comment about David Joliard under oath yesterday for the prosecution. We have those findings as well as the other prosecution witness's statements, but Ms. Beguiles has just denied knowledge of this finding about her husband. We want to know where the truth lies."

Judge Rawlins looked astounded. He turned to Gregor. "And what if that is the case, Mr. Gregor? I will have to allow it in if the defense presses the matter."

Gregor shook his head. He also looked unsettled.

"Your Honor, this is conjecture right now without such a relationship having been put into evidence as fact. If later the defense thinks it's necessary, they can bring in any LA evidence they might have."

"Mr. Stein?"

"Fine, Your Honor, for now."

"Okay," the judge said.

The two attorneys returned to their tables. Vicky Beguiles was still on the witness stand.

Stein told her that was all for now. The judge dismissed her, and she returned to her seat, a quizzical look on her face.

Later, Stein thought things had gone well the first few days. He at least felt better about Henry. During the lunch break, both Henry and Frost Nellums swore that there had been no old bullet wounds on or in Larry Beguiles's body; Patrimos's friend in LA also made it quite clear that the LAPD would come and testify, if necessary, that Beguiles was *not* shot on duty, nor did he have a *pension* being paid to him by the state of California.

This was on the upside of Vicky Beguiles's testimony for the defense. On the downside about jury tampering, the Sheriff's Department notified Stein that they had checked the jury pool selection and there were no aberrations they could find. The two people in question in the audience who had seemed to play to Val's moods, or whom Val had seemed to reach out to, were members of a community service committee that had tried to help Combs find a home. A hung jury would not be in the cards.

At least Stein knew his PI could still be trusted and that was good. A quick discovery during early June had helped cobble together the defense case, but Stein knew that what he was going to be doing with Macy was not a typical defense. It could well depend, as Patrimos told Stein, on his trips out of town, and the facts he thought he might find there about bigger forces at work in the trial.

They were now pursuing a truth that could affect everybody in town, or even the country. It was Patrimos's job to track that truth down, but it was Stein's to bring it into evidence when it would be most effective. Unless something new came up, Stein thought that the trial was not going to be that difficult.

However, after a review of some procedural issues, the prosecution made a surprise announcement.

"Your Honor, the State rests."

The gallery bubbled with delight. Something new was about to begin, and they were aware that a person's life could be at stake, whether by guilt or innocence.

"Is the Defense ready, Mr. Stein?" Judge Rawlins asked, the creases on his forehead relaxing in surprise.

Stein was also surprised. The prosecution obviously thought they had a solid case.

"If necessary, Your Honor," Stein said. "But this has been a trying day for all of us. Could we begin defense arguments tomorrow morning?"

"All right, Mr. Stein," Judge Rawlins said, and rapped his gavel to close out the second day of the trial.

37

Mitch Stein was tired and reluctant to answer the knock on his motel door, but he did. The spasms in his calf had stopped, and with a good night's sleep he hoped for the best. Intense pressure must have something to do with the matter, he thought, since he had yet to spasm like that between trials.

There was a second knock on the door, big and heavy. He opened the door.

"Deputy Vesel," he said. "Come in."

"Sorry to bother you, counselor, but I had a tip about something that might help you," Vesel said, "and I was told by the First Fleckner Bank I would need a warrant to get a look at it."

"Come on in. What was the tip?"

"Something called the *Jubilee Account.* It may have to do with some of the recent issues we have been talking about in court."

"About financial matters here in town?"

"Yes, sir."

Stein frowned. He made a sticker note for himself and placed it on his computer screen.

"Have you given this information to Gregor yet?"

"No, sir"

"We'll ask for it tomorrow," Stein said. "If we can get it easily, I'll look it over first and see what it has to do with what Henry is looking into. Then I'll pass it on to Gregor, although I don't believe he has done any investigation in the money angle here at all. We will have to show a good reason for getting into it, though."

"I was told from a reliable source that the document might be important for an understanding of the role of Calvin Joliard Senior in this town," Vesel said. "That might give us leads on any threats to his children, who made them, and why."

"Okay, deputy, I'll call Henry tonight and I'll keep you in my legal loop as much as possible. It looks like we might have more interrogatories to work up yet. I warned the court of this, with the short discovery period we agreed to."

Vesel closed his folder, stood and put out one big hand. "I'll keep you in my muscle loop too, sir, as much as possible."

Stein burst out laughing. "Of course, of course," he said, putting out his white hand, a hummingbird floating next to a hawk.

Looking up at the bigger man's eyes, Stein saw that while they both seemed calm and in control, they were nevertheless reacting to something larger but unseen, like underground water displaying faint ripples on its surface from a far distant earthquake. Stein could tell that he did not want to irritate Deputy Vesel.

"Enjoy your lunch," Stein said.

"Same to you, sir," Vesel said.

When the deputy left, Stein imagined Calvin Joliard Senior in his old age as a figure out of Dickins, an old man trapped in past dreams, growing old slowly, nursing wounds, wearing clothes of lace hand-knit of Victorian design, with a face like melting wax, and living in an old house filled with spider and dust webs.

While there seemed to be only circumstantial evidence that linked Macy to the murder, Stein thought, there might certainly be more than met the eye, and he had to be careful. Scratch a match in a cave, and you get a quick glimpse of the tunnel in front of you and you take that tunnel. But light a torch and you see many tunnels, all leading in different directions. Which tunnel do you take then?

Patrimos had asked Stein about that riddle many years before, and he still had no answer for it.

38

With the death of LeMace Jacoby, the investigation of the half-murder moved for Neap Vesel into a deeper and more profound territory. He was morose and angry as he drove his Ranger to a part of town where there were rusty manufacturing plants, nasty potholes, and cluttered islands of dirty weeds that did not match, like tiny crowds of international migrants shuffling from place to place where nobody wanted them.

Out of his uniform that night, Vesel stuck his Glock in the belt at the small of his back and left with his truck. He wore blue jeans, a white Guayabera shirt, and a favorite pair of vintage Russian Afghanistan Combat Boots he had bought from an Afghan soldier who had killed a Russian for them.

The neglected houses had unpainted trim, roofs lacked shingles, and rude messages were written on the walls with red spray paint. Abandoned windows outside town looked like knocked-out teeth. The sandstone used to build the houses seemed to have left the mountains, rolled to the suburbs to strive for the big time, and died on the spot. He did not remember such things appearing this way before he left for the war.

In addition, men without work now grew scruffy beards and had hollow eyes; others waited for the sheriff to evict them from the homes they had owned for anywhere from three to twenty years; and no one could make any sense of it. Any news they could get spoke of index rates, study guides, and bad pork futures. They looked haggard and forlorn as they waited to be removed. Vesel knew he wanted to tell them to do something else to spur them on: *Go East and start a crusade; take back Jerusalem, for God's sake!*

Yet it seemed tough times were going to continue. There were increasingly passive people in the hills, like the dead waiting for tombstones.

After a time, it seemed to Vesel that no one was going to take a stand for or against anything but victuals. For the dispossessed, it was all about the next meal. Vesel guessed that if he were alone in Fleckner without a job, and no relative to take him in, he might do the same. History for them was unwinding from meal to meal.

But Vesel wondered if any of these homeless, exiled Flecknerians could be responsible for the deaths in town. Why would they be? What could they gain by doing something like that? They had already lost everything, and now they were in a new and radical freedom. They no longer had the need to deal with businesses, courts, or jails, and therefore there would be no crimes committed that could possibly urge them back into an old, and by then estranged world. He knew right then he could scratch the homeless off the suspect list.

The evening was hot and lonely, but after circling the area several times, Vesel saw somebody who might know something. He pulled to the curb.

"Hey!" he said, shouting out from the car window. "Joanie!"

It was growing darker now. There were fewer streetlights with bulbs than before he left, and Joanie Mapes stopped and tried to see who it was. She swung her bag and sauntered over to him like a girl who liked to make friends.

"Hey, yourself. Who is it?"

"Neap Vesel," he said.

Joanie stepped back. "Hey, I didn't do anything! Just walking."

"I'm after something else here, Joanie."

Joanie paused for a second. "About that man cut-in-two thing?"

"Yes."

"Ah."

"Do you know anything about that?"

"No, but Cayce seems to know a little something about everything, Neap. Find him," she said.

"So, Cayce is back in town?"

"People think he is just a good liar, but I don't. I've seen what he has said turn out to be true more times than not."

Vesel already knew about this. Cayce was a bright guy, and some said he was highly educated. When he talked fast the way he did in a strange accent most people paid attention, like watching a poodle talk.

"Where is he now?" Vesel asked.

Joanie shook her head, and under one of the lamps her blond hair presented dark at the roots. Her face was aging, and her make-up was less effective than it once was.

"All he wants to do is help his daughter, Neap," she said.

"First, I need to know that nobody in Fleckner County did it, Joanie. If it was somebody up here, I am going to have to nail him. Cayce can help by giving me some names. That is all I want. I am not after him. If Cayce did not do it, he can take his daughter with him and leave on the next bus, if there is one, and she wants to go with him."

Joanie looked around. "Okay. At midnight, he is going to play poker at Simmo's. He needs money, and then he will leave town fast. He told me somebody was after him, and I know he did not mean you."

"Who then?"

"He didn't tell me. He just said it. That's what he does."

Neap was quiet for a minute.

"He also said the end was almost here," she said. "That's why he needs money for his daughter."

"*The end?* Of what? What more could happen?"

"He didn't say that either."

"Huh. Well, thanks, Joanie."

"Come by again sometime, Neap," she said.

Vesel smiled at her, then shifted into low and growled away toward Simmo's Warehouse, where there was always an underground poker game run like a church Bingo parlor. Fleckner law did not allow games of chance, even based on skill, although Vesel knew the Sheriff ignored that too; the chance for the town's people making even a small amount of extra cash was an oasis he could not deny them.

At eleven-thirty off Fifth and Third streets, Vesel spotted Cayce. He was a short man, clothed in a black T-shirt, baggy blue gym warm-up pants with a white stripe down the sides, and glossy white tennis shoes. He walked with an easy, low-gliding slouch.

Vesel parked and got out of his truck, keeping Cayce in sight. Cayce helped Vesel when he could because of his daughter. He wanted Vesel to keep an eye on her welfare in exchange for news around town.

But the last time Vesel turned his back on Cayce, the snitch who did not want to be a snitch scampered fast and was gone. Even with the slouch, the little man was good that way. If he got the lead, he could run and hide with genius, find holes, jump right inside and come out escaped on the other end like it was a black hole in space.

"Hey, Cayce!" Vesel called out after starting to run toward him. "Don't run!"

Cayce looked back at Vesel and started running. Vesel, who could run faster, and had anticipated this, caught him by the neck even before Cayce could get into a good stride.

"Cayce, I told you not to run," Vesel said, not even breathing hard.

"You going to hurt me, man," Cayce said, breathing fast. "Not you, but you, you know?"

His hair was shaved on the side and bunched to the top, and his ears were at right angles to it; his long thin nose and small teeth made him look like a hairy rat.

"I'm not going to hurt you, Cayce," Vesel said. "Hold still Goddamn it! Why are you back in Fleckner?"

"I had to come back to get my daughter. I am trying to help her get out. If somebody does not do something soon, trouble is coming back again worse than the last time, when I told them a big hole was coming and nobody did nothing. You were gone then. Nobody listened. I felt like Bob Dylan, and nobody believed me when I sung that song. I hear there may not be anything left in this whole damn country but states fighting each other, and you know what that means. The end of the Republic: *The dissolution of the United States of America!*"

"What? I don't need any nonsense like that, Cayce. Give me some names."

"What can I say? I am cursed. I just wanted to try to help her. I might be gone tomorrow, okay?"

"You may not be going anywhere, Cayce, if you don't talk to me."

"Ah, man, that's it then," Cayce's nose was running.

"I just want you to answer one question, Cayce."

"Who's behind the half-man killing here in Fleckner, right?"

"You see? You read my mind too. I'm amazed," Vesel said, and he was.

But he shook Cayce again as if the little man were in fact a rat. "Think, Cayce, come on now. Answer that question. *Who is it?* Lives depend on it."

Cayce's ears quivered like overloaded antennae. "Ah," he said. "It is the end then."

"The end of what? You won't have to dance here with me anymore, Cayce, if you tell me what you know about the killing. I'll keep doing what I can for your daughter. Okay?"

"Tell her goodbye for me. It does not matter now."

"What doesn't matter?" Vesel said. "I just want to know the killer's name."

"Several years back, at the time of that hunting accident at Joliard's place, when Calvin II was shot. It was an out-of-town contract hit for four people in town. It was accepted here, and so far, three have been hit. There might be some collateral damage. I do not know the shooter, except that it could be someone you know...very near to you, in fact...and big money is involved. Very big money. But behind that is gigantic money! *Jubilee* money! I can tell you it is not over until somebody listens, though."

Casey's shivers picked up, like his TV rabbit ears had suddenly received an even stronger signal from somewhere about something important and the picture was now much clearer.

"Four people? And three are dead? Who is the last one? And until *who* listens, Cayce?"

"Ah, Jeeze," Casey cursed, still shivering. "The listener is some red-headed person."

"Red-headed person?"

Cayce shook his head up and down, yes, but his eyes were stationary.

"Why is *big money* involved?" Neap said.

"It has to be involved!"

"Why?"

"Because it's their problem, don't you see!" he yelled. "Their scheme about money is out in the open and they have to put it back in its box before anybody starts believing it!"

Vesel frowned. "*Scheme about money?* Who is *they?*"

"It's some British thing!" Cayce shouted. "I don't hear everything. I just know it's out."

"A British thing? Keep talking to me, Cayce."

"It's right in front of you, man! You'd be amazed the people they have with them! You're living right through the best and worst of...!"

The bullet zipped through Cayce's forehead, dragging red spit with it.

The sound followed almost immediately, an angry snit, and Vesel fell back and rolled down and over on his stomach.

Another snit went right by him.

Hand-made shells, he thought. He had heard bullets like that before. A fourth one zipped by his ear. Close. Very close. Whoever the asshole was, Vesel thought, he was also a fine shooter. Just barely missed. In fact, it was like he tried to miss. Why?

His service Glock was in his hand and he was looking back toward the parking lot beyond a chain link fence. A car started, and it turned away from Vesel as he leaped to his feet and ran toward it with a gracefulness that could pump his arms and legs in harmony for a long time.

All he saw were the red rear lights. With no further thought, he stopped, crouched, and fired five rounds toward the car, wanting to stop whoever was driving. One...two...three...four...five.

It was the first time he had fired a gun since coming back to the states. The knowledge of it was reflexive, however, and he saw a taillight go out. But the car was gone. When he went back, Cayce was dead.

Ah, man, Vesel thought. He knew he should have paid more attention to Cayce's words, especially that part about *the end*, and he now understood that Cayce meant that it was his own end he was worried about.

Did that mean everything else Cayce said was true? The murderer was in town and maybe Vesel knew him, and he was even close to him? There was already a dead stockbroker, two dead Joliards, a dead hermit, an accountant, and now a dead snitch who had just said there was a murderer still loose, and that an even bigger money problem was coming to town, and it was all going to get worse until some red-headed person paid attention to it. And some desperate states would soon be fighting with each other and all that would lead to the end of the Republic?

These were questions and concerns way above Vesel's usual level of thinking. History and psychology. What could be do about that in Fleckner? Or anywhere else?

He stood sadly in wonder in the middle of the street whose surface looked slick and dark, a light rain giving it reflective depth like oil, an encompassing black that spread over his feet, ran up into the hills beyond the town, touched the horizon, and then leaped into night.

39

On Wednesday the 25th of June, rain fell with a soft whispering cadence, but muffled and slightly unreal, like a sound device for sleeping. Those inside the Sheriff's Department offices wished they could be home asleep. At 9:30 a.m., Homeland Security Investigations Agent Phillip Rainwater, looking reserved yet concerned, walked in the front door of the Sheriff's Department folding a wet umbrella.

"May I speak with Deputy Vesel please?" he asked Ebba. "I understand he is not in court today."

"He's in his office, Agent Rainwater. Down that way," she said, pointing with her hand down the hall toward Vesel's office. "Still has his name on the door."

"Thank you," Rainwater said.

Vesel was on the phone, but he heard Rainwater's heavy tread. He pointed to the chair across the desk from him when the federal agent arrived. He was talking with someone about spousal abuse.

"Corporal, don't let her get so tied up first before you do anything. No, sir, you are easily twice her size. Yes, put your battle ribbons on too. I'll be here, or in the patrol car most weekdays. Good. Goodbye."

"Is it a battlefield out there on Main Street?" Rainwater asked.

"Domestic abuse on both sides. I can't believe it. It's like the new normal came on this town like the invasion of an alien parasite that ate from the inside out, so that what you see walking around are men with no clear emotional reactions to anything except shame and fear. That's my thought anyway. The women are about the same, except they admit it quicker."

The pockmarks on the top of the office desk were apparent. Rainwater saw Vesel's scarred knuckles and derived a conclusion. He had been in Washington at the time when the death of LeMace

Jacoby had been reported. He sat with his legs crossed. He was big, not as big as Vesel, but big. First, he ran one hand over the bare skin of his head, rubbing it with a loose palm like those with bald heads do, and then ran the fingers of that hand through the black tuft of beard at his chin, scratching it.

"LeMace Jacoby," he said. "I heard about him. I am sorry for the loss, Neap. He looked like a good deputy candidate. You did this for him?" he asked, gesturing at the pockmarked desktop.

Vesel did not smile. "It was my fault he was out there alone," he said sharply. "Me, I did it."

Rainwater had dealt with personnel who felt the same way about a dead partner. He had learned that it did not help to give them sympathy. He stared at Vesel for a few minutes, showing no concern.

"I have some things to ask you," he said at last. "Can we do that now?"

Vesel sat back in his chair and frowned. "How can I help you?"

"I know a few of your old Company connections, Neap. Back in the day I was CIA too."

Vesel said nothing.

"I don't want any favors because of them," Rainwater said. "Forget that. But you have people dying here in town, deputy, and I know why some of them are doing that."

"Are you talking stopping drugs, workers, or violence?"

"A bit more than all that."

"How much more?"

"As you may know, Deputy Vesel, after 9/11/2001 the United States Department of Homeland Security was cobbled together out of a number of different agencies. Homeland Security Investigations, my department, is the investigative wing of ICE and DHS; the Secret Service is another wing of DHS, the agency mainly tasked to keep the president alive, and he may well need that, especially these days.

"But as far as Fleckner is concerned, do you know what the connection might be between my being here and the Secret Service, other than both of them being a part of DHS?"

Vesel knew that one of the other duties of the Secret Service was counterfeiting.

"Fake currency?" he said.

"Very good. Can you guess why I am down here talking with you about things like money in a way that the Secret Service would really be interested?"

The deputy could sense something going on here that was not just about Latinos on the loose with drugs, naked neighbors driven into the hills on the other side of the Fall Line, or even other bodies cut in half. Given what had been going on he took a wild guess, thinking of Jessie Joliard's Federal Reserve Note she had called real some twenty years before. He had kept it as a memento of that time, and of her.

"Counterfeit Federal Reserve Notes?" he said, almost sarcastically.

Rainwater stared back at Vesel. "I heard you could do that, see the whole field and what people were likely to bring up about how to run things on it, designs and patterns and such."

Vesel smiled faintly. "Part gift, part DNA," he said.

"Same in battle, right? See the field and all on it and know what to do, except when you don't?"

Vesel unconsciously put his left hand on his right side.

"I am getting older," he said. "And wiser."

Rainwater nodded his head. "They say a man ages out of his skills like a changing moon, very slowly."

"Okay."

"Here is what I need to ask you," Rainwater said.

"Okay," Vesel said.

"You've heard the rumors about Calvin Murphy Joliard the First?"

"All of them."

"If I am not mistaken, it is suspected that he hid gold somewhere in the hills."

"Yes."

"What if I told you it was not gold he was hiding, but that it was a set of plates that could print Federal Reserve Notes worth $10,000 apiece, face value; and what if I told you that the Treasury quit printing those particular large bills after 1934 and started pulling them in after 1945, and there are only about 336 or so known $10,000 Notes held in private collector's hands, now worth about half a million to a million dollars each?"

Vesel nodded without expressing anything.

"And what if I told you that Joliard might have printed 100,000 of them with those plates."

"That's the connection with the Secret Service here? 100,000 fake bills?"

"No, no, partner. They were printed with good plates on good paper, and they are genuine bills. They represent revenue backed by the good faith and credit of the US Government, and they are just sitting out there as an irritant to Treasury. It is an inconsequential amount in a ten trillion a year economy like ours used to be, but still an irritant. That's why I'm here: Treasury wants me to retrieve the plates that printed them."

Vesel went forward in his chair slowly, his eyes on Rainwater. He was thinking of Fellestre's blustery threats about getting the plates. Now they made sense.

"You are not kidding me? They are real?"

"Yes."

Vesel thought of the $10,000 Note Jessie gave him when he had saved her from the vagrant who wanted to rape her. Goddamn, he thought. He had a Note in his scrapbook worth half-a-million or a million dollars? He looked down at his hands. Why was Rainwater telling him all this?

"You think I know where they are," he guessed.

"I think local people have an idea, deputy, better than you might think."

Vesel shook his head. "I once thought I did, but I don't worry about things like that anymore. I'm after a serial killer here."

Rainwater nodded his head. It was clear that he had to offer Vesel something extra.

"What if we can also help you with the serial killer business?"

"Help how?"

"Let's say our agency has access to more labs and computer firepower than you have here. And let's say we might want to share it amongst friends in a non-bureaucratic manner?"

"You're serious?"

"About as serious as I can get."

"How would that work?"

"It would speed up identifying prints, DNA, blood sources. No paperwork. Get it to us, and we'll do workups on most things overnight, if that long."

"I see."

"We can do quicker analyses on anything you are looking at, Deputy. We are on the same side. It will help both of us. We'll know what you know, but you'll know what we know too. There is a Delta agent off the reservation here, and probably after the valuable plates of an old Federal Reserve Note. Am I right? Doing this can speed up our goal of cornering him, and, for you, finding suspects and digging out evidence about other things that may be important in the trial here. Also, you are probably the only person around who could trap a Delta Force soldier and stop him. Old SO soldiers who are still in good shape are getting harder to find, given our problems in the year of our Lord 2008."

"I see your point. And the DEA agent off the reservation is Jordan Fellestre. Right?"

"We'll bring your sheriff in later. Don't mention it to him until then. We'll get the positive name confirmation for the Delta soldier to you, and I'll help you as much as I can, Vesel."

Vesel did not tell Rainwater about the three or more missing and possibly dead DEA agents in black up at the lake, or the warning call from Fellestre about the plates. He was not going to tell everything he knew; in case he was in fact on the wrong side of the fence. However, if he had to choose, right then, Vesel thought that he would prefer the ex-CIA and slick HSI Agent to a rebel Delta Force soldier who had been a problem to him in the past and might be a problem again.

"Have you anything you need answers for right now?"

"Yes," Vesel said.

He was thinking of the cigar they had found in the cuffs of David Joliard's trousers. That would be a good starting sample to see if this would work. He gave Rainwater the sample and after he had left with it, Vesel thought again of his partner, LeMace, who would have learned a lot from that week's activities, had he been there. This did not help his mood, which included the news he got from Abejundio just that afternoon about the last Joliard male, Kurt, who was hunting for something in the woods, about which Abejundio knew more that he was saying, but he was worried nevertheless.

Vesel was growing weary of carrying the grief of others. He had his own grief, and it was heavy enough. But then he was a sheriff's deputy, right? That was his job, like pushing a big rock up a hill and having to push it back down again, time after time. He felt that he and that rock were long-time lovers.

40

Kurt Joliard was northwest of Lake Joliard near its rocky shore ready to start reaping the rewards of a business venture his father had started up but had not fully implemented before he was killed in a dove shoot in the Fall of 2006. His father

Calvin II had an outline of how to handle Russian krokodile drugs smuggled up through Costa Rica. Kurt had decided to make a connection with drug smugglers and Abejundio had helped him do it.

Kurt knew the Mexican landscaper would have preferred not to help him, but the gardener also wanted the house of Joliard to prosper again. He knew this was necessary to the Joliards. Hell was coming otherwise, he thought.

The attempt to make available drugs that would corrode the county was a part of his air of ignorance. All Kurt wanted was the money that could be had. He had a document upon which Calvin Junior his father had carefully arranged a grid of Joliard land to the north and northwest of the Joliard Lake on which to lay out a maximum number of micro-labs. They would last for a week or two as crops were harvested and then they could be dismantled and moved on to the next site where they would stay a week or so, then be moved on, and so forth from the southern to the northern border of his land, which would last about eight weeks. Laid out on a table, the pattern looked like an illustration of a game of Chinese checkers His father believed the entire operation could be repeated year after year until the Joliard fortune was restored.

He knew that the DEA could not prove anything even if it found any of the sites. The Joliards could claim ignorance and blame everything on immigrants. But while that was the downside, Kurt could already tell that the upside could be huge. Abejundio said his past was forcing his future to bend over and become the same as a serpent eating its tail, the same anew, although Kurt did not know what that meant.

Los Zeta was handling the sites and could throw up and tear down a small shack in a day. The members had everything they needed: tools, lumber, nails, as well as the lab material and krokodile ingredients. Kurt was to meet with them again that night at a working site to discuss new schedules and money. The year before he had received $60,000 a week, and he intended that amount to continue during the upcoming harvest.

He was wearing the same LL Bean outdoor clothes he usually used in the woods, but now he was growing desperate. Where the hell was the microlab? He looked again at his mobile GPS device that stuck a red flag right on the site. However, real life did not present red flags at the exact spot. He pressed on, shaking his head, and swatting mosquitos.

When Kurt did reach the lab site, he saw several men he did not recognize. They were working on, or dismantling, something, a bench. Were they throwing up, or tearing down? What the hell?

"Hey! Buenos Dias!" Kurt shouted, raising one hand in salute as he stepped out of the woods with fanfare, as he had been told to do. He had agreed to that, knowing that some of the cartel instructors could be trigger-happy.

"Joliard, Kurt Joliard!"

The two men turned and stared at him.

"Where's Julio?" he shouted, a frown on his face. Julio oversaw all new labs and the financial books for the region. Kurt would be really pissed if Julio was not going to be there. It might mean no money that day. That would be a huge problem for Kurt, and it made him sad and angry at the same time.

While Kurt was fumbling for words, one of the men pulled a .44 magnum from behind the bench and held it like it was a water hose pointing to the ground.

"He's gone, Senor. He pulled out because we are to move. We need to move fast and quickly now. All your little labs are closed. In addition, the big Senorita has paid us to do something here in coin and in other ways that we liked, right Manuel?"

The other man giggled and then spat at the ground.

"No money today, senor. This... is for you," the first man said looking at the big magnum. "Special delivery from her, a lovely queen. Powerful."

"Her? Lovely queen?" Kurt shouted, thinking of his sister Jessie. What was she up to now? Had she been out to the labs and worked with the cartel?

Why? Did she...?

Since he could be prickly in business matters, Kurt became belligerent, swinging his arms like a professor in a classroom full of dumb people. He was not going to take this stupidity, this undercutting maneuver!

"Goddam it to holy hell!" he yelled. "Where is my rightful profit, huh? It was my capital investment."

The two men turned their eyes from Kurt.

"Well?" Kurt said. "Well, what have you got to say for yourselves? Cat got your tongues? No answers, smartasses? No Eenglish?"

The first man, with the gun, frowned and shook his head. He looked at his friend. They both shrugged their thin shoulders.

"And what the hell does that mean, Poncho? A shrug? I'm going to call Julio right now."

Kurt walked right up to the two men and did not even glance at the gun. He felt in charge and guns meant nothing to him. He pulled out his cell phone. These Latinos were children. What did they expect?

"I ask you again. Who put you up to this? Was it Jessie? Who put you up to this robbery?"

The two men were now frowning in annoyance, and a dim awakening appeared on Kurt's face as he stepped back, although he guessed he still had to show his command.

"I said, who told you to do this, my friends? I told her to.... wait...was it somebody else? Who the hell was it? Was it...?"

The Latino answered the question, but the name was lost in the sound of the magnum. A loud, threatening noise.

"It was the *JT*," the Latino said.

The two Latinos took down the rest of the shed. The lumber was thrown in various places nearby, and everything else scattered and cleared. There were four bags of money in one corner of the now barren concrete slab, and they took off with it toward the northeast and were soon lost in the thickening June trees.

41

Early morning, just before dawn, Vesel was caught between dreams and the everyday world. He could sense the enemy just over the horizon with turbaned heads, long dirty shirts, lice, and sandaled feet. They were to attack with their AK47's soon, which he expected. He knew his fireteam could withstand that attack maybe twice, three times before having to call back to basecamp for help.

And then the firing started.

Vesel slowly became aware that his cell phone was ringing with its British double-ring tone. Might be a call from the outpost. Maybe his backup was running late, and that would change the outcome of the mission. He grabbed the cordless phone from the bedside table.

"Yes, sir," he said.

"With a snappy salute too!" said a low voice on the other end that chuckled softly.

"Who is this?"

Vesel was quickly awake and sat up. His wristwatch was on the side table: 5:00 a.m. And then it came to him.

"Sir, your nightmare, sir," the voice said. It had a lisp in it.

This was a voice he did not want to hear, especially not here, not now. He swung out of bed and placed his feet squarely on the floor.

"Fellestre?" he shouted. "You, sonofabitch!"

"Hey, you weren't taught that at SF school, Commando. Shame, shame. But you found that dumb ass the other day up at the lake trying to take over? Amateurs. I won't leave evidence next time. Count on it."

"If you are thinking of doing anything bad in my town," Vesel said. "I promise you I will track you to the farthest reaches of the known world, cut your vitals off, and make dog food out of them."

"If I could have back then, Vesel, I would have ripped your asshole right out of your rear end," Fellestre said. "I already know you, Sergeant Vesel. You killed my woman in country while we were there, then got me booted out of the service. You haven't paid all the way for that yet."

"If it had been your choice, I would have been skinned from head to toe."

"I know. I saw that nice capital T under your armpit. The right one, right?"

"You got what you deserved. I would give you a T of your own, if I hadn't..."

"Hadn't what?"

"I don't do special ops anymore."

As soon as he said it, Vesel was sorry he did. You never give the enemy an advantage.

"Oh? That's good," Fellestre said. "I won't have to worry about that then. Good timing, mate."

"Don't push me, Fellestre. Stay out of my way."

"Details, details. But at least you have a small token of pain, which is nothing like my Abiba being ripped to pieces by one of your IED specials. I have nothing left of her to keep."

"Hey, that wasn't my fault. I had no idea you were humping a terrorist, and I do not control areas of operation. I did not choose to kill anybody but goddamn terrorists in general."

"That *goddamn terrorist* was the key to a year-long operation in that area. That's why I was there, meathead, to keep it all going."

"Why weren't we briefed on it?"

"You were too low on the totem pole."

"Great, so we were working for you? No wonder it all folded. And if you're behind what's happening in Fleckner now," Vesel said. "I will find you, and it will end badly for you."

"Ah, don't forget your promises, Vesel. I have a job here and I haven't finished it yet."

Vesel was at first deadly quiet. "If you even breathe heavy on the phone with anyone I know," he said. "I'll wrap your gonads around your neck and bury you with them."

"*Gonads?*" Fellestre said, laughing. "And you'll do that after giving up doing things like that? Don't bother looking for me, Vesel. You know what mountains can be like, even if you think you know them inside out."

"I'll find you," Vesel said, although he knew Fellestre was right about the confusion of mountains.

"I'll call if I need you. See you at the lake. Good luck, Wimpy."

The phone went dead.

Vesel realized he was squeezing the phone like the handle of a bullwhip. He deliberately let it go, then lay down. But he knew he was through sleeping for the night. He had promised not to kill anyone; but Fellestre needed killing. He kept thinking of the oath every SO soldier swore: *If knocked down, I will get back up, every time. I will never give up.*

But who did that apply to now? Vesel thought. Him, or Fellestre?

42

The next day at the lake Vesel was watching on a sniper scope where one man was dressed in a black outfit, face without camouflage, and two of them were getting into SCUBA gear. They did have yellow DEA letters on their coats, which meant little. Fellestre was not present, or Vesel would have gone for him first. He wanted one of the DEA group, and he silently melted into the woods. Giving himself over wholly to his training, he circled downhill to the next ridge toward them.

Suddenly, to his astonishment, he heard shots to his right, uphill from him. He quickly checked on the team below. The crew had also stopped, and someone motioned with his hand up toward the sounds.

What the hell, Vesel thought.

* * *

Sammy had hidden the gun he found and was back up early that next morning for practice. He was having fun shooting the Glock he had found on the dead man in the hills. It kicked him bad, but he loved it. He had to work the gun with both hands like those he saw on TV, holding the revolver steady. He set up a row of pinecones on top of the trunk of a fallen tree. Out of five shots, only one had come even close to the tree. So, he fired at clouds, waving the gun, hollering at the top of his voice. He felt great.

"Bam! Bam! Bam!"

A big hand clapped over his mouth. Sammy struggled and tried to point the Glock at whoever it was, but he could no longer move. He was big, but whoever had him was very strong and much bigger and hauled him easily to the narrow mouth of what he thought was a cave.

He felt the interior of the cave close in. It was damp inside and smelled of burnt wood, and any sound from outside was muffled. Tired, he quit struggling. Whatever would happen to him, he was too dizzy to do anything about it...

When Sammy came to, he saw a man squatting in front of him. Sammy recognized him.

"Aren't you Deputy Vesel?"

"Yeah, buddy. Relax. You fainted, but you're safe now."

"What?" Sammy said, sitting up. *Fainted?* Where was his gun?

"Where did you get this?" Vesel said, holding up the Glock.

Sammy grew shrewd. "What is it?"

Vesel stared at Sammy and Sammy felt it. He wanted to hide the gun and keep it as his. But there it was in Deputy Vesel's hand. What was he going to do? Absent any other plan, Sammy told the truth.

"I found it."

"Up here?"

"Not far away. Over where the creek is."

"It was just lying there?"

"It was in a man's holster."

"Ah," the deputy said. "What kind of man?"

"A dead one," Sammy said. "I think."

"Black clothes?" Vesel asked.

"Yellow DEA letters on the back?"

"How did you know?" Sammy blurted before he could think about it. The deputy was confusing.

"Okay. So, you found it, and you were trying to practice with it?"

"Yes."

"Hey, that was pretty brave."

Sammy was stunned. The deputy called him *brave*.

"It was?"

"Not everybody would do that. That thing has a kick to it. I respect you for trying. But you also need understanding when you use a gun. It has a purpose, and you should know what that purpose is. Shooting at clouds is not one of them."

"I guess," Sammy said, abashed. But he had never thought of himself that way, as brave. His father never said so. He had never been that close to him, although sometimes he liked to play ball games with him in the backyard. His dad seemed to be thinking of something else all the time, though, even when he was throwing plastic footballs to him.

But Sammy could not think of anything like a gun having a purpose, and neither did anybody else as far as he knew. You just shot it.

"What is your name, buddy?"

"Uh, Sammy."

"Sammy who?"

"Beguiles. Sammy Beguiles."

"Ah, I know your father. An accountant, right?"

"Right."

Sammy was not going to tell the deputy that his father was once an LA cop. That would be too much to tell. He thought of something else to ask about.

"Could you teach me the purpose of using a gun?" Sammy asked. Once he knew how, then he could show his friends what a gun was all about. He could protect himself too. If he knew how, then he could really kill some things.

"Sure," Vesel said. "But first we need to do something about the men in black out there."

"How many are there?"

"At least three, maybe more."

"Was the dead man I found one of them?"

"Maybe, yes."

Sammy thought Chief Deputy Vesel was also a brave man to take on three men with guns. But he also believed it was time for dinner and his stomach was growling bad.

"Can I go home now?" he asked.

The deputy frowned. "I can't leave you here, and you can't just walk out of here with them looking for you. You are with me now. I have several places farther up in the hills we can get to. You will have to do everything I say, though. All right? Can you do that?"

"Okay," Sammy said, growing excited. "Can I use the gun on them?"

Vesel smiled. Sammy took that as a no. Well, at least he could watch and learn. This was getting good.

"Are you ready?" Vesel said.

"Okay."

Sammy thought it was more than smelly inside the cave. The deputy explained a few other things to him and then the two slipped out of the cave into the fresh dark and he was greatly relieved.

43

THE TRIAL, WEDNESDAY MORNING

The hard rains in the commons were worse than the night before. Waters washed down from the top of the mountains to the farmlands to the east and southeast. It filled gutters and ran off the sides of houses in Fleckner; it gurgled from border to border, and weary street drains boiled with the onslaught; through the tall courtroom windows, the steady rain made the outside world look almost as dark as night.

Inside, there was legal paperwork that held the court for a while, then it would be time for Mitch Stein to move on defense and make his best play.

And that time was now.

It was 10:45 a.m. Day Three of the trial.

"Your Honor, the defense calls Marvin Macy to the stand," Stein said.

The audience gasped. Gregor, uncharacteristically, nodded his head in delight. To put the defendant on the stand was a rare event in a capital case. It was the only chance for the prosecution to cross-examine the defendant. Gregor would be able to force Macy in or out of rooms he might not want to enter or leave.

Macy stood and walked to the witness stand. He looked spiffy that day dressed in a blue blazer with a white shirt, khaki pants, and a vivid red, blue-striped tie in an off-center Windsor knot that his newly appreciative ex-wife, who knew his sizes, had picked out for him. Stein approved, although he noticed that the hump on Macy's back was not well hidden by the coat. It gave him a vaguely sinister look.

"Raise your right hand," said the Bailiff.

The Bailiff administered the oath and Macy took his seat. He sat up straight as best he could with his thin hands loosely draped on the arms of the witness chair. Stein had told him to look right at the jury as he spoke, and he hoped that Macy would remember to add volume to his answers.

"Now, Mr. Macy," Stein said. "You have been charged in the murder of Mr. David knight Joliard. Do you understand the charge?"

Macy cleared his throat. "I do," he said.

"Are you guilty of it?"

"No, sir, no I am not."

"All right, but first there are a few things we need to clear up about the alleged evidence."

"Okay."

"Where did you get the gold watch you were wearing when Sheriff Walsh took you to a cell to sleep off your bourbon in the late hours of 6 June 2008?"

"I bought it from Val Coombs for $35."

"Valerie Coombs? The witness we heard from Monday?"

"Yes, sir."

"$35? For a $25,000 watch?"

"I am an alcoholic, and I have been trying to shed drink for years. I was crocked and when Val showed me the watch, she said it was from the bottom of some dumpster and it was hers and did I want to buy it."

"And did you?"

"I did. She knocked on my window at a stoplight. I admit I thought it was a counterfeit rip-off, but it looked okay and it worked. To celebrate, I began to drink more. A little later, I pulled over and put it on with my other watch. I fell asleep, and when he found me, Sheriff Blue invited me to sleep off the drunk in one of his cells. I do that sometimes."

"And you did that until the next day, the 7th of June?"

"It was the morning of the next day, yes, sir, when I woke up. The seventh."

"But before you were let go, the staff noted that one of the watches left in their care might not belong to you?"

"Yes, sir."

"And that's the reason you are sitting here charged with the murder of David Joliard?"

"Yes, sir. That's all. That's it."

Stein smiled. So much for the watch.

The blood work on the handkerchief found in his pocket had revealed that it was Macy's blood from some minor accident, and the prosecution had not introduced it into evidence. So much for the bloody rag. However, before he could make a complete case for Macy, Stein still had to bring out some painful facts about him.

"Okay, we know how you got the watch in question, Mr. Macy," Mr. Stein said. "You bought the watch from Val Coombs. Now, have you had any financial troubles in the past?"

Macy kept his eyes glued to the jury. Stein was not at all sure what he was looking at. Later Macy told him that one of the women on the jury wore some big earrings and he kept his eyes on them the whole time, swaying here and there.

"I have, yes I have," Macy said.

"For example, in 1986, you took out a second mortgage on your house and you used all of it to buy more stock. Is that correct?"

"It is."

"How much money was that?"

"Well, it wasn't a million. It was only $35,000 dollars."

There were murmurs in the courtroom. Wanting to stay on top of any disruptions, Judge Rawlins quickly gaveled it into silence.

"That was a fairly large sum of money to borrow and have in stock at the time, though, wasn't it?" Stein asked.

"In the early eighties, inflation was driving everything up by the month, up and up, including the value of my house, and I was buying on margin in which I could and did borrow half of the money for the stock from my broker, so I had more like $70,000 in stocks."

"Buying on margin? What is that?"

"I bought half the stock at the time for $35,000 with my own money, and I borrowed another $35,000 from my broker on margin. My $70,000 worth of stock in the next few months grew in value to $100,000. I felt it would continue to go up in value. That was my bet."

"What happened?"

"Well, about that margin thing. One, to trade on margin you need a *margin account*, and, two, the money you borrow has to be paid back."

"Okay," Stein said. "And that's it?"

"Not quite. There is a *maintenance margin*, which is the minimum account balance of cash or stock with value you must have in place before your broker will loan you any money. If those stocks fall in value, he can make you deposit more money to maintain the account, or he can sell whatever stock you already own to pay down your loan. When the minimum is passed, he makes what is known as a margin call, and you must pay up or lose the stock."

"Of course, Mr. Macy. But doesn't everything always go well in stock purchasing?"

"Oh, it can get really bad. Buying *long* on margin is the only stock-based investment where you stand to lose more money than you invest. A market dive of 50% or more can cause you to lose more than 100% of your stock value, with interest and commissions still to pay on top of that. I mean, my God!"

"You know your stock language, don't you Mr. Macy?"

"I try to stay up."

"And what you did, that's called *trading long*. Is that right? You hope the stock goes up in value, and you make your money by selling a stock at a higher level than you paid for it?"

"Yes, sir."

"And the other action, *short-selling?*"

"Short sellers are betting that the stock they sell will drop in price. If the stock does drop after selling, the short seller buys it back at a lower price and returns it to the lender with some left over."

"How does that work?"

"An investor borrows a stock from a broker and then sells it at the current price. He holds the income and waits for the stock to fall in price. When it does, he buys the stock at the fallen price and returns what he borrowed to the lender."

"That sounds risky. What is the investor looking for?"

"Short sellers borrow shares in a company at a certain price, hoping that the price falls. The goal is to acquire the shares when they fall to a cheaper price. You can then give the borrowed stocks back to the broker and keep the difference between the first or borrowed price, and the second or cheaper price you have just paid for the stocks. The size of the price decline is profit."

Stein spoke to the jury. "Wow, that's heavy stuff." he said with humor.

"It gets easier after a time."

"Now, Mr. Macy, which way of owning stocks did you choose?"

"Buying long, and I wound up dead in the water. My broker, David Joliard, had predicted that the stock I owned was good. I did too. That would be in early 1987. Usually David was good at prediction. So, I continued to buy long hoping prices would keep going up."

"Did that happen?"

"In October 1987, stocks fell way below the 50% minimum requirement. David gave me a margin call, which I could not cover. To get his money back, he sold all the stock that I had posted as collateral. I had no further assets to borrow against and David was pushing me hard. My lawyer suggested a Chapter 7 Bankruptcy, so I did that."

"So, you owed Joliard money?"

"Yes."

"I see. So, you lost your stock, your house, and your high credit score too?"

"It was bad for everybody back then. I just went too far."

"But David Joliard did not get back all he loaned you?"

"More or less."

Gregor rose to his feet. "Your Honor, what does *more or less* mean?"

"Mr. Stein?"

"He was happy," Macy said. "My account was closed."

"Okay, Mr. Macy," Stein asked. "But do you have any idea about what caused the stock market crash at that time?"

Macy shook his head. "No, sir, I do not. It was, just like that, the DOW crashed 508 points when the high had been at 2722. It was a one-day loss of 22.6 % of the DOW, a historic fall. It almost beat the fall before the Great Depression. Why? Who knows why? It is just the business cycle, you know, and you can't do anything about it. You can *guess* what it will do, of course."

"But your guess was wrong, and so you did not blame David Joliard for the losses?"

"No. David Joliard warned me. He said he had hopes for it to do well, but he didn't know what would happen either, really."

"And that was, what, a little over twenty years ago now?"

Macy looked up at the ceiling and squinted while counting up the years.

"Yes, sir," he said.

"And your inability to make as much money after that, did you blame David Joliard for that?"

"Why should I? I went into insurance sales. That's part of financial business. I didn't do badly. After, let's see, on the sixteenth of next month, he and I were supposed to get together again and talk about another key-man insurance policy for one of his big-money clients. I had five or six policies like that. The last one would have been a huge commission for me. Six times two-thousand dollars a month premium; or a twelve thousand-dollar commission. It would cover my rent until Christmas. Why should I dislike David Joliard?"

"Ok. Thank you, Mr. Macy."

Stein had made clear the attitude of Macy towards Joliard. He showed the circumstantial evidence of the Rolex watch for what it was—weak; and he had shown how Macy made good money since the old bad days. He did not need to blackmail or kill anybody for money. He had a few other points to make with Macy, but that could wait until Thursday. Beyond that, he thought, what was left for the prosecutor to do on cross-examination?

44

The thoughts in Neap Vesel's head were like a rainsquall in spring. But he was not thinking of the heady financial argument made in court that day. He had received a call from Jessie asking him to come up to the house that night, that there were some things he needed to know about Joliard investments which might have something to do with David's death and maybe present an answer to an old question.

Vesel called back and said he would try.

She said, *OK, but please try hard.*

He would try hard, but first Vesel had to see Jim Parsons at the bank cater-corner to the courthouse. He had put that off long enough. As far as he knew, his time at the court was over. He would walk across the street to see Parsons and then go see Jessie. The rain had stopped, and he could walk the distance.

The Fleckner First Bank had been in business for almost eighty years. Still owned by the Parsons family and a small circle of Fleckner stockholders, the bank had emerged after WW II to serve as a stable financial force in the Fleckner County community. Clyde Parsons had opened the bank, and his great-grandson James was now president. It was said that in the early days Calvin Murphy Joliard kept his money there instead of in the bigger banks out of town. Vesel of course recalled that the CIA wanted him to check into whether money laundering could be going on there. It was one way to keep up bank revenues, although illegal.

Vesel had called ahead and Jim Parsons was waiting for him in his office to the right of the front doors.

"Good morning, Neap," said Parsons, smiling and offering a hand to Vesel.

"Hey, General," Vesel said.

Parsons had played football with Vesel; he was two years ahead of him, was a fine quarterback, and the other players had called him *General* for his ability to lead the team. Vesel knew that if he had not played the game there, the General would have been the one to receive all the headlines, although Parsons had never seemed to mind.

"First, let me say how sorry I am that your partner LeMace was killed," Parsons said. "Was there a similarity to the other deaths?"

"Some," Vesel said. He did not want to talk about it.

"I see."

"How's your business?" Vesel asked.

"We almost closed a deal for a huge mall near the Cumberland Gap, but it fell through. There were hidden credit problems. Anyway, that was too far west for us really; we grew up and down the fall line, and we decided to stay near it for historic purposes," Parsons said.

"Speaking of that, are we really going into a recession?" Vesel asked.

"Already there, Neap. You don't keep up with these things?"

"Not unless I have to."

"Well, I've seen some things that are pathetic," Parsons said. "Applied to people *down* on their luck back up in the hollows is almost a hackneyed phrase, as if there was something that would guarantee there would be an *up* to their luck too. It should be changed to *no luck at all*. One of the people living up there right now somewhere is one of our ex-clients, Brad Tillson. His last 401 (K) tanked a year ago. When I had a chance to talk with him recently, I almost cried. He was thin, his hair growing long and uncared for."

"Things are that bad?"

"Don't read the headlines, Neap; read *under* them. It is like a war zone in places no one ever expected it to be. It is not just a city problem, either. Sometimes I think we are hiding several third world countries right here under the thin veneer of our own country, and soon state militias will rise to help their states battle raiding militias from other states hunting for gold, bullets, food, or women. There have already been cases like that in the lower part of the Fall Line. But it will be a lot worse than the Hatfield's and the McCoy's, or Lee versus Grant either."

Vesel frowned. He thought it was bad too, but not that bad. He thought maybe he should get outside town more often. It was true that he had hunkered down after leaving the army and watched little TV news, although he did not think that hurt anything.

"If that happens, Neap, if states go at each other like that, then we are all really in trouble," Parsons continued.

"How so?"

"Well, the constitution allows that kind of militia thing and allows as many guns as you want to use along with them. I can see the banners of the militias with their new rifles carrying dollar-green NRA signs, coarse pennons against the blue air. And if the state militias reabsorb themselves through old connections, gelling together along old lines like the North and South, then we are off and running toward something far worse than a depression. It could be another civil war right here in the USA that could beat the Middle East for bad news."

Vesel recalled what Casey had told him. It was the exact same thing. Maybe there was something to it after all.

"My God," he said. "You think so?"

"At that point, it is possible that small divisions of the country could ask for foreign aid. Think about that: America could be carved up into little pieces asking for foreign aid, pulled together in old groups, or exist as single units and not just as states. They could be taken over bit by bit by other nations under the aegis of protecting those who had asked for their help. Fifty little states, except maybe California, Texas, and Georgia of course, which could be big countries all by themselves. We are seeing this already in voting and loan patterns. Tribalism in action. No more America, land of the free!"

"Damn, General," Vesel said. "I knew you had a good imagination, but wow."

Parsons did not laugh.

Vesel remembered the problem as his snitch Cayce had put it the night he died: The *dissolution of the United States of America.* Vesel had wondered how that could ever happen, and now he knew. If a hard-headed banker could see it happening, maybe it was true.

"Is there something more than just nostalgia driving that kind of talk, General?"

"If you thought like that, Neap, hell, the earliest days were the best days, when we were still colonies and fighting Indians instead of each other and sending money back home for the royal family! We need to go forward, not backward, even if we must fight to get it right. And, Sir, we may have to do just that again."

Vesel did not know whether to nod yes, or wag his head no. He stared at Parsons.

"But, look, Neap. Change of subject. People are worried about that halfway murder business right here in Fleckner too. Is there going to be a conviction? People come in here and talk about it all the time. They are nervous. Chance in financial affairs is one thing, terrorism is another; but put them together and you've got a hellacious problem that could defeat a store full of anti-depressants."

"That is one reason I am here this morning, General, about the murder business. I hope I don't need a warrant, but I need to follow every trail in our investigation."

Parsons sat forward in his leather chair.

"A warrant, Neap? Why would you need a warrant?"

"I need some information from you, and it may be an unusual request, I don't know."

The banker sat back in his chair. "No problem. We can work with you. What kind of information, Neap?"

"*The Jubilee Account.*"

Parsons was startled and showed it. "The what?"

"The Jubilee Account."

Parsons smiled broadly and it froze on his face. He sat silently, trying somehow to outwait Vesel, who was growing angry.

"Get a warrant, Neap," he said at last, with a cheerful grin.

It was Vesel's turn to look startled. The General's words and his facial expression were not the same. What did he mean?

"After what I just told you?"

"Get a warrant," he whispered.

Vesel stood, his face tightening. "We really do need to see that account, Jim."

"I do not admit any such thing exists, but you know who our attorney is," Parsons said, standing up and facing Vesel, still smiling. It was quiet for a moment in the office. One man with a rounded banker's belly over an expensive belt faced one with a flat stomach and a garda belt with a posture that was latent and dangerous, and both stood their ground.

Vesel finally nodded at Parsons and left the bank. He had noticed that while they had been talking, one man in the bank had turned toward Parson's office with great interest.

The running back left his ex-quarterback and crossed Main Street, turning over in his mind what had just happened. He could not make sense of it. Parsons was smiling but challenged him with legal action. Was Parson's bank really laundering money? Was this the result of an old tradition smashed by a new and violent one? But banks were at the center of a community. What happened if they started to go bad? What does the *Jubilee Account* mean? What did it do?

This troubled Vesel more than he wanted to admit, and he left the bank and headed west for what he had always thought to be the peaceful mountains, until he remembered his date for that night.

45

THE MURDERER

Henry Patrimos opened the Tea Shoppe door on Main Street and went in. He walked directly to a table to the left rear of the building and sat down beside the murderer.

"Good morning," he said.

"May I help you?" she asked, wondering why the hell the defense's PI would want to talk with her. He did not look as old as the newspaper said he was. He was trim but well filled out, and she guessed he was not flabby either. He looked a little like Steve McQueen with a thinner head. He had few wrinkles, which suggested he was a hard man all around; he seemed quick and confident in his movements.

"I had a grandfather who was the first person to jump off the Empire State Building," he said. "I don't know if you are old enough to have seen the picture in Life Magazine that said, *Smiling Jumper?* That was him."

"And you are telling me this, why?"

"Well that's central to my purpose, because my grandfather also worked with Calvin Joliard in Chicago in 1929. Any diary or memoir Joliard wrote probably says a lot about my grandfather at the time, and maybe these thoughts will tell me why Calvin Joliard came here and changed his name while my grandfather jumped off a building. I guessed that somewhere there was a memoir of some kind, and now I know there is."

"I have no idea what..."

"Uh-uh," Patrimos said. "You're got it and that's all I care about. Any other matter is between you and Deputy Vesel, who has a good nose for these things. I'm betting that he'll get you in the end for the murders and other things, of course, otherwise I would take you down myself."

The murderer smiled at his audacity, but she was concerned. This man knows about the Joliard *Chicago Diary*, and that I have it? What else does he know?

"I repeat. The diary is all I'm interested in here. Once I have it, I may find answers to many of the questions I have, and I will be very happy. I can either keep it or make a copy and give the book back to you. Your choice. But here," he said as he reached into his pocket and pulled out a calling card. It read: John Henry Newman, PO Box 12-G, Fleckner County.

"What is this for?" the murderer asked.

"Mail me the book using this local post office box number. I should get it in, what, two days at most? Indicate inside if you wish it back. But I certainly don't want it to wind up in some Federal Evidence File where it would be harder to get to and waste my time doing it. Okay?"

"I still don't know what you are talking about."

"Okay, let's say tomorrow morning you are going out to lunch. I'm there waiting with a sniper rifle and shoot you in the ankle. That would hurt like hell and would get you hauled into a hospital quickly and then your cover is blown. Am I right? And you would also have to hobble for a good two or three weeks after that, and I think you are trying to wind up this business soon, and to be laid up for a few weeks and get out of shape would be a bad thing for you."

"What if I call the Sheriff right now," she said, pulling a burner phone out of her purse.

"Please do, but remember, I represent the trial defense, and we have another Bill of Indictment ready to go to the Grand Jury at any time. A Search Warrant for your place could be added quickly enough, and then you would be going straight to jail, but that still would not get me the book, you see."

"And if I wait somewhere for you," she said, "like you just admitted to maybe doing for me?"

"You can do that, but I've had the best in the country try and I'm still here. What do you say? All I want is the book. It may be a key to the one question I have about my grandfather who worked on a conspiracy that failed."

"You've been following me, haven't you?"

"Well, it's not just me, but yes, I have. You must get to know a town and its people before you can do anything meaningful in it. And I've gotten to know you, and I like your efficiency."

"You know about Fellestre too?" asked the murderer. She saw no reason to play dumb anymore, and in fact, she believed him.

"Well, I know more than that," Patrimos said. "But you stay on your side of the aisle, and I'll stay on mine."

"Two days," said the murderer, who was thinking that Patrimos was the kind of man she would like to be, if she were not female. "I won't need it back."

Patrimos nodded, got up and walked out the Tea Shoppe door, leaving a five-dollar tip on the table.

* * *

That night the murderer went over Joliard's *Chicago Diary* again to see if she had missed anything that the PI might find and use against her. She had taken the book from David Joliard when she took the Fed Notes.

The murderer did not care about the actual Fed Notes. She knew something else was motivating her, and she guessed it was probably as dark as an open basement door. What Calvin Joliard Sr. had gone through and endured gave her no solace. His great failure in, and humiliating exit from Chicago, and especially the lack of proof even to himself that he had really done well in his life, or in his goals, in fact, warmed her strangely. The misfortune of people she knew, or might come to know, she thought, did not displease her. She had her own problem to worry about, and it was all about to be concluded.

She quickly finished the *Chicago Diary,* thought it safe enough, and the next day sent it to the PO Box number the PI, Henry Patrimos, had given her. What the man was up to she did not know. But she took precautions that would prevent him from surprising her again in quite the same way. She believed him that all he was after was information about his family. Why not? Let him have it if he stayed away from her and her family.

46

When he received the *Chicago Diary* from the murderer, Patrimos read through it quickly and found a name with which he was familiar: *Pujo*. He Googled the name Pujo and there it was: Before Joliard had been a Keynesian convert, *Arsene P. Pujo* in 1911 had chaired a U.S. House Subcommittee to investigate a rumor about what was called a *Money Trust* that was supposedly working stealthily behind the American financial system at the time.

The missing records of the 62cd Congress (1911-13) that were supposed to have been about the Money Trust contained a special Minute Book for the subcommittee that investigated the activity. In addition, there was a missing Minute Book for meetings of the full committee to discuss the larger results of the investigation about the use of big money in America. That Minute Book was gone too. What had happened?

The *Pujo Report* singled out individual bankers of the time who might have been involved, including Paul Warburg, Jacob H. Schiff, Felix M. Warburg, Frank E. Peabody, William Rockefeller, and Benjamin Strong. The Pujo Report identified over $22 billion in resources and it was believed to be run by one man, J.P. Morgan, through 341 directorships held in 112 corporations.

Patrimos was astounded. *22 billion! In 1911!* To account for inflation, one would have to multiply that amount by 13 or so, and that figure would not consider new monies coming into the trust, nor the difference of values between the pound and the dollar at any given time. Maybe almost 300 billion dollars! In 2008, that was still a huge amount of money.

Neither Arsene Pujo nor Calvin Joliard knew whether the Money Trust had been disbanded after 1913 with the death of J.P. Morgan. Its name seemed to float around in the air whenever bankers gathered, or criminals dreamed of a big hit. Was the Money

Trust still in existence? Did it still pull strings to make things happen, or not happen?

Now he knew. Something like the Money Trust was in fact still alive and well. To Patrimos it was just what he wanted to know, never mind that a known murderer was still wandering loose through Fleckner. He believed he knew what she wanted to do, and it did not affect Fleckner itself anymore, nor any of its inhabitants, except one. When the time came, he would bring her in, unless Deputy Vesel, who was a lot smarter than one would think, did it first, even with what she had on him.

Nevertheless, his belief about what he knew to be an active financial menace was correct. *It was no longer the Money Trust. It was now the Jubilee Trust.* And it was the mention of a new name he had never heard before that sent heat rushing through his body.

...a young man, Gaylon Starks, who works at a local advertising business, made some interesting comments about our mission even though he knew very few details. We sometimes had lunch with him at the restaurant on the corner and discussed our work in general terms. He did not fully understand what we were trying to do, of course, but he was interested.

Patrimos now knew where to go next.

47

THE TRIAL, WEDNESDAY AFTERNOON

After Stein's questioning of Macy that morning, it seemed everyone was in a looser mood, as if the trial were over. The key evidence had been debunked: The defendant bought a stolen watch on the street, and he had no reason to dislike David Joliard or need money from anyone.

However, since the Defense had placed their client on the stand, Gregor now had a chance to go at him. Gregor stood on cross and looked down at some papers on his desk. He seemed to brood for a while. Then he strode toward Macy.

"Mr. Macy, how are you?"

"Fine, thanks."

"Good, good. I bet they are not feeding you in lockup the way you're used to, are they?"

"Actually better."

"Now, you've said that Mr. Joliard did some investment work for you, is that correct?"

"Yes."

"You knew he did investment work for the Joliard family as a whole, right?"

Macy was confused. He glanced at Stein, who shrugged. "Well, sure he did, it wasn't a secret. People in that line of work almost always talk about things like that, you know."

"So, there are no secrets in stock trading?"

"Well, there is always talk on the street."

"Did David Knight Joliard's name ever come up on the street?"

"I suppose at some point, but just in casual conversation about how either Joliard brother felt about stocks and so on. I can't be sure how often, though."

"I know you can't, Mr. Macy, but you lost your stock, your house, your car and, later, your wife. Is that correct? Is there anything else you lost?"

Macy's face turned as red as a rare steak, and Stein leaped to his feet.

"Your Honor, what Mr. Macy lost has already been established. The prosecutor is needling the defendant now."

"Do move on, Mr. Gregor," the judge said.

"Yes, Your Honor. Mr. Macy, in insurance matters, which you have said is now your *forte,* can you tell us what a *beneficiary change* is?"

Macy seemed to squirm in his chair. Stein frowned. What the hell was this about? He knew nothing about any *beneficiary change.*

"Mr. Macy?" Gregor repeated.

"Yes," he said.

"What does it mean?"

"Ah...it's when the name of the beneficiary on a life insurance policy is changed."

"From whom to whom?"

"From one beneficiary to a new one."

"And what does that mean for you specifically?"

"For me?"

"For any policy you might have."

Macy suddenly looked around nervously in a semi-circle as if he had been cornered by a nest of rats.

"Mr. Macy?" Gregor said.

"It was changed...from...my ex-wife...to...David Joliard."

The jury seemed stunned. What did that mean?

"And that was a *whole* life policy, right?" Stein asked.

"Yes, sir."

"And what does that do?"

"As long as the premium is paid, the policy does not lapse, and value builds up inside the policy."

"And a *term* policy does what?"

"Well, after a certain period of time, the policy ends, it *terminates*, whether you pay on it or not, and no value builds up inside."

"So, you changed the beneficiary of the whole life policy you had from your ex-wife to David Joliard and it kept going. When did you do that?"

Macy looked at Stein, who was staring at him like everybody else in the courtroom.

"In early...1983."

"You mean, *before* losing your stock, or your wife, or going through bankruptcy?"

Macy looked down at his hands. "I used it because at that time the policy was new and had no monetary value in it yet, unless I died."

"But your wife, or now ex-wife, would have had nothing to gain from the insurance even if you had died any time after that beneficiary change. Correct?"

"Uh...correct."

"And that policy is still active and has been held by Mr. Joliard all this time."

"Yes."

"I understand that he was paying the premium annually. Correct? Now, when you took out the policy, you were young and in good shape, Mr. Macy. Is that right?"

"Yes, I was in fact in very good...."

"The annual premium at that time was almost $800 a year. Correct? The premium of a whole life policy does not go up every year, and the face value remains the same. Is that also correct?"

"Yes..."

"And so why did it change hands to David Joliard?"

"I wanted to continue buying into the stock market. I would have made a lot of money if only...."

"If only what, Mr. Macy?"

"Well, I didn't make it, did I?"

"No, but before that you signed the beneficiary status over to Mr. David Joliard so he would loan you even more money for stock purchases, right?"

"Yes. There were so many things going on at once back then. To ensure that it stayed active, David Joliard said he would pay the premium if the beneficiary was changed to him *permanently*, and I agreed."

Gregor went back to his desk and shuffled some papers. He wrote something down and returned to Macy.

"Let me see if I understand. You offered the insurance policy you had as an additional assurance to David Joliard that at some point he would get back his money–loaned by him to you for stock purchases–and the change was then made as a permanent change. Correct?"

"Yes."

"What does *permanent* mean here?"

"The beneficiary cannot be changed again unless the present beneficiary dies before the...."

"Before the owner does and then the beneficiary can be changed again, but not before. Now, exactly how large was that policy."

The courtroom was in complete silence, no cough, no murmurs.

"Half-a-million," Macy said in a soft voice.

"How much, Mr. Macy? Speak up so we can hear you."

"Five hundred-thousand dollars."

"Thank-you. Now, you were certainly insurable back then, but what about later, Mr. Macy?"

"Not anymore."

"Because of your current health problems, correct? The alcoholism and all? Excessively high blood pressure? Diabetes Type 2? Things like that?"

"Your Honor, Relevance?" Stein said. "His health has not been entered into evidence."

Gregor turned and pointed to the rear of the court. "We could call his physician Dr. Bevel up to testify, if you wish, Mr. Stein."

"No, Your Honor," Stein said, sitting back down.

"So, again, Mr. Macy, has your health prevented you from buying any further life insurance?"

"Correct."

"You can obtain no more insurance, really, except for tiny, very expensive burial policies that require no medical questions, so that one large whole life policy was it for you, as far as getting any larger life insurance coverage was concerned. Right?"

"Yes."

"And for anybody else to receive any of the insurance money from your old policy, Mr. David Joliard would have to have been willing to sign the beneficiary rights back over to you, or to whomever you now wanted. Is that also correct?"

"Yes."

"How willing was he to do that, Mr. Macy?"

"He was...."

"He was, what? Not in favor of the idea?"

"No."

Gregor returned to his desk and found a sheet of paper. He looked at it and walked back to Macy.

"Mr. Macy, who is Melissa Hartridge?"

"How did you...?" Macy said and then froze.

"Your Honor, I have here a copy of a wedding certificate for Marvin Macy and Melissa Etta Hartridge. They were married last year in Fayetteville, North Carolina. She still lives there near the army base where she and her late husband lived, before he had to go overseas and from which he did not return alive. The husband had a small military life policy, but that was it. For any new marriage, I am sure that the benefits of a large insurance policy going to somebody other than the new spouse would be a matter of lively discussion, right, Mr. Macy?"

Macy looked as if he had just choked on something.

"Judge, we saw nothing about this in discovery," shouted Stein.

"Mr. Gregor?" the judge said.

"Just as Mr. Stein says he is doing, we have also been establishing larger grounds for the commitment of murder, Your Honor, but by the defendant, Marvin Macy. We did not think it was relevant at first, given where we stood in the trial, since we could not cross the defendant about it then, but since he is open to cross now, we can bring it out. That's what we are doing.

"My assistant found this marriage material in North Carolina. Marvin Macy may or may not have continued to hate David Joliard for past events, but he certainly wanted to show a new wife that she would receive a half-million if he died. My assistant found that, according to her work mates in a small Doctor's office there in Fayetteville, she in fact had made it quite clear to Mr. Macy that the marriage depended on such a large policy having her as the beneficiary.

"When Mr. David Joliard would not give the rights back, Mr. Macy had a strong motive to murder him for that purpose alone, Your Honor, so the right to name a new beneficiary would revert to him. In fact, we discovered that he has already notified the insurance company to that effect. Melisa Hartridge-Macy is now the new beneficiary. Right, Mr. Macy?"

"Well...yes. But David Joliard *is* dead now, and it is a policy on me. My wife will need the money if something happens to me."

Macy's ex-wife was sitting in the audience and had heard of the new wife at the same time as the court. Her eyes were narrowed, and she was thinking of the best way to kill him.

Because of these revelations, the courtroom sat in an icy silence. Stein was shaking his head. It was not always bad that a client lied to his lawyer, but not mentioning an important thing like a new marriage could be disastrous. If Macy had not brought up a large insurance policy, a new wife, and a change of beneficiaries with his defense, what else had he not brought up? Maybe Macy was guilty as sin after all; the district attorney knew it, and that was why the case had been pushed to trial despite the apparent lack of hard evidence.

Stein was also upset that Henry Patrimos had not found those facts first either. Stein saw his pursuit of Joliard and the monetary forces behind a financial rollercoaster go up in smoke. He had to admit that Patrimos might after all have let him down. He suddenly felt old and shrunken, his leg aching again. He tried not to show his despair but failed.

"Any more questions, Mr. Gregor?" Judge Rawlins asked.

"Not today, Your Honor."

"Redirect, Mr. Stein?"

Mitch Stein stood and leaned on his desk. He believed he had to at least man up and put a bigger name on the list of people other than Marvin Macy who might have wanted David Joliard dead and gone. That would really begin tomorrow. However, he had to immediately move the jury's attention from this incident to another one more favorable to his client. Whether it would work depended on how well the jury could follow such an argument; but what did he have to lose, after his client's surprise admission of needing badly something the victim had been unwilling to give up?

But first, he had to make his client's position clear.

"Mr. Macy, did you kill your broker because of an insurance policy?"

"I did not!"

The thin hunchback seemed to have recovered sufficiently to sound genuinely indignant at the suggestion.

"Thank you," Stein said.

Later the judge gaveled the end of court. It was Wednesday, and it had started well, but ended badly. Stein hoped that Thursday would not be the same. In fact, it would be their biggest day, and it would involve very big money.

48

Wednesday night, Patrimos called Stein and told him what more he had found in Chicago, and what he now believed were the facts in the Macy case. After hearing about the surprise in court that day, he pointed out to Stein that it would have made no difference in the case had he tracked the marriage change down and presented it to Stein before the prosecutor's office did.

"Remember, Mitch, even if you had known in advance about this, you had already decided to make your defense an offence by putting Macy in the Witness Chair. You still had to explain what role Macy played in all events. The news would have simply been less of a surprise. If that had happened, I would have ferreted out all the facts very quickly, but the case is no worse off now given what I've just told you."

"I suppose not, Henry, but if that happens again, if something else rises out of left field like that, I may have a goddamn heart attack right there in court."

"You've been through a lot worse, Mitch."

Stein shook his head. He knew Patrimos was right, but he still needed to know what his client was going to say before he or any body else asked him. But after listening to Patrimos's discoveries on the road, he knew that the trial had in fact already taken a major turn, and it had nothing to do with an insurance policy. The two pushed Macy to the sidelines. They were both certain that the hunchback's involvement in the murders was tangential at best.

"And I think I have at last found what role my grandfather played in all this business," Patrimos said. "And much of it will be backed up by the banker I found who has currently unknown facts about the Great Depression. Michael Houston's financial testimony tomorrow can explain a lot about the real background of this case."

"From what I've already learned from Houston over the phone, I believe you may be right, Henry."

"You know I have stayed awake many nights over the years, worrying about this. What was Walter really thinking? What was he doing up there on top of the Empire State Building? And then after re-reading all these articles in the final issue of his journal, it hit me, as did the new evidence I found. I mean, Jesus, why had I not seen this before?"

"And what was that, Henry?"

"What he was really thinking at the time."

"And that was...what?"

"The key has been in my room at home all this time. A footnote in the Chicago Diary said it. The footnote quoted a brief statement from Calvin Joliard about his fiduciary duty as the head of a financial company."

"And...?"

"I'm getting there, Mitch."

"Okay."

"It was in two of the essays in his *Chicago Business Journal*, which was to be the summer issue in 1931 but was never published, as you know, because he died that summer. He had rolled up a proof copy of the journal and secured it in his coat pocket. He might have left it at home, or thrown it in a trashcan, but he took it with him and left it there on top of the Empire State Building just before he jumped, or was pushed, although the outcome was the same."

"I remember," Stein said. He knew the hot-button question that bedeviled Patrimos: *jumped, or pushed*, but he was not going to bring it up himself.

"Because of that event, my father gave the proof copy to me when I was in high school. For some reason I liked English courses at the time, and in my senior year we had a seminar on the mechanics of publishing, and I learned about things like proof copies. I actually took that proof copy to school on a show-and-tell day."

"You found the key there at school?"

"No. It was still meaningless at the time. The school assignment was to bring in something of value that belonged to someone you knew, and even better if that person had a certain notoriety. That was the teacher's request. The teacher wanted to juice up the course. She wanted big concepts and big names if possible. She was a good teacher. So, the *Smiling Jumper* picture made the cut."

"I see."

"Now a proof copy as such is important in the publication process, Mitch, as you know, and it is complicated in a meaningful way; but it is only a means to an end. A proof copy is marked for changes, typos, re-writes, and things like that before the final edition is set to print. So why would he so carefully preserve the proof copy knowing that he was going to be dead in the next few minutes, and the journal would never get printed anyway?"

"There was something in the proof copy?"

"You got it, Mitch."

"What was it?"

"Wait a minute, Mitch, let me grab the proofs."

Stein heard a drawer open and close, and Patrimos retrieved the phone.

"Okay. Here. The two essays by Walter himself. He disguised his authorship by using his initials as the author of the articles: WLP. If you did not know his name, you would skim right over it and see nothing that would mean anything. He called one article, *The Mystery of the Business Cycle*, and the other one, *Black Michael: Queen Victoria's Last Lord Chancellor of the Exchequer.*"

"What?"

"I repeat, *The Mystery of the Business Cycle,* and *Black Michael: Queen Victoria's Last Lord Chancellor of the Exchequer.* Neither title is particularly striking, except for the name *Black Michael* and the suggestive words *mystery* and *last.* The last mystery of Black Michael, and so on. A bit catchy, don't you think?"

"Okay, so what was in them?"

"The first article itself is almost gibberish, Mitch. In the real world, the only way it would have been published was because Walter was the goddamn editor! And the fact that there were errors of certain kinds in the essay meant that correction would be required. But what kind of correction?"

"Don't tell me the book is full of anagrams to be unraveled, puzzles, or clues to be discovered in mysterious old books found in odd places around the world, Henry. I don't need that."

"What? No, Mitch. But by reading it closely, skipping over all the gibberish in the first article that was mushy and mysterious, you find that what in fact he was saying was that *business cycles were not meant to be read in the way you were reading that article.*"

"He did?"

"Except for the jump from the building, Mitch, my father said that Walter was the most rational man you could know. His earlier essays all used straightforward rational discourse. So why did Grandfather Walter write that irrational bullshit like he did at the end? Was he really crazy?"

"I don't know."

"Rhetorical question again, Mitch. In one of the footnotes on reason and Keynesianism in the other article, he cited Calvin Joliard on the nature of the rational! He said it because he wanted to attract attention to the real nature of the business cycle.

"The amount of money Calvin Joliard insisted on printing was one billion dollars, and it is recognized by economic scholars today, as Michael Houston will note in court tomorrow, to have been a sufficient figure to stop the depression in its tracks, had that kind of liquidity been in circulation at the time."

"This is starting to make sense, Henry."

"Damn right, Mitch."

"Thus, the question: How could your grandfather even know about Keynesianism in 1931, not long after the concept of Keynesianism itself was generally known just after WWI?"

"Now you're showing the prosecutor in you, Mitch. I couldn't ask a better question myself. My grandfather believed that they could have considered the need for the one-billion figure in 1929 *only by assuming the opposite belief for the times, that business cycles were* not *mysterious*, which is what Keynes basically said."

"So, business cycles were rational, and in 1929, your grandfather rationally figured that the amount necessary to stop the coming depression was one billion dollars, and so he and his friend Calvin Joliard set about to print up that amount?"

"Exactly. And if the movements of the market are rational, then the irrational aspects of all that had come from those who want to profit from it being irrational. You could divert almost any amount of somebody else's money from the stock market and say, *Hey! It's all irrational anyway. Nothing I could do! Go back home and suffer quietly!*

"My grandfather and Calvin Joliard, like John Maynard Keynes, knew that somebody or something rational was behind what was going on in the world of finance, and a rational man could figure out who or what it was. My grandfather did not agree, at least until the end."

"My God," Stein said.

"Correct, Mitch. But even with all the Wall Street books about the subject, something still wants us to accept an irrational belief that a business cycle can seduce people's money into the system in a bull market, and then force others to commit suicide in a bear market that seems inevitable, but is not. We accept that viewpoint when we believe that nobody can do anything about it; and victims accept it to be their fault anyway, like throwing darts at a county fair and missing the board. You win some, you lose some. It was all chance, they thought, and so they even *deserved* the failure they got. That's what my grandfather saw the idiocy of."

"But to stop Joliard and your grandfather back then, there had to be even bigger muscle than we thought," Stein said. "Was J.P. Morgan still alive and kicking and able to silence Joliard, and stifle any questions about what was going on?"

"In a way he was," Patrimos said. "That's where the other article comes in. The one about Queen Victoria, who died in 1901. It was about the man who was the Lord Chancellor of the Exchequer when she died, Sir Michael Hicks-Beach, known as *Black Michael* for whatever reason.

"At the height of the British Empire, high-lighted by Queen Victoria's Diamond Jubilee in 1897, the sixtieth anniversary of her reign, London was at the center of finances in the world and Queen Victoria and Hicks-Beach intended that it stay that way. Victoria was evidently a hard woman who always followed through on a plan once she had settled on it. In this case it was the formation of a vast financial conspiracy that would continue long after her death."

"How?" Stein said.

"In 1897, Victoria and Beach agreed on a strategy. Knowing Victoria was dying in late January 1901, Hicks-Beach, who knew Junius Morgan—J.P. Morgan's father—from prior dealings with his banking firm in London, Peabody & Company, struck a deal with both the Morgan's, father and son, to structure an even larger entity to ensure that both country's finances remain strong no matter what happened in the world.

"It was a vast pattern that would weave financially behind the scenes so that the key assets of the British Empire remained long after Victoria's death, insisting that it was working for British subjects around the world, even in its largest ex-colony, America."

"Damn."

"A decision was made by Hicks-Beach and J.P. Morgan before Beach left office in 1902 to shift huge assets from the trust he built, the *British Empire Trust*, to America to balance swings in the business cycle that was brewing in both countries. Morgan then helped merge the two entities before he died in 1913, and that was when it was known by a new name, *the Jubilee Trust.*"

"TJT!"

"Yes, and that means that the Money Trust Arsene Pujo exposed right before the outbreak of WW One is still around, Henry, but in a new guise and with the much larger addition of old British Empire assets. If there is a conspiracy here, and I am convinced that there is, then its fear of exposure would go a long way to explain to a jury why Calvin II and David Joliard were killed."

"The jury will have to go with this now," Stein said eagerly, excited about the discoveries as he envisioned them.

"I agree," Patrimos said. However, the grandson of Walter Patrimos had a different outcome in mind. He was eager for revenge in the coming death of Hector Rulotto, Jr., but he kept the focus on other matters and did not mention that part of the scheme.

"There may be more people in danger now, Mitch, and that includes me and you."

"I wonder why the JT allowed Calvin Senior to live and not hound him for the money he was supposed to have printed?" Stein said.

"It was a part of the bargain for him to drop everything in Chicago," Patrimos said. "If he had printed money, he could keep it for his family. That way they had the chance to squeeze him if he ever wanted to start talking, which he never did. He in fact earned that money by closing his mouth about it and becoming a recluse the rest of his life."

"And that money was supposed to be hidden somewhere here in Fleckner?"

"Well, there is a street myth about that, Mitch. Hidden gold and all. There may be a connection, but it is less of a concern for us. All we are after is the narrative of danger to certain real citizens living in Fleckner."

What Patrimos did not tell Stein was how he had learned what he did in Chicago when he talked with Millie Masters' daughter. Nor did he mention Byron Crumb, or the break-in at the Crown Exports Offices; or later, the torturing of Gaylon Starks. Whatever the information was, the point of it was its usefulness, not how it was achieved. Thus, the long-looked-for object of his revenge was drawing closer. He hoped Stein would understand.

"Do you still have your old Luger, Mitch?" he asked.

"Yes, I do," Stein said.

"Well, before I fly down, I have some business to do here while you decide how to lay it out for the jury. But from what he told me–and you have my digital tape of the Houston interview–when you have Houston on the stand, I think he will do a fantastic job about making the terms of the conspiracy clearer," Patrimos said.

"I have listened to that Houston recording several times already, Henry, and I agree with you. My closing argument will use it extensively."

"Good, Mitch."

Stein paused for a moment and then smiled. "By the way, a woman called this morning and wanted to leave you a message."

"What woman?"

"Delores. Just Delores."

Patrimos shook his head. *What the hell,* he thought. He knew that this court case could come down to a split with Mitch if she had said anything about that night at her place in Chicago. Christ! She must have puzzled it out after hearing about it on some news feed: *A murder trial with the celebrated Stein and Patrimos team.*

"A message?"

"Yes."

"And that message is..."

"'Tell Hector hello for me when you see him Friday night.'"

Patrimos relaxed. He would have to commend her later for being discreet as well as signaling that Hector Rulotto was in fact going to be in Fleckner the end of that week.

"No need for me to know who Claire or Hector Rulotto are, is there, Henry?"

"No, Mitch, it has nothing to do with the case," he lied. "Now, about your luger that you still have. Keep it handy throughout the trial. We may soon be at endgame. If we can pin down the possibility of an outside force acting directly in Fleckner, then the jury will no doubt free Macy, and we can proceed to find out who or what *TJT* is really up to, although, as you noted, we may still be in trouble ourselves."

"I will do my best," Stein said.

After Patrimos hung up, Stein lay down and stared at the white scalloped ceiling of his motel room. He considered all the economic conspiracy theories about the Great Depression that had come out of the woodwork since 1929, only to be laughed at and tossed away. Could this be the real thing at last? The one true economic conspiracy of our time? The *Jubilee Trust?*

The colorful attorney turned off the lights and drifted into a troubled sleep, after thinking that Henry could still lie so well about everything but women.

49

It was 9:10 p.m. When Vesel knocked on the front door of the Joliard Mansion, Pauley opened it.

"Evening, Pauley," Vesel said.

"Come on in, Mr. Deputy. Your raincoat, please. Jessie in the den," she said, dropping verbs as usual. Vesel thought she did that deliberately.

Jessie stood upright beneath her grandfather's portrait as if she wanted a witness to something important that was to happen there that night.

"Neap," she said.

"You had some news for me?" he asked.

"Yes. I have a copy of a poem about the house under the lake. It will help you find the plates. We'll go over it, and I'll give it to you before you leave."

"A poem?"

Because of the chilly rain outside, there was a fire in the fireplace, and knots of wood were spitting and flaring. Vesel remembered the large Serapi Hand-Knotted Rust/Ivory Area Rug with intricate red, blue, and gold designs covering the center of the room, always partially hidden in shadow.

Jessie was dressed in a form-fitting saffron silk dress, and it showed her radiant auburn hair as the late streaks of a summer sunset. Vesel could not help moving his eyes over her. He imagined in one quick moment what the man he had killed had seen in Jessie many years before.

"Yes," she said, walking to Vesel slowly, her eyes on his. "An interesting poem."

"My God," Vesel finally said.

She stepped closer and Vesel could smell a faint scent like honeysuckle. He could see her earrings twinkle golden from the fire in the semi-darkness.

"Do you know what I thought those years ago, just after you saved me," she said. "When I was a witness to what you did for me."

"No."

She placed her hand gently on his cheek, stepped closer and Vesel could not move from her. She caressed his cheek and the back of his neck.

"I thought, this is a man who has killed for me. Why was I just standing there, crying? And by choice, I have not seen him in fifteen years? Why?"

Jessie parted her lips to breathe rapidly, softly.

Vesel moved his face toward her as she closed her eyes. Her golden earrings were quivering. In her high heels, her hair was still beneath his chin and he could feel the warmth of her stomach on his hips. His lips touched hers. They clung together until Jessie pulled gently away.

"But then I have a senator of the United States."

"And I have Grace."

Vesel slipped out of his blue rainproof jacket, blue shirt, and his V-neck undershirt; she rubbed the hair on his thick chest as he unhooked her dress and let it fall. He was breathing quickly now as he stepped back and slipped off his uniform slacks, tossing them to a pile on one side. His memories of Jessie at the age of nineteen, when he was fourteen, came back to him urgently. She was standing in front of him, exposed and afraid, and now here she was.

"We...should..." Jessie said, her hand still on his cheek.

"Yes," he said.

His nostrils flared at her touch and he reached his left hand forward and touched her hip. There was something about her face that blurred and came together at the same time. It was perfect, and he could not restrain himself. He parted his lips and put a hand on her right hip and pulled her with him down to the racing, intricate designs of the Persian rug.

Now words seemed to have no purchase in their actions, nor in their natures. When they paused for the first time, he lay by her breathing deeply. Then he resumed kissing her lips, her eyes, and the tops of her breasts. He kissed her thighs and bit her stomach. He felt her nails in his hair and her breath on his forehead. Her legs embraced him again. Time ceased even as the rhythm increased, faster, faster, and then like the symbols in the Persian rug all was a consuming mystery.

Later, after another stillness, he put his face between her breasts and kissed the salt of her skin. He believed he was at the beginning of time with the first beat of his heart as she whispered his name softly:

"Neap, Neap."

For Vesel, neither Grace nor Jessie was from the river of the girls of his youth, and he thought he could treat the two of them as anomalies. He could transact with them the mayhem of love's heat, but not with the cool forgetfulness of those earlier times. This emotion and its significance seemed to be much more important to him and his life now, even though later he understood that it was not, and that the river of women was more important than he could ever have guessed.

50

The next day, Thursday, Vesel noted on his calendar that Vicky Beguiles needed a visit from the department as a courtesy call about the death of her husband, and he knew he better do that before something else came up. He was tired from the love of the night before, but he also had to tell her about Sammy. He would have to explain the whole thing, meeting Sammy, and what he was trying to do for him.

After the rain it was another 105-degree day, the third in a row, and Vesel knew he would be sweating before he got to the Beguiles' front door.

He was about to get out of the car when he glanced at the house and thought he saw Mrs. Beguiles in the front bedroom, but then he saw he was not at the right address. Shaking his head, he pulled down to the next house and parked. He knew he had been forgetting names recently, as if everybody was the same and names were just, well...names. He wondered if he should talk to Dr. Bevel about it sometime; but then, he thought to himself that at that point he might not mind a little dementia in his life.

Vesel adjusted the holster on his belt and wiped his forehead. He knew the moisture in the air came from the lake that affected everything in Fleckner. He thought of mentioning that to Jacoby, until he realized his fellow officer was just a name on a list now. This pricked Vesel's anger, but he had to hold it in. Mrs. Beguiles would need something else from him.

Two cars were in the carport driveway, an old black Volvo sedan, and a recent green Chevy SUV. He walked slowly up the walk to the front door, noticing that the grass needed cutting. He wondered if that had been Larry's job, or Sammy's.

He rang once, twice, three times, and was about to go when Mrs. Beguiles opened the door. She was disheveled and her eyes were red. She had a damp handkerchief in one hand and was wiping the corners of her eyes with it.

"Yes, Deputy?"

"Mrs. Beguiles, may I come in?"

She stared at him. "Yes, do," she said, opening the aluminum storm door.

Wearing a puffed-out white dress, several of the red buttons unbuttoned, her hair in a medium cut with displaced curls over the eyes, a little styling visible, no glasses, she motioned for Vesel to have a seat on one end of the red sofa in the living room. She sat on the other end and made no motion to hide her tears.

Vesel cleared his throat.

"Mrs. Beguiles, I want you to know that the Fleckner Sheriff's Department sends you its sincerest condolences for your husband's death and that the hunt will not stop until his murder, and that of more than four other Fleckner citizens, is cleared. I know you will miss him."

Beguiles looked at Vesel with raw eyes and broke again into full tears.

Vesel was hesitant to ask the next question, but he had to.

"I know this is difficult. It was asked in court. Did anybody have a reason to do something like that to your husband?"

"No," she blurted.

"We want to do whatever we can to help you. Just let us know."

He sat silent for a few moments in shared sympathy with her. He believed he had intruded enough. He stood.

"Well, if you can think of anything, Mrs. Beguiles, call us."

Beguiles dried her eyes and stood too. She stepped toward Vesel awkwardly, put her head on his chest, and linked her arms around his waist and squeezed, hard.

"Thank you," she whispered.

She held on to Vesel a long time, gripping him tightly. She had just seen her oddly butchered husband down at the morgue, Vesel thought. He would want to hold on to somebody tightly too.

"Goodbye," she said as she stepped away and began sobbing again.

Vesel stepped out into the steamy afternoon and drove slowly back to the Sheriff's Department with lots of thoughts, none of them productive. With so much on his platter now, the murders, the trial, and a buried passion for Jessie coming to the surface, his brain was worse than a covered pot of hot jumping beans, all banging at the top to get out.

Later, he remembered that he had totally forgotten to ask Mrs. Beguiles about Sammy.

51

Thursday morning Sammy was fishing in a new area with a small lake, the light wind rippling the surface with long rhythmic lines. He and Deputy Vesel were high in the mountains, and the sun was out. Sammy could see down below the dark clouds moving slowly over Fleckner before heading east. It was raining down there, but not up in the taller mountains.

Vesel had been talking with Sammy about his schoolwork, possible big endeavors, and about why he might soon have to be gone most of the next day and night. With some spare time, Vesel showed Sammy how to handle his family shotgun to bag squirrels or rabbits, and how to clean and fry them, although scooping out the organs and intestines was an unhappy event, while cooking the flesh was good.

Sammy looked across the beautiful lake the deputy had brought him to and whipped his line out as far toward the center as he could. He was not great at fishing, since his father did not like it. But he was getting in some good practice now, and he had learned that fresh fried fish tasted better than Army food anyway. Even squirrels did.

He raised the pole and brought the line back towards him.

"Watch this," he yelled at Vesel. "I'm going to cast a huge one if I can get the hook!"

Grabbing and jerking at the line, Sammy caught the fishhook in the webbed skin between the thumb and the forefinger of his left hand.

"Oh, damn it!" he yelled.

"Hold still," Vesel said, after running down to see what it was. He looked at the problem, went back to his cabin and found wire cutters and alcohol. He cut off the tip of the hook and ran the wire back out and threw it away. He poured alcohol over the hand and showed Sammy how to squeeze blood from the wound. He had no antibiotics or bandages and tape to fit over that part of the hand. He had meant to get some, but the need had not come up before. He would have to go to his house to get what he needed.

"I have to get some supplies, and I'm going to try to see your mother," Vesel said. "She needs to know you are safe."

"Why?" asked Sammy, holding his hand and squeezing blood out of it where the hook went in.

"Fleckner is in a shut-down mode right now because of the killings. People stay in their houses, and I'm sure she has tried to find you, alerted my office, or put something in the newspaper."

"You think so?"

"Stay here under the biggest bushes," Vesel said. "Keep pressing blood out of the wound if you can. I'll be back very soon. Keep watch. A single bad man should not stop a big guy like you, but the black team can be a problem if you let them find you."

"Okay," Sammy said. He liked being called *big guy*.

"I also need to check in at the Sheriff's Department to see if anybody at the trial needs me. I think I am through though. All I had to do was tell about Val and the Rolex watch."

"Okay, hurry," Sammy said, holding his wrist.

Before Sammy could blink his eyes, Vesel was gone. Sammy wondered how he did that so easily.

He crawled into, and lay beneath, some heavy bushes and waited. His hand was beginning to throb, but he could hear squirrels chittering, birds whistling, and he could smell the raw earth upon which he was lying. He could feel things under the leaves pushing around and trying to find out who he was, and what he wanted.

It occurred to him at such times that he did not think any more about TV, comic books, or killing little animals. Why was that? He felt a part of things here in the light green June woods; it was dreamy and silent. His dad had never taken him out to the woods overnight, and his mother could not care less about things like that, although he wished she would. Sometimes he believed his mother never thought about him at all. What was she planning for?

Sammy knew that he had not told Deputy Vesel all there was to know about his house, so he was glad the deputy was not going there. He did hope that Deputy Vesel would come back okay. He knew the lawman had not yet taken him through all the basic training he had been discussing, but Sammy sure wanted him to.

* * *

The rain was white and coming straight down heavily enough to obscure the black road ten feet in front of her. The murderer thought it a bother, but it should at least relieve the mugginess in the air. Near the Indian Mound she was driving through a dense pine forest with trees of a single height and size, a nest of clones. It was a genetically altered, fast-growth forest owned by Champion International Paper and used for timber harvesting with clean cuttings every dozen years. It was a wooden army of paper, all brothers and sisters of the same age, bred to be cut down all at once by an army of blades.

The trees made her think of what happened with her family, and that made her feel alone; not lonely, but solitary. That was one reason she connected with her fellow Flecknerians while driving during the night. She could see what they were doing without her being seen. She found that people never looked for a driver in a car. They may look at the car and make a judgment of some kind: Too old a car, too small a car, a low- or high-status car. There was no attention left to waste on the driver. That helped her. There had been several instances when she was coming or going on business, and someone looked up straight right at her, but did not see her, as if she were only another tree hidden in a stand of cloned pine.

She loved her red car. She had let the looks of the outside go, but the front seat of her car was well padded, and the mechanics of the seat braced her lumbar region well. She rode and enjoyed the motion of the car. It was smooth and well lubricated. Perhaps it was the feeling of a clean, legless gait that called her to drive and watch so much. It was comforting.

The murderer knew that a chain of huge volcanoes along the east coast built the Appalachian chain several hundreds of millions of years before, and the erosion in those mountains over the millions of years since had shaped the farmland and coastal plains, grain by grain.

She had once seen a vein of rock at the coast with the slippery look and feel of an eel, while the lip of the sea sucked tirelessly at it, reducing it. The two motions revealed to her at the same time a sense of the rock's vast uncaringness about its destiny, as well as its sturdy beauty and peace, and the sea kept moving over it. There was acceptance in the rock, but justice in the sand.

Carefully the murderer picked up a cell throwaway and dialed a number with the one hand, heard the call answered, said nothing, ran down her front window, and tossed it out into the rain.

52

Scouting his house from the foothills that surrounded it in a horseshoe fashion, Vesel quickly recognized that it was under surveillance, and by several different units. He saw them from the ridge that fell away into his backyard like a slide, although from his vantage point, the trees were dark with rain.

He saw there were four men in two different cars. The *DEA? ATF? ICE? CIA?* It was not the Sheriff's Department, because with the Sheriff despondent, his deputy trainee Jacoby dead, Himons basically inadequate, and raw recruits still learning how to stop a car to give a ticket, Vesel was it. He was the department and he had been spending his time between his office, the court, and where Sammy was hidden.

He did not risk it. Instead, he moved around the top of the horseshoe and headed through the woods toward Vicky Beguiles' house. She should have what he needed to help her son. There was no car there, nor any lights on. He remembered after Larry died when he had been there to console her and had forgotten to mention Sammy. Did she worry at all about Sammy? If she were not home, he would have to slip into her house, get what he needed, and leave a note.

Fifteen minutes later Vesel was inside the house. He taped the flashlight's beam into a small slit, so he could use it and not worry about it being seen from outside. He went to the closet in the bathroom off the hall and looked for iodine and bandages. He found Band-Aids of various sizes, some tape, and antibiotic cream. That should do it.

He also saw on the top shelf a box of hypodermic needles. He looked at the small glass bottles near the needles. Steroids. Were they for Sammy? His dead father? He would ask Sammy about that as soon as he was back in the hills.

While looking in the closet near the floor, he also noticed two vertical cracks in the back. He would check it later, but first he needed to write a note to Mrs. Beguiles so she would not worry about her son.

He went to the living room and a dark wood writing desk that stood in one corner. He looked through a drawer full of papers. He looked in another one and took out a yellow note pad. In another, he found a beige Catholic Church pen that said on one side, Building Hope for People, and on the other side, Father Tim, who had officiated at Larry's funeral.

Vesel noticed under the yellow note pad four annuals from Fleckner High School for the years he had been there. Strange, he thought. As far as he knew, neither Larry nor Vicky Beguiles had gone to school in Fleckner. He opened one annual out of curiosity. He knew where he was: in the sports section. He stopped when he saw his signature scrawled under a picture of himself running through the goalposts. A note said: *To Vicky. Neap. Running for you!*

Most of the girls brought their own blue or black pens with them for him to use, but this one was written in red.

This one's for you!

Uh-oh, he thought. He grabbed the other annuals and found roughly the same message with his signature under pictures for four different years. All the signatures were in red.

Damn, he thought.

He remembered her as being slim, but with appropriate curves for a girl that young and almost unsatisfiable, which was odd for him. He recalled at the time that she seemed to know exactly what she was doing.

"My god," he said. He counted back through the years. The last note had been written fourteen years before, two months into the season.

His head was in more of a turmoil than ever, but the crack in the closet bothered him, too. There was something unnatural about it. What was it? He went back and opened the closet door in the bathroom. There were boards serving as shelves in the closet, but they looked removable and Vesel did that, pulling out the medicines first, and then the boards, and carefully laying them out on the bathroom floor.

Vesel examined the baseboard of the closet's back wall. A close look revealed a horizontal crack at the bottom. There was no line at the top. He traced a continuous line on the sides that almost formed a square except for the top.

He looked closer at the floor and saw a wire leading to a protrusion from the base of the square and it had a knot at the end. He pulled it up as far as it would go, and a square door opened toward him revealing a dark hole that headed down into the earth. He noticed a hook on the left side of the closet wall and saw that the wire knot he was holding was long enough to twist around the hook and so hold up the door.

Vesel explored the tunnel, which was tall and thin. It forked in the middle and one tunnel went to the carport of the first house, and the other one went to the bathroom in the house on the corner.

When he was finished, he put the annuals back and left without writing a note. The antibiotic cream and Band-Aids were in one pocket of his camo cargo pants.

He ran all the way back to where Sammy was, dodging trees as if they were defensive football players.

* * *

Vesel fixed the boy's wound, and then he and Sammy headed even farther up into the mountains where Sammy would be safer and would give Vesel himself an opportunity to figure out something that seemed to be changing his life before his eyes.

When they were settled again, Sammy asked him if he could tell the deputy something.

"Sure, big guy," Vesel said.

"That man cut in two, David Joliard?"

"Yes?"

"I saw him that night behind the mall."

Vesel was silent for a minute.

"So, you were there and also saw the homeless person and she saw you too?"

"Yes."

"Did you see anybody else?"

"Yes."

"Did they see you?"

"I don't think so."

"Did you recognize the person?"

"No. He looked big and mean though."

"As big as me?"

Sammy thought about the possibility, and that he was way up in the mountains with a murderer, if it was Vesel. But he sincerely believed the deputy was way bigger than the person he had seen in the alley, and that he was no murderer.

"No."

"Did you touch anything?"

"No."

"Was the dead man wearing a watch?"

"A gold one. I saw it."

"You left when the homeless person saw you?"

"Yes. It was a woman, as far as I could tell. I think it was."

"Okay," Vesel said. He knew he would have to call Stein as soon as he could. This would make it clear that Joliard was in fact wearing a watch. He did not want to put Sammy through interrogation, but it was an important fact to be able to sustain.

"There is something else," Sammy said.

"What is that?"

"My mother made me remember something, and I was supposed to say it when anybody asked what I was doing with my life."

"Really? What is it?"

"I want to *elevate my life by a conscious endeavor.*"

"That's good," Vesel said, nodding his head.

"She said it was by a man named Thorough."

"Thoreau?"

"Yes, like that."

"That's a good ambition, Sammy. Do you have one?"

"One what?"

"Conscious endeavor."

"Not yet. She said it would come in time."

"I see. Good," Vesel said. "Good, Sammy. But, until then, look, I don't know if you will be needed in the trial about what you saw. I'll do what I can to keep you out of it, though."

Sammy smiled. He really trusted the deputy now. He was going to be protected by him. But why would the trial want him in the first place? He had done nothing wrong, except find and shoot a Glock. Since it was almost officially summer, he could not even share all this with many of his friends who were going to be out of town visiting their grandparents to save on food, they said. Trials were things he saw on TV and the innocent always got off after a scare, except sometimes when there was a great sadness in the final lines of a show like *Law & Order* about how some legal solutions were not as easy or right as they should be. He usually ignored the final lines, though. The possible conceit of a good crime itself is what made it attractive to him. But Sammy felt good and did not want to worry about the trial anymore, even if he knew how it would end, which he did not.

53

Back in Chicago late Wednesday night, Patrimos was at the pier where the Crown Export Company had its headquarters. He had a few things left to learn and some punishment to mete out. It was time. The whole of his career had built to that moment. Revenge for the death of his grandfather was long overdue, and so was an answer to the big and final question: Was Walter Patrimos pushed, or did he jump? And if so, why, in either case.

Hector Rulotto's office was on the sixth floor of the Export Building, but Patrimos had been unable to determine if he were there or not. His ex-wife had been certain that he was going to be at the Fall Line on the East Coast that week. If he were going to be there, it would be the opportunity of a lifetime for Henry Patrimos.

According to the materials in the boxes he had lifted from Hector Rulotto's attic when he had been there, the Crown Import/Export Company had a slush fund of close to two hundred million dollars. For what? On paper, the company had a strong balance sheet as an importer of vodka from Russia, contraband ivory from Africa, and jewelry from the Arab Emirates. It paid the owners close to a million a year. Why would they need a slush fund? Tax evasion? Operating expenses? What?

He would have to find out, and the stolen papers revealed that the main building in front of him was the site of all the Crown Exports accounts. The excess money had a specific purpose, and he was about to learn what it was. If he got Rulotto too, that would be the cherry on top.

Moving silently through the night parking lot, Patrimos saw only one guard on duty at the door. Outside, he sprayed sensors black and disabled others with tape. After showing his new company ID at the door, the guard opened it. Three seconds later the handle of Patrimos's .38 hit the guard's forehead and the man was out. Patrimos found the control center and flipped off the sensors for maintenance service. That gave him five minutes to work inside without alarms.

He sat at the desk on the sixth floor with the AL Express Crossplex computer. It was, as Patrimos knew, the fastest mid-size computer outside of the military. Why would they need that at a small import company?

Unfolding a sheet of paper, he tapped in the ID numbers, 12111098, and the password HECTOR. It opened to three images: a deer in a forest, an oyster lying on a beach, and an eagle flying above clouds. Patrimos touched the eagle and was taken to a pyramid and asked to count the numbers of steps on it. Since most of the pyramid was under sand, he responded *insufficient evidence.*

The computer switched to Accounts and there were thirty-one of them. Patrimos pulled out three: 24, 29, 31, and put them on a 10G flash drive. He glanced at his watch. Two minutes to go. When he left, he turned the internal sensors back on.

Back at his motel with more time to look, Patrimos ran the flash drive. The first folder was about the structure of the Crown Export/Import Company. The first two pages told him what he suspected: It was controlled by the Rulotto family out of Detroit. It was an outfit that sat like a squid on top of Midwestern rackets; it was their money that went into the Crown Export extortion schemes too, and evidently back out to them at a seven to one increase. Not bad. He believed that the slush money came after big incomes to almost twenty-five members.

Patrimos guessed that this line of extortion had started with the S&L crisis in the eighties. It started with the Midwest Federal Savings & Loan, a federally chartered savings and loan based in Minneapolis, Minnesota, that failed in 1990. The St. Paul Pioneer Press called it *the largest financial disaster in Minnesota history.* It was a family fraud, and the Chairman of the S&L and his daughter and a few executives were convicted of racketeering. However, not all the racketeers had been caught. The Rulotto Family, for example, went on from bank to bank like aliens sucking worlds dry, and they were evidently still at work.

It was the second folder that most engaged Patrimos. The opening page had on it the golden letters TJT.

"Well, well, well," he said.

After checking the third folder, which contained sites where money pickups were made, Patrimos spent the rest of the evening trying to determine how close the one group was to the other. After a time, he saw that the TJT folder was the template upon which the much smaller Crown Export/Import was based. That was it. That was what he had been looking for. The fraud, the scheme, the entity that had forced his grandfather over the wall of the Empire State Building was the Crown Export/Import company, not the Jubilee Trust.

With all the self-doubts and hatred over the years, Patrimos now felt exhausted. But he knew where Hector Rulotto would be Friday night, and he would be waiting for him. The trial was not yet over, however, and Patrimos replayed the verbal message sent by Stein stating that Thursday would be the financial day that everything else depended upon, and he wanted to be sure of Michael Houston's presence.

Patrimos called Houston, who was their defense witness for financial matters.

"Michael," he said. "This is Henry Patrimos. We have you down for Thursday, early."

Houston was silent for a minute. "I'll try to be there in a motel tonight, if the rain doesn't get any worse."

"Okay, good."

"Oh, another thing, Mr. Patrimos," Houston said. "I want to warn you. The people we are talking about work in private and they can bribe anybody in the proceedings at the Fleckner trial to change their minds, vote a certain way, or hang the jury. Jurors, court officers, the defendant even. Watch out for that. It may make things more difficult for you to get at the truth."

Patrimos thought about that. "You said Mitch and I could be in danger because of this information too. Aren't both you and your cousin at risk yourselves?"

"Well, as far as we know, the Jubilee Trust has no knowledge of the papers at the Chicago Bank and therefore will not be looking in our direction. The risk is with whoever has the papers about real events in 1929, and the decade that followed, and can do the most damage to them with those facts, and right now that's you, Mr. Patrimos, and Mitch Stein of course. My cousin Lana and I are too small to make any big ripples now. Even if we were bigger, I am sure they will soon know who is of greatest danger to them."

Patrimos checked his notes again. "Okay. I've got you down for Thursday morning, 9:00 a.m. at the courthouse," he said. "Mitch may want to see you tonight if you are going to be there. I'll give you his number if you want to get with him once you have arrived."

"I think that would be a good idea. He told me he would like to have a brief review before court started about how we would structure the presentation. I'll stay there until I'm no longer needed."

"Great," Patrimos said.

He ended the conversation, passed the information on to Stein, and returned to the Crown Import computer files. He still wanted to know monetary details concerning his grandfather. Who put out a contract on him, and what did they offer?

Patrimos worked that angle much of the night before falling asleep.

54

THE TRIAL, THURSDAY MORNING

Court was in session and Mitch Stein was pleased that Michael Houston had been able to be in Fleckner on short notice. This was going to be the Big Kahuna, the major fireworks display, the time for snapping the right necks, or finding some big money and see what it could do.

They had talked late into the night the evening before, he and Houston. It meant that the trial could go forward under a good head of steam. Stein felt better than he had prior to that point, and he stood smartly dressed in front of the jury.

He wore the bowtie he liked best, the one that looked like the American flag. The jury remembered that he had worn a new bowtie each day of the trial. There was a polka-dotted one; one with a galaxy full of stars; one with a puppy face looking out at whoever looked at it; and then there was the American flag bowtie that he wore that day. He had not yet picked out his bowtie for Friday.

"We have heard testimony to the effect that David Joliard was a financial advisor for the Joliards," Stein said, talking to the jury. "And that the original Calvin Joliard was a banker who worked in Chicago at a turbulent time in American history. My next witness will tell us about a great-uncle of his who worked with Calvin Joliard. We need to explore the nature of what he did and show that current actions may have gone back to relevant events in the Great Depression involving a new slate of potential suspects in the murders for which Marvin Macy is on trial."

The prosecutor shot to his feet with indignation. "Your Honor, the *Great Depression*? This is most certainly a fishing expedition!"

Nevertheless, the judge was in the mood to learn more about the Joliard's past. He had grown up with the same myths about them as everyone else. The tragedians, the comedians. This, he thought, was great stuff. *The great stuff I signed up for when I first ran for judge here!*

"As I recall, Mr. Gregor, the door on financial matters was opened on cross when you asked Mr. Macy if he knew about what David Joliard did for the Joliards. Overruled, but, Mr. Stein, guide us carefully here so we can appreciate the significance of this approach."

"Of course, Your Honor. We call Mr. Michael Houston for the Defense."

Houston stood and walked up front. The public looked at one another and wondered who this was. No one knew him. He wore an expensive suit, was short, had combed and brushed white hair, and a pink face with a big jaw.

After Houston was sworn in and seated, Stein turned to him in the witness stand. "Mr. Houston, please tell us about yourself and your great-uncle Michael Houston, for whom you are named."

"I live in Philadelphia. I am a retired banking officer. My great-uncle Michael Houston worked during the 1920's for the Federal Reserve Bank in Chicago as a bond analyst. One thing he told us—the Houston family—about his time there always disturbed me; it happened when he worked with Calvin Joliard just before the stock market crash of 1929."

The temperament of the jury and the gallery seemed to change instantly. *Calvin Joliard worked at a Federal Reserve Bank before the Great Depression?*

"Was there a cordial relationship between the two?"

"Yes. My great-uncle said that Mr. Joliard was a very bright and honest man."

There was another murmur in the crowd. Most of them had grown up thinking of Joliard as a skinflint scam artist, who was always hiding gold and finding trouble.

But Stein knew he would have to stay on tiptoes to keep them on his side. "Okay, now, your uncle resigned from his job there in the summer of 1929, is that correct?"

"Yes."

"Do you know why he resigned?"

"I do."

"And would you please tell the court what that was?"

"He resigned because of a financial conspiracy he helped design, to stop the Great Depression before it could start."

The courtroom burst out in surprise again. People were asking each other what he had just said, and the judge began banging his gavel.

"No more, or I clear this courtroom!"

Since no one wanted to miss this, a tense calm settled over the room. But Gregor was angry. Goddamn it! He leaped to his feet. He could feel a simple case slipping away. Is this what the Attorney General was waiting for?

"Your Honor, again, what does the Federal Reserve System in 1929, or any kind of conspiracy, have to do with this case?" he asked.

"If that is a plea for the prosecution Mr. Gregor, it is denied. Do you want to move your witness along a bit faster, Mr. Stein?"

"Yes, Your Honor. We are attempting to lay the groundwork for other motives beyond those of any Fleckner native who may have hated David Joliard enough to kill him. There were in fact other motives, and for far different reasons than a Rolex watch, or an insurance policy for a new wife."

"Proceed, Mr. Stein."

"Thank you, Your Honor."

Stein returned to his desk and took a sip of water from a cup. He walked back to Mr. Houston. He was not going to play the recording of Houston with his cousin from Chicago, Lana Gibbs, who currently worked at the Federal Reserve Bank in Chicago. She had taken notes and other information about that time from a forgotten vault in the bank and hoped no one there would find out. But Stein wanted all of this to be clear and guided by him so the jury would follow the logic.

"Now, Mr. Houston, was I correct when I heard you say there was a conspiracy before *Black Tuesday, 1929*, that your great-uncle was a part of, to try to prevent what followed, and that what is known now as the Great Depression in fact occurred as a result of this activity not happening?"

"Yes."

"Would you tell us about it, please."

"My uncle worked with Calvin Joliard. They were cordial and were worried that what appeared to be ravishing Europe after WWI—austerity coupled with a tight money supply causing very high inflation rates—would strike America too, unless monetary steps were taken to prepare for and prevent it."

"What kind of steps would those be?"

"Keynesian steps."

"Explain that for us too, please."

Michael Houston spoke in clear terms about Keynesian economics. He had a strong voice and his years as a banker had given him a way of speaking to clients that was soothing and informing at the same time.

"It was the birth of a new monetary policy. John Maynard Keynes was an economist who worked with the British government at the Paris Peace talks in 1918. His job was to help work up economic terms for ending World War I with the Germans. It was common at the time to charge a fee for having started a war that caused the other side to be stressed economically, and WW I was a huge war that killed sixteen million people worldwide and wounded twenty million. It was a strong temptation to make the Germans pay and pay for starting such a war.

"But Keynes saw a problem in forcing such a huge settlement: It would keep Germany on its back for years to come, and the resulting bad economics could affect far more than the Germans. Keynes resigned when it was clear that harsh terms would win the day, and he returned home to England to write his now famous *Economic Consequences of the Peace.*

"Sure enough, bad times in Germany stretched throughout the twenties and Adolph Hitler came to power in the thirties promising to end it. WWII followed, and Keynes was right: More than the Germans were affected by the bad monetary settlement of WWI. If they had followed his system, things would have been a lot better than they were."

"How does Keynesianism work?" Stein asked.

"It says that if interest rates are high and money supply tight, the consumer does not have the capital to buy goods, and businesses do not have the capital to supply goods. The flow of capital freezes up and bad times ensue, like this country in 1929 until 1943 when we entered the war against Japan and Germany and before war production started.

"According to Keynes, in a recession, only the government has the ability to prime the pump. In slow times, the government can borrow money to heat things up, and when the economy is humming again, revenue will flow back to the government in taxes to repay the loans it had made. Good times ensue. Like post-WWII America until the seventies, when the system was locked up by high oil prices artificially hiked by an angry Saudi Arabia."

The courtroom was dead silent when Houston finished. Stein could feel it: the jury had followed the layout. Did they believe it?

"And exactly what was the conspiracy set up by Calvin Joliard and your great-uncle? How would it work?"

"They wanted to print enough valid Federal Reserve Notes to ensure liquidity when Midwestern farmers needed to buy seeds to plant in the spring. Since that part of the country is vastly agricultural, when the harvest came in, farmers would pay back the loans and the bank would pull out the new bills. But they could use them again and again, if necessary. By using those Federal Reserve Notes to serve as security, bankers in the community would be able to make sure that there would be no anxious runs on banks to withdraw funds: No fevered bank runs, no depression."

"For this to happen, how much new money did Joliard believe needed to be printed for that to work?" Stein asked.

"It was calculated by Joliard that it would require at least *one billion new dollars* in the Midwestern system to beat a depression, and maybe that amount could expand elsewhere."

"Thank-you, Mr. Houston. Now, if your uncle agreed with this approach, why did he resign before it could be put into play?"

"If a single key person had not unexpectedly learned of it and come out against it, my great-uncle would have proceeded with Joliard, and it may have worked. But a key-man did come out against it. My great-uncle heard that a negative vote was coming, and he told Joliard that he would say nothing about the conspiracy, but he would resign in protest of such an action by the Fed Board."

"Who was the key person who came out against it?"

"The Governor of the Region Seven Federal Reserve Bank at the time, James B. McDougal."

"Do you know why?"

"Not exactly, but my uncle told me what he thought."

Gregor shot to his feet. "Hearsay evidence again, Your Honor? Surely this is...."

"Denied, Mr. Gregor. Let's hear this out."

"And what were his suspicions?" Stein asked, a warm feeling growing in his chest.

"In 1911, before WWI began, J.P. Morgan was called to Washington and questioned by the US Congress about something called the *Money Trust* that Morgan was supposed to have put in place. It was a huge conglomerate of companies, banks, corporations of all kinds, like a spider web of which Morgan was at the center, pulling strings, keeping things working. What exactly was he up to? Even though he had personally bailed out the US Treasury several times before WWI, Congress was afraid Morgan had too much financial power for a democracy, and they wanted to stop him.

"Both Calvin Joliard and my great-uncle believed that such a Money Trust could be behind the depression they saw coming, and that the Chairman of the Federal Reserve wanted it to happen, because he was a part of the Money Trust too."

The jury was intrigued now, and Stein knew it.

In fact, he thought it might be time to call a recess so the jury could catch its breath. He needed some downtime too.

"Your Honor, this might be a good time to have lunch. We have much more detail and we will need time to play it out."

Judge Rawlins sat back in his chair and nodded his head. "The court is recessed until 2:00 p.m." he said and banged the gavel hard.

55

THE TRIAL, THURSDAY AFTERNOON

After lunch, standing near the witness chair, Mitch Stein went right back to the intriguing part of the affair. "How big a something was behind this remedy for that solution coming down the road, Mr. Houston?"

"The entity had to be more powerful than just the Governor of the Federal Reserve Bank, or of the billion dollars Joliard had intended to raise."

"Why would the entity want a depression to happen?"

"For one thing, there was very big money involved."

"In what way?"

"The simplest way to describe this is as an event, and it is roughly like Mr. Macy's comments on margins and margin calls I understand he made in court this week. In all sales negotiations, the ideal principal is: Buy low, Sell high. But there is a difference in stocks. If someone schedules a financial crash in advance, and you know about it, everything on Wall Street is overvalued, and you sell short and make huge money when everything falls in price and you snatch it up and hold it. And later, if you know the same people are arranging an upward surge, you could buy long and make big money as all the stocks you hold rose in value. You could make massive money both ways. Up and down. It is the biggest insider trading of all time.

"But in this case, the insider trading is rigged by the Money Trust: Neither the government nor the consumer has anything to do with it. The timing of its actions belonged to somebody else, and that somebody else need not have *our* best interests at heart, so you can see the problem."

"Okay. About how much massive money could be made, using the entire stock exchange as an example during the 1929, and other recessions up to today?" Stein asked.

"Oh, that would be a major guess, but certainly trillions of dollars."

"*Trillions?*"

"Without auditing the exact manipulations of the stock market during those times, who knows? Three, four trillion? That amount is based only on what we know now."

Trillions? The courtroom was simmering with curiosity and horror. Something wanted the Great Depression to happen so it could make money off its distortions of financial matters?

Most of the people in the courtroom, especially the older ones, believed that a depression was like a tornado, which nobody could start or stop. Now they were hearing that such things could, in fact, be manufactured and manipulated.

"And that's the reason the Joliard conspiracy failed?" Stein asked. "This group that wanted the depression to happen did not want Joliard or your great-uncle to stop it?"

"That's what great-uncle Michael believed."

"Why do you think this is important in this particular case?" Stein asked.

"There were people behind the group that shut down Joliard's conspiracy that would not want any of this to come out at any time, then or now. It might cause probes and investigations about the truth, like this trial, and perhaps others like it."

"And you think they would kill to stop this from coming out?"

"They probably already have."

This caused the public gallery to simmer near an explosion. They were hearing things they never considered before. After all, there was currently a crime wave in Fleckner. Why? Because of something that was also behind the Great Depression of 1929? And people in Fleckner *were dying* because of it too?

But at the first sound, Judge Rawlins raised his gavel.

This time the onlookers in the courtroom knew to calm down immediately. This was a big front-row seat to a championship-boxing match, and no one wanted to leave in the second round. When all was dead silent again, Stein continued.

"If there is danger in knowing about this, why have you come forward?" Stein asked.

"It is clear in retrospect, as stated in the lost minutes of the pertinent congressional committees, that except for one decisive, biased vote of the Chicago Federal Reserve Bank Board on September 15, 1929, the Great Depression need not have happened, and the public need not have gone through what it did in the thirties," Houston added.

"And in addition, in my opinion the public need not go through the current recession, or worse, one that may be coming. I think that is important to know."

"So, do I, Mr. Houston. So do I. Thank you. That's all, Your Honor."

"Any cross, Mr. Gregor?"

"No, Your Honor."

Apparently, Gregor did not intend to add to the defense narrative of a big outside force murdering people in Fleckner to make money on the stock market. Gregor might not be buying Houston's testimony, but he was not at all sure that the jury was not.

"Mr. Houston, you may step down."

Stein looked at his watch. It had been a tough day of testimony.

"Your Honor, before the defense begins closing arguments, perhaps we should recess?"

"Friday, 9:00 a.m.," Judge Rawlins said, hitting the gavel.

He went to chambers and called Martha, his wife, to have some hot clam chowder and sweetened iced tea ready for an early supper.

56

Sammy was ensconced in a small ravine hidden between several hills farther to the west of Lake Joliard, the highest yet he had seen. He watched carefully where they were going as they climbed from the old site to the new one.

Vesel gave Sammy to use the camo tent he had used in Afghanistan. It would do nicely, and Sammy thought it was sweet stuff. Vesel taught him how to use a smokeless fire stove to warm the military MRE's, Meals-Ready-to-Eat, of which Vesel had plenty. He had almost come to like the taste, except when fresh fish and game was available to fry.

On his part, Vesel hoped the men he had seen at the northeastern side of the lake would be uninterested in anything other than what they were doing now. He figured Rainwater knew by then about the dead DEA agent in the stream, whose gun Sammy had found, and about Fellestre, and about the influx of the Krokodile drug in the county. Vesel would take no action absent any other way to handle the situation. He was fearful about the Krokodile drug when he heard that the drug gave a great high and was instantly addictive. It was perfect for the pusher. His concern was even more for what the drug could do to the habitual user. Patches of skin turned green and sloughed off, exposing muscle and bone, and making a user look like one of the walking dead.

However, after court Thursday when he was already in camp watching Sammy fry fish he had caught, Vesel received an unexpected cell phone call that came through at that altitude.

"Neap? It's James Parsons."

"I hear you, James."

"You must think it's strange for me to call you after kicking you out of the bank the other day."

"What can I help you with, James," Vesel said.

"You know where I live?"

"Out on Gleason Street in the flat part of town."

"Can you meet me at the softball field the next block over?"
Vesel was silent. How serious was this?

"You want the truck or the cruiser?"

"The truck," Parsons said, without laughing. "9:30?"

"9:30 it is, General."

* * *

At 9:30 p.m., Vesel was at the softball field where he saw
Parsons, wearing a gray hoodie.

"Hey, Neap," Parsons said, slipping into the truck and
buckling up. "Let's get out on the interstate and drive a while."

"Okay," Vesel said, puzzled, but willing to let it come out as it
would.

On the anonymity of I-95, Parsons spoke. "Have you ever
heard of the Jubilee Trust?" he asked.

Vesel looked at Parsons.

"Yes," he said.

"How?"

"From Henry Patrimos. He believed his grandfather jumped
from the Empire State building because of it. But Patrimos could
never find the group itself. He's still looking for it."

"That's the thing, Neap, no one sees any of these people. It is
always a voice on a phone or a tape message, never a paper
document either, and especially not a person. How can you grapple
with something like that? Through economic manipulation they

seem to be involved in almost every aspect of our lives, and *we don't know it.* Only a few even know its

original name, the *British Empire Trust,* yet I have to give them my final word on the Fleckner First Bank today."

"Your final word? On what?"

"They called the bank a month before the killings started in town. They wanted to buy my majority stock in the bank. I said no at first, but I told them yesterday I would."

"Oh? You think they are behind the killings?"

"I don't know, Neap. You know my family opened that bank after the Great Depression so that Fleckner would not ever have to go through that kind of domino effect of bank runs that make a depression worse. We have been in business successfully for three generations now. The JT people want to end that and use the bank for money laundering, or something close to it, or even to just shut it down and let Fleckner die, I do not know why."

The speed of the truck picked up and Vesel noticed that the landscape was moving faster. He slowed and concentrated on driving as well as on what Parsons was saying.

"They called yesterday and said they would give me through Friday to sign contracts. After that, they would buy up all available Fleckner Bank stock in town and dump it on the market. I checked. They can do it. Jeremy Brown and Oscar Delinda want to pull money out anyway for something else to get into, and I can't stop them long."

"In other words, the bank is gone anyway."

"It would just take longer. I think the Trust has a deadline of some kind they don't want to run past, and I'm the better bet to forestall that deadline."

"That's why you would not give me the Jubilee Account information?"

"They have been spying on what I do, so they would know about it and probably move faster to close it all down."

"First, Jim, what is the Jubilee Account?"

Parsons coughed and cleared his throat.

"It was started by Calvin Senior with my grandfather. It is an account funded by Joliard money, a lot of it, to underwrite Fleckner County government services, like the Sheriff's Department and the Free Clinic. Joliard wanted the town to work even in very bad times. I think it was a way for him to make amends for earlier economic matters he had been unable to prevent in 1929. He never said what that was, but I believe it involved a battle with the Jubilee Trust at the beginning of the Great Depression."

"And if JT got its hands on the Jubilee Account?" Vesel asked.

"This town would no longer be a ghost town, it would be a cemetery, and we could never come back."

"Why call it the *Jubilee* Account?"

"Calvin Senior's parents attended the 1897 Diamond Jubilee in celebration of the sixty-year reign of Queen Victoria. They had family there. By their return, they had become great Anglophiles. Calvin grew up with his ears full of stories of the British Empire, and he studied the mementoes his parents brought back from their trip to England. He was soon an Anglophile too. That was basically it, I believe. He named the account, and my grandfather said, fine. Joliard wanted our bank and Fleckner to have a long and happy reign, like Queen Victoria's."

Thinking of his old contacts with the CIA and their concern about money laundering, Vesel knew he had to go through it now.

"Is that money undeclared, General?"

"You mean has my family been laundering untaxed funds from Joliard all these years?"

"Yes."

The General shook his head. "No, Neap, old Joliard showed us how every penny that went into the Jubilee Account was fully taxed. I have the number of the IRS contact that I work with whenever that question comes up. The account is kept secret for the good of the town and its citizens. It is kept secret for good reasons, but not for money laundering purposes. It's all good."

"But now the Jubilee Trust wants to shut that down, along with the bank? That's what they want to be able to do?" Vesel asked.

"I think so, Neap. Closing down the banks of a series of towns like Fleckner could cause a huge negative ripple regionally, or even nationally, whenever they choose to do it. I assume that they then could leverage big bucks from just about everywhere by raising and lowering stock prices and values anywhere in the country."

"That does not sound like what Queen Victoria would want," Vesel said.

"I don't think they care about that, Neap."

"Okay, but why wait to tell me about this until today?"

Parsons smiled ruefully as if to say he thought that might come up.

"It was a hard decision. Selling the bank to them would be a denial of everything for which we built the bank, but I'm not going to risk my family for it."

"They would go after your family?"

"Yes. They called last night. That's when I called you using my son's cell phone. What else can I do?"

Vesel stared at the stretch of I-95 in front of him. That was a good question, what could he do in the face of that kind of threat?

"I can't guarantee anything, James."

"Don't be long, Neap. A man will do a lot of things before he puts his family at risk."

"Look, do you still remember your play calls?" Vesel asked.

"Sure. Every damn one of them, even if all I ever had to do was hand the ball off to you. Why?"

"Well, two things. One: We know they want the bank for some reason."

"Yes."

"And: two, I might have a way that will force them to have reps here to buy the bank, even if they have never done that before. That gives us a chance."

"How?"

"If we can get some representatives here from JT, I know some Federal people already here in town from whom we can get some tremendous help to deal with them."

"They talk like sane maniacs, Neap. How do I bait the hook to get them here?"

"I'm going to talk with Henry Patrimos. I think we can get them with the same Federal Note plates that Calvin Joliard almost sunk them with in 1929."

"Good God," he said. "*Real* Federal Note plates?"

"Yep," Vesel said. "And TJT already knows about them."

"So, do you have them?"

"Not yet, but I believe I may by tomorrow night."

Parsons faced the road in front of them and inhaled deeply and exhaled with a whoosh. "Well, if that's the only way, let's do it, Neap," he said.

Vesel nodded his head and immediately started making plans like the blunt but intricate attack designs for success he used to make for his old fire-team in battle.

57

THE TRIAL, FRIDAY MORNING

Early Friday morning Marvin Macy demanded to see his lawyer and told Mitch Stein he was going to change his plea. He wanted the judge to declare a directed verdict of guilty. Stein argued with him but to no avail; in fact, Macy went so far as to threaten to fire Stein as his free attorney if he did not set it up. Stein arranged an ex parte meeting with Judge Rawlins in chambers before court was to begin that morning.

"I did it, Your Honor," Macy happily declared as if he were now going to summer camp. He danced around with his arms swinging like he was the Hunchback of Notre Dame. "I want to change my plea!"

Judge Rawlins frowned and said he would take it under advisement. He was not bound to accept such a plea, especially since everything had moved in place for almost a week and was about to close. Why a change of plea now? The fascinating story of the Joliards was coming out as well, and it was not finished. He said he would dismiss the jury that day and rule on it by Monday.

Stein immediately thought Michael Houston was right. Houston had said that somebody might pay Macy to do the time for somebody else and keep his mouth shut. Macy probably was promised he would be kept safe in prison too.

Angered, Stein called Alex Gregor for a sit-down that afternoon. This surprise plea could not be allowed to re-plug the gaps in the JT they had worked so hard to make. It was dangerous, but Stein believed that if the world were collapsing, he at least wanted to go down fighting.

* * *

Preparing for the supper meeting that night, Stein was taking a shower at his motel when he heard the phone ringing. It did not stop. Dripping water, he pulled a large towel around his now pudgy middle and went to the phone.

The conversation seemed to him later like an extension of a dream he had when he first heard of the *Jubilee Trust* affair.

"Hello, Mr. Stein, it's good to talk with you at last. I've been hearing a lot about you and what's going on in Fleckner, and I want you to know we are on your side."

"Who is this?"

"The name's not important. I'm with what we call the *Jubilee Trust.*"

"Oh?" Stein said. He came to quick attention. Was his investigation to help the Marvin Macy case getting to him? Was he hallucinating? James Parsons' was being forced to sell his bank to the JT that night, and now the bad guys were calling him? Why? Were the two things connected? He had to be careful not to give anything away here. Could they know he knew who Parsons was and what was going on with the bank? He thought he would say as little as possible about that.

"Nobody knows if you exist or not," he said. "Why should I listen to you?"

The voice chuckled but retained a steely tone. Stein wondered if it was a computer-generated voice. "You and some of your friends have unknowingly walked right into one of the biggest heists since 1998 and the dot.com bubble, and you want to discuss gossip?"

"A heist? In Fleckner? What are you talking about?"

"You and I need to discuss what's happening right now in the U.S. Senate and the military-industrial complex. Someone is financially shorting almost every stock on the market except weapons systems, which are going long, to make a mega-bloody fortune when war blows up again, and when financials go down the tubes, and the rest of us are back to shelling peas for a living."

"Okay. Which war? Tell me something I don't know."

"A senator on key panels is about to force a war in north Africa that will draw in every terrorist group in the Middle-East. It would be to help his military-industrial friends sell more new arms overseas to the Israelis, the terrorists, and to our own military, which will of course fight that war too. It will destabilize America for another generation, but it will generate a lot of wealth for the senator and his cohorts. They might even own the government after that."

"So?" Stein asked, unsure what else to say.

"So? A war for wealth? Is that what you want? I thought you would be interested since the senator we're talking about is engaged to a friend of Neapolitan Vesel, Jessie Joliard, there in Fleckner."

"Jesus," Stein said. "You mean Senator Jackson Miles?"

"I do."

"I can't do anything about him. He's in a different league."

"It's all connected, Mr. Stein. You have been thinking about it: The distance between a miserable society and a rich one. It is only a gradient. But happiness and unhappiness are two sides of the same emotion, and it is not always about money. Money is too easy to blame.

"However, if you want to work to restore a society from a miserable state to a balanced one for those in the center, you will find that you are standing right beside us. We try different things until we find a balance. That is the way Queen Victoria worked. The Jubilee Trust is on your side, Mr. Stein," the voice said. "And since you and some people you know are trying to find us like we were a Nazi submarine to blow up, I wanted you to know that."

Stein was still puzzled and, frankly, shocked.

"You are on my side?"

"It might take me some time to explore all that with you, Mr. Stein, which is surprising, since economics is the simplest way for people to communicate. It involves how we interact, get and spend, and so forth, all public acts. Do you understand?"

"I don't know," he said.

"Balance makes economics as natural as the balance of nature. Take wolves and sheep. If the wolves eat all the sheep, wolves die out because they have nothing else to eat, so the preservation of sheep becomes a rational proposition for them, hypothetically at least. A Darwinian balance in money, maintained properly, could work in the same manner for all of us, don't you think?"

Stein considered the thought.

"If you are a sheep, Darwin can be tough," he said.

"That's true. That's why you need us."

"How long have you been doing this?"

"One part of the JT in this country has its roots in the Great Depression of 1893 when the DOW lost 30% of its value and stood at 28. After that, when we merged with the American Money Trust and were fully involved, and there was a Bull market that lasted to the September of 1929 and pushed the DOW up to 381, until it went bust again in the Great Depression, which was scheduled."

"*Scheduled?*"

"Yes. The 1893 depression in America scared many people, as it did in Europe; if it all went bust and the masses gave up, there would be no one left to buy the cars, stoves, or furniture the middle-class made. Since 1893, fear and loathing in economics has led to the formation of a balancing force that would chart the best times for ups and downs in such an economy.

"You've heard this before. Victoria was Queen of what was the huge British Empire in the latter part of the nineteenth century, a time when *twenty five* percent of the earth's population were her subjects, and she wanted that empire to remain in good shape after she died.

"Sir Michael Hicks-Beach, one of our chief British founders, served as the Chancellor of the Exchequer twice during Victoria's reign. He helped strengthen the framework for the trust and the

Queen approved it the year of the 1897 Jubilee, just a few years before she died in 1901, after which a healthy percentage of the empire's wealth went into its startup formation. Any displacement in the usual economy at the time was attributed to the negative effects of her death.

"WWI was the beginning of the end for the old empire. It also threw our plans off the rails for a time, which forced us to take a more proactive view of what we were doing. We knew with Keynes that the demand to exact a large War Fee from Germany for that war would unfortunately lead to WWII, which we regretted. Between the wars, we tried to decide who should win the next war and why. We had to make starker choices for our tactics to work."

"Wait," Stein said. "Before you tell me the tactics, tell me your strategy again."

"There will always be the tendency to fluctuate, but we choose to keep a level base. So we put money in when needed and take it out when it is not."

"That sounds like putting choir robes on girls at a brothel," Stein said.

The voice paused and seemed to chuckle.

"In some ways, you're right. But it is all more than that, of course."

"How many of you are there in the JT?" Stein asked.

"Enough."

"No one has ever seen a JT representative."

"There is a good reason for that. How can you be hidden if you are not hidden? I want you to keep that in mind, Mr. Stein."

"But why the mystery about the Trust at all?"

"If there is any mystery, it is the mystery of mathematics, the rule of the *vital few*, in which large numbers fall out in certain predictable ways, and it jibes with what the science of the time was seeing. In a pea patch, 20% of the peapods contain 80% of the peas. In a population group, 20% of the people will create and hold 80% of the wealth. Meanwhile, those who land on top of the pile, the vital few, naturally want to keep the game going to ensure that the porridge stays warm enough for the other 80% to be happy, eat, procreate, and keep working."

"Your scheme forces this balance?"

"I confess that this sometimes requires stealth behind the scenes, but it cannot be helped. In addition, the narrative of a worthwhile struggle toward the top of the heap helps keep class violence to a minimum; we know that violence is a subject some of your new friends there in Fleckner have thought about for themselves and have sworn to stop where they can."

"You mean Neap Vesel?"

"He is one of those. Another one is an old friend of yours, who also likes William Wordsworth."

"*Melody Turner?*"

"She teaches the way of the Vital Few in her classes, and in what you would call her lifestyle. I think you can understand that, since you know her. Our way releases the energy of steam like a kettle to alert us, so that fewer get hurt. After all, a fuss in the newspaper is better than bombs at a building site."

Stein did not want to think of Melody right away. He was thinking of what Patrimos had told him about the shifty work of the JT.

"I've got evidence about your actions...," he started to say.

"Evidence? I doubt it but should you and your friends succeed in disturbing the current balance of the American GNP, the 20% will still love you, Mr. Stein. At least things will be moving, and not freezing up like a wounded limb healing in so bad a position that it cannot move later without a world of pain."

"Let's go back to 1929," Stein asked.

"Ah," the JT man said. "In 1929, things almost went bad for us in a different direction, as I've mentioned. Our balances dictated that 1929 was the time for a bubble and a depression, and it did happen; but it was also scheduled for a long bull run, after we got through the war. And this is where your concern comes in. There was a problem in mid-1929 that might have stopped that balance, which would have led to a much bigger blood bath later in WWII, and no bull run after that. It may have led to the loss of a world to a side that had a different view of things. It would have been a 20% world of Adolf Hitlers."

"So, you backed a side in World War II?"

"Yes. The JT could see that it would have to take sides to help America and Britain fight two major countries that were already battle-ready, Japan and Germany, and we could not have helped that fight during a depression. Therefore, we had to be sure the depression came earlier, in 1929."

Stein took a guess. "You're talking about Calvin Joliard's attempt to stop the Great Depression before it started, right?"

"Yes."

"You're the muscle that was behind him being shut down?"

"Yes."

"Why?"

"I just told you. To keep the long-term balance going. Calvin Murphy Joliard Senior agreed with us later that it was better to have crashed in 1929 than in 1939. He preferred to live out his life in isolation in your town, saying nothing, and we respected that."

"Calvin Joliard agreed that it was better to have a huge depression in the 1920's instead of having it later during what turned out to be WWII?" Stein asked.

"Yes. He saw war coming too."

"What about Walter Patrimos?"

"The first to jump from the Empire State Building?"

"Yes."

"In a way he caused the American Great Depression to come earlier than planned. His actions forced our hand sooner rather than later. We tried to persuade him, although he was quite determined. We tried to stop him from jumping at the last minute but failed.

"As I told you, it was better to have a financial cleansing at the right time than during what would later be World War II years. His pricking of the forces behind the financials forced the Great Depression even earlier than our timing; but it worked well, and so Walter Patrimos did better for his country, and the world for that matter, then he imagined. His reasonings set a better course for you. You should tell that to Mr. Patrimos."

"I will. But then, why did you kill the others?"

"Who?"

"David Joliard, and several others here in Fleckner."

"You think we did that? No, sir. We only police our own, senators like Jackson Miles, and sometimes we remove those who get too close to an important turning point and cause an imbalance, like Mr. Joliard, but I told you why we respected his isolation in Fleckner. We had nothing to do with the recent murders in Fleckner."

"Then who...?"

"There are some things you and the local Sheriff will have to do for yourselves, Mr. Stein. We do not do séances, either."

Stein again heard a computer-like chuckle.

"Why are you telling me all this?" Stein asked. His head was still full of the morning's incidents at the courthouse, and he had not mentioned what was planned for later that night at the bank.

"We admire the way you have tried to manage things in your private and public lives through the law, Mr. Stein. It looks like you can successfully walk a very thin line and possibly help others do the same.

"But one last thing: Beware of false prophets, and remember that a flea on an elephant's back is not a major problem, although if you helped wash the elephant down from time to time, it would force the elephant to be grateful."

"What?" Stein said. "False prophets? Fleas? An elephant? Grateful? I don't...."

"Goodbye, Mr. Stein."

Stein held the phone to his ear until the nagging beeps became jolting. He replaced the cordless receiver to its base and pondered the question of attribution. It was frustrating. If the halfway murder was not committed by JT people, he thought, who did kill Calvin II, David Joliard, Kurt Joliard, LeMace Jacoby, Larry Beguiles, and Vesel's snitch Cayce? What was the common thread? And what about Parsons and his bank? Was the killing over, or just beginning?

Along with this disheartening but hopeful sounding disclosure, Stein had to consider his own failure. If he were using this trial just to stop a conspiracy, would the defendant Macy be in the same trouble he was in this late in the trial? Was his Defense Attorney nothing more than a hypocrite, wanting others to go down for a good reason while he would not?

The answer was not long in coming.

58

Dressed for battle that evening, Vesel nevertheless went by to see Grace. Marriage to her moved through his mind like a ride down a jungle stream with flickering lantern posts on each side lighting the way. It was a mating in his dreams.

But there were now two important women in his life. What should he do? Which should he choose? Grace or Jessie? He could not tell Grace about this decision yet. He had to think about it, brood about it even, create new lines of thought.

He rang the bell.

Grace opened the door in surprise.

"Neap, how nice! Come in, please."

"I can't, Grace. I've got to run. But I've missed you. I'm sorry all this is happening, but I believe the trial will be over soon and we can get back together and then we can talk more. Okay?"

He had not mentioned Sammy to her, and he thought it best not to tell her anything about him yet. Things were getting complicated, but he believed one day Grace would like to get to know Sammy. She would love it up in the deep mountains at their new camp. They could become a simple, decent family with the best of ideals. Maybe they could build a house of their own up there and live high above all others in Fleckner.

"Of course, Neap."

He had developed a strong relationship with Grace, but the thought of Jessie was intense like heat lightening just over the horizon, announcing itself in brief flashes, coming closer and c;oser. He could already hear the rumbles.

"Now I have something to help you with in this business of the murders, but it will not be easy to..."

"Grace, right now I have to check on trouble up north of the lake. I will be back at my place later tonight. Wait there for me. Okay? We will talk all about it then. You'll be safe there."

"There is trouble at the lake?" she asked, thinking of what Fellestre had told her.

She had hoped she would be able to tell Vesel about Fellestre before he caught up with him. Still, she also needed to do further research on the murderer in Fleckner County. She believed she was close, and maybe only a discussion away from knowing for sure who it was. In fact, she had called that morning and left a message on that person's phone answering machine. If she was not the one, no harm done. But if it was her, Grace had to make her confess in a public place. Maybe she would be willing to be put in a stockade like in the old days when consequences could be easier seen, and guilt cleared in stark fashion.

"I'll tell you about the lake business later, Grace. It might mean a lot to Fleckner," he said.

Grace rose on her toes and kissed Vesel's chin. He bent down to kiss her and draw her as close as he could like that, touching her softly until he pulled reluctantly away, intoxicated by her smell.

"We'll talk," Vesel said softly.

"I hope so, Neap."

"I love you and we'll make everything right. Okay?"

"Okay," Grace said, placing her ear against his big chest. "I can hear your heart," she said.

"I hope so," Vesel said, smiling, but in a hurry now. He had to reach Sammy and prepare for a bigger fight without killing anyone.

"Bye," he said.

"Bye, Neap."

* * *

The murderer thought Grace was on to something. She had just received a phone message that was very suggestive:

I think I know what you are doing.

See me at 10:30 this morning at the Fall Line Park.

Grace

Neither had heard yet about Marvin Macy's announcement in court, and the murderer was waiting for Grace when she arrived. She noted that the younger girl wore a gray short-sleeve shirt, tight blue jeans, and light blue, orange-laced tennis shoes. With her deep black hair and tanned skin, she thought Grace looked gorgeous, a dusky Latina. She could see what Neap Vesel saw in her, even though he did not seem to know about Fellestre, who shared her with him. Pity.

They met and walked down beside the river away from town. At that early hour, there was nobody else in the park. But there were plastic cups and napkins with dried mustard and ketchup on them littering the grounds, and she pointed them out.

"It's a damn shame," she said. "This is part of the problem right here."

"What is?" Grace said

"All this stuff."

"Why?" Grace said, and she did not mean why people threw away coke bottles and hamburger wrappers in the park.

"Because Calvin Joliard Sr. cheated everybody who lived in Fleckner."

"But the clinic he donated!"

"There were a few things good, yes, but all very tax-deductible. He cheated the United States of America in 1929 big time. He made a lot of money and kept it for himself."

"You don't know that!"

"Of course, I do. I have seen the documents and the figures from Calvin II's legal papers. The people in town watching the trial learned this from a banker yesterday. I hope it opened eyes like cataract surgery."

"You have facts?" Grace asked.

"Of course. When I was in college I majored in both Sociology and Colonial American History, to learn how things work in revolutions, population shifts, and the like, and the reasons for it. Using court documents, I did a land survey in this area and discovered who used to own property here, when it was sold and by how much, who owns it now, and I see clearer reasons for who built what for whom. The Harris family once owned almost everything around here of any value, including the land that would soon turn into a lake."

"It was the Joliards that owned all that!" Grace exclaimed.

"No, but they acquired it, illegally as far as I can tell. Calvin II used loans and foreclosures to make the Harris's liable in court at least. The family has since been selling off land like crazy to hide the lake's provenance. Drug cartels own a lot of it now, for drug production. The Joliard boys like to gamble in the stock market, too, hoping to hit it big so they can be on their own. But there are groups who balance things on a larger scale, as I've told you, outside of all this," she said, gesturing at the park and the town beyond it, and even beyond the town itself.

"And such a group has helped me in my work to correct the situation. It will take a while to tell you about it, but come, let us walk up to Patriot Point where the old water wheel is, and I'll tell you more."

Grace glanced at her watch. "Okay, but I have to be back at the fashion shop soon. I am supposedly out getting coffee right now."

"Not a problem," the murderer lied, feeling the weight of the syringe in her pocket.

"So, you are really doing all this like Robin Hood? Take from the rich and give to the poor to correct land theft?" Grace asked.

"Well, I mainly want to wound the rich."

"Wound? Or kill?"

"Well, who knows."

"You'll have to talk to Neap. He'll be fair."

"I want the story known, Grace, and when the people know the facts, what do you think they will do?"

Grace thought for a moment.

"Study the problem. Suggest some answers?" she said.

"Do you really think so?" the murderer asked.

"Yes. Why not?"

"The past."

"What about the past?"

"Exactly," she said.

"What do you mean?"

"Nothing was done about it then, either. If I confess, do you think it will all change into a problem solved, just like that?"

Grace shook her head.

"I'll listen," Grace said, reaching one hand into her blue jeans pocket looking for her cell phone. "But now that I think about it, I want you to come see Neap with me right away, okay?"

The murderer knew this was a ploy on Grace's part. She believed that Grace did not have a vast intellect; nevertheless, the murderer had to continue covering her tracks. She had one more Joliard to tend to before reaching the end and then that would be it.

"Of course. Yes. Let us go see Deputy Vesel now. Why not? It's about time," she said, trying to sound humble.

Grace nodded her head, seemed to feel better, and pulled her hand back out of her pocket. They turned and headed back to the parking lot, and the litter seemed to disgust them all over again.

"Ah, see that huge cup on the ground beside you there, Grace? Gross. Pick it up and toss it away in that green waste bucket just ahead, would you? God, it looks awful. Then we'll go."

"Sure," said Grace, stepping off the walkway and bending over to reach the cup.

Following Grace, and quickly pulling the syringe with high-dosage Thorazine from her pocket, she removed the cap and, squirting a spume, she jabbed it like a dart into one of Grace's buttocks, right through the blue jeans and panties. Grace spun around to face the murderer, awareness dawning in her eyes.

But the murderer grabbed and held Grace in a strong grip, struggling, her hand over her mouth, until she grew listless. For a time, they looked like ardent lovers embracing, inventing new moves.

"Good, now let us go for a drive," she said. "This is not a time to tell anybody about anything, you know. Not quite yet anyway. Here, let me help you walk. Just put your arm around my neck. "There."

59

THE SECOND DESCENT

Vesel learned about Marvin Macy claiming he was guilty after all, but returning to the mountains, the deputy had a much bigger problem. He lost the digital feed up high in the mountains, and he did not have the time to look for the plates and then find Parsons and let him know if he had them or not. He would have to improvise, although he believed the whole town might soon be sluicing down a grim and pathetic toilet and stopping it all depended on his finding what he was not at all certain he could find.

Preparing himself, Vesel retrieved the copy of the poem Jessie said might be critical in finding the valued plates.

In the house of three pines it is best

To be cautious of the box below.

Rise up to secure the chest

With plates which you should know

Are for my family, the Joliard nest.

Considering the poem's third line, the place to look for the plates was logically upstairs in the house, not down. Jessie said that neither the senator nor the hired diver knew about the second line. That would explain the first diver with a two-by-four rammed through his chest. But before he left for the lake to find the plates in the underwater house, Vesel talked with Sammy man to man.

"You're going to have to lie low for a while now, Sammy. Do you know why?"

"Yeah, the men around the lake in black clothes."

"When they are around, avoid them, hide, keep out of sight. You are good in the woods, Sammy. You can explore around up here while I am gone but stay close and watch for anybody else coming. You know where the food is. Okay?"

"Okay," agreed Sammy, who liked that comment about him being *good in the woods*. He was beginning really to like the big man, Deputy Vesel, who was supposed to have played football at the high school. He would have to ask him about that sometime. He knew that he was already beginning to feel differently about things because of him.

"I'm off," Vesel said. "Keep a watch. I'll find you."

"Yeah. Sweet."

"You can hold down the fort?"

"What?"

"Keep everything in the right groove here."

"Oh, sure," Sammy said, feeling important.

"I'll be back," Vesel said, and vanished into the woods.

* * *

By late afternoon, nothing was happening at the lake. Vesel did not see the tall Fellestre. He hoped he would not hear the other shoe for killing drop, but he was now prepared for it. He would not let Fellestre hurt anybody again, but he had to act soon to be on time.

He could see a smaller DEA group at the site of the house with three pines in front working with SCUBA gear. There were three men on duty in all. He wondered where the agents from the previous time were. There were no perimeter defenses, for example. They were like boy scouts at camp, and if the fake fireteam was that sloppy in basic duty, Vesel figured, it had to be equally sloppy in others, like finding metal plates in the old house underwater.

He stalked the one man left for a watch and took him easily and learned what he needed to know. The plates were supposed to be underwater, but when they went down the first time only bad plates had been found. This was their second hunt, this time to look everywhere else down there, but nothing had been found. Fellestre was supposed to be on his way there later to check on their progress.

The other two men, cleaning their SCUBA equipment, were also taken and bound by Vesel. He hid his gear and put on one of the SCUBA suits. He took a Halogen underwater light with a yellow handle and slipped into the dark water. SCUBA diving had been part of his SF training, and the guard had told him to look for an old house fifty feet below the surface and one hundred and fifty yards out from the camp. There would be a large Welcome Home sign and the stumps of three antebellum pines in the front yard that would mark it for him.

The three pines were easy to find and then the Welcome Home sign appeared as if by magic out of the dark water.

Vesel carefully swam into the large house. Small fish the color of maple syrup brushed by him, and drowned leaves lay scattered on the floors. He could tell the inside had been disturbed recently, and it was clear to Vesel that something bad had happened in the basement. The missed clue from Jessie was to:

Rise up to secure the chest...

He saw the impaled body of the diver with a suit like his. That, he thought, was at least one member of the missing DEA team. Vesel kicked off and looked through the front of the house. There was nothing he could see but some few pieces of old furniture left behind perhaps in haste before the waters came, and were now themselves ghostly parodies of themselves; there was an old bed set in the back room with horizontal springs looking like clever performance art. He noticed that someone had carved the word GARAGE on one wall in the room.

Glancing up the stairs in the old house, Vesel maneuvered slowly, watching carefully for rotted spots that could betray him. The upstairs rooms did not look disturbed and Vesel was careful and slow, and he almost missed noticing that the ceiling of one of the closets had a hatch in one corner that had to give access to something even higher up in the house. It was easy to miss.

Carefully, Vesel raised the hatch and was able to float up into the small space. The green water was heavy like a narcotic dream from which it would be difficult to wake. The strong halogen lamp he held picked out a few possible objects of interest to the rear of the attic, and he floated over to see.

It was a skeleton, and it had to have been there a long time. Someone from before the land was flooded maybe, or someone diving just after it was flooded. He noted that the skeleton had no sign of diving gear of any kind. Whoever it was must have come down the old-fashioned way and gone up into the attic by holding his breath. Did that mean that he had not intended to come back up? Was this Calvin Murphy Joliard III, Jessie's oldest brother?

The mountain hag will get you like Calvin 3, if you don't watch out, and you don't try to see.

Vesel wondered if maybe the son had something he wanted to hide out of shame for what his father Calvin, II, had been doing with the dam and the flooding of lake properties, plowing up owners who may have been prominent land owners, and selling tiny plots to family groups from out of town. But he was now looking for a box that would be able to hold metal printing plates in it.

So, where would that box be?

Like right there maybe, he told himself as his light reflected off a waterproof oilskin wrapped around a container a bit larger than a box of shoes.

Son of a bitch, Vesel thought.

He silently thanked Calvin III, retrieved the box, and negotiated himself down and out of the house, coming ashore at a different location. He quickly removed the oilcloth and there it was: *U.S. Treasury* in raised letters on top. Stripping off his black wetsuit, he thought of Calvin Joliard Sr. This box of currency plates had to be the rumored gold of his youth. But why had his son chosen that old house to put them in, and whose old house was it anyway? And why hide just the plates? To keep them from his own father?

Before leaving, Vesel checked the guard who was bound with tape on his mouth. Vessel wanted to be sure he would be able to eventually work out of the bonds and so leave with the other two. But the man had an odd look in his eyes, and Vesel knelt to check. The man's throat was cut clean. Vesel quickly checked the other two men, and it was the same. Fellestre is here, he thought, looking around the camp.

He could see no one and, dry after retrieving most of his clothes, he put the Treasury Box in a rucksack he found in the camp, dressed, and began stealing through the darkened woods, the rucksack carried on his back like a German Alpine climber. As Vesel ran with the Treasury Box, he was careful and paused occasionally to watch for any sign of a follower.

He ran through the trees like a feral dog, loping, his mind focused on the importance of what he had found. He would gather Sammy and go into town to find Parsons and Rainwater. This would soon be over.

He felt giddy as he ran.

60

Jakie Knotts and a fishing friend with muddy black boots came into town and they told Sheriff Walsh about finding what they thought were the remains of the last Joliard brother, Kurt. The body was up near the extreme northeastern shore of the lake, and it had a big hole in the middle of its chest. The almost untouched monogram on his shirt was what gave away his identity: KMJ.

Sheriff Walsh shook his head in despair. In case there was any danger, he deputized the two fishermen, armed them, and sent Himons with them to collect the body. He knew he would have to call Judge Rawlins, and Jessie Joliard, who had already suffered enough with the loss of her father and another brother. She was now the last Joliard.

It was early evening and he drove up to the Joliard house himself to tell her, but she was out. He saw Abejundio at the potting shed and told him what had happened, that Kurt may have been dealing with the Los Zetas cartel, and they had shot him, although it did not sound right even to him. Why would they do that if they were making money with him, as he suspected?

Abejundio said Miss Jessie would be back soon and he would tell her the bad news. He said he knew how to tell her without too great a sorrow. He had shaken his head and seemed nervous about the cartel, but he did not tell the deputy the real reason he was nervous: That near where they were talking, two dead DEA agents lay buried in mulch. He was deeply sorry for helping Kurt Joliard in his drug business. He had known how it would end, but that was over now.

Sheriff Walsh had done all he could and left, looking forward to the day of his retirement and a cozy cabin in the hills, not at the lake which seemed to have taken on an air of malice since he had come to town years before.

* * *

A solid blow to the back of Vesel's head shot him into rough ground and a wet blackness. Later, with repeated slaps to his face, he rose to the surface. For Vesel, it was hard to breathe.

"You with us now, eh, big guy?" a sibilant voice said.

Vesel tried to shake his head. It hurt. He remembered nothing of the blow and falling; he remembered only that he had been running to reach Sammy.

A big hand with orange rawhide gloves slapped his face playfully.

"So, stay with me here, Sergeant."

Vesel jerked to life, and he was immediately aware that he was tied to something big.

"That's better, Sir," Fellestre said. "I figured that was you on my men back there at the lake. They were neatly tied up the way Rangers do it. Good thing I found them when I did, sir. They were dismissed without pay. You were underwater at the time, and I figured you would head on back up this way to your last camp very quickly if you found anything worthwhile.

"When you started out fast from there, I knew you had something, and I came ahead to set this branch-link trap you might remember from SO training camp. There was a narrow passage through a rocky gap, and you had to go right through there to reach your place. The limb shot loose and bam, you were up to your face in the muck and rocks. Bingo."

"*My* place?"

"Yeah, there was nobody at the camp. I came back here to find you and, guess what, I did."

"Nobody there?"

"What?"

"At my camp?"

"I just told you. You were gone, cowboy, but I could tell that you had packed up enough supplies to stay out there a long time, and that you weren't going to abandon it overnight."

Vesel let it go and spat blood.

"So, it's a freaking Fellestre again, is it?" he said.

"It's a big name in Louisiana, my man. We knew Arsene Pujo down there. We knew about his investigation of the Money Trust JP Morgan set up. He said it was real and Morgan was laughing all the way to the bank."

"Oh?"

"Yes. I used to be like you, a player in foreign countries to kill a savage enemy for patriotic purposes. Now I am paid a lot more for doing the same thing in this country. And guess what? I find the Great Neap Vesel, Fleckner's famous football and Super-Ops man. Right? Well, you got lazy tonight, eh? A tad over the top maybe? Gotten soft as a lawman? I warned you."

"Eat it."

"Hey, you want a jelly-filled donut? They are good! I need to thank that Puck person who recommended them to me. I will have to see her later to thank her in several more ways. You sure you don't want one?"

"Leave Puck alone, you son-of-bitch."

Fellestre smashed the raspberry donut on Vesel's forehead and ground it in, the sticky jelly moving slowly through the deputy's left eyebrow and down his cheek as if they were bloody tears.

"OK. If you are not going to be nice, then we will go at it in earnest," Fellestre said, observing the mess while wiping his gloves clean with a wet towel. He grabbed Vesel's shirt and, using his knife, slit open the right side and examined beneath it the scarred skin that looked like a capital T.

"My, my, even with plastic surgery it shows. Where did they get the skin to cover that? Your legs? Yeah. Wow, I bet that smarted. Goddamn rug tops. Maybe we can fix that tonight, you know, even reverse the damage? We'll have those retreads right back where they should be."

Fellestre lightly poked Vesel's side with a finger, and then jammed a pointed thumb into it.

"That doesn't hurt anymore, does it?"

"No," Vesel lied, trying to show no emotion.

"You sure?" Fellestre laughed.

"What do you want in Fleckner besides what's in the box I have?"

"*Did have* in the box," Fellestre said. "And since you may not be leaving these hills, I'll tell you."

Vesel strained against the ropes with his thick neck, chest, and legs. Fellestre had bound him standing erect against a rough-barked Walnut tree. His chest was bound loosely, but the legs were wrapped tight with three lengths of rope and his wrists were tied behind the tree. A slack double strand of rope stretched around his neck and served as a noose: He knew if he struggled, or slumped into the loose chest ropes with fatigue, he could choke himself while also tearing up his back against the tree's wrinkled bark.

Fellestre seemed pleased with himself.

"First, I'm glad you found the box with the original plates. That is outstanding work, Vesel. You get battle stripes for that. The box holds a real treasure. Genuine US currency plates for a rare denomination of Federal Reserve Note. You can print as many as you want, clean and uncirculated. It's a collector's dream! Now I can have as many as I want. Screw Senator Miles and Screw Rainwater. Thy will never find me."

"So, you can outfox the colonels, huh?" Vesel said, which meant in Special Operations speech, that someone was not thinking far enough ahead.

Fellestre slammed Vesel's face with another left hand.

Vesel spit blood. He felt woozy and his legs were weaker than normal. There was a time he believed this could never happen, and Vesel suddenly realized this might be his last battle. His strength, his fighting skill, his will to win. All gone. Fellestre was good, he thought; but while gathering the plates, he had forgotten his own training and focused on something that was not the major goal, and he was paying for it. He cursed as he kept testing the bonds on his wrists behind the tree. He *was* getting soft as a deputy of the law.

"I wouldn't try that," Fellestre said, noting Vesel's straining neck. "You are tied so that only one of three things can happen: You will either be eviscerated by your opponent trying to secure information from you; you will choke yourself to death trying to get away; or, you will die of hunger and thirst up here where few go, not even Captain James Thaddeus Kirk."

"You piece of shit," Vesel said, still straining.

"Hey, let's get back to your choices of how to die."

"All three," Vesel said, yanking against the ropes.

Fellestre slapped Vesel several more times with his gloves.

"First I want you to pay attention. I need some information about something else that lies somewhere here in your hometown. Does Jessie Joliard have the 100,000 notes old Joliard printed with these plates?"

"I haven't a clue," Vesel said, and he meant it.

Fellestre stared him in the face. He at least knew the truth when he saw it.

"Ah, well, I'll see Miss Jessie next and see how well she holds up under a similar interrogation," Fellestre said. "But I have a question. I have surveilled her, and there is something odd about her face. Her eyes maybe."

Fellestre's voice showed the usual split attitude toward Jessie of lust and levity.

"What I said about Puck, that's true for Jessie Joliard too," Vesel said. Vesel knew Fellestre must have been surveilling him for probably a week at least and must know about Grace. Why had he not threatened him with her? He did not know. For Grace's sake, he would at least keep that information to himself.

"Neap, so far you're doing fine, and I'm proud of you. SF School graduate summa cum laude, making useless threats at a useless time!"

"Go fuck yourself," Vesel spate out.

Fellestre tore open Vesel's sweaty shirt and spread it out. "Okay, let's count that last question as a no."

Using Vesel's own very sharp Afghan Khyber Dagger, Fellestre began to carve a small upright V into Vesel's skin on the left pectoral muscle of his chest. Vesel tried not to, but he screamed and felt weak. It brought back memories of the Afghanistan flaying in a way nothing else could: of the periodic laughing and talking of them to one another while his side was being skinned.

At that time, in an extraordinary effort of will, he had not cried out once; he could resist the pain then, but not now.

"Shhh, Shhh, Sergeant, the real question is this: Do you want to die this way, slowly, completely skinned to the waist, or quickly?"

Vesel spat, drooling. "You should never have made...Delta Force. You are a...disgrace...to the name."

Fellestre was rattled and again slammed a fist into Vesel's face, and his nose unleashed more blood spreading down past his mouth like a map of the rivers of Africa, and onto his chin and off to the ground.

"Ah, man," Fellestre said, wiping the front of his shirt where blood had spurted on him. "I just bought this thing. Damn. Well, your time is up anyway, Vesel. So, say goodbye."

Neap Vesel's mind spiraled as he saw his mother and father and his friends at school. He recalled every game in which he had ever played. He thought of the Jubilee Trust and understood it could level Fleckner to the ground financially like it had done to so many other small towns in America.

It was a Gothic tale when one heard it, attractive and chilling, but past belief; and then one found it was a real story from the next town over, and then it became a fear of how to survive with his loved ones and friends when it came to his own town. Everywhere could become part of a vast intermingled wasteland.

Given what Parsons had told him, he imagined how it could happen, how a huge country like the United States could become a scattered country with discrete little pieces and without many telephone poles left standing. But why did it *have* to happen?

As Vesel descended deeper and deeper into a black hole out of which he knew he would never rise, he slumped and swelled his chest and neck, straining against the heavy rope. He could see a dark pool opening before him, waiting for him to slip in. He would take the warrior's way out as he tightened his neck toward a better death than the one Fellestre had in mind. He would not again submit to torture.

He was sinking deeper, deeper into the pool.

Into utter darkness.

Silence.

Boom!

Vesel felt something sting one cheek and his eyes snapped open.

Fellestre stood briefly in front of him without much of a head and then fell sideways to the ground.

Standing behind Fellestre to one side, Sammy held the shotgun in his hands, still aimed at where Fellestre had been, his eyes bigger than boiled eggs.

61

Mitch Stein was waiting in the Mountain View Lounge fifteen miles from the Fleckner exit up I-95 North. At 5:45 p.m. Gregor arrived. He had his PI Arnie Nichols with him, and they joined Stein at his tab to the rear of the lounge. He had tried to get Vesel too, leaving messages at the Sheriff's Department, but there had been no response.

"Mitch," Gregor said, nodding at his adversary. "Where is Patrimos? I thought he would be here with you."

"He's with Parsons at the bank, preparing for a meeting tonight."

"Well, this is my right-hand man Arnie Nichols. I can barely afford him, and he's as good as Patrimos is, in a different kind of way."

Stein pursed his lips and looked at Nichols with interest as if he could see whether he was as good as all that. The man was all straight lines, whether horizontal, like his red eyebrows and lips, or vertically, like his nose and posture. He had sandy-red hair, smoothed back, his face expectant, like a baby fox whose head was rising from hiding and glancing around for problems while eagerly waiting for momma to come back with lunch.

"Don't take him seriously," Nichols said.

They shook hands and ordered drinks.

Stein reminded Gregor of Macy's change of heart that morning.

"Yes, you may be out of a job just as you were starting to get some traction. I am sorry to see that happen," Gregor said.

"Don't give it a thought," Stein said.

"You behind the change of heart?" Gregor asked.

The conversation hesitated for a minute when the drinks arrived. After they were passed around, the waitress left, and Stein smiled at Gregor.

"You didn't even let the drinks arrive good, did you? Right now, I can only guess why Macy did it. I have some suspicions. Patrimos and I thought that we should all talk about it, and I don't mean just about Macy, either. Then if we agree, we can talk to Judge Rawlins. This trial needs to proceed for reasons other than just getting Macy off."

"Why shouldn't we just kick him free?" Gregor asked. "He confessed, right? It's another notch in my gun."

"You remember court yesterday when Michael Houston spoke about his family's knowledge of this matter?" Stein asked. "The same conspiracy that ran during the Great Depression is now running through us with a similar link to our financial problems. A bad recession started up last year and continues this year, and if we don't act, it looks like 2007-08 might be another major financial disaster that might rival the Great Depression, with no end in sight. If not that year, one year soon.

"In addition, there might be another war, and that and a recession don't go well together at all. We may have to deal with the Middle East again, but at the cost of what, and to whom?"

"Good question," Gregor said.

"We need to know who is behind this, whether it is just crisis management by Chase Bank, which is a worldwide organization, or something bigger and darker that needs to be exposed as soon as possible."

"Are you accusing JPMorgan of being behind the murders in Fleckner County, for Christ sake, Mitch?" Gregor said.

"Marvin Macy is just a minor beneficiary of this conspiracy, Alex, and the group behind all this is even bigger than Chase. We think someone offered my client money to do the time and keep his mouth shut. He is not guilty, but he sure does not mind somebody paying him to say so. He could claim insanity, and with good behavior be out in less than seven years, collect his money, and move to Borneo."

"Borneo?" Gregor said.

"And if that group–whoever it is–did this once, why could they not have set up and executed the same deal many times over since 1929 to make huge money, forcing booms or busts whenever they wanted them, and keep the odd person like you silent by bribery or death about what they were doing at the time? These people threatened Calvin Joliard with exposure, with a charge of treason even, to take him off the table.

"Henry's grandfather Walter was trying to help, but he went over the edge of the Empire State Building, and Joliard Senior was depressed here in Fleckner for the rest of his life.

"Now, there have been recessions and panics throughout economic history," added Stein. "Normally, you would rely on study and good luck to help you in the stock market. If you have advance knowledge, however, you can make money in a big way, and that would be like dropping an A-bomb on an unsuspecting economy."

"An A-Bomb?" Gregor said.

"Class lines are predictable. Right, Arne? One class works for minimum wage. One works at a professional wage and stores up some small wealth in the stock market, in 401k's, or in pensions. Then there is a small 1% class up above that which seems to oversee the other classes. But there may be another group yet, outside class structure itself, pulling the strings on financial movements that affect all three classes. The world needs to know about these things, Gregor, and those who care about these things need to pursue them. I want you two to help me, starting now."

"And my boss?" Gregor asked. "The Attorney General of the state here?"

"I talked to your boss, and he was here to see how this trial would play out. He was forcing these people's hands by pushing this trial hard, and he is willing to send you both into the mess because it is important. This country doesn't need another crash; it needs another chance at a middle-class and a lower-class that may need bungee cords to practice with while trying to get out of the muck."

"Ah, so that was why he was here in Fleckner," Gregor said.

"Yes."

"Did Patrimos tell you the name of that group?" Nichols asked. "Was it the *Jubilee Trust?*"

Stein stared at Nichols. "How did you know?"

"I've run into them every now and then. They don't like to kill ordinary people, but they will weed out those who are inside the organization and make mistakes or play scams on the side. It is an international group, and they like to think that what they do keeps everything in the world on an even keel. Stiff upper lips and all that. It certainly makes the world safe for the old Queen's Empire, if you have ever wondered why London remains the financial capital of the world."

Gregor glanced at Nichols. "My friend here has a Ph.D. in economics for some reason, but he prefers bringing bad people to justice for economic misdeeds. He calls what they do *economic terrorism*, although it looks just like a mainstream American playground full of bullies, and he does like to fight bullies. If I bought him an Uzi, he would cheerfully use it against them."

Stein raised his eyebrows. "Really?"

"Right," Nichols said. "But an economic fight like this, as you are describing it, is maybe both winnable and unwinnable, like the war in Afghanistan. You are not made quickly aware of who is really against you. There are bastardized groups that try to be JT and sometimes it works, sometimes it does not. The people who are with the Jubilee Trust are well entrenched, like the Taliban, and you need good fighters on your side just to avoid being played by them, and they never come out into the open. Never."

"Well, we're trying to bring them out tonight," Stein said as he glanced at his watch. "In fact, Vesel may already be there by now with the door prize."

"Do you need another hand?" Nichols asked.

That is when Stein thought that Nichols might well be as good as Patrimos was. They would certainly need him if this all led where he thought it was going to lead: right into the basement of the American economy. Henry Patrimos and Arne Nichols already had a common trait— their red hair, although he did not mention it. He figured that if Nichols was that good, he had already noticed.

"Okay, but we have to leave by seven-thirty," Stein said.

"Thanks," Nichols said. "I have a suggestion to make on how to start that big a front. Doing a statistical survey of bond and stock exchange activity for the last one-hundred years should give us a good overall look at the size of this war. I don't think anybody has ever attempted that scale of analysis on the markets yet, but we need to do that to show there is a war going on, and that it is not just in Afghanistan, and that it will take a specialized approach and a room full of Cray supercomputers to throw some light on it."

"Good point," Gregor said.

Stein leaned forward. "When whoever they are get what they are after, they seem to fade back into the woodwork until the next time. We need to research this business using our half-murder case as a portal, because without solid legal powers like witness- or duces tecum-subpoenas, we cannot easily find out what we will need to know."

Stein thought it best to keep to himself the telephone conversation he had had with the JT voice the day before. Were they that good in what they did— an economic balancing act–or was all that just a spiel? He thought he would keep that to himself and see what happened that night.

Gregor assumed his courtroom face. No blinking. Intimidating.

"I suppose we could ask for a continuance in the Macy trial claiming new evidence on conspiracy that will take time to fully unearth. You stay on Macy as your client, but we are really after the group that wants to pay him to take the fall, the JT, is that right?" Gregor asked.

"Right," Stein said.

"But what paper evidence do you have for a judge to back up a conspiracy plot, all this about the 1% or so of Americans actually caught at play?"

Stein slid a folder across the table to Gregor. "These are copies," he said.

It was the lost minutes of one of the Congressional Banking and Currency Committee meetings in the early thirties. Michael Houston had given it to Stein. Before Macy broke his change of pleas, Stein had intended to place the material into evidence in court.

Gregor opened the folder and scanned the material. When he finished, his eyebrows raised, he passed the folder to Nichols, who read the material quickly, nodded, raised his eyebrows too and looked at Gregor.

"This stuff was supposed to have been lost," Nichols said. "It looks real. The Library of Congress keeps a collection of typewriters going back more than a century. From a 1911 Underwood with double-shift carriage, to different ones in the twenties and thirties and so on. It won't be hard to match the lettering here with what would have been used by a congressional committee back then, just to check on its authenticity, you see."

"Good thought," Stein said.

"So, you have access to the originals?" Gregor asked.

"Yes," Stein said. "All of the major sheets and much more if no one in the opposition figures out where they are stored first. But I think we have enough pages in a safe place to make our point."

"OK," Gregor said, "You got some time, you say? Let's talk."

Stein glanced at his watch and gestured to the waiter to bring another round for everybody.

At 7:15, after eating, Nichols and Stein left to join Patrimos and Parsons at the Fleckner First Bank. They understood that Deputy Vesel should be there too, although they were not sure.

62

The silence was dramatic, even after the shotgun blast.

"He was going to hurt you again," Sammy explained, as the sound of the blast diminished.

Vesel had been holding his breath. He let it out carefully. He knew he had been hit somewhere too, maybe his left cheek, but he did not care.

"Sammy!" he shouted.

Sammy's Mohawk hair and everything else on him seemed to be shivering with adrenalin. He was frowning as he pointed at what was left of Fellestre.

"He came to the camp, but I hid. I did not think he was expecting anybody but you to be there, so that was easy. I followed him and heard him yelling a lot, and so I came to see what it was. He rubbed a jelly doughnut on your face and said bad things. He was hurting you again so I...."

Still woozy, Vesel pointed his jaw at Fellestre's knife. "It's okay, Sammy, we'll talk about that in a minute. But first, can you get my knife he has and cut these ropes?"

"Sure," said Sammy, who carefully parked the shotgun on a fallen log facing away from them and, using the deputy's knife, hacked at the ropes, and got them off.

"This is one sharp blade," he said, wiping it on his pants leg.

"Thanks, Sammy," Vesel said, rubbing his wrists and then wiping the raspberry jelly off his face as best he could.

But Sammy was preoccupied. He had suddenly bent over and was vomiting.

Vesel went to him and patted him on the back. He recalled with vivid detail the time he did the same thing in front of Jessie

Joliard. "You did what you had to do, Sammy, but it doesn't mean you have to like it."

Sammy looked up, clotted drool hanging from his mouth like a pearl necklace. He nodded his head.

"I...hope not," he said.

There was some worry now. Vesel knew that if Delta Force found the body, they could identify it by barcode tattoos; but the question of why Fellestre was here at all could never come up, because it would involve questions about Delta and DEA activities in the USA, and like the fact that Fellestre was off the Delta Force reservation, and yet he was still acting as a federal agent. But Vesel did not believe that anyone would ever demand a real search to find him.

He wondered if Patrimos really knew who the halfway murderer was as he had said when they talked. It might just as well be Fellestre now, and he was dead. Who would know, unless there was a new murder with the same MO.

Burying Fellestre as best they could, digging a trench deep in the soft earth and filling it back up with Fellestre, rocks, and dirt, they took care to cover up the area to look unused for years. Then Vesel and Sammy returned to their last camp.

Vesel kept the U.S. Treasury plates in the waterproof rucksack he had used to bring them from the lake. He checked them. They just fit. No leaks. He looked at his watch. He had maybe an hour and thirty-five minutes left, and he still could not get Parsons on the phone. He tried again and failed: Still no random coverage that high up. Vesel quickly treated his chest wound, smeared antibiotic cream on it, covered it with a pad, and taped it down. He washed his face with cold water and felt the places where there would be bruises. He vaguely worried that if he did not hurry, his eyes would be so swollen shut he would be unable to help anybody.

Rope burns covered his neck and chest. His nose had not been broken any worse than it had in football, and he rapidly fashioned a support tent for it with gauze and Band-Aids. It would heal. But he knew if the people of Fleckner could see his face now it would be as the mask of a savage, and if anyone saw him like that, he hoped he would have the time to explain.

He mentioned that to Sammy who suggested that he shave his skull and allow enough hair left to form a Mohawk strip on his head too. Vesel laughed and thought about it. Why not?

But time was running out. Vesel knew that this could be the most important run of his career, spotting the enemy before they saw him and taking them out, making rapid decisions not knowing all the facts. In fact, it was way past time, and he had no idea about what Parsons would do or had yet done. He might arrive at a dark, abandoned building already lost, doomed in its quest to keep small communities free of the ravages of low liquidity and high inflation.

"Hurry, Sammy, keep up with me as best you can. I'm going to have to find a place to keep you even safer while I do something in downtown Fleckner."

"No, no," Sammy said. "I want to stay with you."

"People are asking where you are, Sammy, except your mother. Do you know where your mother is?"

Sammy shrugged. "She's done it before."

Vesel paused. "And your father, Larry, he did it too?"

"He went out more, but I don't think he was my father."

"Why not?"

"Mother said something to him one time when they didn't know I was there. She said my real father would have done something about something, I forget what it was."

Vesel looked away for a minute. He saw himself gliding through a goalpost and signing an annual for a young girl: *This one is for you!* But, why had the *same girl* been able to secure annuals *four years in a row,* and why had he not noticed that, four years in a row? Why had she been able to get his signature and later the mating games four years in a row, when there were so many others to be had? She was certainly determined. He slowly shook his head in wonder more than with regret. He did not know what he would say when he saw Mary-Vicky again.

"Look, if you go back to your house tonight, Sammy, do you think you can stay there for a while, and be okay?"

"Sure."

"But I don't want this to get out, Sammy."

"What get out?"

"This business of your blowing a man's head off, for example; we need to keep it quiet, because otherwise the law will have to come in to look around—I know, because I'm the law now. You did it to save a life, mine, but that is going to take a lot of explaining that I do not think we need to do right now. Do you understand?"

"It's worse than a movie," Sammy said.

"Yeah," he said. "Let's go. I'll have to branch off to town before we get there, though. You can take care from there on, right?"

"Yes," Sammy said as they began to run. He noticed quickly that while he could run fast, Deputy Vesel could move it on out.

"Good man," Vesel said, not breathing hard at all and holding back with him.

"Sweet," Sammy whispered, and ran with him as best he could until the deputy he now admired branched off, waved, and headed southwest toward town.

As he ran, Vesel was wrestling with another thought about the killing of Fellestre. Who really had done it? Who had pulled the trigger? Sammy had shot Fellestre. Sammy had killed Fellestre for him as a stand-in; had that fact released him from his own oath not to kill again? Had Vesel violated this oath after all, using Sammy as a surrogate?

And if he had violated his oath, what did that mean now?

63

THE LAST BANK

At exactly nine o'clock that night, there were three loud knocks on the front door of the Fleckner First Bank. The strength of the blows made Parsons think it was Vesel doing the pounding, if he was thinking at all. The events that night were not what bankers normally schedule. But if that was them beating upon the door, they were right on time.

With a nervous look, Parsons opened the inner door with one key; the middle door with another one and spoke to the two men through a slim opening in the outer door.

"You are Rulotto and Jaffee?"

"Yes," said the taller of the two men, Hector Rulotto, Jr, who handed Parsons two cards with their names on them. The only other information on the white cards was a silver JT in a circle, centered above the names.

"This way," Parsons said, opening the outer door and pointing to the right, through a trellis advertisement for car loans at low rates. The two men entered, and the banker followed.

The lobby in the bank where normally there would be people lined up to cash checks or to make deposits, was hushed and dark. Parson's office was to the right of the entrance and Parsons followed the men in and pointed them to two chairs sitting in front of his desk.

"Nice office, Mr. Parsons," Rulotto said. He was taller than Parsons and carried an acquired sense of gravity about himself; the other man, Jaffee, was short and thick, dressed in a badly fitted suit the same color as his brown hair, which looked dyed.

The Parsons family had built the bank just after the First World War. The ceilings were tall, the polished wood on the floor was from original pine planks, and the desk and chairs were heavy wood. The colored windows on the street side were from old churches. The exterior was gray rock from a local quarry; the streetlamps allowed them to look out on Main Street, and they could see the huge water oak in front of the courthouse on the far corner.

"This is a very unusual meeting, Mr. Parsons," Rulotto said. "We have had only a few personal meetings in JT's history. There are reasons for that, of course."

"I can imagine."

"Do you have the items we are here about?"

"Let's do the first thing first. My bank and the money for it," Parsons said.

"Good, you made your choice," Boris Jaffee said.

"I wasn't of the opinion that I had a choice," Parsons said.

"Yes, you do, but one of them is not good for you, your bank, or your family," Jaffee said, standing and removing a slim metal box from one pocket. He walked around the office with it in one hand, nodding his head.

"No listening. No video," he said to Rulotto as he sat back down.

"Good. You can never be sure, can you, Mr. Parsons," Rulotto said.

"You got that right," Parsons said.

"So," Rulotto said.

"I don't want any of this to get out," Parsons said.

"You mean selling your bank behind your neighbors' backs? You should be very happy, Mr. Parsons. You are getting out in front of the curve. Last year five banks like this one failed. This year maybe four or five times that will fail; next year the number of banks knocked over will probably be well over twenty-five thousand, mostly small-town banks. It's called Bush-War Bowling, and it won't stop any time soon."

"My God," Parsons said.

"It's not us. It's your government," Jaffee said. "Money is drying up because they want to buy another war. But we are paying you above the going rate for your private stock, and then you can be a retired banker with lots of time to do whatever you like and watch all the other bankers squeal like pigs as things get worse and they can't find buyers."

"And what of Fleckner First, if I go now?"

"That's our business," Jaffe said. The man's shoulders were solid, and Parsons could see his knuckles toughened through use as he worked his fingers over them.

"In other words, Fleckner First will become an outlet for money laundering?" Parsons said.

"Those words imply criminal activity. The Trust has no criminal activity," Rulotto said.

Rulotto looked very much like a banker himself, with a black suit and vest, and a white, blue-striped shirt whose sleeves protruded out the cuffs of the suit a full inch. He had arranged his facial hair in a scrupulous Edwardian manner, with a thin black mustache and a crisp van dyke beard. His shoes were polished, and his socks matched the suit that was, Parsons guessed, Artic black.

"You don't have criminal activity?" Parsons asked. "Do you mean you are not subject to laws?"

"Well, not to your laws."

"American laws?"

"There are no longer any island nations with separate laws," Rulotto said. "There is only a globe. You should know that. We know you covered that information at the Financial Officers seminar in San Francisco three years ago."

Parsons sat back in his large leather chair. "I recall that I did not agree with the idea then either."

"Mr. Parsons," Jaffe said. "Do we have a deal, or not? We can buy up all extant shares at high rates, let the bank's finances slide, and then allow the feds to close it. No big money for you maybe, but we will be able to pick up other little banks like this one, here or there, to make it still worth our time being on the fall line. What do you say?"

Parsons opened the top drawer of his desk. It was still a bad time, and he hoped the others would agree. He pulled out a fat letter-sized envelope and handed it to Rulotto, who opened it, checked the sheets, and Parson's signatures on them. He noted the observations about the bad condition of the bank.

He noted the spaces marked with an X where he was to sign for one of the many shell-companies of JT. He nodded his head.

"A pen, please," he said.

Jaffe handed Rulotto a Faber-Castell ink pen. Rulotto signed in three places of the first set of notes. He returned Parson's copy of the papers with an additional item, a receipt for five and-a-half million in bearer bonds.

"That's a nice payment, Mr. Parsons," Rulotto said. "And now the Series 1918 plates for the $10,000 Federal Reserve Note. That's why we are here after all."

It was a big moment. Everything hinged on the lost plates of Calvin Murphy Joliard Senior.

Parsons looked nervous. "You must know that I have not checked them. I don't know how to authenticate them."

"May we see them?" Rulotto said.

Parsons pushed the bag toward him.

Rulotto took the bag and opened it. Inside were front and back plates. He examined the front carefully, noting that there was only a single leaf shooting up above the others on each side of the Salmon P. Chase picture. He also examined the blue certificate on the front plate. He then scrutinized the back plate, reading it slowly and rubbing it with one thumb for a minute of silence.

"They're good," he said at last, smiling.

"How much extra, Mr. Parsons?" Jaffe asked.

"Extra?"

"You said when we agreed to this meeting that you would tell us the extra price of these plates if they were good."

"Price is a problem?" Parsons asked.

"Of course not," Rulotto said.

"One-hundred Notes when you print them," Parsons said.

"That won't be until this fall," Jaffee said.

"Boris!"

"So, it is your intention to continue printing with the plates and move bills through the system as you wish to?"

Rulotto's eyes narrowed and he glanced toward the door behind him as if he sensed men waiting somewhere out in the darkness. The eyes returned to Parsons, and then he looked at Jaffee and was about to say something. Parsons held his breath.

At that moment there was a loud battering at the thick windows on the street side of the bank. Val Coombs, wild-eyed, her light hair tousled, stood outside the bank yelling something, beating on the panes, screaming at them.

The two JT agents were stunned. "What the hell," Jaffee said.

Parsons jumped to his feet. "That's goddamn Val Coombs," he said. Looking angry, Parsons seemed to be yelling at the window.

"Gen Center 22. Right!" He shouted.

With their eyes on the windows, and before either Rulotto or Jaffee could react, a man whose black and blue face looked like a jungle mask with a Band-Aid teepee on the nose, followed by five big men, two of them Henry Patrimos and Arnie Nichols, were through the door and on Rulotto and Jaffee. Mitch Stein hurried in as fast as he could. Vesel pinned Jaffee's arms to his side and yanked him up with the chair, elevating his feet off the floor. Nichols quickly reached up and stretched tape over Jaffee's mouth while another ICE agent cuffed his hands in front.

Simultaneously, Patrimos slapped duct tape over Rulotto's mouth and pulled him to one side away from the others while handcuffing him too.

Parsons was on his feet, his mouth open as he stared at the swift efficiency of what was happening.

No one said a word. An agent with thick glasses carefully reached into Jaffee's vest and altered the code of the detonator on the explosive bundle. Jaffe's eyes widened. The agent nodded his head at the door through which they had entered. Agent Rainwater came in silently. He indicated to Parsons not to speak. The agent with glasses pulled out of his coat pocket a device that looked like a cake frosting tool. He rolled up the right pants leg of both men, searched lightly under the knees with his fingers, moving like a spider, and found the bugs; he lowered the disengagement tool to Rulotto's leg and carefully extracted the bug with an excision followed by a strong suction. The agent repeated the action with Jaffe, who was still dangling in the air, his feet no longer kicking.

The Secret Service agent then applied ointment to the wounds on the two men and rubbed a square bandage on them. He put the removed bugs into a lead container and closed it.

"Thank you, gentlemen," Rainwater said, breaking the silence. "We needed to have a few of these live bugs of yours to play with, if in fact they are live. Nevertheless, it is a felony to engage in activity like this. Taking the bugs from you prevented full knowledge of what just happened here, and possibly prevented a demolition signal coming in from outside. A little reverse engineering might even help us find your headquarters, whatever that is, and I suspect that it might be real."

With the detonator now safe and Jaffee's foot trigger inoperable, Vesel let him down, and told him to sit on the floor. He did.

But then things changed. Patrimos yanked Rulotto farther away from the desk and the others. He stood beside him, the muzzle of his .38 revolver pressing hard against Rulotto's ribs. "Hey, you wanted to find the person really behind all this crime, right?" Patrimos said. "Please meet Hector Rulotto, Jr., Head of Crown Imports extortion operations out of Chicago. You remember me, Hector?"

"No."

Patrimos hit him with the .38, the handle of the gun dancing back and forth on his forehead.

"I'm the man who raided your office in Chicago on the waterfront, the Crown Export/Import Company. I also met your ex-wife. You should have kept her. She had a lot of information of yours in the attic. It was not her fault. It makes for interesting reading."

Rulotto struggled. "You ass," he said.

"I'll say hello for you the next time I visit her. I trust it will go as well as the first time."

Rulotto continued to struggle. Patrimos had a killer's smile and hit him again.

Vesel knew what Patrimos was going to do. He should have guessed it was not just information the PI was after. He could tell by the man's manic look that Patrimos was answering to something that had been growing somewhere and calling to him for a long time, like the flayed capital T on his own side. It was *revenge*. He was after simple revenge.

"A contract on my grandfather went out in early 1931, Hector. Your father signed for it. Walter Patrimos then either jumped from the lofty tower to get away from him, or your father pushed him."

Rulotto was silent.

"Your father probably laughed about it, Hector. The *May Day Hit* was what you called it later."

"It was business," Rulotto said.

"Either way, I know now why his group did what they did. It was in your father's business book, and in Calvin Joliard's *Chicago Diary*. It was all about the imitation of great masters, *the Jubilee Trust*, and how to become like it."

Patrimos hit Rulotto above the right eye with the stock of his gun. The man kneeled and fell to the floor as Patrimos swooped on him like a bird of prey. "Your little Crown Export/Import group is nothing more than a bunch of imitating thugs. You are not the Jubilee Trust. Walter Patrimos did not know that, and you drove him over the edge, you and the other Rulotto's. You were not like Walter Patrimos who wanted a balance between reason and nature and finally settled on reason down the road since he had failed, so he left some answers to me. You would have pushed Parsons and his bank over the edge for money, if you got away with it."

Stein suddenly remembered what the man from the JT had told him earlier: *Beware of false prophets, Mr. Stein, and remember that a flea on an elephant's back is not a major problem.*

A flea on an elephant's back? He had thought. The Rulotto's are fleas to the gigantic elephant, JT? Does that also mean that we were meant to stop them? To wash them off the elephant?

For the first time, Hector Rulotto looked up at Patrimos with a frightened look on his face.

"So, it was you who nearly killed Marmon in that hot tub? That was you who did that?"

Patrimos hit him again. "He'll get over it, but I don't think you will. You owe me a death for what your father did, and tonight I get to collect."

"Patrimos," Vesel said.

"Back off Deputy."

Vesel felt the irony keenly. He and his son Sammy had just killed a man earlier that day; how could he express the importance of not pulling a trigger to Patrimos? How could he tell him with a straight face not to kill anyone? Yet it was not called for. This would be a cold-blooded murder, and that was not good for the man Vesel had come to admire as an investigator and a good representative of SO personnel.

"You can shoot him right now, as far as I am concerned," Vesel said. "That's not the problem. The problem is I'm very tired right now and I would have to track you down. And I would do that, no matter how good you might be at evasion. That's my training.

"And here is the bigger problem: If Crown Exports/Imports *is not* the Jubilee Trust, then who is? We need you to help us track *them* down too, and you cannot do that if you're sitting in one of my cells on a murder charge. That would be the end of your search for justice for your grandfather and your family too. Don't waste it."

Patrimos thought: Did he really want to do what the deputy wanted him to do? The idiot savant, the good soldier, the hero, as opposed to his own use of transactional ethics?

"Well, let's see," Patrimos said. He looked down at Rulotto and up at Vesel.

"Well, if you don't mind my shooting," he said, pointing the revolver at Rulotto's left ear.

"Okay then."

"Bang!" Patrimos shouted.

Rulotto cringed and folded inward.

"Oh, wait, that wasn't the gun at all. It was just me. Well, here's the damn gun."

He aimed at Rulotto and pulled the trigger.

Click.

Patrimos looked around the room at Vesel, the banker Parsons, Arne Nichols, Rainwater, Mitch Stein, who had a shocked look on his face, and the Federal ICE Agents. He shook his head. He felt suddenly a sense of vertigo, and he steadied himself as he held Rulotto. What the hell, he thought.

"I've got evidence about this, Agent Rainwater," he said. "He is an extorter of scared people, like my grandfather, and like this town, and Parsons there. If you have that evidence, will you promise me Rulotto and his bunch will get justice?"

"Oh, I most certainly will," Rainwater said. "Full justice. Extortion is a Federal crime. We have enough on them right now, although there is more to find, I'm sure."

"And what I was about to do here?" Patrimos asked. "What was that?"

"*Dark interrogation,* which, under the statutes, is no longer a crime," answered Rainwater with a straight face. "But work on that. It sets a bad example."

Patrimos stood and put his .38 back into his shoulder holster. "It ends here for you and the Rulotto's, you prick," he said to Hector, and kicked him in the ass. It felt satisfying, so he did it again.

Vesel nodded and yanked the tape off Jaffee's mouth, glad to see that it brought a swatch of hair and skin with it.

"Well, Rulotto," Rainwater said. "You may have bought this bank too soon; so anyway, Mr. Jaffee here did not have to blow himself up."

"You guessed that I didn't have a bomb too?" Hector said. Red bumps from the pistol whipping were already appearing on his forehead.

"No, we didn't guess. The new micro 3D/HD fluoroscope in the front door, through which you entered the bank, showed us that the switch Jaffee wore was a foot trigger. You did not have one. It might have worked if Jaffe could have stamped his heel on something solid, which he could not do anymore, being up in the air like that. Did you know that, Jaffee? Would you really have used it to blow yourself up when Rulotto here told you to, so he could get away?"

Jaffee frowned and looked at Rulotto.

"Oh," Rainwater said sarcastically. "Did he tell you your bomb vest was a fake, and the real one was somewhere else, and you could detonate it from a distance for a getaway? He did? Too bad for you. Anyway, the only man I know that could have held you up off the floor in the air like that is Neap Vesel here. Thank him for your life. It looked like a good balancing act: His solid feet on the ground; your evil ones helpless in the air. Yes, sir.

"Of course, there were the bugs you had in you. The trellis out front was a new piece of airport security gear loaned to us by DHS to see if it works. It does. So do the new bugs you could not find with that old detector, Boris. We have no video with them yet, but the audio allowed us to strategize next door, record everything while you were lying about things in here and prepare Val outside to be ready to start banging the window on cue. The General's shouted numbers gave us the coordinates of how you were positioned so we could apply the right force at the right time, and then we turned Neap loose."

"The General?" Rulotto asked.

"A long story," Vesel said.

Rainwater stopped smiling and addressed the two men formally.

"Hector Rulotto, you and your partner Boris Jaffee, suspected to be agents of a criminal enterprise, are both under arrest for suspicion of terrorist activity and money laundering for such purposes in the United States of America," Rainwater said. "Executive Order 13224, signed by President George W. Bush on Sept. 23, 2001, 'authorizes the seizure of the assets of organizations or individuals designated by the Secretary of the Treasury to assist, sponsor, or provide material or financial support or who are otherwise associated with terrorists.'

"In addition, the HSI charter grants us the ability to investigate such financial crimes for the DHS, like the one you wanted Mr. Parsons to engage in; that is, selling a bank to a terrorist group for purposes of illegally manufacturing US currency and distributing untaxed dollars to launder them."

Hector Rulotto said nothing. Rainwater finished and directed his assistants to further restrain the two men. The formal business was over.

Stein took back the ruck sack with the plates inside. He handed them to Rainwater. "Last night I had a good chat with a spokesman for the real Jubilee Trust," he said to Vesel.

"You did?" Rulotto said, overhearing the remark.

"Yes, presumably, the real one, and he had some very good ideas."

"I don't believe you."

"Yes, sir," Stein said. "True as Dick Tracy. I now know that your front office is not the front office of the JT. You know why I know that? Because you became *visible*. Their spokesman reminded me that invisible means you are *never* seen. I think they know you have been hitchhiking on their back, a false prophet, like a flea on an elephant's back? They may not like that. I think I will give them a call and tell them how successful we were here to get rid of a few fleas."

The two men on the floor glanced at one another as if they had already been thinking about that but said nothing further.

The Secret Service Agents had them in arm and leg chains. They then frog-hopped them out to join the SWAT team that had moved in tight to check for and contain other members of the group just in case the original plan had not worked.

64

The men in the banker's office were thinking about what had just happened. They better understood the danger of it after the fact.

"My God, Neap," Parsons said, sitting down behind his desk after the SWAT team left. He still had sweat on his brow. Only Vesel, Parsons, Nichols and Rainwater remained. Stein had gone to continue some legal proceedings in the trial in progress and have a late date with Melody Turner. Patrimos said he had some further business in Illinois.

"I was afraid they had smelled a rat there at the end," Parsons said. "And the whole thing would be called off, and they would do some other bank somewhere else. And then he said the words, *show you something*, and I knew I was a goner. If it had not been for Val Coombs at the window, and the play-call telling you where I was, and where the one with the real bomb was sitting, we might all have been blown up by a nervous Jaffee."

"I'm sure they planned to use that ruse to cover an escape," Nichols said, smiling, palpably happy to have been part of the action.

"Your play call came through loud and clear, General," Vesel said. "I'm glad you figured out on short notice what was going on. We really did not have the time to rehearse."

"Close, very close, Neap, but you are still the same goddamn acrobatic bull I recall, even though somebody laid a few bad boys on your face, I see."

"You should see the other guy, General," Vesel said, thinking of what was left of Fellestre's face. He did not want to go into it any further than that, however.

"Well, it had to be done this way, Mr. Parsons," Rainwater said. "To be legally safe, we had to have a signed agreement between you and Rulotto first, a verbal statement of intent to continue terrorist activity with what he was buying next, and finally the intent to print more Fed Notes illegally. You did good on all those points. I will need the receipt and the Bearer bonds back, of course."

"I doubt they are real, but they are all yours," Parsons said, handing him the envelope with the signed contract for the bank and the receipt for the Bearer bonds.

"But what can you do by taking out just those two agents?" Nichols asked Rainwater. "There are more people like that out there, right?"

Rainwater nodded. "In an economy like ours, some people are willing to believe in almost anything to get back what they had. As you found out, however, these two were not the Jubilee Trust, so we still have the real JT to worry about. We need to know exactly what they are up to. At least these scam artists are gone, and we can shut down a number of other outlets like theirs we think we know about."

"Listen," Vesel said. "Val was eager to help once we told her you would be here, Rainwater. When you're through, go out there and tell Val she did well. I hear she thinks you're cute."

"A little soap and water, she'll be cute too."

"Stein said he came away liking the real JT spokesman," Vesel said. "They say they help us keep our financial balance sheet straight, and we believe they are bending us over. Which is it?"

"I go for the latter," Rainwater said. "But then that's my job."

"To see what the JT is up to, Stein, me and Nichols here will not stop going after them," Patrimos said. "I owe that to my grandfather at least, and Nichols tells me he likes to go after economic terrorists too."

"Fine with me," Rainwater said. "But keep in touch."

"Neap, thanks for all your help. Somebody's got to have a backbone," Parsons said.

"My pleasure, General," Vesel said. "Just like old times."

"Yes... it was," Parsons said. "And it felt good even though it will never really be the old times again, will it, Neap?"

"I'm afraid not," Vesel said. "But look, it's been a long couple of days, and I need a soft pillow. We can debrief in the morning. Rainwater, have you got a place to sleep?"

"Vesel over there just told me Val thought I was cute, Neap. Maybe I'll find out."

"In a dumpster?"

"Well, no, there are better places hereabouts, right?"

Vesel shook his head and looked at his watch. "Good luck."

"Night, Neap," Parsons said. "I'll close up here."

Vesel told the others goodnight and figured he would go by the Sherriff's Department first, and then go have a long, long nap with Grace.

65

It was 9:45 p.m. when Vesel started to the Sheriff's Department. He could see lightning in the distance, but he knew he would hear no thunder yet. Sweating hard, he called the department, his cruiser AC on high. It had been a long two days.

"Blue?"

"Yes, Neap."

"Glad you're still there. I will be by in a few minutes. I know who the murderer is. I'll talk with you about it then."

"What? The murderer? Okay."

The Sheriff looked at the receiver before putting it down.

"Neap said he'll be back here soon, Himon," he said. "He says he knows who did the killing here in town."

"Did he tell you who?"

"No."

Ten minutes later Vesel came in. Both men worried over his battered face, but Vesel seemed to ignore it.

"It's Vicky Beguiles," he said. "And she has been missing for several days now."

"*Vicky Beguiles?* Okay, I'll call Judge Rawlins and get a warrant," Blue said. "We'll go after Vicky at home. We'll have her on suspicion of murder at least."

But Vesel suddenly felt very uneasy about something. He had not thought of this before. He had sent Sammy straight to his mother's house. Was his mother there? Would Sammy be safe with her? What happens if they break in and arrest his mother in front of him. What had he been thinking? He should have kept Sammy with him.

Ah, god, he thought. Then he grabbed his hat.

"Neap?" the Sheriff shouted. "Wait! We'll go together!"

"No. Patrimos is right, Blue. It was not just politics or Federal Reserve Notes behind these murders. It is long term revenge, and it was not just Patrimos working on it. I have to be by myself on this, Blue. You wait until I call."

"No! Wait for us. Neap!"

But Vesel was out and gone. He was halfway to Vicky's house before the Sheriff could get Judge Rawlins on the phone.

Driving to her house quickly, Vesel thought that Vicky's hate and willpower would have had to be intense for her to dig the tunnel he found and to use it regularly. He could imagine her brushing through the narrow passage as he had several times to check it himself, going back and forth like a gopher from house to house. For her, inside it, the claustrophobia must have been intense. But it was a good cover for what she did.

She could come and go without notice in her disguise and successfully doing whatever it was she was doing.

66

Vicky Beguiles knew Neap would be close behind her. So far, he was showing her the wisdom of her choice. He had to show up soon. But she could no longer think of Sammy as separate from Vesel, and therefore she worried that he was no longer a safe bet for her to use. No matter what she thought and felt about Sammy, her struggle now was with his father. Her strategy was to play on his father's weakness: his honesty and military training would lead him to the final test even if he could not actually pass it.

She felt physically equal to Vesel, no matter his training. Over the span of fifteen years, she had prepared herself for her status by vigorously training in every aspect of evasion, the tracking and killing of a foe, and the art of offense as well as defense with, of course, steroid help. The same was true with all of them. Once she knew Fellestre was surveilling her, she in turn surveilled him too, and without his knowledge. The same was true of Patrimos, a strange man.

Sweet, she thought, using a word of pleasure Sammy used a lot. She felt as ready as she would ever be. If Neap were no longer up to game, then he would be the one in trouble; if she was the one to die first, then that was all anybody could expect of a woman, and Sammy would have a real father at last.

* * *

Vicky had used their son against him. He had been made to live for fourteen years as somebody else's son. Was Sammy now faced with deciding between him and Vicky? This burned Vesel even deeper than the flay master in Afghanistan. After knowing about Sammy for just a few weeks, Vesel could see his genes in him, could see the man he might be. He would not give that up. If Vicky thought she was going to run away with Sammy, she was wrong.

However, perhaps she had carefully prepared Sammy for a specific role in the same way she had manipulated everyone else around her into a role— her husband, her town, him, he guessed. What was Sammy's role to be?

Vesel detoured rapidly to his new storage locker in town and secured the Hun Gabon. He looked at it and put it in one pocket of his uniform. He picked out several other objects and, armed with what he thought he would need from the locker, he headed fast toward the Beguiles's house.

Sammy was his new, almost fifteen-year old son; and Sammy's mother was the Fleckner murderer. He had no real clues about why she did what she was doing, but now was the time to separate the murderer from the herd and capture or kill her. He hoped he would have the chance to ask her why she was doing this, on a personal level if not a public one; the former was what a father had to do, but the latter was what an officer of the law had to do.

* * *

Vicky went to Sammy's room and sat down on his bed. She was wearing one of her tight-fitting vermillion workout suits.

"Where did you get all those bug bites," she asked, already knowing the answer.

"Where I usually do," he said. "Outside."

"Well, we need to talk," she said.

"Why?" Sammy said.

"It's about your special endeavor."

"Oh."

"Do you feel all right now?"

"Maybe."

"Well, I need your full attention here, Sammy."

Sammy frowned. He was sullen and withdrawn.

"Deputy Vesel will be here soon and we need to be ready."

Sammy pointed to the gym bag standing next to his shoes on the floor. "I'm ready."

"No, you're not," Vicky said.

"I like him."

Vicky paused for a minute. She knew this could be difficult. He still did not know Neap was his father, but she knew Neap had found her annuals and the tunnel under her house, so he knew. And maybe Neap knew about her goal and Sammy's role in it; and maybe Sammy wanted Neap to be his father. But her goal was so close now. Except for whom his real father was, she had never lied to Sammy, but now she had to.

"He killed your father, Sammy," she said. "He has to have some punishment for that."

"He wouldn't do that."

"Your father told me so."

"You were there?"

"Well, I found him, and I asked him, and he answered who it was before he died."

Sammy said nothing.

"Now, do you remember what to do?"

"Yes."

"Remember, Sammy, war plans change in the first battle. That may happen here, so keep in close contact with me. Okay?"

"Okay," Sammy said, and he straightened up.

An unsettled calm fell over the house and the two again went over what they would do to be certain of their actions.

* * *

Vesel observed the house for half an hour and saw nothing move, no lights, no parting curtains, but he did see the rusty red Ford at the house on the corner. The other cars were in the main house carport. She was there, somewhere, waiting.

He knew he would have to go in through the front door. He visualized the floor plan of the house from the short times he spent there: A front living room with a sofa, and a chair sitting beside a small writing desk in one corner; the living room opened to the den; and a door to the right led to a short hallway connecting the two bedrooms, and between the two bedrooms was the single bathroom where the tunnel was. Hardwood floors and throw rugs covered the front living room and the bedrooms; the den floors were linoleum designed like steppingstones, and a sliding door exited to the backyard with a grey wood deck. A garden and a workshop stood in the left corner of the backyard.

Vesel crept to the front door of the Beguiles house, keeping a low profile. He did not know what he would find, but he had to be careful in his firepower because of Sammy. He lay down under the windows on the front porch and reached out slowly to rattle the knob of the door, and as quickly withdrew his hand.

The first blast of the shotgun blew a hole in the middle of the front door; the second and third shots continued across the windows scattering glass across Vesel's back.

"Vicky? Vicky, was that you? We need to talk!" Vesel yelled. No answer.

Vesel had to get into the house to get to the tunnel. He charged through the front door and rolled across the laminate floor to the front of the sofa, its back facing the den. No shotgun blasts. He gingerly moved to the door leading to the hallway with the bathroom in the middle. No shotgun. Once inside the bathroom, he saw the escape door was open, but there was no sign of the two.

Before he entered the tunnel, he wanted to be sure his back was still safe. In front of the sliding door in the den, Vesel lined up a semi-circle of drinking glasses from the kitchen cupboard. He did the same for what was left of the front door. The glasses were a rough warning system; they would be hard to see in the dark and would make some noise if she came in from either of those directions and ran into them. He could be up and out of the bathroom before she could get far, and he would shoot her on sight.

But what if it were Sammy?

He did not think about that.

When he finished arranging the glasses, the rest of the house was clear. He assumed that Vicky, probably with Sammy, was already in the tunnel at the end of one of the two tunnels where they forked. He knew that might be a way to draw him in quickly, and she could ambush him either way.

Vesel still wondered about Sammy. He had not seen any thoughts of this kind of thing in Sammy while he was in the mountains with him. Had Vicky drawn him into her goal and made him a fishing lure, making Sammy see that as his conscious endeavor, as he had said? Had Sammy been playing him all this time?

Vesel was just into the tunnel, which was narrow, about five by three, and he had to crouch or crawl. He heard sounds from near the other end of the tunnel where it turned ninety degrees and bent up into the ground near the carport, as he recalled.

"Sammy?" he shouted. "Sammy, it's Deputy Vesel. We just went through some bad times. You saved my life. Did you tell that to your mother? That seemed like a grand endeavor to me. Not everybody can save somebody's life. Is what you are doing now part of that endeavor too? Who will be saved? Ask your mother. I'll wait."

There were sounds of quiet argument ahead. It ended as Vesel crept closer.

Sweat ran down his forehead and burned the wounds on his face, but he was still able to see. He was lying flat on the tunnel floor as a blast came from around the end of the tunnel.

"Vicky?"

There was silence. The tunnel itself was a quarter of a football field long in a straight line with tiny white Christmas tree bulbs strung along the top for minimal lighting. Vesel wondered whether to return fire. It might be Vicky shooting, and his hesitancy might make her think she was safe from him because of Sammy. She could wound him badly before he could get off a shot.

He leveled his Glock semi-automatic straight ahead toward the end of the tunnel where it should do no harm. He squeezed the trigger just as Sammy poked his head around the turn of the tunnel and raised one hand.

Christ thought Vesel.

But the shot was done and gone. Sammy snapped his head back behind the turn. Vicky heard the shot and hurried down the tunnel from packing the car.

"Sammy," she whispered. "Are you all right?"

Sammy shook his head. "He wasn't trying."

"Let me have that," Vicky said. She took the shotgun, loaded it, stepped out into the tunnel opening, and fired both barrels.

Vesel saw her, but he was still on the floor of the tunnel and ducked his head. The smell of gunpowder filled the tunnel. He then fired five shots at where he thought she might be.

But Vicky had already moved back around past the opening, and she was cursing.

"Goddamn it, Sammy. He was lying down. We have to get him standing up. Here, take the shotgun and go around the back. Go in the den and then to the tunnel opening. He'll stay in the tunnel trying to get to us and won't be prepared."

"Remember, Sammy, he just shot at you."

"But he didn't really try to shoot me, mom! He would not miss. I told you!"

His mother slapped him hard across the left cheek. He pulled back and bared his teeth.

"Sammy Beguiles, I raised you to have one great moment in your life to test you and that you would be able to remember it always and use it to your advantage. This is that moment, Sammy, and I will not let you give it away! Do you understand?"

Sammy shook his head. He was big, but his mother was bigger. He could not remember a time she did not wear long sleeves and pants to hide her arms and legs. However, he could see her now in a close-fitting gym suit and what she had been hiding, and he could tell he had better do what she asked, even though he wanted to run from her and deny what was coming.

"Sammy, this is war now, and hesitancy in battle is fatal. I'll finish loading the car and wait at this end for you. When you fire from behind him, I'll be in the tunnel to shoot as he turns back toward you. If he doesn't look back at you, you shoot him for me, Sammy, and for yourself. Okay?"

* * *

Vesel's eyes were slits from the beating by Fellestre, but he could still see well enough. He backed up in the tunnel a bit and noticed that his face was on fire in sync with the capital T below his right armpit, and his angry feelings about what was happening felt the same. She was using Sammy as a stalking horse. Their son! Whatever feelings he may have had for the mother of his only child was lost at that point.

Now he had to save Sammy from her. But how was he going to do that?

Ten minutes later, he heard a glass knock over back on the den linoleum. Moving as soon as he heard, he was up and out of the bathroom closet and flat against the wall near the hall door to the den. He froze and waited, knowing the other person could not slip up the tunnel from the garage port, since he could defend either outlet from where he stood. The one coming from the den was the one who would move first. Which one of them would it be?

The shotgun appeared from around the door. Vesel waited One, two, three. Then he slammed the shotgun barrel up with the protective sleeve of his left forearm, wheeled around, and pointed his automatic pistol directly at his son's frightened face.

"Shhh!" Vesel said and motioned with his head for Sammy to back up into the den. Vesel took the shotgun.

Sammy had his arms hanging to his side and his eyes were misty with fear and sorrow.

"I didn't want to do this," he said. "But my mother said I needed to fulfill my grand endeavor. I told her I didn't want to shoot you."

There were tears in the boy's eyes. Vesel knew this would be tough for him as a man to cry in front of another man. It might be better for a teenager. He could tell Sammy still did not know he was his father. Vicky must not have wanted him to know. Why? For this, for him to be able to murder his own father? Should he tell him now?

"Tell me what you were supposed to do, Sammy," he said instead.

"I was to come around behind you and call out. I would fire a warning shot when you looked back at me, and at the same time she would come out and shoot at you as you stood up and moved around toward me."

"Where did all the dirt go, Sammy?"

"What?"

"All the dirt that was dug out of the ground to make the tunnel, where did it go?"

"Oh, ah, first to the garden in the back yard, and then to the old Indian Mound outside town, I believe. It probably fills that workshop out back too, but I've never been allowed inside to see. There is another place she goes to, takes dirt to, and does something with, but I have never been there, although I think it is out near the lake. She's been doing this a long time, even before I was in the first grade. Early on she had a truck. She said the digging was all part of *her* grand endeavor."

"Okay, Sammy, now for the big question. Do you agree with your mother about what she is doing?"

"Are you a deputy now?" Sammy asked.

"I might be, Sammy, but she is doing things nobody would agree to. You have to understand that."

Sammy shook his head. "It was all just something she did, and since I grew up with it, I was supposed to help. It was just a tunnel, you know. I didn't know what it was going to be used for."

Vesel closed his eyes. So, Sammy did not yet know the big picture of what Vicky had been doing. He knew about the killings in town, but not that Vicky had killed them, or that she had probably killed many more in preparation for her role.

"Did you know what she was planning to do here, right now, tonight?"

"If we failed to kill you, to make you follow us up to the lake."

"Why?"

"I don't know anything about that part. She wouldn't say. All of us have to go through with it though, whatever it is."

"All of us? Do you know why she is after me?" Vesel asked.

"She said you killed my father."

"Your father? Larry?"

"I told you, he wasn't my father."

"Well, I didn't kill him either."

"Oh."

Vesel thought for a minute. "Okay, look, you know where I live?"

"Over on McNoughton Street near the park?"

"Right. Can you get there okay?'

"With my moped, sure."

"Good. I'll want you to go there after you have fired. I'll want to see you there later tonight and tell you about something very important. Okay?"

Sammy nodded his head. "Okay," he said.

"There may be someone else there, Grace, my friend; and if so, just explain this, and tell her that I'll be there as soon as I can. Okay?"

"Okay," said Sammy. "You're not going to kill my mother, are you?"

"Not if I can help it, Sammy. But I'm going to have to arrest her and ask her about some things that have happened in town."

Sammy's eyes opened wide. He was thinking of the half body of David Joliard now, and of the muscular person he had seen with it.

"You don't think..."

"I have to find out, Sammy. Are you ready?"

"Jesus," he said, with a new wonder in his eyes. "I guess."

"Okay, here we go."

Vesel slipped back down at the beginning of the tunnel where he had some shelter from the other two ends and waited. And waited. Had Sammy returned to the other side of the tunnel and gotten with his mother again? Had he misread his son's intent?

Then he heard Sammy holler the word deputy and fire a shot in the bathroom.

* * *

Vicky Beguiles heard the shout and the shot. Her son had done it, she thought, his conscious endeavor is fulfilled! Now it is time for mine.

She clutched the two H&K .45 automatics and stepped out into the narrow tunnel. At first, she did not see him, since he was no longer lying in the tunnel, and then she saw his half form at the other end and she shot in rapid succession, but Vesel had fired too. She felt a spear of fire and pain in her right leg that knocked her back while shooting. She dropped one of the H&K's.

Limping back to the tunnel opening, she climbed up and snipped the wire to the light in the tunnel and it went dead. She crawled out and used both arms to help her swing into the car. She put the automatic on the passenger seat. The carport light was off too. Two old garbage bags leaned against the wall next to the kitchen door in the carport, and there was the stench of garbage and the less putrid smell of sawdust and oil.

Vicky did not know what had happened to Sammy, but she had to have faith in his ability; and she had to fulfill her own goal one way or another. She cranked up, backed out of the garage port, and headed northeast toward Lake Joliard, slowly at first so she would not lose Vesel.

* * *

Vesel heard a car cranking, and he hurriedly turned in the now dark tunnel and made his way back to the front door of the house and ran to his cruiser down the block. In the distance he saw a solitary car that had a red rear light missing, and he thought of the night someone shot his snitch Casey and drove that car. It was now going west toward Lake Joliard. He turned on his lights and siren and pushed the Crown Victoria hard.

Vicky must have customized her old car, he soon thought, because it stayed way ahead of him in his efforts to catch it. The drive to the lake was fifteen minutes from Fleckner on small roads that paralleled the Murphy River which ran into the lake and over the dam's spillways and turbines and flowed east past Fleckner.

He was sure that he had hit Vicky and drawn blood. He had no idea how bad it was, or if he had hit an artery. But he did know that with him after her, she would have no time to treat the wound. His vision limited by the road with curves, he thought he was nevertheless gaining on her. They were nearer to the lake itself now and Vesel wondered what she was doing. She was speeding up and slowing down, as if looking for something.

He almost rammed her car while coming off a climb that hairpinned at the top. With tires screaming, he stopped past her and backed up to the red Ford. Getting out carefully, he could not see Vicky. He checked the rear light of her car and he could see the bullet damage.

Vesel saw drops of blood at the edge of the road and he tracked it for a space into the woods before turning back to get his gear. If he were going to track her, and if she were in better shape than anybody had thought, as Pauley had told him, he would have to consider her a capable enemy even with a wound. He guessed what was ahead, given the time she had to prepare it, and pulled from his trunk what he might need in such a situation, checked all his weapons and ammunition, and turned to go after Vicky.

* * *

Vicky sped to the wild northwestern edge of the lake. This was the place where she started to get ready for that day almost ten years before, near the underwater house, but concealed far enough away from the lake to throw off any casual hunter. There were swamps, mud flats, and berms; the lake was a half-mile beyond the road and in the woods, traps were set up along the way.

She would soon see who was better for her purposes: her, or Neap Vesel. Her leg was starting to hurt badly, but she was used to pain, and she moved on until she reached the first trap.

* * *

Vesel assumed that if Vicky was not wearing one earlier, she would be wearing a Kevlar vest now, and he assumed it was the latest kind, as was his, made with boron-carbide, and Under that vest was a cotton T-shirt processed with boron carbide nanowires that were five times stronger than Kevlar. He also had a rebuilt .45 armed with a sulfur phosphate armor piercing bullet. She would not have one of those, he hoped, and he would have to be careful with it, choosing just the right moment, if he could find one.

He heard the high-pitched electronic signal that the games had started. He knew because he had helped set up many of them for the SOP overall testing range at the Army's Fayetteville unit. He also knew what was coming.

He ran ten feet and immediately dropped to the ground.

Overhead a yard-wide set of shot went speeding by with a fearsome buzz. Not bad, Vesel thought. He noticed she had it angled perfectly just for him, no taller, no shorter. He would adjust accordingly.

The next test was easy and that made Vesel think. It was meant to be the kind of test that made the subject feel confident by getting through an easy test when he should not be confident at all. The first was a punji trap easily avoidable. But beyond that? He slipped off his backpack and opened it. He left the Hun Gabon sphere and chose three shiny black balls and closed the pack. He threw one ball to his left another to the front, and the third one to the right. He pushed a plug into his ear and listened for a few minutes. The 3D ball scanners located the trap just beyond the bungee test. It was an IED with a motion switch.

Vesel bypassed the Punji trap and carefully followed the image of the IED until he was beyond it. Then he threw a rock back at it. When it exploded, Vesel quickly moved closer to Vicky and the lake.

The next test was fiendish. His night-vision spotted a small white shape lying on the grass. He crept to it and immediately wanted to pick it up and see if it was still alive. However, he stopped and looked closer. No, it was a dog, but it was not Alexander the Great, thank God. It was a Toys-R-Us model. This was one way to catch a sentimental soldier, but he did not touch it, nor let it explode. He could neuter the IED strapped to it later.

Vesel guessed that Vicky may be after a bit of direct power now. She would add a little something extra. A sniper shot. She was crippled a bit and he was not. So, he had to be crippled a bit as she was.

Vesel knew the testing sites would become more dangerous as he came closer to the lake, and the possibility of Vicky adding something extra to the test was real. The most dangerous test was the random test, one that was not necessarily taught, nor used in normal training. Nevertheless, no soldier graduated from SO school without knowing how to counter the random test. This was why Vesel had not bent to check on the dog but passed it by defensively. He checked an area beyond it that had flattened out and was not as full of underbrush as before. He lay down.

He carefully removed from his pack an inflatable sex doll, which he had always kept with his army gear for deflating prolonged stress in the field, as a joke for his men when they had been stressed almost to the limit. He took pains now dressing it in light camo gear. He had time. Vicky was not going anywhere during this test. He knew she was probably waiting for at least a wound shot, and he would find out soon.

Finished with the doll, Vesel raised his hand slowly and carefully tossed it like a glider a few yards into the clearing to give the effect of a leaping body falling into position. With the camo clothes, it would show up on her night vision. She would have to come closer if she wanted to check to be sure, but then she was not going to have that chance. Vesel pulled his .45 with the armor-piercing phosphorous bullet.

He did not have to wait long. He knew she would be surprised by the effect of the shot on a leg. It would deflate and she would dwell on that for a minute too long. Vesel was checking for the shot using the angle of the doll. He saw the flicker of the rifle to his left and shot the phosphorous bullet right where Vicky's chest would have to be.

Vicky screamed. The phosphorous blossomed quickly into a bright sun as seen through a night scope. The figure leaped to its feet and began racing as best it could toward the lake, the burning phosphorous and the bullet wound received in the tunnel at her home hampering her flight.

Vesel tossed the phosphorous gun aside and went for her. He knew the lake was only maybe one-hundred feet from there, and he knew she would head for it to immerse the phosphorous under water, where it might settle down, or it might not. He took off after her, but slower to avoid any additional traps or ambushes.

* * *

The phosphorous was eating through her vest. She knew it worked fast, but if she could endure a few more moments, she would reach the lake near where her temporary SCUBA gear was.

Now the final event could occur, and she and Neap both needed to be there to ensure Sammy's place in life.

* * *

Vesel was close enough to see Vicky dive into the lake, and he watched as the burning phosphorous fell through the water with her. He found the SCUBA gear he had used earlier in the day, checked and saw that the oxygen was dangerously low, but he had no choice now as he stripped off his camo gear and slipped into the diving gear. The mask fit too tightly over his bruised and swollen face and nose, but he made it fit. While doing this, he wondered how she had gotten outfitted so quickly. But he did not think he would need a weapon now. He was there to retrieve her burnt body from the water.

He sank quickly into the murky water and entered the front door next to the *Welcome* sign. He floated through the first part of the house and saw the fading but still brilliant light of phosphorous to the rear of the house. The water had not yet settled the phosphorous, and by then it would have eaten through Vicky, the camo and SCUBA gear. He was uncertain what he was supposed to feel about this. She had killed many people, and yet she was the mother of his son. He would have liked talking with her about that.

Vesel floated into the old bedroom and saw the white blur on the bed. He watched for a while and then moved closer to her. When he reached her, he knew he had made a mistake. Vicky was not on the bed. That was just her vest with phosphorous, but without Vicky. She was somewhere else.

Vesel spun in his SCUBA suit and saw Vicky in the doorway behind him, pointing something at him. From its size, he guessed it was a Woody's Sawed-Off Spear Gun. She was wearing red underwear and a sports bra now and she was getting oxygen from a tiny Spare Air unit held in one hand, meant for short-term use only. He could see phosphorous burns on her hands and arms, random holes on one large bicep, and the bullet wound he saw in her right leg; in some places, he could see what he thought was exposed bone. She had to be in tremendous pain.

But her body was clearly no longer dumpy or slack. Vesel guessed that long before she had arrived in Fleckner, she had been hiding her true physical shape with floppy matronly clothes, and that was the reason she had been able to trick him and others earlier. Now he knew why she had not required an accomplice in what she had done; she was physically strong and had prepared herself well for the fulfillment of her plan. He recalled her hard grip when he had been there for her husband's death, to give her sympathy. That should have told him something. She had hugged him fiercely, perhaps knowing the end that was soon coming for one of them.

He bet that if he went back through both of her houses, he would find laboratory materials, drugs, medical supplies, a work area for sewing up cadavers, a supply of hospital booties that would leave no footprints, and a good gym with weights.

But Vesel knew she had him now. The spear gun was a lethal underwater weapon.

He raised his hands palm up as if asking a question: Why?

Vicky smiled.

Vesel frowned. He was not following this. What was she doing?

Vicky moved to one wall and pointed at a word that he remembered seeing when he had retrieved the Reserve Note plates earlier:

GARAGE

Her eyes behind the mask suddenly looked strange and forbidding, but her aim was steady as she stared at Vesel. He could see there were two more words carved in the wall now:

OUR SON

He did not remember the words Our Son having been on the wall from his previous visit. They were new. Why?

He knew she had beaten him to the house, but what was she waiting for? She smiled and, holding the spear gun pointed directly at him, she gestured at the words again and removed the small Spare Air tank from her mouth.

"No!" Vesel screamed to himself.

He watched the bubbles from her mouth move upward, and at the end, she dropped the spear gun and floated to the floor. He did what he could, but she was gone before he could even try to give her air from his tank.

Her face was soft and misty in the water and looked peaceful.

He wondered if he should just leave her there. No one else knew where she was, although Stein and the Sheriff would guess. Vesel was a Chief Deputy Sheriff and he had a duty for the trial to have its way, and an innocent man–Marvin Macy–released. The phosphorous gone now, Vesel cradled the mother of his son and probably the murderer of at least six people he was aware of, and rose to the surface with mixed emotions, following a narrow shaft of light upward.

67

Vesel carried Vicky back to where her car and his cruiser were. The whole of that area to the lake was now a crime scene. After calling the sheriff, he found an envelope inside Vicky's rusty Ford with his name on it. She had written it in a neat hand that went forward with purpose. He could already tell she had been ready for what had happened from the very beginning, even as a fifteen-year-old girl in Neap's car after at least four big games during a four-season period, and the thought sent a chill up his spine.

Neap,

Congratulations. You must have made it through the entire test. I did not really plan to kill you, because a son needs his father, but I knew I would have to lure you to my family's old house in a convincing manner.

I always knew what would happen to me.

Please take care of Sammy. He is our son. I could not tell you before. I know you have been with him recently, and that is good. I always wanted the best of you for him; I loved you for what you were–strong. I think Sammy will have the best of us both, being strong and determined, which will be necessary in the new world.

Why did I do it? Sharp things are needed now, Neap, more than ever. The half-body in town showed what can go wrong if good people delay making good choices, make bad choices, or no choices at all, even after knowing all sides of things. I placed the body near a public place, so the town's people or newcomers could see it if they wanted to as in the old days of stockades and true shame.

There were others outside Fleckner who helped me, but we had only a common purpose. I used their money for equipment and tools and such, and they agreed about killing the Joliards, whose past activities had made them mad or angry or both. The same was true for me. The Joliard family ruined my family starting back in the nineteen fifties. They ruined the blood of my generation. Check the courthouse records. It was my family who owned all the land the lake came to be on, and my folks should be living in a mansion today, not theirs. Jessie's father rigged the deal so they would be out. So when young, I knew I had to change the equation for Sammy's sake.

Some say that true climatic change is coming, Neap, and the Atlantic Seaboard Fall Line is moving east toward the ocean rather than moving west and away from it the way you would think. Maybe the oceans are rising again after all, Neap, instead of falling. Maybe one day we will all be covered here with water. What can I say about us then, except that to be saved, we as humans must scramble ever higher into the mountains that remain above water.

Soft sand moves to the sea, Neap, but hard mountains remain; I have always lived on the high hard edge of the world and wanted the best for my family, including you.

Love,

Vicky Mary Harris

Vesel knew he had been right about the identity of Sammy's father. *He* was the father. But if killing was the one conscious endeavor Vicky had been using to elevate her life, Vesel could not imagine what Thoreau would have thought. He knew that Vicky had gotten what she wanted: revenge on the Joliard family for forcing her ancestors from the status of their land and then covering it with water. But the law had been against them from the beginning, and there was no return. Her family had become hardscrabble farmers without distinction, and in effect, penniless.

However, Vesel knew she had not known about Calvin II being the sole problem; she had wiped out almost an entire family because of the one member she should have blamed.

When the Sheriff and Patrimos arrived, they saw Vicky's oddly burnt body lying on the hood of the Ford. Vesel was sitting and waiting for them. He handed Vicky's letter to the Sheriff.

"Here, Blue, this is evidence for the halfway murder, and others. Read this letter carefully. Note the signature."

Puzzled, the Sheriff took the letter and began reading.

68

That night, Jessie Joliard was alone in her big house; dark ivy clung to the outside walls, and deep shadows from thick surrounding trees hid the mansion in gloom. Pauley and Tommie remained close in their onsite cabins, waiting for whatever was to come.

Abejundio and his family remained in their sites too, even though she explained carefully that she could not pay them as much. She knew the few tax-free utility bonds left in her name would carry her only to the following Thanksgiving and then be gone. She would have to put the place up for sale soon if anybody could afford it. She did not know if Neap Vesel would stay with her if that happened. She had been unable to call him. She heard that her ex-fiancée Senator Jackson Miles had been killed in an auto/truck wreck near his home in Maryland and CNN had run a brief video obituary on him. She knew it was the JT that killed him. They policed their own, Neap had said, and she did not feel as bad as she thought she would.

But depressed over the things for which people had unjustly blamed her grandfather, and things she had said or done, she felt bleak and destructive. That Friday night, Jessie drank and went out on the roads in her big silver S-Class Mercedes-Benz. She circled the lake on small dirt roads, dust spuming behind her like invisible horizontal tornadoes.

Tiring of the back roads, Jessie went to US 1 and took off south, hitting potholes by choice, then turning left off to I-95, and speeding back north to the Fleckner exit at over one-hundred mph, hoping some Highway Patrol cruiser would spot her and give pursuit.

None did.

Later she caromed up the road to her house, crunching gravel and almost flying off the road several times like a pinball in a tilted machine. Turning at the last minute, she headed at full speed for the garage, its doors open and lights on. She hit the brakes hard just before it was too late, and yet the stout Mercedes sedan plowed into the back wall of the garage anyway, almost splitting it open.

Abejundio heard the noise and was alarmed. He ran to the garage and found Jessie slumped in her seat. He called Vesel, who was heading home to Grace after finishing some late paperwork on Vicky Beguiles at the Sheriff's Department.

"Yes?" Vesel said.

"Deputy Vesel, this is Abejundio. There has been a wreck. It is Jessie. I think she needs you badly."

Vesel was on top of the mountain at the Joliard Mansion inside ten minutes. Jessie was okay, with only minor bleeding at the scalp. They were sitting and thinking of what might have happened in the garage if she had been unable to stop and had bashed even through the heavy garage wall all the way through the timbers to the outside, revealing some of the old inner walls of the garage.

He stopped in mid-thought. He remembered Vicky had been pointing at an underwater wall at the time of her death. There were a few words carved into the wall: GARAGE. OUR SON. At the time, he had no idea what that meant. He had thought it a nonsensical event created perhaps by different divers taking advantage of the disaster of the old house underwater to disfigure it in fun. But now he thought he knew what it meant, and he had a deep feeling of huge, invisible events riding roughshod over him. Stunned, he blinked and asked Jessie an obvious question.

"Are there working tools here somewhere?" he asked.

"Umm, sure," Jessie said. "Yard tools are in that storage chest. Abejundio keeps everything sharp and in shape. Why?"

Vesel went to a drawer in the tall chest standing next to the door that led to the walkway to the big house. He looked in the drawer, pushed something around, and found an old pit axe. He glanced at the walls in the garage, which was of a three-car capacity. There were very few boxes or storage cases lining the walls inside. He noticed several patches that looked like someone had torn the wall and then plastered over it. Confident now, he chose a spot he could reach near the front of the car where it had already broken through the wall. He began swinging at it.

"What are you doing, Neap?" Jessie said, her voice rising.

"Hitting this place here," he said, tapping at a place on the wall under which the Mercedes sat immersed like an unexploded bomb.

"Well, okay, Neap," she said. "I don't know what you mean but go ahead if you want to."

Vesel had swinging strength like his landscaping father, and he held the axe with two hands and sank its keen edge deep into the wall. It was solid pine behind the later addition of mortarboard and paint, but the front of the car had already fractured one section of it.

"I hope insurance covers this, Neap," she said. "I'll need it."

"We'll see," Vesel answered.

Vesel wound up and attacked the wood again. He chopped at the wooden boards, running at an angle to the floor, and in a major split opened more room allowing him to see there was something stuffed behind the boards.

"Come here, Jessie," he said.

"What?"

"Take a look."

She stared at the hole for a minute. Then she saw it.

"What the hell!" she said in wonder.

"You said your grandfather knew how to put money away for you when you really needed it?" Vesel said.

"Pawpaw!" she screamed.

Stepping up to the battered wall, Jessie ignored splinters and tore away boards. She reached in between them and began to pull out handfuls of Federal Reserve Notes. She started laughing and she screamed for old Abejundio, who had been afraid that she was hurt when he had called Vesel.

If something bad had happened to her, what could he say to old Calvin, who had saved him? He stared in amazement as he saw

Jessie pull from the broken garage walls handfuls of large Notes, the fresh blue seals on the front giving an arresting accent to the green swirl of large bills falling around her like a Welcome Home parade.

Jessie waved at Abejundio and urged him to grab some bills, but he shook his head. "It is yours," he said, smiling, as if he knew all along that it was there, waiting for her.

She did some quick arithmetic in her head, something she had always been good at doing, and she figured that if she used the collector's minimum value of $300,000 for each good Note of the one hundred thousand if sold separately, it seemed that she faced the prospect of having over *thirty-billion dollars* in her goddamn garage walls.

Thinking about it, she laughed and figured pawpaw would not mind if she turned him in to the Treasury Department for, first, printing and hiding the Notes; and then, second, paying no taxes on them for almost ninety years; then third, not paying any of the accumulated fines and penalties since then either.

She knew the IRS paid taxpayers for turning in people like that, even if they were relatives. She just knew Grandfather Calvin already approved. Thirty percent of the face value of just one billion dollars, or 300 million, she mused, would be a good starting point for a Finder's Fee from the Treasury Department. She was sure Jim Parsons could help negotiate for it. She danced for a long time with knees jumping high as she tossed the bills up in the air and danced under them. She yelled that Neap Vesel had saved her. Her face seemed radiant and full, unmarked, as the Federal Reserve Notes fell like confetti on her goddess form. Vesel and Abejundio watched her with great happiness.

69

PATTERNS

Bone-tired, Vesel finally wished Jessie well and kissed her with as much passion as he could muster. She laughed at his bruised face but commiserated with him and kissed him on his chin so it would not hurt. He then headed home, not knowing what he and Jessie were up to and not caring now. He was ready to sleep for two or three days if Grace would let him. He could not recall any football game in which he had been more tired. Even periods in the mountains going after the Taliban gave him at least a few moments to relax in between attacks. He could barely move, but he was happy and believed he could make it home without losing his sight.

At his house, the lights were on and the front door was open. A football was sitting on the living room floor. Vesel went in and called Sammy's name.

No answer.

He went to his bedroom. Grace sat against the headboard in the big bed.

The lights were on and she was facing the door with the smile that Vesel loved. She wore a gray blouse, jeans, and orange-laced tennis shoes, her ankles crossed. Alexander the Great lay sideways beside her but made no sound. She seemed to be staring at the door as if she had been waiting for Vesel to come for her.

"Hey," Vesel said. "Sorry I'm so late. Did a young guy, Sammy, come by here recently?"

Vesel wondered what was wrong with the Shih Tzu, who had not barked at him in jealousy as usual.

"Grace?" he said. "Grace!"

Grace did not blink.

Vesel was quiet as he searched for a pulse for maybe half a minute, then his eyes grew salty, and his mind dark. He realized he had come to love two women and had not been able to choose between them, and now one was gone forever; perhaps the other one might be gone too, now that her money problem was solved. He might say his life was now split like the body of David Joliard, and he wondered like Joliard perhaps did, what it was all about.

After the recognition of Grace's death, Vesel picked up Sammy's football. Sammy must have come in, found Grace, knew what had happened, and fled in fear. Broken-hearted, Vesel tracked Sammy in the mountains to their last fish camp where the boy must have felt safe. He explained to the fourteen-year-old that he was proud to be his father and had come to love him for many reasons. They spent the night in the large, strong mountains together, talking. Vesel would deal with Grace's body later; but that night, his troubled son came first.

* * *

The next day Vesel called Miss Melody Turner, the retired schoolteacher who had given his search a push when it needed it. He had promised her he would call when he had answers, and he believed he was always going to keep his promises. He told her who the murderer was, Vicky Beguiles, but not the full story. She probably already knew since Stein had told him that she was a member of the Jubilee Account. Before she said goodbye, after he gave her the message, she said:

"You're probably grieving in several ways, Neap."

And he was. With the loss of Grace, he saw more of Jessie and they took Sammy and traveled up and down the fall line before school started. Their marriage would be that year at Christmas time, and they would live together in the old family mansion after formally adopting Sammy. Vesel was extremely happy with Sammy, his and Mary's child.

Vesel retired from the Fleckner Sheriff's Department but promised he would find a replacement, and he did, a woman DEA Special Agent Phillip Rainwater recommended.

Vesel and Jessie pledged to Jim Parsons that the Jubilee Account money to help run the town and the clinic, to help its citizens through bad times, would continue as it had since 1929. The question about what this money could be called only came up a few times. Since the intent was to protect and preserve people in Fleckner from bad times, and since there was no taxpayer pay-back due, none who knew about it were angered.

Pauley and Tommie were delighted at the new sounds in the Joliard mansion. They would swing as they worked, reinvigorated in time's passage.

Vesel had to admit to himself that he felt better about how things turned out when he heard from Doc Bevel that Grace had been pregnant, but that DNA tests revealed that it was not his child. It must have been Fellestre's. This mitigated his despair at Grace's loss, although it seemed to some who knew him that despite this proof of her betrayal, and the anticipated marriage with Jessie, Vesel still grieved for what he and Grace might have had together.

70

Matters settled down in Fleckner, but Vesel now felt the compression of a plan, something icy in his life. He knew that Mary Harris, or Victoria Beguiles, had planned all this from the very beginning, when she was very young, sitting beside her grandfather in an old courtroom in Fleckner and learning that courts were not the solution.

She must have learned from someone early on–perhaps from someone whose grandfather had helped build the addition of the garage to the house in 1929, or her father, who was evidently a local historian and teacher–what might be in the walls of Joliard's garage, and she was determined to remove all Joliards who might otherwise stand in the way of connecting Vesel and her son Sammy directly to Joliard land and money by the father's marriage to Jessie Joliard, and she would have her vengeance, her just inheritance, her class-standing, all returned to her family line at last.

Sometimes, in battle, Vesel believed that all hard-driving urges in life were blind, and killing was one of them, and whatever was pushing hard in life in one direction or another was unknowable and could not be consciously handled; they could only be managed.

Vesel had mastered plans and patterns all his life, as a football player and an active soldier, and now patterns must have mastered him as he could feel the grasp Vicky's plan had on him long after she was gone, and he had no way of stopping it. He grew slim, and spent his days running the mansion's simple life, a well-ordered business, although he wondered from time to time what had happened.

This came even closer to an explanation when he learned the meaning of the Pashto words *Hun Gabon* from a man who passed through Fleckner one day looking for his parents. He had been an ambassador to Pakistan and spent one evening at the mansion with the Vesel family and told them stories about that part of the world, which seemed little different from what Vesel knew. But the man had studied Pashto language at the University of the Punjab, in Lahore, one of the oldest institutions of higher learning in Pakistan, and he said the Pashto words meant, *Hurry to the center.*

Vicky and Queen Victoria, Vesel reasoned, were evidently masterful at creating compelling patterns that brought things to their centers: The *Jubilee Trust* for the Queen, and for Vicky Mary Harris, a son and heir in line to inherit money and a huge estate. Those were the goals. They were good solid values made of money and influence, and he was only a soldier in that army.

Vesel assumed that all heroes triumphed when young, but as they grew older, they married and passed on a heroic line, and then they died.

He wondered if Mary Harris was the real hero, and his resistance to the unfolding of her plan and his part in it faded. He was not fully unhappy, but he still felt Mary Harris's influence in everything he did, and sometimes it stung. The trapped words repeated themselves often: *This one's for you!*

* * *

Patrimos returned to his grandfather's burial place in Palatine, Illinois, and arranged for an updated brass plaque like one he had seen in Rome, and held a private ceremony for a man who had sacrificed himself for this distant moment in time.

WALTER LEEDS PATRIMOS

1882-1931

Semper Campii Expansum

Patrimos stood for a time silently explaining to Walter what he had done for him and why, and for his friend Calvin Murphy Joliard as well. The PI felt good. With investigations into the nature of the *JT* now underway, he believed his grandfather Walter would be proud of him. It seemed an appropriate ceremony for himself as well, a man starting his career to understand his grandfather's leap from the Empire State Building and winding up not only understanding the deed, but also validating his grandfather's sacrifice. For him, persistence had won, and he felt the high nature of his calling by finding the truth by whatever means possible. The opposite thought did not occur to him. He did however think, for penance's sake, that he did not need to retire, and maybe that was not his and Stein's last case together after all.

* * *

Before returning to Fleckner, Patrimos went by 223 Parsons Street and saw the fair-haired Ginger Masters. She smiled when she saw him, as if she had been expecting him. She reminded him what she had said about him when he had been there before, that he was on a wheel and would always be back. He walked in the front door and was tempted to close it for good.

END